W9-BPE-333

Praise for

KAYTE NUNN

'The whole book is a delight . . . Perfect reading whilst sipping a G&T in a beautiful garden somewhere in the sun!' Rosanna Ley

'*[The] Silk House* is at once eerie and evocative . . . Utterly spellbinding' Natasha Lester

'This book is the best kind of escapism: thoughtful, colourful and meaningful' Sophie Green

'*The Silk House* is an elegantly woven ghost story that both chills and delights . . . this evocative tale of mystery and secrets continued to haunt me long after I turned the last page' Joanna Nell

'A sweeping and exotic read. I was completely swept away. Perfect for readers of Kate Morton' Lorna Cook, on *The Botanist's Daughter*

'I loved this exquisitely written novel and drank in every word. *The Forgotten Letters of Esther Durrant* is a reminder of the redemptive nature of love, and that it can be found in the most unexpected places' Fiona Valpy

Also by Kayte Nunn

The Botanist's Daughter
The Forgotten Letters of Esther Durrant
Rose's Vintage
Angel's Share

The SILK HOUSE

KAYTE NUNN

An Orion paperback

First published in Australia and New Zealand in 2020 by Hachette Australia

First published in Great Britain in 2020 by Orion Books,
an imprint of The Orion Publishing Group Ltd
Carmelite House, 50 Victoria Embankment
London EC4Y 0DZ

An Hachette UK Company

3 5 7 9 10 8 6 4 2

Copyright © Kayte Nunn 2020

The moral right of Kayte Nunn to be identified as the author
of this work has been asserted in accordance with
the Copyright, Designs and Patents Act of 1988.

All rights reserved. No part of this publication may be
reproduced, stored in a retrieval system, or transmitted
in any form or by any means, electronic, mechanical,
photocopying, recording, or otherwise, without the
prior permission of both the copyright owner and the
above publisher of this book.

All the characters in this book are fictitious, and any resemblance to
actual persons, living or dead, is purely coincidental.

A CIP catalogue record for this book is
available from the British Library.

ISBN 978 1 39870 0185

Typeset by Born Group
Printed and bound in Great Britain by Clays Ltd, Elcograf S.p.A.

www.orionbooks.co.uk

For Charlotte, who loves to scare me
with her own stories.

'Love, thieves and fear make ghosts.'

GERMAN PROVERB

ONE

Now

Thea heard the sound first, the ghostly echo of female voices raised in song. Soprano, alto and contralto effortlessly harmonising, a clear, pure stream that drifted from the open windows and across the slate rooftops, along the old red-brick walls worn smooth by centuries of wind and rain, over the manicured playing fields and towards the wide, tree-lined path where she stood. Gooseflesh rose on her arms as the wind gusted around the corner of the building, bringing the sound closer, louder. As she glanced to her left she saw shadows, blurred shapes against square-paned windows. In the darkening gloom the effect was ethereal, other-worldly. An angelic choir. The words, 'and give you peace . . .' swirled around her, hanging in the air.

She stopped, pushed her glasses up on the bridge of her nose and gazed up at the edifice before her. It was everything she had ever imagined an English public school to be, wearing the weight of its history in the honeyed stone, thick with ivy and wisteria, immaculately kept grass (doubtless tended by a phalanx of gardeners) bordered by neat rows of purple-faced pansies and white alyssum, the tall gates, the arched portico, the heavy oak door studded and banded with iron. The entire place reeked of tradition, privilege and money. Among such imposing buildings the feeling of being a slightly scruffy imposter was as sharp as a slap.

The singing faded, and she carried on, dragging her suitcase behind her and cursing under her breath as it caught on the gravel.

The bus had dropped her off half an hour earlier in the town's wide, gently curving high street and she hadn't needed directions, having made a flying visit to the college for her interview three months ago. She was nearly there, but the gravel was making the final steps of her journey more difficult than they should have been. She suspected that most visitors arrived by car not, as she was, on foot, the drive crunching pleasingly under expensive tyres.

With a final yank of her suitcase, she reached the grand stone portico. She spotted a handle and grasped it, leaning her shoulder against the door as the catch released. The smell of beeswax, sweet lilies, old books and, faintly, sweaty gym shoes – her father would have called them plimsolls – was overwhelming.

As she walked in, the door closed behind her with a thud that reverberated down the vast hallway. She found herself standing in the high-ceilinged entry room. To one side was a rectangular table, polished to a high sheen, and on it sat the lilies she could smell, arranged in a tall cut-glass vase. The blooms were exquisitely formed, petals curling outwards, creamy and unblemished, bright orange pollen balanced on each stamen. Another few days and they would have wilted, begun the journey towards decay, but for now they were perfection.

She looked past the flowers to the end of the hallway where a wide, curving stone staircase with an elaborate balustrade stretched upwards into darkness.

'You're late.'

The voice was low and ponderous as it boomed towards her out of the shadows. Thea strained to see where it had come from, and a moment later a tall, spare man with slicked-back hair and a face as runnelled as a dry riverbed emerged from the gloom. His old-fashioned frock coat hung on him as if it had been made for someone larger, but his tie was sharply knotted and high against a clean white collar. Heavy brows shaded his eyes, and his shoulders were hunched as if to ward off imaginary cold. He didn't meet her eye.

'Sorry . . . the bus was late leaving the station.' She checked her watch. 'But only by about fifteen minutes.'

'Of course, you're from the *colonies*,' he said, as if that explained everything. 'We were expecting you yesterday, Miss Rust.'

Thea bristled. 'I thought the students arrived tomorrow?'

'They do, but nevertheless we were expecting you yesterday,' he repeated slowly, as if she were dense as well as foreign.

She went to apologise again, but he had already disappeared into the gloom.

No sooner had she opened her mouth to call out than he returned, holding a heavy iron circle on which a set of keys was strung. 'There are three of them. One for the front door, one the back, and the other . . . well, I expect you'll work it out. That's if you've got anything about you.' He held out the keys to her with one hand and rubbed his chin with the other. There was a rasp as flakes of skin drifted onto his lapels, and she suppressed a shudder.

'The *girls'* boarding house is back towards the high street, number fifty-eight.' There was a wince in his voice as he spoke, as if even uttering the word *girls* caused him physical pain. 'I have been reliably informed that you will be a guest there, for the first term at least.'

Boys – the sons of gentlemen, so the school's website boasted – had been educated at Oxleigh College since the mid-nineteenth century. According to Thea's reading, it had been founded as a last-ditch effort to save the town. Once a popular stop on the road to Bath, Oxleigh went into a sharp decline when the railways proved to be a far quicker and more efficient means of transport from the capital to the spa town. A former coaching inn had become, and still was, the Master's House and the rest of the buildings grew up around it. Then, as the school thrived, so did the town once more.

This was the first year, however, that Oxleigh had deigned to admit girls. It had held out far longer than other schools of its ilk, which had begun accepting them several decades ago, but enrolments were dropping and the school had been forced to move with the times, or so Thea surmised. It was clear that this man, whoever he was, was far from happy about the situation.

She held out her left hand for the keys and then stuck out her right to shake his. 'Thea. New history teacher.'

'Of that I am well aware, Miss Rust,' he said with a withering grimace – it couldn't be called a smile – and ignoring her outstretched hand. 'Battle. *Mr* Battle to you. Porter.'

'Yes, of course,' said Thea, withdrawing her hand as he turned, dismissing her.

'I'll head back to the high street then, shall I?' she said, keeping her tone deliberately light.

'It's the green door. Next but one to the George and Dragon. Don't get lost,' he muttered over his shoulder as he disappeared into the shadows again.

Instead of leaving the room right away, she took a step forward, curious to see a little more of her surroundings, for she had not had the chance to take in much on her previous visit. Her eyes had now adjusted to the dim light and she could make out several large oil paintings of learned-seeming men hanging from the wood-panelled walls. One, with a tonsure of short dark hair, was seated behind a desk and wore round wire-rimmed spectacles and sported a small moustache, a pen in his hand. Another wore an academic gown with a scarlet hood and a mortarboard atop his head. Yet another, more contemporary this time, showed a youngish, sandy-haired man sitting on a bench with a labrador at his feet, the college gardens and buildings behind him. She moved closer and read the inscriptions. All of them had the word 'Master' above their names, and then the dates they had served. The sandy-haired man, Dr Alexander Fox, was the present headmaster; *2011* was inscribed after his name but no end date. She had met him at her interview, and had liked his open face and unstuffy attitude.

Oxleigh College was a bastion of the British establishment in the heart of the English countryside, but Thea might as well have applied to teach on Mars, for she had no experience in such a place as this. She had been surprised to get past the first interview. There was, of course, another reason she had been looking at the college's website in the first place, had impulsively decided to apply for the job she'd seen advertised there. But now was not the time to dwell on that.

As she went to leave, she turned the keys over in her hand for a closer look. They were large and smooth, their metal surface worn, the result of many years of use. One had the shape of a pentacle, a pattern familiar to her, the points of a star enclosed in a circle at the top. The second featured maze-like intertwined circles with a star at their centre and the third a quiver of arrows with a twisted-thread effect along the shank. She ran her thumb over the pentacle and wondered briefly when it had first been made, why such designs would feature on this set of keys.

She put them into her jacket pocket, shouldered her bag, grasped the handle of her suitcase and pulled the door open. The wind rustled the trees lining the grand avenue and her stomach growled in response. Lunch had been a plastic packet of sandwiches and a watery coffee on the train, many hours ago now. There was a chocolate bar somewhere in her bag, but she could hang on for a few more minutes. She should retrace her steps to the town and find her new lodgings.

The path to the school gates was illuminated by spotlights at ground level that cast long-fingered shadows from the trees across the gravel. The sound of cars from the road was a far-off murmur.

But there was something different now and at first she couldn't work out what it was. Then, the quiet struck her: the music had stopped. She recalled Mr Battle's words. If none of the students had arrived yet, then who had been singing?

TWO

September 1768, Oxleigh

The first thing Rowan noticed was the man's waistcoat, for it was embroidered with a pattern the like she had never before encountered: orange flower petals that glowed in the afternoon light, leaves in a twisting green curve. Then, breeches as snowy as the underside of a magpie, white stockings and polished leather shoes with shiny silver buckles. A wealthy gentleman, by all appearances.

He approached her with a swagger, pausing to stuff something in his pocket. She smoothed her skirts, applying a smile to her face and quelling the urge to run and hide. She wished her boots were not crusted with mud and her red cloak – once her mother's – not so tattered and patched. She hastily tucked her hands behind her, for they were streaked with green sap from the herbs she had picked on her journey, and cast her gaze to her feet.

'You, girl. Are you strong? Healthy?' he enquired, looking down, for she was slight and he stood a foot or more taller than her.

'Aye, sir.' She found her voice. 'Have been maid and laundress for a household of nine for the past two years.' Rowan omitted to mention that the household was that of her aunt and uncle and she had not been paid for her work. She wanted him to think her more experienced than she might appear. 'And not a day's sickness.'

'I had hoped for a manservant,' he sighed, casting a glance across to the other side of the village green where several people huddled in small groups, the women holding mops or brooms, the men scythes, hoes or shovels. Rowan noticed that scraps of bright blue ribbon were evident on the breasts of most of them – signs that they had already been hired. 'But it appears there are none to be had at this late hour.'

The town held an annual Michaelmas Mop Fair, drawing those in need of employment from near and far in the hopes of securing a year's work, and Rowan had made the two-day journey on foot from her village of Inkpen, sleeping in a hollow by the roadside as night fell and continuing on as dawn broke. The sun was now well past its zenith, and she had been standing beside the green since early that morning, but so far those who had come in search of maids, washerwomen and cooks had caught sight of her face, the scarred left eye that drooped at the outside edge, and moved swiftly on. She wondered why this gentleman had not been among them, but thanked her stars that he had not, for the hollow ache in her stomach reminded her of the grave nature of her situation. If she were not hired, she had not the fortitude for the long walk back to her aunt's house, nor would she be offered a welcome there if she did return, for she had been sent to earn a wage to pay for her brothers' keep.

From where she stood, Rowan had a view of almost the entire town of Oxleigh spread below her. It was the largest place she had ever seen: so many houses, one after another, of all types and sizes fitted together like pieces of a puzzle, many of them brick, with sturdy tile roofs, not wattle and daub and thatch as the cottages of her village were. The high street was wider even than any river she could imagine and curved gently downhill like the peel of an apple. She was awed by the size of it, much as she was by the gentleman standing before her.

'I suppose a housemaid will suffice.' His words brought her back to where she stood and she allowed a small hope to grow. He paused, considering her, and she tried not to flinch under his gaze, to meet it with a steadfastness she did not feel, for her heart was racing faster than if she had run a mile. He made no sign that he had noticed her ruined face, the spider's web of lines that radiated out from the corner of her eye.

'If my wife is in agreement. Come.' He motioned to her and she gathered her bundle containing a spare set of clothes and a few small treasures – everything she owned – scrambling to follow him as he paced in the direction of the main street. A market threaded its way along the centre and she took in the swarm of people, stepping quickly out of the way to avoid being jostled as they examined fat marrows, cabbages larger than a baby's head, baskets of eggs, heavy sacks of grain and malt, towers of apples, chickens with necks twisted but feathers and feet still attached.

Being sure to keep the man firmly in her sights, she dodged tables laden with blocks of butter, curds and whey and all manner of cheeses, spotted a hover of trout, their eyes bright, skin stippled and silver-brown, bunches of watercress, herbs and flowers, crocks of honey, folded lengths of ribbon. She spied courting couples sidling near a fiddler working his instrument into a flashing blur. He was a good one, judging by the crowd that had gathered around him, tapping their feet and swaying to the music. Here were people of all types and sizes: short and broad like a bread oven, round like a wheel of Wiltshire loaf or thin as a pane of glass.

She almost tripped over the crust of a pie, discarded on the ground, missed by the press of boots. It had been a very long time since her breakfast the day before. Glancing around to make certain no one saw her, she ducked down, plucking the pastry seconds before it was ground into the cobbles and cramming it into her mouth before anyone noticed. When she rose again, she had almost lost sight of the man in the bright waistcoat and had to force her way through the crowd to catch up with him.

She was fair dizzy with the industry of the town, the foreign aromas and strange calls, the noise, snippets of conversation as tantalising as the smell of a stew on a cold day. In Inkpen, she had recognised the faces of everyone, known them all by name and they her, but now . . . who knew there could be this many unfamiliar souls contained in one place? She caught a glimpse of a butcher's boy, running errands through the throng, his handcart laden with joints of meat, strings of sausages, a flitch of bacon. Something in the turn of his head, the curve of his jaw reminded her of Will, the eldest of her brothers, and she felt a sudden pang of homesickness for the cottage she had left behind and the quiet of her village.

The man stopped suddenly at a large dwelling set back from the road and she halted a pace behind him. 'Here we are,' he said, a note of pride evident in his voice. 'Hollander's Fine Silks.'

Rowan stared at the house. It was bounded by two smaller dwellings that leaned up against it like buttresses. As wide as it was tall – which was plenty – it was made of red brick with a steeply gabled tiled roof. Two large square-paned oak-framed windows looked out from either side of a broad doorway and a painted sign depicting a pair of shears swung above the lintel. Even from her swift survey, it was clear it was one of the town's most impressive buildings.

The ground floor was a shopfront, and displayed in the window to her left were bolts of fine cloth: plain, striped and some that were richly woven with exotic birds and flowers. It was to be several months before she would learn that the colours that so delighted her were turquoise, chartreuse, violet and vermilion, but only a few weeks before she would feel fine silk fabric between fingers that had previously only known coarse linen and broadcloth.

Rowan dragged her gaze away from the fabrics and craned her neck skywards. The house was so tall it seemed to touch the sky. She counted three sets of windows, one atop another, those of the first floor paned with diamond-shaped glass. There were six chimneypots and four dormers jutting out of the pitched roof, and she knew from the height of it that there would be a great many stairs to reach the very top.

The man retrieved a set of keys from the pocket of his coat and beckoned her into a small entranceway. Doors led off it to the left and right and a passage continued on towards the back of the house, which was dim and shadowed. 'We live at the back and upstairs,' he explained. 'Your room – if you meet with my wife's approval – will be at the top of the house, with Alice. Now follow me, for Mistress Hollander should be hereabouts.'

He ushered her along the passageway and into a large, square room. Sconces lit the panelled walls and her boots sank into the thick carpets laid upon the floor. At the far end was a grand stone fireplace the colour of honey, where a fire burned smokily, the green wood spitting and hissing. She knew that there was a better kind to use.

Beside the fire, a young woman sat reading in a chair. Her hair, dressed in loops and curls, shone fair, and her skin glowed, struck with firelight. Her gown was the colour of autumn cider and lace frothed at her slim wrists like a syllabub. She had a smallish, pink mouth, and a pointed chin that sharpened her otherwise serene features. A mole at the high point of her cheek, which might have been mistaken for a courtier's beauty patch, drew attention to her round, china-blue eyes. Rowan had never encountered anyone quite like her before: she was so clean and dainty; she looked as though she might snap at the slightest pressure.

'Ah, my dear Caroline,' the man said, rubbing his palms together as if he were unsure of himself. 'What do you think to our new maid?'

'Rowan Caswell, ma'am.' Rowan spoke up, for Mr Hollander – she presumed that was he – had not bothered to ask her name. She remembered that a curtsey might be in order and bobbed self-consciously.

His wife turned and put down the book she had been reading, now studying Rowan with a languid curiosity. Rowan was grateful that her face was in shadow, that her scar might not be seen so clearly.

'This will not do. It will not do at all.'

Rowan's spirits sank to the thin soles of her boots.

'Were we not after a boy, someone we could train to be your valet?' She shook her head, as if the fact of her husband returning with something other than he intended was not an unusual occurrence.

'There was no one suitable.'

'What? Not even early this morning?'

'No, I am afraid not.'

But there had been; Rowan remembered several boys of about her age, as well as older men, waiting to be hired.

Caroline Hollander sighed, and inspected Rowan more closely. Her eyes narrowed, and Rowan knew that she had seen her scar. 'She is no painting, but that is perhaps a good thing,' she said. 'All right, if there really was no one else, she will have to do, for now anyway. We shall have to get her clean, for I doubt the girl's seen a bath for a good while. Probably lousy and with goodness knows any manner of other infestations.'

The unkindness of her words was tempered by a sweet smile, but Rowan was affronted, though she knew better than to show it. She might be the worse from her long journey, but she used a tincture of rosemary, peppermint, clove and geranium that kept the lice at bay and her hair shiny. When necessary, she also rubbed a paste of fenugreek seeds and mustard oil on her body, which wasn't as sweet-smelling, but was certainly efficacious. She might be a simple girl from a poor village, but she was no peasant.

'Have Prudence arrange it tonight. But for heaven's sake, Patrick, make sure she is fed first; the scrawny baggage looks like she hasn't seen a meal for months.'

Rowan allowed herself to breathe out. It seemed that she met with Mistress Hollander's approval, enough to be employed on a trial at least.

'And she will need new dresses. I'll not have my servants clothed in rags. She can have an old one of Alice's for the time being.' Caroline Hollander picked up her book again, as if they had already taken their leave.

'Of course, dearest,' he replied. Then, to Rowan, 'Come along, then, I'll show you upstairs.' He took a glass lamp from a sideboard and led them back along the hallway. Rowan glanced behind her as she left the room, seeing shadows gathered around her new mistress. She blinked and they disappeared; she told herself it was simply the effect of her unfamiliar surroundings.

THREE

Now

A light rain had begun to fall, spotting the pavement, and Thea sheltered under the lintel in front of the house as she juggled the keys, trying to decide which one might open the newly painted front door.

The house was at the far reaches of the long high street, just before it narrowed and curved upwards towards distant hills she remembered seeing on her first, daylight, visit. It was three storeys tall and square-fronted, with red-brick walls and a rust-coloured, lichen-spattered tiled roof. Four dormer windows were set in the steeply pitched roof, with chimneys at each end. Wide white-framed, multi-paned windows flanked the front door and a smart plaque next to it proclaimed the residence to be 'Silk House'. A smaller sign underneath in black lettering, which looked to have been recently added, warned that it was 'Strictly Private'. Not a single welcoming light shone from within.

Thea had passed several pubs along the way to the house, hearing the roar of conversation and smelling the aromas of log fires and bitter ale seep from one as a couple entered, and she'd been sorely tempted to stop for a drink and something to eat, but thought better of it, even when it had begun to rain. Priorities, she reminded herself.

She turned her attention back to the keys, selected one and then moved to insert it in the lock, but the front door now stood ajar. She stared at it, certain it had been shut a few seconds earlier. Pushing it with her fingertips, gently in case someone stood behind, she called out, her voice a question.

'Hello?'

A streetlight on the pavement nearby gave some illumination, but the interior of the house was pitch black. She couldn't shake the feeling that she was being watched, and glanced behind her but saw nothing. She stepped determinedly over the threshold and sniffed – the air inside the house smelled smoky and sharply herbal, as if somewhere a fire had been lit using damp wood. She didn't scare easily, but an empty house on a dark night in an unfamiliar town was enough to give her pause. Swallowing the first inkling of a misgiving, she walked on, pulling her suitcase behind her. Once she was further inside, she set the case upright and shrugged off the zippered bag of hockey sticks that had been slung over her shoulder. She turned back, feeling along the wall by the door for a switch. Her fingers closed around a round dome and she pushed down on the button she found there. A light flickered and then glowed dimly.

'Miss Rust?'

She jumped when she heard the voice behind her and swung around.

Standing at the other end of the passageway was a tall, gaunt woman, her silver-grey hair pulled back from her face, glasses shading her eyes. The light cast dancing shadows about the hallway, so that the woman's body seemed insubstantial, melding with the gloom around her.

'Yes, I'm Thea. Thea Rust,' she said, ignoring a desire to turn back to the pub she'd passed, to the light and the warmth and the life there.

The woman seemed to glide across the floor before stopping a few inches from her. The oversized, opaque-lensed glasses and severe hairstyle were at odds with her delicately patterned blouse. 'You look hardly older than the girls we're expecting. Mrs Mary Hicks. Dame of Silk House,' she added, tucking her hands behind her back. A large cat the colour of smoke curled about her feet, disappearing and reappearing from under her skirts, hissing furiously at Thea.

Now the woman had come closer, she was less intimidating, but nevertheless there was something about her that sent a shiver down Thea's spine. 'Very nice to meet you, Mrs Hicks,' she said, doing her best to sound sincere. 'I wasn't sure if anyone was here – it was dark . . .'

'Well, of course I would be here, Miss Rust. The girls arrive tomorrow. I have been so busy readying the house that I didn't have time to turn on a light at the front. That is all.'

Thea bit her lip at the condescending tone but said nothing. She didn't want to make an enemy of the woman before they'd had a chance to get to know each other.

'What a lovely cat,' she said, trying to be friendly and bending down to stroke it. The cat slunk beneath the Dame's skirts once again and Thea straightened, feeling foolish.

'Isis. A damn fine mouser.' Her lips twitched and she eyed Thea, as if silently evaluating her. 'Be careful, though – she scratches.'

'Got it.' Thea had only a sketchy knowledge of Greek mythology, but knew the cat was likely named for a goddess not the Islamic State.

'Well now, we should get you settled. Your room is at the top of the house,' Mrs Hicks said, pointing in the direction of a staircase further along the passageway. 'Turn left at the top, second from the end. I am at the back, to the left, on this floor. The girls will be on the first, second and top floors, with the communal rooms and breakfast area here on the ground. There's also a garden at the back, off the breakfast room, and at the end, past the fishpond, is a gate in the wall that leads to the river. Going beyond the gate will be strictly out of bounds.'

Thea sensed that dictate extended to her as well.

'And in future, I would prefer if you call me Dame Hicks. It's an Oxleigh tradition.' She smiled, but Thea had no way of knowing if it reached her eyes or not – the glasses made her quite inscrutable. 'I'll give you a full orientation tomorrow,' she added. 'You'll need to be up to speed before the girls arrive.'

'When will that be exactly?' asked Thea.

'From three; enough time for them to settle in and unpack before supper at the house.'

Thea knew from the copious briefing notes she had been sent, that the girls – fourteen of them – were to eat their early and late meals at the boarding house, but would have lunch and dinner at the main school with the rest of the pupils.

'And Mrs Jackson? The housemistress?' Thea had met her at her interview, a lovely, warm dumpling of a woman who smelled of talcum powder and peppermints. It occurred to her that if Mrs Hicks, or the porter for that matter, had been on the interviewing panel, she might have had second thoughts about taking the job. She could only hope that Mrs Jackson would smooth her path.

'I'm afraid there's been a slight hiccup there. She rather unfortunately injured herself playing badminton last weekend. Tripped over the shuttlecock. Has put her back out, so it seems,' Dame Hicks said. 'The school was obviously unable to employ anyone to replace her at such short notice, and I have been informed that you will stand in for her until she is recovered. Which will be quite some weeks, I am told.'

Thea, who had been momentarily distracted by the thought of the chocolate bar in her bag, started. Had she heard correctly? She was to take responsibility for the new girls? The Dame sounded as happy about the prospect as she was and her mood plunged as she realised that it would mean being involved with their wellbeing and welfare. She loved teaching history and sharing her passion for the subject, but she had precisely zero experience in pastoral care, and had little patience for the petty dramas and emotions of teenage girls. She could still remember what it felt like to be sixteen years old, pivoting from crippling self-doubt to boundless self-belief, sometimes in the same minute. Although it was probably considered a step up in responsibility, she mused, it was not one she had planned on.

'Obviously, I shall also be here,' said the Dame. 'But my role is to ensure the house runs smoothly, supervise the kitchen and cleaning staff, oversee the laundry and so on. Come along, then,' she said, glancing at her watch, 'and bring your bags. Let's not waste any more time.' She marched off at a smart pace, flicking on another light as she went, not checking to see if Thea was following. 'On this floor we have the dining room – it was the hotel restaurant before the school bought the house.' The Dame indicated a room off to the right and Thea looked through a half-open set of double doors, seeing two long tables and rows of chairs flanked by a serving area. Cheerful patterned curtains hung at the windows and she could smell that the room had been recently painted.

'The kitchen is behind there,' she said, pointing to a set of double doors at the end of the room. 'Now, follow me upstairs.'

A wide oak staircase, the time-buffed newel posts carved into acorns, led to the first floor. Thea hefted her suitcase and bag up the uneven treads, glad that she hadn't given in to the temptation to pack more than absolutely necessary.

They reached the first floor, where a long landing ran towards her right, off which were five doors, two on one side and three on the other. 'The girls will sleep two or three to a room.' As the Dame opened a door Thea peered around it to see twin beds, made up with white cotton duvets and thick pillows, and two desks with comfortable-looking chairs filling the space. Pinboards were fixed above each desk, a circular rug lay between the beds, and a wall of cupboards lined the back. To Thea the room looked, for the moment anyway, rather antiseptic, the only accessory a curious disc about the size and shape of a large pebble on one of the desks. Thea's own teenage bedroom had been a similar size, though plastered from skirting board to ceiling with posters of hockey players, glossy thoroughbreds and tennis stars. She remembered with embarrassment a crush on Andre Agassi that had endured throughout her teenage years and wondered if the girls would be allowed to personalise their space. She suspected they might be limited to the pinboards.

The Dame indicated a smaller staircase at the end of the hall that twisted upwards into darkness. 'That leads to the attic, and also runs all the way down to the ground floor – I believe it was the original servants' staircase. Two girls will share the larger room up there, and then there is your room, and a study for your use as well.'

'Super. I can probably take it from here, thank you,' said Thea, anxious to find her room and set down her heavy bags.

'Very well. I will see you in the morning, then.' As noiselessly as she had appeared, the Dame disappeared.

Thea shifted her suitcase to the other hand, shouldered her hockey bag and carried on along the hallway. The first room had the names of three girls affixed to the door: Aradia Bianchi, Morgan Addington-Clay, Sabrina Fox. She opened it a few inches and saw a large space with two dormer windows that faced the high street. Despite the sloping walls, there was ample room for three beds, desks and a large wardrobe. There was even space for a pair of red gingham-upholstered armchairs, which were arranged around a low table. In one corner was a washbasin and a table on which sat a kettle, mugs and a couple of storage jars.

Satisfied that she had seen all she needed to, Thea withdrew, closing the door behind her, and then hauled herself and her belongings up the final staircase to the top floor, where she found her rooms at the end of the corridor, past a door marked with the names Fenella and Camilla. She wouldn't have been surprised to have also seen an Arabella, Henrietta or Clarissa affixed to the doors on the lower floors, such was the type of girl who was to attend Oxleigh College. She stopped herself. Her own name – Theodora – was hardly very different.

As she wheeled her suitcase into the room, she took an inventory of her surroundings. There was a single bed, made up as the girls' had been with a ticking duvet and a navy tartan blanket at the end – thank goodness they hadn't gone for pink – as well as an armchair placed next to the single dormer window, and a large dresser. On the dresser sat the same pebble-shaped ornament she had seen in the other rooms. Curious, she picked it up, noticing a string of blinking lights around the circumference and the word 'Ekko' printed along the side. It seemed to be one of those smart devices, the ones Thea was convinced listened in to your conversations, fed information back to God-only-knew-who. She put it down, supposing she could always remove the batteries.

She made her way to the far end of the room, where the walls sloped together to form a point and where she could only just stand up without hitting her head. There was another door, which she opened to discover a tiny bathroom. The floor creaked in complaint as she walked on it, groaning like a geriatric levering themselves out of a chair. It was also far from level, and in fact seemed to be skewed on an incline that made her feel as if she were in a ship's cabin rather than on solid ground. She shrugged. It was an old house; it was to be expected. As a historian it thrilled her to be staying there, for the building appeared to date from at least the eighteenth century, judging by the exterior and the off-kilter floors.

Thea set down her sports bag, unzipping a side pocket and retrieving a somewhat worse for wear apple and the chocolate bar. She had noticed one more door at the end of the corridor, which she assumed was her study, but she would get to that later. For now, she kicked off her boots and flopped back on the bed, taking a large bite of the apple and chewing thoughtfully.

Every muscle in her body ached, the combined effect of a long plane journey followed by two days' sightseeing in London scoping out museums for potential excursions for her classes, and her normally level spirits had dipped along with her blood sugar. It was probably this that made her suddenly wonder if she had made a mistake in coming. This school, with its ghosts; the privileged boys – and now girls – who attended it; the other teachers who were doubtless cut from the same cloth as Mr Battle – what would she have in common with any of them?

Sometimes she really didn't understand herself.

Restless, she finished the apple and threw the core in a wastepaper bin on the far side of the room, the slam-dunk bringing a brief smile to her lips. She got to her feet, tossed her glasses on the bed, and went to wash her hands and face in the sink, standing on tiptoes to peer short-sightedly at herself in the mirror. Deep purple circles ringed her eyes and her long, straight brown hair had separated into lank strands. As she stared, she saw a shadow flit behind her, and she whirled around but it disappeared before she could make out what it was.

Nothing but the rattle of the windows in the wind.

Tiredness and the lukewarm welcome were making her paranoid. *Get a grip, Rust.*

She dried her hands, replaced her glasses and went back into the corridor and to the room next door. It was small, scarcely more than a box room, though there was a window that looked out over the back of the house. She opened the curtains and peered out, though in the darkness she could see very little. A smear caught her eye, which on closer inspection turned out to be a handprint, the finger marks widely spread. She rubbed at it with her sleeve, but it didn't budge. It must be on the outside of the glass, though how anyone could have got that high up she had no idea, for the top floor – the attic, she supposed – of the house was too tall for even the longest ladder.

She turned back to the room, seeing a wooden desk, chair and a wastepaper basket. A multicoloured rug took up half of the tiny floor space, and there were hooks on the wall that must have been newly drilled, for there were small piles of dust on the floor beneath them.

A stack of buff-coloured folders sat on the desk, and she shuffled through them, curious. Each was marked with the name of a girl – the new Oxleigh students. She took them back to her bedroom, placing them on the bedside table to look at later. Her first priority was to unpack, and it didn't take long to stow her clothes in the dresser and organise her toiletries in the bathroom. Reaching the bottom of her bag, she pulled out a cylindrical tin, a small photo in a wooden frame and a couple of books, all of which she placed on the small bookshelf at the end of the room. She opened the top book and looked at the faded ink script on the flyleaf, reading the inscription she knew by heart: *HAR, September 1965, Mill House, Oxleigh College.*

HAR: Henry Adam Rust. The reason she had been looking at the college website in the first place, and the deciding factor in impulsively applying for the job.

A sudden memory of her father rose, unbidden. She was sitting with him on the back verandah of their suburban house in Melbourne as he patiently applied whitener to his Dunlop Volleys in anticipation of his regular Sunday afternoon knockabout (which he nevertheless played with the commitment of a Wimbledon wildcard). There was always a cigarette burning, its ash growing ever longer, and a bottle of beer beaded with condensation next to it. She frowned as she recalled his competitiveness, never letting Thea or her younger sister, Pip, get the better of him. 'Take no prisoners!' was his favourite cry whenever they faced each other across the net. Desperate for his approval and his attention, they submitted to countless drubbings. She didn't think either of them ever managed to best him, at tennis or cards or chess or anything else, for that matter. Just as well, for he hated losing; it would put him in a temper for days.

She closed the book and was about to go over to the bed when she was suddenly plunged into darkness. A heavy silence descended and the hairs on the back of Thea's neck stood on end. Then, from somewhere deep in the bowels of the house, came a spine-chilling screech.

FOUR

September 1768, Oxleigh

In contrast to the rest of the almost silent, dim house, the kitchen was ablaze, and a not inconsiderable amount of smoke billowed from the wide fireplace, where a haunch of meat turned slowly on a spit. It was by far the warmest and most welcoming of all the rooms Rowan's new master had led her through.

'Lawd save us, what have we got here?'

A short woman stood in front of the fire, almost as wide as she was tall, her arms the size of Wiltshire hams and generous hips bound by a greasy apron. Wisps of hair the colour of a new penny escaped a mob cap and her cheeks were veined and russetted, like autumn windfalls. She appeared to Rowan very much like a ruddy, slightly wizened pippin.

'Prudence, this is the new maid-of-all-work,' said Patrick. 'She will be seeing to me from now on, while Alice will serve Mistress Hollander.'

'Very good, sir.' The cook wiped her arm across a forehead beaded with sweat as she scrutinised Rowan. 'She's skinny enough. Looks strong all right, though. Whatever happened to your eye, girl?'

'Caught it on a meat hook, mistress,' Rowan said shyly. The truth was more obscure than that, for Rowan had been born with the injury. She never knew if it had been inflicted as she emerged from her mother (a difficult birth by her account), or if she had simply grown like that, misshapen and warped. She'd learned that it was better to offer the easier explanation, for those born with deformity were often regarded with suspicion. There was enough reason for people to view her as different, without that too.

The cook winced.

'Mistress Hollander has requested that she bathe. After supper will be perfectly acceptable,' Patrick said as he left.

'Sit down then, girl,' Prudence said, indicating a seat at the large table that took up most of the kitchen. 'Did they not feed you at your last place? Even an urchin would have more meat on her bones.' She placed a bowl of barley studded with carrots and dark with shreds of meat in front of Rowan and passed her a slice of bread from a loaf on the sideboard.

Rowan did not wait to tuck in. 'Is there nothing I can do to help you?' she asked, mumbling through a mouthful of food, wanting to prove her usefulness straightaway.

'You'll be busy here soon enough, girl. I've managed on my own in the kitchen for near seven years now, another day won't harm me. First with the master when he was in London and now here.'

'He lived in London?' Rowan swallowed. She had heard cautionary stories about the capital, a city of thieves and cutpurses, strumpets and beggars, press gangs and bodysnatchers, thrilling tales of loose morals and avarice. She regarded the place with a mix of outright terror and fascination. Oxleigh was a bustling town that fair exhausted a quiet soul; she could scarce imagine another twenty times larger.

'Aye, before he was married.' Her voice turned brusque. 'Now, enough idle chatter, for it profits none of us.'

Rowan took another spoonful of barley porridge, scraping every last morsel of food from the bowl. For the first time since she could remember, the fullness of her stomach pressed against the coarse fabric of her dress.

When she had finished, she watched, fascinated, as Prudence busied herself about the kitchen, hauling pans, draining steaming water and setting out serving dishes with impressive alacrity. Rowan had never seen so much food as the feast that was assembled. And all that for two people. She counted herself most fortunate to have found a wealthy employer.

The warmth of the kitchen and the nourishing food made her drowsy, and she laid her head and arms on the table, thinking to rest for just a moment.

'Come on, sleepy head.' Rowan felt a gentle tug at her sleeve and looked up stiffly. She blinked, seeing that the kitchen now bore little evidence of the cook's earlier industry. 'Let's see about a wash, shall we?' She disappeared into a passageway that ran off the back of the kitchen but was gone so long that Rowan began to wonder what had happened to her. Eventually she returned, carrying a cotton shift, a folded square of fabric, a scrubbing brush and a cake of pale brown soap. 'There's a trough in the scullery, down the passage to your left. I've filled it with water from the pump outside,' Prudence said, giving Rowan the items. 'I don't hold with hot water, brings in all manner of ills.'

Rowan's mother had felt the same way.

'Get on with you, then; there's no time for dawdling in this house.'

'Yes, Prudence.' Rowan hurried in the direction of the scullery.

After she had scrubbed every inch of her body, her teeth chattering with cold, then dried herself with the cloth, wrung out her hair and combed it through with her fingers, Rowan put on the shift. It was obviously once a fine gown, though it was darned at the wrists and dragged along the floor, the sheer fabric soft as thistledown against her skin. She gathered the extra yardage up with one hand, bundled up her soiled clothes in the other and returned to the kitchen.

'Oh!' Rowan nearly dropped the bundle she was carrying. Sitting at the table was the butcher's boy she had seen in the town earlier that day. 'Begging your pardon.' A crimson blush rose up from her neck, and where she had once shivered she was now only uncomfortably warm. She wasn't used to being seen by strangers, at least not in her nightwear.

The boy looked at her as if he'd seen a ghost. 'Who are you?' he asked when he had recovered himself.

'Rowan Caswell. Maid-of-all-work,' she said, liking the sound of her new position as it rolled off her tongue.

'Tommy Dean, what are you doing here?' Prudence had returned to the kitchen and plumped herself down at the table.

In her hand was an onion-shaped bottle containing a clear liquid, some of which she sloshed into a tumbler next to her.

Even from a distance, Rowan could smell the unmistakable aroma of gin, for her aunt had also liked a glass or two.

Prudence then noticed Rowan and gasped. 'Your hair . . .'

Rowan put her hand to her head. Prior to bathing, it had been hidden behind her cap. She knew what had caused Prudence's sudden intake of breath and the boy's reaction, for her hair was of a colour that was rarely seen: white-blonde, and as fine as gossamer. It hung over her scarred eye and fell almost to her waist. Rowan's brothers had teased her for it: 'Queen of the snow, nowhere to go!' they would chant until she chased them away, laughing as they tripped over each other in their haste to escape. In the evenings, her mother would comb out the snarls and when it caught the light from the fire, even her father stared.

Prudence regarded her warily, for it was common knowledge that those with such hair often brought an ill wind – some said outright bad luck – with them. She pursed her lips but said nothing further about it. 'You'd best be getting upstairs, and mind sure no one sees you. Here –' She handed Rowan a men's dressing gown, and Rowan immediately wondered if it had once belonged to Mr Hollander; the wool was finely woven, a tiny frayed edge on the cuffs the only sign of wear. 'Put this on first. That shift's barely decent.'

Rowan gathered the gown about her, but stopped, curious about the boy. He seemed to be in pain. The expression on his face gave nothing away, but Rowan sensed an overwhelming hurt radiating from him as though it were heat from a fire.

It wasn't the first time she'd had the foresight. One afternoon, the summer she turned ten, she had been out in the fields with her brothers, when she had a sudden urge to run home. She tore up the path to their cottage and arrived to see her mother's hand stained scarlet with blood, her face a rictus of agony. 'Fetch me a cloth,' she hissed at her daughter. Rowan returned with a smock, the first thing she could find, and helped bind the wound. 'Knife slipped,' her mother explained through gritted teeth.

Afterwards she asked, 'How did you know to come?'

Rowan shrugged. 'I felt it, as if something had sliced right through me, and then before I knew it, my legs had carried me here.'

Her mother looked upon her, considering. 'You have it, don't you?' she asked. 'The sight?'

'The what?' Rowan looked at her blankly.

'Your grandmother had it too. You will always have to be on your guard. Especially with your hair so fair. Don't breathe a word of it, not even to your brothers or your father, do you hear me? For people will surely believe you to be a witch.'

The word struck fear into Rowan; she well knew what happened to those accused of the craft. They were shunned, blamed when the crops failed or livestock died, when ill fortune or ill health was visited upon a person. Those suspected of witchcraft, even if there was no proof of it, were driven from their homes, outcast from their villages, or worse, locked up in the nearest gaol. Whispers became gossip became fact in less than the blink of an eye.

Not so many years ago, her mother had told her, witches were drowned, or burned on a bonfire while the rest of the village looked on in terror and awe. At the very least, they were tortured, pilliwinks used to crush the bones of their thumbs until they confessed to their crimes, whether real or conjured from the faintest suspicion. Merely being outspoken meant being harnessed with a scold's bridle, a metal bit pushed between your teeth to stop you from speaking. Everyone knew the story of the Malmesbury witches, three women who had been blamed for causing sickness, branded as 'cunning women' and hanged for concocting potions and casting spells. And her mother had been but a girl when the Handsel sisters – four Danish girls living in Wilton, a village not far from Inkpen – were accused of bringing pox to the village and were bludgeoned to death in Grovely Wood without so much as a hearing.

Not all the ducking stools – inflicted on harlots, scolds and witches – had been destroyed when the laws against witchcraft were repealed. Some were still hidden away in byres and sheds, attics and sculleries. Rowan had never seen one, but she shuddered as she remembered her mother telling of the thick leather straps that held a person down as they were lowered into the water, could imagine the terror they would face, unable to move, unable to breathe. She had always been fearful of water: fast-flowing rivers, streams that wound their way across pebbles and sticks, deep pools formed by storm-felled trees.

Her mother had already been instructing Rowan in simple medicines, made with herbs and plants foraged from the hedgerows and hillsides, but after the incident with the knife she began to teach her a number of enchantments, and Rowan knew without having to be told again that she was not to speak of it outside the house or to the rest of the family.

The boy shifted on the seat and Rowan felt the pain radiate from him again; there was something very wrong.

'My sister will wonder what's become of you,' Prudence scolded the boy. 'Come hoping for some supper, by chance?' she asked.

'No, Auntie Pru, look.' Tommy gingerly swung his left leg out from under the table.

The cook, who had taken a swig from the beaker at her elbow, spluttered out a breath. 'Lawd sakes!' she cried. 'How the devil did that happen?'

A round welt had formed on his shin and below that a deep gash was oozing blood, the skin around it already discolouring. 'Kicked by a horse,' he said, gritting his teeth against the pain.

As he spoke, Rowan went to where she had left her bundle of belongings and found a pot of salve she had brought with her. 'Here,' she said cautiously, holding it out to Prudence. 'This might help. He'll also need to bind that; keep it clean. Is there some cloth about?' Surely in the house of a fabric merchant there would have to be.

'I've muslin that I use for straining sauces,' said Prudence, a note of doubt in her voice.

'As long as it is clean, please fetch it,' Rowan replied, surer of herself now.

'But where'd you get that from?' Prudence pointed to the pot in Rowan's hand.

'It's mine. I mean, I made it,' she replied. When the summer just past had been at its height, Rowan had ground comfrey, yarrow, lemon balm and calendula, adding lanolin extracted from lambswool gathered from the hedgerows. Her mother had taught her well; she could make the salve, and a number of other healing balms and poultices too, using the herbs of the wayside and field mixed with beeswax and honey, soaked bran and bread. She had not forgotten the knowledge of other, stronger remedies, though when she and her brothers had been taken in by her Aunt Win, the woman had insisted upon 'none of that kind of magic' under her roof. After that, she had stopped making all but the simplest remedies.

The cook raised a disbelieving eyebrow.

'My mother taught me. She was . . . she knew about such things.'

Rowan looked at her as innocently as she knew how, hoping to dispel the flash of mistrust she had seen in the cook's eyes.

'Out with it,' said Prudence, her expression narrowing with suspicion. 'Are you a hedge witch?'

Rowan held her breath. A hedge witch was the name for someone who dealt in herbal tinctures and healing potions, not magic exactly, but she did not dare admit to even this, for the slightest hint of anything untoward cast a long shadow. She was still a stranger in this house and had yet to prove her worth and good character. 'It is but a common remedy,' she said quietly.

The cook hesitated for a brief moment, then held out her hand. 'Right. Give it here, then. And you'd best be off to bed, girl. You've a long day ahead of you tomorrow.'

Rowan passed her the precious pot of ointment and turned to leave.

'Thank you, Rowan Caswell,' Tommy said.

She glanced back and flashed a grateful smile at him – he reminded her so much of her brother Will. He had the same shock of tow-coloured hair and eyes the colour of filberts and she couldn't help but like him. ''Tis no matter,' she said, before scampering up the back stairs.

When Rowan reached the top of the house she found the attic room again, though still no sign of the mysterious Alice. It was a small, shadowy space with a sloping ceiling and a dormer window that looked out onto the street. It contained an iron-framed bed made up with a patterned counterpane, linen sheets and a pair of thin pillows; a linen press and a chest of drawers on which sat a wide basin and a jug made up the remainder of the furniture. To Rowan, who had slept on a pallet in the kitchen at her aunt and uncle's house, and before that shared a bed with two of her brothers when they were small, it appeared very grand indeed.

She placed her scant possessions on the floor next to the bed and lay down on the side furthest from the door. Though the mattress and pillow were thin, they felt like goosedown to Rowan after a night spent in a copse on the way to Oxleigh. She lay, luxuriating in the feeling of them against her skin, her mind a tumult of the day's experiences. Then, remembering, she reached into her bundle and pulled out a small cross fashioned from two twigs bound in the centre with a strand of wool dyed red with crabapple bark. The twigs were from the rowan tree, for which she had been named, and her father had made it when she was little, indeed had made one for each of her brothers too. As she touched its familiar surface she heard her mother's words. 'For protection,' she had said when she handed it to her. Rowan hoped the charm her mother had placed upon it had not lost any of its power, that it would keep her safe in this strange new place. She clutched the cross in her hand and was seized with a sudden longing to be back in Inkpen, curled by the embers of the fire, her brothers, like a tangle of pups, close by. Before she had time to dwell on the thought any more deeply, she was so soundly asleep that she did not stir when a young woman crept into bed next to her many hours later.

FIVE

1768, London

The petals were studded with tiny beads that, when looked upon closely, reflected a world turned upside down as if by a conjurer's trick. Mary-Louise Stephenson sat at a table by the window in her drawing room and adjusted the flowers in the vase in front of her, loosening the tight knot she had wound them into when she gathered them and being especially careful not to break the remaining dewdrops.

Earlier that morning she had offered to go to the market, walking the few short streets from the house in Spital Yard in search of a turnip and some carrots, and on the way home she had picked these wildflowers, for they grew in tangled profusion in the ditches thereabouts. She favoured them above all others, which was just as well, for the household's meagre income rarely stretched to the purchase of meat, let alone the flower-seller's luscious roses, blousy peonies and the lilies that almost made her swoon with their perfume as she passed. Later, her sister Frances would add a handful of grain and some water to the vegetables that she had left in the kitchen, making a soup for their supper to have with a loaf of yesterday's bread. With care, they would stretch this meal until the end of the week.

Ignoring the knot of hunger in her stomach, Mary turned the flowers this way and that, searching for the best angle of the sunny yellow coltsfoot and the purple flowers of wild violet. She had in mind to design a pattern from their contrasting forms and complementary hues. She worked by painting the flower first and then tracing a pattern from which to embroider a repeat of the flower onto fabric. Her ability with the needle was not of sufficient quality for her to imagine seeking employment in that area, nor were the wages – sevenpence for a day that often began at dawn and did not end until late at night – something to aspire towards. But it enabled her to demonstrate how the design might work when woven in silk. At least that was what she hoped.

It was her sister Frances who had suggested Mary turn her fondness for painting into a more profitable pursuit. They lived on the edges of the city's weaving industry, on the outermost of a grid of streets barely a half-mile square, where almost every dwelling housed a loom on its upper floors, presided over by a journeyman or master weaver, and the air sang with their clack and clatter from sunup to sundown and beyond. Silks and damasks were woven and brocaded with showy patterns of flowers, exotic fruits and leaves. There was lustred taffety, corded paduasoy, silk tabby, damask and velvet; the most expensive silks were shot through with fine gold or silver thread. Patterned silk commanded a price more than double that of its plain cousins, for it required far greater skill to weave.

'A few extra shillings in the household purse would indeed be a blessing,' Frances had said. 'For I do not know how we will afford the rent after this year.' She insisted that Mary was as talented as any of the men. 'More skilled too, once you learn the particulars, I'll wager. It should be but a short step from painting and embroidery.'

Fabric design, like so many interesting – and better-paid – activities it seemed to Mary, was generally the province of men, and the pattern-drawers, mercers and silk weavers behaved like proprietary lovers, not allowing outsiders to come within sniffing distance of their work. There had been but one female pattern-drawer in recent decades – the revered Anna Maria Garthwaite – but she had been buried five years past now. Mary dreamed of one day taking her place, wished she were still alive to share her wisdom.

The sisters were fortunate in that Frances's late husband, Samuel, had been a journeyman weaver, and they had friends among the legion who plied their trade in the surrounding streets. Frances had appealed to the good graces of one of them, Guy Le Maître, a Huguenot whose father had fled persecution in Lyon, to initiate them into the mysteries of weaving. One morning, he led them up into his loft, a sloping space filled with light that streamed in from long windows set into the angled walls. There he demonstrated the workings of the lashes and battens, the needles where they sat on guiding springs, and how the weft and warp threads were set up, using the pattern on the squared paper before him as a template. 'We have a flying shuttle,' he said, his expression serious as he pointed in the direction of a draw boy who sat atop the loom sending a small object on a wheeled track hurtling across the silk threads. 'Now we can weave fabric wider than the span of a man's arm. It is a great saving.'

Mary nodded, intoxicated by the dry, earthy smell of the skeins of silk thread and the lightning-fast movement of the shuttle. 'Why, it is as fine embroidery, not weaving,' she said, drawing as close to the loom as she dared. 'How is that possible?'

'The detail,' he said. 'The most intricate patterns can take weeks to mount.'

Mary's eyebrows knitted together in confusion.

'To set up,' he explained. 'This particular design is such that we can see enough of a repeat of the pattern whether used on a waistcoat or the skirts of a ball gown.'

A glimmer of understanding lit Mary's mind as she marvelled at the rich colours of the silk thread wound on the bobbins that lined the room: buttercup yellow, the crimson of rosehips, peach, bright scarlet, and a purple–blue almost the exact hue of iris petals.

'The more detailed the pattern, the more lifelike it is, but also the more difficult to weave without making an error, dropping a thread. We must strike a balance,' he said. 'The pattern-drawer ought not to be a stranger to geometry nor proportion, as well as art,' he added.

'And how much of this fabric will you weave?' she asked, though Frances, who stood nearby but said nothing, had already explained some of the workings of the trade. Mary had determined to appeal to Monsieur Le Maître's sense of importance, to flatter his ego so that he might be forthcoming.

'Generally only enough for four gowns, as much as the mercer has requested and knows he will sell. Each gown will use between nine and sixteen yards of material.'

'So, between thirty and sixty-odd yards of one design in total,' said Mary, calculating the sum in her head.

Guy's eyes widened momentarily at her quick accuracy before his expression assumed its usual dour impassivity.

'And how long will that take?'

'Several months.'

'I can see that a lady would not want to meet another wearing a gown of the same fabric,' she murmured. 'And why it commands such a high price.'

'Exactly.'

'Who chooses the colours? The weave? How exactly do you decide on a pattern?'

'The weaver will sometimes commission a pattern-drawer; other times it is the mercer who decides what is to be woven. I have to admit, however,' he grumbled, 'that at times the pattern-drawer is unaware of the limitations of the loom and we have, on occasion, been forced to halt the weaving until it can be altered. Sometimes even scrap the entire commission.'

'I can well imagine the cost in lost time and materials,' Mary sympathised.

Guy nodded, seemingly unfazed by her endless questions. 'The mercer provides us with the order, although we might make up a length of fabric in the hope of finding a buyer,' he continued. ''Tis never good to have the loom lying idle.'

'It must be difficult to translate a drawing onto paper, no?' she asked.

'It is at first,' he admitted. 'But here, let me show you on this twill . . .'

~

Mary left the weaver's loft that day with her head spinning, as visions of how she might transform her naturalistic sketches of plants and wildflowers into patterns that might take the fancy of grand lords and ladies – perhaps even royalty, she allowed herself a fanciful dream – danced in her mind.

She spent her waking hours sketching and painting until her eyes strained, her fingers were numb and the candle stubs burned to pools of wax. She painted primrose and crocus, and then, as the weather grew warmer, cornflowers, cow parsley and foxgloves. She copied these onto fabrics, embroidering them until they appeared almost to possess three dimensions. From these she attempted to draw the pattern on the point paper as Guy had shown her, which the weaver would use as a template. Her first attempts ended in frustration, as she struggled to transfer her curling designs onto a grid. But she persisted, finally creating several that she thought might work.

'They are quite fresh and lively,' said Frances as Mary showed the portfolio of designs to her. 'Why, I would be delighted to wear a gown woven with such delicate and pretty flowers.'

'But they are so very different from the work of the other pattern-drawers,' Mary said doubtfully, wondering suddenly if she might have been wasting her time with such common plants. Would they not appear ridiculous on sumptuous silk, as a damask relief or picked out in silver and gold threads? The flowers of the verge and byway that were dismissed as weeds?

The fashion was for showier blooms, roses, lilies, camellias and the like. No, she reminded herself sternly, her wayside gleanings held a beauty of their own. She would persuade the weavers to use her designs. 'My work will stand out as original,' she declared, a note of determination in her voice.

'I certainly hope you are right,' said Frances, a worried expression not leaving her face. 'For we will be down to our last few pounds 'ere long.'

Mary refused to let worry about money sway her from her purpose: to assemble a portfolio of sketches and patterns that might be woven onto silk to grace the backs of the finest ladies and gentlemen of the city.

It was only in the early hours of the morning that doubt weaselled its way into her churning mind and kept her awake until the first birds began their melodic twittering. Who was she, a spinster educated in a parsonage, to imagine she could force her way into a man's world, let alone succeed at it?

SIX

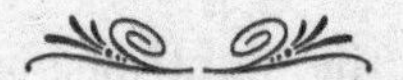

Now

At first, Thea couldn't remember where she was. Disorientated, she reached for her glasses and staggered from her bed, pushed aside the curtains and peered onto the street far below. It curved gently downhill, and in the grey morning light she could see the outline of the roofs of the college buildings at its far reaches, and beyond that, the green of the playing fields. Several trucks rumbled heavily along the other side of the road, crunching their gears as they descended towards the belly of the town.

The night before, after the lights had cut out, she had been on the point of feeling her way downstairs when they flickered on and off again, finally staying on. Putting it down to the dodgy electrics of an old house, and the spine-tingling screech to a cat shut indoors, she had nevertheless been unable to quell a prickle of apprehension as she settled down for the night. Despite her exhaustion, it had taken her longer than usual to fall asleep.

She left the window and glanced at her watch: still plenty of time before her meeting with the headmaster. She reached for her phone and pressed the button to turn it on but the screen remained resolutely black. She checked the charger and the lead. Nothing. Perhaps the socket didn't work, or there'd been another power cut in the night? She silently cursed. She had wanted to check her emails; make sure she didn't miss anything ahead of her first day. She was on her way to the shower when a crumpled shape in the corner of the room caught her eye. Her jacket. She could have sworn she'd hung it up on the back of the door. She must have been more tired yesterday than she realised. Next to it was a chocolate wrapper on the floor – she hadn't managed to land that in the basket – and she knew that her first priority, after a shower, was breakfast, preferably not in the company of Dame Hicks. She needed to fortify herself before facing the inscrutable woman again.

~

The kitchen was large, clinically clean and, happily, empty. A clock on the wall showed the time at a quarter to twelve. Thea didn't need to check her watch again to know that it had stopped quite some time ago.

She walked to the rear where a doorway led to a short passage and then a back door. Unbolting it, she saw a long, narrow garden bound by high flint walls. In the centre was a complicated-looking flowerbed with sections marked out in old bricks and pruned low hedging: a knot garden or parterre perhaps. Beyond that was a small fishpond. She stared at the flowerbed, her brain taking a few seconds to catch up with her eyes until she recognised the shape it made and where she had seen it before. It was a pentacle, the same as on one of the keys Mr Battle had given her. The wind scattered the last of the leaves on the damp grass and she shivered in the cold morning air.

Back in the warmth of the kitchen she rummaged in drawers and cupboards, not finding batteries for the stopped clock, but discovering tea, bread, jam and assorted boxes of cereal. A brace of large refrigerators was generously stocked with, among other things, butter, milk, cheese and vegetables. Cupboards yielded cups and plates, and cutlery was in a long drawer to one side of the room. Cheering up at the prospect of food and a cuppa, Thea toasted bread and boiled a kettle for tea before settling herself at the end of one of two long oak tables in the dining room, basking in the bright sunshine that now streamed through the two bay windows.

She had no sooner taken a bite of her toast when the door opened and the Dame appeared. The woman looked slightly less formidable in the daylight and was dressed in a similar blouse to the previous night, but this time with a pattern of red berries. Thea was wearing a pair of grey tailored trousers and a simply cut shirt in anticipation of her first day in the job, had even added an unaccustomed swipe of lipstick, but she was sombrely dressed compared to the Dame. She put her toast down, hastily swallowed, and wished her good morning, resolving not to be intimidated.

As moments of silence stretched between them, Thea noticed an unusual round pewter brooch affixed to the Dame's collar. It featured an arrow-shaped design, not unlike one of the keys Thea had been given. Intrigued, she wanted to ask about its origin, for it looked antique, but held her tongue. The older woman's countenance did not invite personal questions, though when she spoke her tone was a few degrees less frigid.

'I trust you are rested.'

'Yes. Thank you. Though little could have disturbed me – I slept like the dead.'

The Dame looked at her sharply. 'Perhaps we might find some time before the girls arrive to discuss the running of the house and where our responsibilities lie?'

Thea nodded. 'How about eleven?'

'Very good. I have to supervise the delivery of the remaining provisions, and the kitchen staff are due to arrive after lunch, but that will give us enough time to run over everything.' She left Thea to her breakfast.

As Thea was clearing up in the kitchen, the door creaked open, followed by a high-pitched meow. Isis. The cat immediately began rubbing herself against Thea's legs, doing figure of eights around her ankles. It seemed the cat, like the Dame, was far friendlier this morning. Thea reached down to stroke her and was treated to a rumbling purr. 'Was that you yowling last night, hey? What was all that about?' she crooned, casting about to see if there was anything on the floor that might be a bowl. 'I'd better not feed you, puss,' she whispered. 'Can't risk getting into trouble on my first day.'

She looked at her watch. Eight-thirty. Enough time to explore before her meeting. She'd had no opportunity to stroll through the town after her interview several months earlier, because she had been hurrying to get a bus to the train station, and she was now anxious to see what it might hold. These were, after all, the streets her father had spent much of his boyhood wandering; nearby were the playing fields he had battled on, the theatre he had performed in, the boarding house he had slept in. She and her sister had heard how he would run five miles before a cold shower and breakfast on icy winter mornings, how he'd been rapped over the knuckles with a wooden ruler for minor misdemeanours, wiping away the blood when it was over.

How they had been some of the best years of his life.

Her father had described the twice-weekly market that snaked its way down the centre of the wide high street – 'Third widest in England,' he had impressed upon them. 'Built so that a carriage and six could turn a circle.' He had talked of foods foreign to her and Pip when they were young: savoury pork pies, scotch eggs the size of a baby's head, lardy cakes studded with currants and orange peel.

Occupied by these memories, she left the house and crossed into the middle of the road, where, after walking only a few metres, she spotted a baker's stall piled high with quiches and tarts, empanadas and, yes, scotch eggs and pork pies. Her lips curved in a smile, and if she hadn't just demolished an extra piece of toast, she might have been tempted.

A few minutes later, as she walked through the archway that led to the school grounds, she noticed a number of other women and men of varying ages and sizes hurrying towards the Master's House. She caught the eye of a woman wearing a flowing skirt cinched by a wide belt and a brilliant tangerine and scarlet blouse, moving with a long, confident stride and a sheaf of papers tucked under her arm. 'I hadn't realised we were all to be at the meeting,'

Thea said, recognising one of the art faculty, Claire McGovern, who had shown her around the school before her interview.

'Oh, hello there,' said Claire, her face lighting up with pleasure. 'Yes, we all get the summons on the first day of term. Well actually, tomorrow is the official first day, but you know what I mean. Anyway, welcome, and I don't mind telling you how glad I am that you got the job – you should have seen the other applicants,' she said quietly, wrinkling her nose as if she'd smelled something particularly unpleasant. Thea couldn't help but laugh. Perhaps the school wouldn't be as daunting as it first seemed.

'I'm still not sure I'm ready for this,' she confided in a whisper.

'Don't worry – it's not all beating, bullying and buggery these days, though there is a story that any master found to be raising their arm above shoulder height when applying the cane is to be fined a case of French. I'm sure it's a myth, though.' Claire winked at her, speaking almost as quickly as she walked. 'Come on,' she said, slowing her pace a fraction, allowing Thea to catch up. 'The headmaster hates it if we're late.'

It was a good thing the headmaster's rooms were large, for Thea and Claire were among the last of the dozens of teachers to squeeze in. There was a loud hum of conversation from those present as they caught up with each other after the long summer break, but it soon hushed as Dr Fox made his entrance. She had to crane her neck to see him over the heads of those in front of her. He was young to be head of such a school, mid-forties, and he had a smile that seemed to warm the room. Her apprehension eased a little more.

Six months ago Thea hadn't been looking for a new job, let alone considering leaving Melbourne, or Australia for that matter.

She'd been teaching at a progressive, multicultural state school in the city's outer suburbs and, despite the woeful lack of funding, stretched resources and the constant staff-room politics, she had loved her job. But the opportunity to come and work in this area had drawn her like a magnet. Quite apart from her father's connection, it would mean she would be in the ideal place to further her doctoral studies. Before she had time to think twice, she had sent off her application for the post advertised on the school's website. A month or so later, she had been surprised to be contacted for an interview, and booked a trip to England with hardly a backwards glance.

'Good morning, staff,' Dr Fox called out, breaking into her thoughts. 'I am very pleased to be standing before you on such an auspicious day: the sesquicentennial year of Oxleigh College, and I look forward to sharing our plans to celebrate this milestone in the weeks to come.'

Thea had only a vague idea what sesquicentennial meant, but almost everyone else in the room was nodding as if it were obvious.

'However, first, an especially warm welcome to the newcomers. Perhaps you might raise your hands so that everyone can know who you are?'

As Thea put a tentative arm in the air she cast about her, relieved to see that three others had done the same and she wasn't the only newbie. As the hands were lowered, she noticed a stocky man a few metres away from her, his bright copper hair a beacon among the sea of browns and greys. He had the solid build of a sportsman, wide shoulders and narrow hips – rugby, if she'd had to guess. He caught her staring at him and she registered disarmingly bright blue eyes before looking away quickly and refocusing on the headmaster.

'Right, then,' said Dr Fox. 'As you are all well aware, this is a momentous day. For the first time in the school's hundred-and-fifty–year history we are welcoming girls to our student body.'

There was a murmur of voices.

'There will, no doubt, be a period of adjustment, but I expect each and every one of you to go out of your way to make the fourteen new pupils in the Lower Sixth feel at home.'

Another murmur, louder this time. Thea noticed the expression of one of the older masters; he didn't seem exactly pleased, and she heard the words, 'females . . . upset the apple cart . . .' and '. . . beggars belief'. Another grumbled, 'Where will it end? There'll be a headmistress next instead of a headmaster,' followed by a titter of anonymous laughter.

Thea blinked, but worked to keep her expression neutral. What era did they think they were living in? She should have been surprised, but she wasn't. These crusty old men would naturally be resistant to change, and the influx of women and girls would be nothing short of a seismic shock to them. The teacher with the arresting baby blues looked in her direction again, raising his eyebrows and rolling his eyes at the other masters.

She felt Claire by her side. 'About time the college joined the twenty-first century,' she whispered in Thea's ear.

'Who's that?' she asked in a low voice, her gaze flicking to the blue-eyed man.

Claire took a moment to follow her gaze. 'Gareth Pope. PE.'

'Right.' Thea recognised the name; she would be working with him to help coach the senior hockey teams.

Dr Fox spoke again, outlining the achievements of the previous year and his expectations for the coming one. The school focused strongly on academics – the entrance exam was reputed to be one of the most exacting in England – but even Thea was astonished to hear of the number of A-starred results. When he spoke about the music, art and drama achievements as well she began to wonder how the pupils coped with such pressure to achieve, and what happened to the ones who faltered. She thought briefly of all the boys who had passed through the school, whose character had been shaped, for better or worse, by it – for there were cabinet ministers, scientists and explorers among the legion of Oxleigh old boys, as well as those who led simpler but no less valuable lives, but there also had to be those who buckled under the weight of all that expectation, the constant comparison to others who flew higher, achieved more. A school such as Oxleigh left its stamp on you for life, of that she was well aware, her father having often repeated this fact. There wasn't much time to dwell on the matter, however, as Dr Fox wrapped up his speech and someone opened the doors to let them all out.

Thea turned to follow the other teachers, but felt a hand at her elbow. 'One moment, if you wouldn't mind, Miss Rust.'

SEVEN

Now

Dr Fox. She hadn't seen him approach, had been too caught up in the throng of other teachers, but there he was at her side. 'I wonder if I might have a word.'

Thea nodded. 'Of course.'

She hung back and waited until the room had cleared. Claire was one of the last to leave, giving Thea a questioning glance as she departed. She waved at her and mouthed, 'See you later,' before turning to the headmaster.

'How are you settling in?' Dr Fox asked when everyone else had left. Not waiting for her to reply, he continued. 'Now, to Mrs Jackson's unfortunate accident. It is inconvenient to say the least.'

'Indeed,' agreed Thea.

'I have my concerns regarding your lack of pastoral experience, but we are in somewhat of a bind because we have been unable to secure a replacement at such short notice. I imagine you will only be required to hold the fort for half a term at most.'

Thea nodded, doing her best to give the impression that she was up to the job. It was only to be for a few weeks; she could surely cope with that. Anyway, she'd hardly been given much of a choice in the matter.

'Oxleigh College prides itself on its exceptional sports results, no less than it does its academic achievements. We believe in the triple-A advantage: academics, arts and athletics,' said Dr Fox. 'I'm sure it is no surprise that what helped to secure the position here is your own considerable expertise in the sporting arena.' He smiled encouragingly at her.

Thea had known when she was offered the job that it wasn't only her qualifications as a history teacher that the school sought. Her years playing hockey for Australia as a junior, though now a decade or more past, and more recently as a coach of the state under-nineteen team, not to mention her father having been an Old Boy, had swung things in her favour.

Likewise, the newly enrolled girls who would make their way to the school later that day were not average students. All sixth-formers – sixteen- and seventeen-year-olds – they had been selected for their academic and sporting prowess, as well as their close links to the school; most had brothers at the college, or fathers as 'OOs' – Old Oxleighans. Though Thea had been initially conflicted at the notion of teaching such privileged students, feeling that she should be using her skills to help those who had greater need, taking up the position had served another, rather more selfish, purpose.

'Obviously, you will have a reduced academic workload, to compensate for your new responsibilities,' he said. 'Your timetable has been updated to reflect this.' The headmaster spoke in a far more formal manner than Thea was used to, but he fixed her with a warm smile. 'I cannot stress enough how important it is that these girls settle in well. The future of Oxleigh College depends on it. Your role will be instrumental in achieving that. You will be aware that my daughter, Sabrina, is one of the new intake.'

Of course, Sabrina Fox. Until that moment Thea hadn't made the connection. 'Understood, Headmaster.'

'If you have any issues, any issues at all, please see that you come directly to me.'

As he continued to speak, Thea's eyes roamed the room, noticing, now that it was empty of the other teachers, the inscribed lists of boys' names and dates lining the oak-panelled walls. The earliest ones dated back a hundred and fifty years, a time when her country was still being settled by deported thieves and miscreants.

There were the names of Oxbridge entrants, scholars and exhibitioners, and then a roll of previous head boys. Her eyes travelled down the gold-leaf lettering until they stopped on one. *1970 Rust, Henry.*

Thea still couldn't believe she was really here. Standing on the same ground that her father once had, quite literally walking in his footsteps some fifty years later. Perhaps she might even teach in the same classroom where he had once sat, eat at the same long dinner tables that she had spied in the college refectory on her earlier visit. She doubted that much would have changed.

'Any questions, Miss Rust?' asked Dr Fox.

'No, none, thank you. I'm sure it will all be fine,' she assured him.

'Good. I have no doubt that you will rise to the occasion,' he paused, regarding her with a grave expression. 'I was very sorry to hear about your father. I never had the pleasure of meeting him but he was, by all accounts, a great man. A credit to Oxleigh.'

'Thank you,' she said, colouring at his words. 'I only hope I might live up to him.'

She pushed down the memory of her father's funeral; the confusion of feelings, of which grief had been only one.

The headmaster cleared his throat. 'Well, you'd best hurry along. The new girls are due to arrive with the other pupils later this afternoon and I am sure you have much to occupy yourself with before then.'

~

'I thought we said eleven, Miss Rust?'

The Dame stood in the shadows beyond the doorway, as if she had been keeping a lookout.

Thea, who had walked from the school as fast as she could, glanced at her watch. Five past. 'The headmaster kept me,' she explained, refusing to apologise for something that was beyond her control.

'Come along, then, we've a great deal to do before the girls arrive.'

As they reached the dining room and sat down Isis padded in, curling herself about the Dame's ankles, purring like a V8 engine. 'The bell sounds to wake the girls at seven – you will have noticed the smart connection in each room that we use for all communications – then breakfast is at seven-thirty . . .' The Dame continued, talking about study times and sport afternoons and weekend activities and Thea began to wonder if she was expected to remember everything. She wished she had thought to take notes.

'Any questions?'

Thea shook her head. She was sure she'd figure out the rest of it herself.

'I hope you will consider me someone you can turn to if need be,' the Dame's voice softened slightly and a faint smile lifted her thin lips. 'But you will take care of communications with the parents, liaise with the girls' teachers and keep an eye on their academic work. You will also be the first point of contact for the girls if they have any concerns, either academically or personally.'

'Dr Fox explained some of that, and it all makes sense,' said Thea, trying not to feel too daunted.

The Dame nodded. 'Now, do you have any questions about the girls themselves?'

Thea had briefly studied the profiles left for her. Each had been affixed with a photograph, together with details of the girl's recent examination results, co-curricular achievements and reports from her previous school. They were all, without exception, high achievers. Bright, sporty girls with peachy complexions that spoke of youth and good nutrition, she thought ruefully, aware of her own sun-scalded, freckled arms. Three in particular had stood out: Morgan, who with her twin brother was to be the sixth generation of Addington-Clays educated at the school; Aradia Bianchi, a dark-haired Italian girl who, in addition to her near-perfect examination results, spoke three languages fluently; and Sabrina Fox, an only child whose father just happened to be the headmaster, Thea now knew. Morgan, Aradia and Sabrina had been at the same girls' school together for the past five years before transferring to Oxleigh. The three of them, along with one other girl – Fenella Wildash – had all chosen to study history, and she was pleased to see that she had been assigned as their tutor.

'I've read the reports,' said Thea. 'Is there more than that?'

'Not really. I believe you are also continuing with your studies while you are here,' said the Dame.

'That's right,' said Thea. *And how exactly did you know that?* she did not add aloud. Perhaps the Dame had been given a file on Thea, similar to those of the girls. 'Out of term time, mostly. I'm interested in persecution ideologies – specifically witchcraft in sixteenth- and seventeenth-century England.' Her university thesis had also been on that subject, and she was well aware that Wiltshire had seen more than its share of women – mainly old and poor – accused, hanged or drowned because of the suspicion that was cast upon them. Generally, Thea knew, they were scapegoats – blamed when crops failed or sickness spread – and she looked forward to finding out more about some of the lesser-known incidents, for she had yet to determine a specific focus for her study.

'So, you believe in magic?'

What a strange question. 'Not in the slightest. Such women might have had special skills and knowledge, but supernatural powers? Those were the allegations of people who were afraid of what they didn't understand or couldn't explain.'

'Indeed.' The Dame paused and looked as if she was about to confide in Thea, but then said blandly, 'Well, I'm sure you will discover plenty to interest you in that regard hereabouts. Now, as long as you're up to speed, we can leave it there.' She stood up to leave and Isis followed her out of the room, tail raised in the air like a question mark.

Had she had bitten off more than she could chew? Thea had no doubt of her teaching ability, but being a housemistress – even a temporary one – to fourteen teenage girls was an entirely different undertaking. That said, she had never been known to back down from a challenge, uninvited or not. Her father had seen to that.

EIGHT

September 1768, Oxleigh

Almost before Rowan knew it, Prudence was shaking her awake. She breathed in the comforting aroma of cinnamon and mace, overlaid with a stale reek of spirits and remembered where she was.

'Now, girl, I'll not stand for slatterns in this house. Splash your face and then dress as quick as you can. You'll need to clean out the fireplaces in the dining room, the drawing room and the parlour and relight them. I'll show you where to find wood and the kindling. You do know how to light a fire, don't you?'

Better than some in this house.

Rowan rubbed her eyes and blinked in the dim light of Prudence's taper. There was no sign of Alice; indeed, the other side of the bed appeared as if it had not been slept in, the sheets pulled tight and the thin pillow smooth, but Rowan thought she had felt someone next to her when she rolled over in the night. 'Yes, of course,' she replied, more awake now.

'Good. Then please start by opening the curtains and shutters downstairs. Be up with you, the day's waiting for no one.'

Rowan pulled back the covers, shivering at the cold air that rushed in. It dispelled any lingering sleepiness and she dressed quickly in her spare set of clothes, gathered her hair under her cap and fastened on an apron that Prudence had placed at the end of her bed. 'Mind you keep that hair covered,' Prudence had warned her the night before. ''Twill not please the mistress to have a whitey in the household.' Rowan did not need to be told twice.

As Rowan passed the main stairs, she paused for a moment to trace a finger over the large acorn on each newel post, marvelling at the detail, for she had never seen such a thing so artfully carved. Hearing a distant noise, and anxious that she not be caught dawdling, she hastened to the dining room.

The air in there was stale with the smell of tobacco, and as she threw open the shutters a pair of handsome wine glasses, pooled with deep red, and an empty bottle caught the morning light. Another, also empty, lay on a side table, accompanied by a discarded clay pipe, ashes spilling from the bowl. A hand of cards lay abandoned on the chaise, their faces upturned and scattered as if someone had tossed them down in disgust.

She swept out the fireplace and cleaned it with black leading, then buffed it dry. As she re-laid the hearth, she was careful to choose only the driest logs, and placed them on a pair of iron fire dogs so that air would draw underneath the wood. She held a taper to the kindling until it caught and then pumped the bellows that lay beside the fireplace, coughing at the smoke that drifted towards her but pleased when a blaze began to warm the room.

When she was satisfied that the flames had taken hold, she went to the small parlour where she had met her mistress the afternoon prior to repeat the process, though in that room the fireplace was of stone and so did not require the time-consuming blacking. Then to the dining room where, after she had pulled up the festoon curtains (she had to call Prudence to show her how, for she had never encountered such a thing – so much fabric and flounce she could scarce believe it), she knelt down to roll back the hearth rug. As she did so, she spied a small object in a shadowy corner of the room and rose to retrieve it. The metal was black with tarnish, but as she picked it up and held it close to her ear she heard the faint sound of dried beans knocking against each other. A baby's rattle. An odd thing to find in a house with no children. She placed it on the sideboard, thinking to polish it later.

Once Rowan had attended to her chores, she returned to the kitchen, where Prudence stood at the range stirring a large pot, the smell of kippered fish coming from the pan that sizzled next to it. 'Come and sit down, girl, have some breakfast,' said Prudence. 'Rowan, this is Alice; Alice Picken.'

The girl sitting at the table was perhaps a year or two older than Rowan and was eating a bowl of porridge, spooning the food into her mouth with an automatic action.

If she had a more pleasant expression on her face she would have been considered pretty, for her eyes were fringed by thick, black eyelashes, two pansies in a perfectly oval, olive-skinned face, and her lips were wide and full. Dark curls escaped the linen cap she wore and her hands were delicate and fine. Rowan felt suddenly coarse and ill attired by comparison, a Welsh mountain pony in the company of a lady's mare.

Alice did not seem at all pleased to see her, wearing a sour expression at odds with her fresh features. Rowan nodded cautiously at her before taking a seat a little way along the table. In return, Alice tilted her head in acknowledgment, her eyes lingering for a second on Rowan's scarred face, before she returned her attention to her porridge.

Prudence placed a steaming bowl on the table. 'For me?' Rowan asked.

'Well, Alice already has hers.'

The cook's tone was indulgent and Rowan couldn't help a small grin. She had never seen so much food for one person, and though she had eaten well the night before, she wasn't surprised to find that her appetite had returned. Hunger had been an almost constant state of existence since she could remember; a full stomach was a novel experience.

As Prudence bustled out of the kitchen towards the scullery, Rowan seized the chance to make an overture of friendship to Alice. 'Have you been here long?' she asked.

'Long enough,' Alice said through a mouthful of food. She scowled at Rowan, leaving Rowan wondering what she could have done to vex her so.

She tried again. 'Is it a pleasant household?' she asked.

'Depends what you mean by that,' came the reply.

'Are they kind? The master and mistress?'

Alice appeared to give the matter some thought. 'You expect kindness?' she said with a snort of derision. 'You really are a bumpkin.'

Rowan gave up trying to make conversation and turned back to her bowl, then to her surrounds. The sun was now shining through a window that overlooked a long, walled garden. There appeared to be a host of growing things, though at such a distance Rowan could not properly identify them. Were she to have a spare few minutes to venture there later in the day, she could investigate properly.

Prudence continued to bustle around them, and when they had eaten every last speck of porridge, she bade Rowan carry the breakfast serving dishes into the dining room.

She bore them carefully along the dim hallway, anxious not to trip, and then entered the room, placing them on a sideboard, managing only the slightest rattle of pewter on wood, but then narrowly missed colliding with her new employer as he bowled into the room in a fluster of movement and energy. 'Thought I could smell kippers,' he said as he lifted the lid from the dish furthest from her and peered in. Rowan murmured a brief, faintly embarrassed, 'Mornin', sir,' but Patrick Hollander's attention was focused on the food before him and he barely seemed to notice her.

She hurried back to the kitchen, seeing Alice disappear in the direction of the scullery. Prudence was wafting clouds of flour as she kneaded and stretched a mass of dough in front of her.

'Prudence?' Rowan asked warily, for she was uncertain whether raising the matter would cause more trouble than it was worth.

'Yes?'

'Is there some reason that Alice dislikes me?'

'Don't mind her,' Prudence replied. 'She thinks that there's more status in looking after the master; that she's better than a country maid. She was none too happy when she found out you had been hired and that she will no longer see to Mr Hollander.'

'I see,' said Rowan. 'Well, I can only hope that she might come to see that I pose no threat.' But how best to overcome Alice's ill will towards her? For she did not wish for there to be trouble between them.

'Give her time, lass. Now, the mistress'll be down soon enough. Go to the master's bedchamber and straighten that. Draw the curtains, air the bed, empty the pot and refill the washstand. It's upstairs, third door on the right.'

'Yes, Prudence.'

'When you've done that, sweep the staircase and polish the mirrors. You'll find everything you need in the scullery.'

'Yes, Prudence.'

'You'll learn soon enough what needs to be done, without me having to tell you.'

'Yes, Prudence.'

Rowan looked longingly out at the garden again. Her exploration would have to wait.

~

Later that day, when the mistress had summoned her to stoke the fire in the drawing room, there was a commotion in the street. Going to the window to see the source of the hubbub, Rowan spied a cart directly below. A large object, protected by a thick cloth, was lashed to the boards. As several passers-by stopped to watch the spectacle, her master emerged onto the street and began gesturing towards the house.

'Whatever is it?' asked Caroline languidly, not moving from her seat.

'I'm not sure, mistress. But it's awful big.'

'We are not expecting a delivery. It cannot be silk, for that comes on the London coach, which is not due until next week. Are you certain it is for us?'

'I don't know, ma'am, but the master seems to be in charge of it.' Rowan continued her observation, noticing that whatever it was had now caused half the population of Oxleigh to cease their business and watch.

'I suppose I had better see what is going on,' Caroline said. 'If my husband has anything to do with it, I cannot begin to guess what is to be visited upon us.' She raised herself from her chaise, smoothing her skirts, the pale colour of which reminded Rowan of a newly unfurled leaf, and joining Rowan at the window. Mr Hollander, the driver of the cart and several other men seemed to be discussing how to move the object, pointing at the upper floors, particularly it seemed at the window from which Rowan and her mistress were observing the scene. 'That's not coming in the house, surely?' Caroline asked. Then, under her breath, 'What the devil has he gone and done this time?'

Rowan watched carefully as two ladders were produced and the carter held up what appeared to be a large pulley, together with a length of rope as thick as her forearm. He and another man leaned the ladders against the front of the house, one on either side of the bay window below, then went back for the ropes and the pulley, and entered the house. Rowan felt the drum of their footsteps on the staircase and then the two entered the drawing room, closely followed by Patrick Hollander.

'What is all this to-do?' Caroline asked her husband. 'Have you taken leave of your senses?'

He greeted her with the expression of someone who was about to play a great trick, his eyes alight with mischief. 'Wait and see, my dear, for when it is revealed you will be as excited as I am, without a doubt.'

Caroline pursed her pretty mouth, and Rowan could see that her mistress did not share her husband's anticipation. 'I shall reserve judgment until I am informed of whatever it is that you have purchased,' she said. 'Though I doubt that we can afford it,' she added under her breath.

'Hush now, I have had some luck with the cards,' he said, bestowing on her a grin that gave him the appearance of a cheeky urchin. 'So, do not worry yourself about such matters. You will not be disappointed, of that I can assure you.' He brushed off her concerns and gestured to the two men who accompanied him, 'Look lively, let us make a start.'

They moved forward and Rowan and Caroline stood back, watching their actions, Rowan with wide-eyed interest, Caroline with an expression of faint exasperation.

'We must open the windows as wide as they can go, but I estimate there will be enough room,' said the carter.

The men got to work securing the pulley and, once it was affixed to their liking, they slung the rope over it. One man disappeared down the stairs with Patrick while the other held the end of the rope, winding it around his waist and tying it off amid shouts in the street that brought another two men, seconded to help, into the room, where they were instructed to grab hold of the rope as well.

Rowan stood to one side of the window, still peering out to where her master and the carter were fixing the rope to those that bound the lumpy object sitting on the boards. Then they climbed the ladders and, together with the assistance of several more bystanders, began to haul the object up the side of the house. There was much shouting as they fought to prevent it smashing against the brickwork, and Rowan heard words that nearly set the air blue and her ears to burn.

Slowly the object was hauled upwards until it was level with the window. More men had been drummed in to help and now the drawing room was crowded with people. Caroline and Rowan looked on, staying out of the way but fascinated by the activity. The men, sweating and heaving, guided the shrouded bundle into the room, where it was lowered to the floor with a bump followed by a gentle twang.

'Splendid,' said Patrick Hollander as he raced back into the room followed by a small, dark man whom Rowan had not seen before. 'Oh, splendid work!'

The stranger began to undo the ropes and covering, muttering to himself as he did so. The carter entered, carrying another, much smaller, wrapped bundle and placed it on the floor.

'Everyone out now,' Patrick commanded, handing each of the men a copper coin. 'Even you my dear,' he said to Caroline. 'For I want you to see it only when it is perfect.'

'Really, such a disturbance,' she replied, rolling her eyes. However, there was an amused tone to her voice. 'I shall be in my chamber.'

Rowan followed her mistress out of the room, and as Caroline climbed the stairs and she turned towards the servants' passage, she came upon Prudence lurking in the shadows.

'What do you think it is?' Prudence asked, her eyes alight with intrigue.

'I've no idea,' said Rowan as they went to the kitchen.

'A painting perhaps,' suggested Alice, who was shelling peas at the table. 'Though I'll wager it will not make her happy, whatever it may be,' she muttered when Prudence turned her back.

Rowan was shocked at the maid's scathing tone, but kept her counsel. She was very aware she was new to the household and had yet to learn its rhythms and peculiarities. Living with her aunt and uncle for two years after her parents died had taught her that every household had them, in one form or another. ''Twas not of the size and shape for a painting,' she replied quietly.

'We'll see it soon enough,' said Prudence. 'Now, enough of your dawdling, girls, for there's work to be done.'

~

Several hours later, Patrick summoned the entire household to the drawing room for what he grandly called 'the great unveiling'.

The object was still covered with the cloth that it had been wrapped in, though it was now more loosely draped. Four legs peeped from underneath the cloth, two set wide at the front and two narrowly at the back. The thing had a broad, flat top, but that was all she could make out and it gave her no clue as to its purpose, if indeed it served one. Perhaps it was a new piece of furniture? It took up a great deal of space in the room and was certainly commanding.

Rowan stood next to Alice. She looked for the rattle she had placed on the sideboard earlier that morning, and was surprised that it was no longer there, but any further thoughts were soon chased out of her mind by the anticipation of discovering what exactly it was that Mr Hollander had brought to the house.

When he was certain he had their attention, Patrick tugged on the cloth with a flourish and let it slither to the floor. The assembled maids, cook and even the groom sucked in their breath almost as one. The wooden box-like object was shaped like a bird's wing and its surface had been buffed to a brilliant sheen. Rowan imagined she would see her own reflection in it if she dared stand close enough.

'A harpsichord?' Caroline asked, a touch of disappointment colouring her voice.

'I can see why you might think that, my dear, for the two are similar in form, though the sound is quite, quite different, as you will soon discover.' Patrick went across to the object and lifted the top panel until it was at an angle, securing it open with a thin prop that mysteriously – to Rowan at least – emerged from the belly of the instrument.

'Well,' said Caroline, examining it carefully. 'It has only one keyboard. And what are these pedals? It is far plainer than a harpsichord.' She did not sound altogether impressed.

Rowan drew as near as she dared, spying thick strings and pads of felt filling the body. She had never seen such a thing, had no idea what it was for. There was a seat to sit at – that she did recognise – and the white rectangles interspersed with thinner black ones looked designed for fingers to touch.

'It is a pianoforte,' Patrick said triumphantly. 'The latest instrument, all the way from Paris. I saw one in a salon when I was in London last and had to have one exactly like it. I know how much you love music, so I thought it a suitable gift to mark our fifth wedding anniversary, my dear.'

Caroline made no comment, but a faint smile curved her lips.

'Why not play it? Then tell me how much you like it.' He danced around his wife in excitement, gesturing to the stool in front of the keyboard.

She hesitated, but then proceeded to sit down, lifting her skirts out of the way and settling herself on the stool. 'I am sure I do not know how to get a tune from this contraption,' she protested, but nevertheless she placed her fingers on the instrument. She began to press a few keys at random and Rowan felt as well as heard the sound vibrate across the room towards her. It was like the buzzing of a bee in the low notes and the whine of a mosquito in the higher ones. The only musical instruments she had hereto seen were fiddles, pennywhistles and drums, nowhere near as impressive as this.

Her master clapped his hands at his wife's notes and looked around at the servants, encouraging them to join in.

''Tis a very pretty harmony indeed, sir,' said Prudence at a pause in the music.

Caroline, who hadn't looked up from the instrument in front of her, barely paid the rest of them any heed, slowly coaxing a melody from it, experimenting with the pressure on the ivory keys. 'Why, it can be played louder and softer,' she exclaimed. 'That certainly makes it superior to any harpsichord.'

'Only the best for my wife,' Patrick declared proudly.

Rowan noticed the expression of pure joy on her mistress's face that transformed her entirely, one that barely faltered as her master declared that he was to return to London on the morning stage. Alice's countenance, on the other hand, was blank, as if she were deliberately trying to show no emotion. Would nothing please the sullen maid?

NINE

Now

Thea observed the thirteen girls gathered around the two tables. Not the expected fourteen, as one girl – Camilla – had been diagnosed with glandular fever two days before the start of term and would not join them for several weeks. With the exception of a couple of quieter ones, they seemed to be getting to know one another, indeed some of them were already well acquainted and chatted away, barely pausing to eat. Earlier, Thea had watched as the girls exchanged flurries of goodbye hugs and kisses with their parents, and for a brief moment she had envied the easy and obvious affection. Now, as the meal progressed, the noise level rose, and they were laughing and talking, animated by their new surroundings, none of them showing any signs of homesickness, outwardly at least.

She clapped twice, and was pleased to see that the effect was almost instantaneous silence and eyes turned her way. 'I've met most of you now, and am delighted to be your housemistress until Mrs Jackson has recovered from her unfortunate accident,' she said, surveying their eager faces. 'I'll also be taking some of you for history, and for those among you who are hockey enthusiasts, I'll be assisting the sports master, Mr Pope, in forming a mixed team. I'd encourage you all to try out.' She watched several of the girls – Fenella, Joy and Morgan in particular – as she said this, remembering the details of their sporting skills, and was pleased to see them react to the news with enthusiastic smiles.

'You've got a big day ahead of you tomorrow, so after we are finished here, I expect you to return to your rooms to finish unpacking, and lights out will be at nine-thirty.' There was a groan as she said this but she held up a hand. 'I know most of you have boarded before, but for those of you who haven't, an early bedtime is a rule we strictly enforce here.' She noted their seemingly guileless expressions. 'We also ask that you all place your mobile phones in the charging station at the end of the dining room. They will stay at the house during lesson times and you will be allowed access to them after school every afternoon. I'm sure most of you have noticed the smart alarm in your rooms – it will wake you and alert you to mealtimes and so on. Your rooms must be kept tidy and beds made before you come down to breakfast. Tomorrow morning I will walk you all over to school and show you to your classrooms. Does anyone have any questions?'

There was a murmur of voices but no one raised their hand, so she resumed her seat. There were so many more rules to get her head around than she was used to but, aside from the early bedtime, most of the girls seemed unperturbed by them.

She was about to reach for the water jug when a crashing sound made her jump and silenced the chatter. She turned to see Fenella, a worried look on her face, shards of broken glass at her feet.

'I didn't touch it, honestly,' she muttered, embarrassment colouring her features.

Thea got to her feet, but the woman from the kitchen who had served their meal was quicker, descending with a cloth in her hands. 'Don't worry,' she said with a sympathetic look. 'Accidents happen.'

As the woman moved to collect the glass, Thea caught the blurred blue of a tattoo on her left wrist, the flash of a shape that looked like an arrow.

~

Quarter of an hour before lights out, Thea did the rounds of the girls' rooms, pleased to see that most of them were in bed, reading or quietly chatting. When she reached Fenella's room, she was greeted by a maelstrom of clothes and books strewn across the bed and on the floor.

'It looks worse than it is, I promise,' Fenella said, casting around dispiritedly at the mess.

'How about I give you a hand?' said Thea. 'That way we've half a chance of creating some order in the next ten minutes.'

Fenella folded the pile of clothes on her bed and together they straightened the books and papers.

'You were right,' said Thea when they had finished. 'It wasn't as bad as it seemed. Now try to get a good night's sleep. I know it'll be strange at first, but don't worry, we'll all get used to it. I'm sorry you're without a roommate, as Camilla's sick, but it does give you more space to yourself for a while.'

Fenella shrugged as if it didn't matter one way or the other.

'You know, you're not the only one who's never boarded before,' Thea added. 'I'm new to it all too.' She was reassured to see a small smile from the girl as she went to leave. 'And I'm only down the hall if you need anything.'

~

Returning to the kitchen after lights out, Thea ran into Dame Hicks. 'I missed you at supper –' Thea began.

'I thought I mentioned: I take my meals in my room,' the Dame interrupted, her tone brooking no objections.

'Oh, okay then.' Thea didn't recall her saying anything about that, but didn't see that it was worth questioning. 'I'm going to get an early night. We all need to be on our toes tomorrow. Can't have the girls being late to school on their first morning,' she said, realising that the responsibility for that now fell to her.

'Exactly.'

'Good night, then.'

Thea climbed the two floors to her room, a dim nightlight was all that illuminated the corridor. She stumbled to her bed and found the lamp, cursing as she nearly knocked it over. She clicked the switch and was relieved when the room was light again.

~

Thea woke suddenly, in the dark, early hours of the morning. She lay still for a moment, thinking she'd heard a sound. She sat up in bed and listened again for a clue as to what might have roused her from sleep. There it was again. The distant notes of a piano. She had seen the instrument in the girls' sitting room on the ground floor, but she couldn't believe that any of them would be up playing at this time. Then footsteps, a muffled cry. Alarmed, she reached for her dressing gown and thrust her feet into her slippers. Using the torch on her phone, she eased the door of her room open and crept into the hallway, listening carefully.

A shushing, whispering sound. She took a few steps towards the door of Fenella's room and paused. No noise coming from there. She went towards the top of the stairs. Nothing. Then footsteps once more, louder this time. She inched her way down the stairs, wincing as one of the treads creaked under her weight, her heart thudding against her chest.

Stopping on the first-floor landing, Thea listened again for the footsteps, but the sound had stopped, disappearing into the shadows. Had she imagined it?

Then suddenly she felt something brush against her bare legs and she nearly jumped out of her skin. She looked down: there was a shadow at her feet.

Her heart rate slowed to normal as she realised it was only Isis.

As she crept down the main stairs towards the kitchen, there was the chink of glass, the soft thud of a cupboard door closing. She turned on the light and there she was, standing by the sink, frozen in the act of getting a glass of water.

Thea let go of the breath she had been holding. 'Fenella,' she whispered, mindful of the sleeping house.

'Thirsty,' the girl said, holding up the glass. 'Sorry, did I wake you? I was trying to be quiet. I promise I won't break this one.' She gave her a rueful look.

'It's fine.'

Fenella gulped some of the water as Thea reached for her own glass. As she opened the cupboard door, a cloud of tiny moths fluttered out and she jumped, startled, as she waved them away with her hand. 'Ugh.' She filled her glass at the sink. 'It's not easy, sleeping on your first night in a new place.'

'I'll be okay.'

'Sure?'

Fenella nodded.

'Try to get some rest, then.'

When Thea returned to her room, she found the door shut. She thought she had left it ajar when she went downstairs, but it was now firmly closed. She turned the handle, pushing hard as the door stuck in its frame before it swung open. She looked around the room as she entered. Everything was as she'd left it, but she couldn't shake the feeling that someone had been in there in her absence. A disturbance in the air, the faint scent of flowers . . . Her imagination was working overtime.

She climbed back into bed, but sleep was frustratingly elusive. Eventually, she resorted to a podcast – on Egyptian antiquities, the most boring one she could find – and let the disembodied voice lull her into oblivion.

~

As the girls assembled in the dining room the next morning, adjusting ties and doing up the stiff buttons of their new blazers and overcoats, Thea prepared to walk them over to the school. 'I'll show you where your lockers are and take you to your classrooms and from there you'll go to chapel. You should already have your individual timetables,' she said, before being interrupted by a loud knock on the front door.

'Just a minute, girls,' she called over her shoulder as she moved to open it.

Standing in front of her was a tall, dark-haired man, a camera with a large flash slung around his neck. 'Jeff Damer, official school photographer,' he said, thrusting a card under her nose.

'Oh,' said Thea, taken aback. 'No one mentioned this.'

'I was told to get a few frames of the girls on their first day. For the annual report, you know.'

Thea didn't know, but his card bore the school crest and so she stepped aside to let him in. 'How long will this take?' she asked, thinking anxiously of the time.

'Only a jiffy,' he said, giving her a smile that showed a set of higgledy-piggledy teeth.

'All right, then,' she said. 'Everyone's in the dining room, to the left.'

'Hello ladies,' he said brightly, as all of the girls stopped their chatter and turned to look at him.

'This is Jeff.' Thea introduced him. 'He needs a quick photo for the school's records, if you could oblige him.' She turned to the photographer. 'It's a bit dim in here; perhaps outside in the garden might work?'

He nodded enthusiastically. 'Super.'

'Er . . . girls?' Without exception, all of the girls had pushed their chairs back and were making their way out of the room and up the stairs. 'The garden's not that way,' she added.

'Just got to make sure we look okay,' said Aradia, brushing past her. 'If I'd known about this, I'd have got up earlier to straighten my hair,' she complained.

Thea sighed, exasperated. 'Be quick,' she called after them. 'We *cannot* be late this morning.'

After ten minutes or so, while Thea fretted over the time, the girls trooped back down the stairs, looking, to Thea's eyes at least, no different than when they had left.

'All right, stand in three lines, against that wall there if you would.' Jeff directed the girls into formation. 'You too, Miss,' he said, motioning for Thea to join them. As he was about to start snapping, Thea glanced across to her left and saw Dame Hicks standing on the other side of Fenella and gave her a quick smile.

Jeff was as good as his word, and wrapped up the impromptu photo shoot in under five minutes. 'Hurry up, girls,' said Thea as she waved him away. 'We need to leave right now. Collect your bags and we'll get moving.'

Thea had woken early specifically to study the school map, for the grounds were extensive and she still wasn't sure where all of the classrooms were located. 'You'll all be familiar with the layout of the school from when you came for orientation, but each of you has been assigned a guide from among the boys in your year,' she said as they walked along the high street.

Aradia wrinkled her nose at this.

'Don't worry,' she said. 'I'm sure they'll be friendly, and you'll soon find your way around. I believe there is also a map, among other instructions, waiting for you.'

'Will we all be in the same class, Miss Rust?' asked Joy, a quiet girl who wore blue-framed glasses and a serious expression.

'No, not for the first period of the day, but you will be in two all-girl pastoral groups, and then of course for your academic subjects you'll be in different groups. It's important that you mix in with the boys, even though there are far fewer of you than them. It'll all become normal in a very short time, I'm sure,' she said, doing her best to reassure them as they passed through the school gates.

When they reached the block housing the senior classrooms, Thea consulted her list. 'Fenella, Aradia, Sabrina and Morgan.' She checked they had heard her. 'The four of you are in Dr Adams's class, up those stairs there.'

The girls went in the direction she indicated and she carried on with the other nine, depositing them at their classrooms in turn. Congratulating herself on successfully completing the first job of the day, Thea made her way to the staffroom, running into Claire on the way.

'Getting your bearings?'

Thea nodded. 'I think so.' She adjusted the bag on her shoulder. 'My first lesson isn't until ten, but I feel like I should go over my notes again one more time.'

'You'll be fine. It took me a while to get used to the place.'

'I know,' Thea said. 'That's exactly what I told the girls; I should listen to my own advice.' She rummaged in her bag. 'Ouch!' She withdrew her hand and saw that she'd managed to nick the skin on her thumb. 'Paper cut,' she explained, sucking on the blood that welled up from it.

'There are plasters in the first-aid kit somewhere, I think,' said Claire. 'Come with me.' They walked into the staffroom, where Claire lifted a large black box from a shelf on the far wall.

'Everything okay?' It was Gareth Pope, the sports master.

'Just clumsy,' said Thea with a wry smile as she stretched the Band-Aid over her thumb. 'But it's all sorted now.' She crumpled the wrapper in her other hand and tossed it in a nearby wastepaper basket. 'Right. I'd better go and find my classroom,' she said, squaring her shoulders. 'See you later.'

~

There were ten pupils in Thea's A Level history class, including three of the new girls: Sabrina, Morgan and Fenella. Thea introduced herself and then listened as the students told her their names. Most regarded her with curiosity, a couple with a faint challenge in their eyes as if they were waiting for her to prove herself. 'Okay, then. Why study history?'

A couple of hands shot up.

'To know what happened in the past?' offered one of the boys. Edward, she thought he had said his name was.

A snicker went around the room.

'It might sound obvious, but Edward is right,' said Thea.

'To prevent us from making the same mistakes in the future,' said Sabrina.

'Though people and civilisations don't always do that,' said a boy named James.

'True.' She smiled at him. 'Anyone else?'

'To balance understanding and knowledge and to learn to think independently,' said Fenella.

'Good,' said Thea. 'That's a start. And what is the first rule of historical analysis?'

'No one is impartial, not even a participant or witness,' said Fenella again. 'There are two sides to every story.'

'Sometimes more than that.' Thea thought of her father. He had been held in such high esteem, but her feelings about him were rather more complicated. The face he'd presented to the rest of the world was different from the one he showed at home. He hadn't always been an easy person to be around; he had little patience for shortcomings of any kind, and she and her sister had spent their early years terrified of disappointing him. He had been known to lash out in frustration if he thought Thea or Pip weren't trying hard enough, and she had been on the end of many a humiliating whack to the shoulder or backside when she was small. As she got older, she'd become better at burying feelings of inadequacy, but they were still there, a knot in her stomach whenever she faced a new challenge, the fear that she might fail and he would be proved right.

She swallowed and looked around the classroom; now was not the time to dwell on such things. 'There are the known facts. And then there is the interpretation of those facts. We have to examine the situation from every angle, sift and analyse the material – primary and secondary sources – to gain a thorough understanding of events and determine their importance, before arriving at a conclusion,' she said.

Sabrina's hand shot up. 'Isn't it a bit like peeling away the layers of an onion, to get at the central truth?'

A few of the other students nodded.

'It can be,' agreed Thea, though she couldn't help thinking that sometimes you kept on peeling until nothing certain, nothing true was left.

TEN

December 1768, London

Mary tucked her sheaf of drawings, embroidery samples and dot patterns under her arm and prepared to knock on the door of every master weaver on Spital Square, Old Artillery Ground and beyond.

Few would admit her.

Some drew their shutters at her approach, as if they had been forewarned of her purpose. Others – especially the French weavers – pretended not to understand her. Most scoffed at the notion that a woman might have the required artistry and technical understanding, and refused to let her so much as open her sketchbook. Those who did take a glancing look at her designs dismissed her scornfully: 'Who would pay to be dressed in the flowers of the field?' was the comment from more than one. 'What is embroidered cannot so easily be woven, surely you must understand that,' said another. She was given no opportunity to argue her case.

The light was fading by the time she found herself back at home at the end of her second week of knocking on doors. She dragged her blistered feet up the steps and flung her sketches to the floor in anger as her sister approached. 'Why did I even think this would amount to anything?' she cried, as Frances's hopeful expression turned to one of dismay.

'Oh my dear,' Frances replied, taking in Mary's slumped shoulders and downcast demeanour, 'we will think of something'. She gathered up her sister's work, smoothing out an edge that had become crumpled and running a finger over the fine pencil strokes.

~

Mary did not remain despondent for long. She believed her designs were good, she simply had to persuade someone to take a chance on her work and everything else would surely fall into place. In any case, she had no choice but to keep going, for she could foresee no other way of adding to the household income, at least not in a manner befitting a woman of her class. True, she might manage to secure a position as a governess, but as she would not dream of leaving Frances, that ruled out that avenue of employment. Besides, she knew herself well enough to realise that she did not possess the required patience with children. She was considered – with no small sense of relief on her part – too old to think of making a suitable marriage. The institution held little appeal for her: she had no wish to live at the mercy of another, to promise to obey. All she really wanted was to design and draw and paint, and enjoy the quiet company of her sister. Was that too much to ask?

She would apply herself anew, work harder and master the craft. Resolute, she dipped her paintbrush in her jar of water and contemplated the wildflowers before her. She was on the point of applying the brush to the thick watercolour paper on her desk once more, when a sharp rap at the door disturbed her peace. She paused, brush held aloft. No one was expected. Frances, who spent her mornings at the French hospital caring for those less fortunate than themselves, had yet to return, leaving only Mary in residence, for they could not afford to keep even a single servant.

Mary sighed at the interruption, set down her paintbrush and brought her hands to her hair. It had a habit of curling riotously from the confines of its simple arrangement and she patted it back into place, hoping that it was at least presentable. When painting, she generally wore a cotton smock so as not to damage her gown, and she hastily pulled her arms from its sleeves as she went to answer the door.

'This is the home of Miss Mary-Louise Stephenson, is it not?' asked the man standing on the front step. 'She will be expecting me.'

He had clearly taken her for a maid, such was the humble nature of her dress. 'May I say who calls upon her?' she asked, pretending servitude.

'Mr Patrick Hollander.' He paused, as if expecting her to know who he was, but Mary merely raised her eyebrows.

'I am afraid, sir, that I have no knowledge of you,' she blurted, forgetting her charade in the face of his penetrating gaze.

'Miss Stephenson?' he asked, realisation dawning on him.

Noticing the finely woven silk of his waistcoat, the cut of his breeches, his unmuddied stockings, the rich leather of his shoes and their gleaming buckles, Mary became even more aware of her dishevelled state, for underneath her painting smock she wore a simple linen jacket that she had remade from an old gown of Frances's and a patched petticoat. The lace that was visible at her neck and wrists was spotted with paint. Her hand went to her throat in a vain attempt to cover herself, though in doing so it only drew attention to the sullied cuffs of her chemise. Here was a man of obvious substance on her doorstep and she looked for all the world no better than a serving wench. For once, she was at a loss for words.

'Madam. My sincere apologies,' he continued, bestowing a smile of such warmth that his words sounded far from remorseful. 'I sent a letter, not a day ago, advising of my visit. It was not my intention to arrive unannounced or catch you unawares.'

Although ill at ease, Mary could not help but be charmed. The smooth timbre of his voice, with its rounded country vowels, was most pleasing to the ear and he spoke at a languid pace, his words as if honey dripping from a comb, implying that he had all the time in the world.

'It is no matter. How might I be of assistance?'

'I have come from Wiltshire, the town of Oxleigh.'

Mary's eyebrows flew higher. They were not in the habit of receiving callers from so far afield. Though she knew approximately where this was, she had never ventured south, or west for that matter, of London in all of her thirty-five years. Her knowledge of geography, as with many other things, came from the schoolroom, not from experience. 'That is a very long way indeed.'

'I confess I made the journey some four days prior. I have had some business to conduct here.' Again, the smile, but Mary was still no wiser as to the reason for his arrival on her doorstep. 'Perhaps we might talk further inside?' he suggested, swivelling his glance to indicate the prying eyes of her neighbours. A shutter flapped across the lane, and at an upper floor opposite, a window sash lowered.

It was a most unusual situation, for no one had called on her in the time she had been living with Frances. She made a quick decision to trust him. 'Of course.' She opened the door wider and ushered him in. If he had come such a distance, then she could hardly turn him away without allowing him the opportunity to explain himself. As she led him along the hallway and into the room that she and her sister fondly called the drawing room (it was the only room they occupied, save for a shared bedroom and a communal kitchen at the back of the house), she became newly aware of the shabby furnishings, the peeling paintwork, scarred card table and threadbare rug that were in such contrast to the gleaming presence of her visitor. She did her best not to think of it, nor of the time she would lose with her painting and wondered instead what his business might be.

He was tall and had to duck his head to avoid cracking his brow on the lintel as he entered the room, but he moved with an enviable, loose-limbed grace.

She indicated two high-backed chairs that faced the card table. 'Please. Have a seat.' Now that she was indoors, Mary felt on surer ground.

Patrick Hollander did not appear surprised that no maid or housekeeper would be attending to them, and was apparently unperturbed by the impoverished surroundings. Mary decided it was his good manners that prevented him from acknowledging either. She, too, did not draw attention to her situation. 'Perhaps I might offer you some tea?' she said instead.

'That would be most agreeable.'

She returned to the room several minutes later carrying a tray laden with Frances's finest silver teapot, bone china cups and saucers and a small jug of milk. She had scooped the last few precious leaves from the chest and prayed it would make a strong enough brew. There was no sugar, not a scrap in the house, and she hoped that he would have the manners not to request it.

He rose as she entered the room and placed the tray on the table with a slight chink of china. She arranged her skirts and sat down opposite him, indicating that he might also resume his seat. 'My sister, Mrs Wycroft, is at large, but I expect her back shortly.' It was a warning that they were not likely to be alone in the house for long.

'No disrespect to your sister, but it is your good self that I have come to see.'

'I am quite certain that I cannot imagine the reason why.'

'You are the artist that the apprentice weavers whisper of, are you not?' he asked. 'I hope my intelligence is correct, for that is what brings me here today.'

She started. *Were* they talking about her? If so, it was most likely to gossip at her presumption and her ignorance. 'I would not go so far as to make that claim,' she said modestly. 'I am attempting to become a craftswoman at best. A pattern-drawer. At least I would be if I could persuade the mercers and the weavers to take my work seriously. They are inclined to scoff at my efforts, I am afraid.' Mary bit her lip in an effort to stop talking. She had admitted more than she intended, especially to a complete stranger, but nevertheless she felt herself relax under his frank regard, for his open face was as wholesome as a loaf of fresh bread.

'It is a ridiculous custom to exclude women,' he declared. 'But an opportunity for me, eh? Perhaps a path to fortune for us both.'

Mary poured the milk into the cups first – essential to prevent the delicate china from cracking – then lifted the teapot. As she poured, she studied Patrick Hollander from under her lashes. He was younger than her by at least a decade, but she was surprised to find herself appreciative of the fine specimen that he was: clear skin unmarked by pox, broad shoulders that stretched the seams of his coat, hands square and strong, and the sheen of chestnut hair as an escaped lock curled over his forehead. She chased away a flicker of unease; he appeared perfectly pleasant, and she could not say what it was about him that worried at her. It was likely the result of him calling unannounced, and she being unaccustomed to visitors, she reminded herself.

He noticed her surreptitious study of him with amusement and she started, catching the spout of the pot against the rim of a cup and nearly upending it.

'Might I assist?' he asked, putting his hands over hers. She let him take the teapot from her as, for a fleeting moment only, she relished the feel of his skin. She rarely experienced the warmth of another being and the sudden touch invited an intimacy that awoke a most disturbing sensation.

'Am I to understand that there is not a Mr Stephenson?' he asked.

His boldness was unexpected and for a moment she was unsure whether to take offence. 'You are rather well informed for a stranger,' she said, deflecting the question.

He inclined his head. 'Forgive me, but I have been making enquiries.'

'My father had not a fortune to settle upon a marriage,' she surprised herself by elaborating. 'Besides, I find I prefer my independence, such as it is. Rather a city spinster than a provincial wife. I am not certain I could find myself beholden to a man.' His bold gaze unnerved her. Being not in the habit of entertaining gentlemen callers, she was perhaps not as guarded as propriety would have dictated.

'You do not mince words.'

She inclined her head. 'I do not.'

'Good. I am pleased to hear it. I respect forthrightness, whether it be from a man or woman.'

'That is not something many would admit to, for it is a world made for men, is it not?' she replied.

'And you would have us a petticoat government, I suppose?'

'I would not perhaps go that far.' She flashed him a conspiratorial grin. 'Not this year.'

He gave a bark of satisfied laughter and slapped his thigh. 'Miss Stephenson, I see I have found my match.'

She took a sip from her flowered cup, returned it to the table and met his eyes. 'Then perhaps I might enquire as to the purpose of your visit today? The path to fortune, you said? Those are strong words, and I have to admit I find myself intrigued.'

'Indeed. I will speak plainly if I may.' He looked her directly in the eye. 'I have a proposal for you.'

'Oh yes?'

'It is in the nature of an exclusive proposal.'

'I am not in the habit of receiving proposals,' she replied, unable to prevent a note of playfulness entering her voice. 'Particularly from strange gentlemen.'

'I would hope we might not be strangers for much longer.' His voice lowered, became intimate. He too was teasing. 'I am a humble silk merchant. The town in which my business is located is a popular staging post on the way to Bath and we deal in some of the finest fabrics produced throughout the land. We supply the best dressmakers and upholsterers in all of the southern shires.' There was no small amount of pride as he spoke, making his use of the word *humble* rather ridiculous. 'We also have a number of clients from the Americas. Indeed, I am recently returned from across the Atlantic where I have been in Boston, Philadelphia and New York.'

'I see,' Mary could not help but be impressed, but did her best to keep the tone of her voice even and not give away the excitement that arose within her at his words, for hope flared that he had come to see her about her designs.

'I am an ambitious man, Miss Stephenson, and undertake to engage only the finest designers on an exclusive basis, to create bespoke fabrics for our most *discerning* clientele.' He leaned heavily on the word, angling towards her at the same time, as if inviting her into a private club.

'What is it that you know of my work that causes you to seek me out?' Mary asked. 'There are sufficient talented pattern-drawers other than myself, are there not? And men at that.'

He laughed again and she noticed the evenness of his teeth, the rosy colour of his lips as they parted in a smile, the fine sheen of his skin. 'I am surprised you consider this a laughing matter, sir,' she said, a hint of reprimand in her voice.

He straightened his expression. 'No laughing matter at all, let me assure you, madam. I merely find your modesty most amusing. Your designs are the talk of the apprentices, were you not appraised of that? Their masters might not appreciate the fresh breath of air that your designs bring, their originality, but they – and I – certainly do. I have been searching for something different, Miss Stephenson, something that will set Hollander's apart – and I do believe I have found it.'

'You have seen my work? Where?'

He glanced over to the desk where her portfolio was open. 'I took the liberty of examining it while you were absent. I do apologise for my forwardness, but I could not wait to see if what they say is true. And it is. How is it that you are not aware that, though your stature is small, you stand head and shoulders above your fellow artists?'

It was heartening to hear such words spoken aloud by another, especially after being told by so many that her work was worthless. She had suspected that the weavers and journeymen were more concerned with protecting their own interests than objectively judging the merits of her designs, but the slights had nevertheless hit their mark.

'I have seen the beauty and originality of your drawings,' he continued. 'You have a natural genius.'

'Sir, you do but flatter me,' she demurred. 'Pray, tell me why should I offer my services exclusively to your good self?' Mary might be delighted by his words and – she forced herself to admit – charmed by his presence, but she still had her wits about her. She was not about to leap at the first offer he made, no matter how desperate she might be.

He spread his hands, the picture of ease. 'Of course. I understand that you might think that way, but what if I were able to offer you more for less?'

'More for less?' Mary frowned and glanced over at the watercolours and her brushes idling on the desk across the room.

'A successful designer can be expected to create upwards of sixty pieces a year. I can promise to halve that workload while doubling the payment.'

It was Mary's turn for mirth. 'You will surely bankrupt yourself running a business in such a way,' she declared.

'Who is running a business in such a way?' Mary's sister, Frances, appeared at the door, pulling off her bonnet and gloves, a burst of chill air coming into the room with her. 'Oh, I see we have a visitor. How do you do, sir?' she added.

Patrick Hollander rose from his seat and took her outstretched hand, bowing low over it. 'Madam.'

'Mr Hollander is a silk merchant from Wiltshire,' Mary explained. 'He has come to ask me to work for him.' She widened her eyes at her sister, imploring her not to reveal her lack of experience. 'Exclusively.'

'Indeed,' said Frances, her tone and her expression neutral. 'Please, do not let me interrupt, but I too should be pleased to hear of your proposal.'

'Of course,' Patrick said. 'There is nothing I have to say that cannot be heard by your good self also.'

'Let me fetch another cup, Frances,' said Mary.

'Thank you,' Frances replied, taking the far seat.

When Mary had returned, Patrick began to outline his offer. 'A steady income, guaranteed money every month, no waiting for the merchant to pay you once the fabric has sold.'

All she had to do was produce twenty-five original designs a year. That meant a little over a fortnight for each one. It was, she considered, manageable, and the payment would enable them to buy fuel for the rest of the winter and keep food on the table. Her mouth watered at the thought of a chicken in the pot.

'Why, pray, should I agree to that?' she said cautiously.

'I think you are an intelligent woman, Miss Stephenson. It is a fair offer; you will get no better.'

That much is certainly true, Mary thought wryly.

'And how are we to know that you are who you say you are, that you can honour such promises?' Frances interrupted.

'I have my bona fides and you are welcome to peruse them,' he said, producing a flutter of paper from inside his coat and extending it to her.

Frances took the paper, her mouth pursed in concentration as she read the spidery script.

'I can advance the first payment as we speak today, a gesture of good faith,' he promised. 'After that, I shall visit every month and examine your designs. Guy Le Maître is well known to me;

he shall be the one who will weave them. Though, I have to confide, I do not think that family has laughed for more than four generations, he is nevertheless a fine craftsman.'

The three shared a smile at the comment.

'Shall we shake on the agreement?' Patrick asked.

For Mary the idea that someone wanted to use her work and was willing to pay so handsomely for it was more than she could have imagined. That the offer came from such an engaging man made it irresistible.

ELEVEN

December 1768, Oxleigh

Six weeks into her new life in Oxleigh and the calluses on Rowan's hands had grown thicker and the muscles in her body ached as if they had been dragged over the stones embedded in the stream at the bottom of the garden. She came to bed each night almost asleep on her feet, seldom seeing Alice, who generally kept later hours.

She had quickly learned precisely how the master liked his clothes arranged, the most efficacious way to brighten the brass candlesticks and clean the bone-handled cutlery, how to efficiently black the fireplaces and – most importantly – to avoid spilling the slops from the privy when emptying them into the cesspit at the end of the lane. She had even made a reduction in the pile of clothes requiring mending. Much to her dismay, she had, however, made no progress in forming a friendship with Alice.

The maid avoided her whenever she could and answered Rowan's questions with as few words as possible, usually accompanied by a grunt or a sigh. 'I have no wish to take your place,' Rowan whispered one evening as the maid slid silently into bed.

'Do not think that you will ever be his favourite,' Alice replied. 'No matter how well you might please him.'

Rowan stiffened, 'What can you mean by that?'

Alice did not reply.

Rowan tried to go about her work as unobtrusively as possible, and the idea of her master or mistress having a favourite among the staff had not occurred to her. 'You have no reason to be concerned by me,' she said. 'None at all. I have no interest in being anyone's favourite.'

Alice snorted and rolled over, pretending sleep.

Since then she'd had very little time to ponder the matter, but when she came upon Alice leaving the master's chamber before supper one evening, she felt a flicker of suspicion, for she knew of no reason why the maid might be there. Alice brushed her off, muttering something about a shirt that required mending and refusing to meet her eyes, and in that moment Rowan began to think that there might be more reason for Alice's animosity than she had been given to understand.

Patrick Hollander was often away conducting business in London or, when he was at home, about the town on mysterious errands. From what Rowan was able to observe, her mistress did little other than sit at the pianoforte or read by the fire, and Rowan had grown accustomed to hearing the sound of music floating through the house as she went about her work. There was one tune in particular that Mrs Hollander returned to time and again. Rowan recalled her mother singing the same notes as she rocked her littlest brother, Albie, to sleep. A lullaby. And each time Rowan heard the notes she thought of the tarnished baby's rattle she had found on her first morning, and noted the flat stays under her mistress's gown.

Accustomed as she was to a house overflowing with bodies and chatter and movement, Rowan found the merchant's house unnaturally quiet, and she was left alone with no one to oversee her for many hours of the day, though she did not dare slacken in her duties. She used her precious free time to wander the garden, a long strip of land bounded on two sides by a high brick wall, and which delighted her with its climbing honeysuckle and thorny rose bushes. At the rear was an orchard, a thicket of apple, damson and medlar trees, and then the stream, which was choked with watercress and marsh marigold, mallow, oxlips and willowherb. She also discovered a kitchen garden where a number of herbs and other medicinal plants, including her favourites feverfew, lemon balm, costmary, hyssop and chamomile, grew. She resolved that when she had the time she would gather peppermint, comfrey and rosemary to make an ointment to soothe her aching muscles, dry the witch hazel to make a balm for her skin, and dig out the teasel root that grew in abundance, for ailments of the stomach and nerves. When summer came she would gather wild rose petals and lavender buds for fragrant water to sprinkle on the bedsheets.

One afternoon, she spent near on an hour searching for the ingredients for a tincture for Prudence, for she had noticed that the cook had developed a cough that sounded like parchment rasping over stone. Prudence's bedchamber was next to hers and Alice's, and they would all sleep more soundly if her throat were soothed.

At the rear of the garden, beyond the orchard, the garden sloped away and as Rowan explored more thoroughly, she came to bushes of rosemary and sage along its edges. She tore off a few leaves from each plant, tucking them into her pocket, taking care not to bruise the tender young sage leaves. Then, in a far corner, what she had been hoping for: rosehips.

She was returning, a handful of the bright fruits gathered in her apron, when she saw Prudence standing at the back door, a long broom in her hand. 'Whatever are you doing out there, girl? I've been calling for you for some time – did you not hear me? Come in at once, for you'll catch your death; 'tis a bitter wind blowing.'

Rowan had been so absorbed in her explorations that she'd barely noticed the cold. She pulled a handful of the bright fruits from her pocket. 'I might brew a decoction,' she said. 'For your cough.'Twill ease it.'

Prudence eyed her doubtfully, weighing up the benefits of such an endeavour. 'Seeing as how your salve helped young Tommy,' she said eventually, 'I'll say that's most thoughtful of you. But mind you leave things as you find them and do not make more work for me.'

Later, Rowan boiled the herbs and hips in fresh water drawn from the well until she had a dark liquid to which she added a drizzle of honey and a splash of vinegar. The window fogged with the steam from her potion and the room was warm from the range. It was a most pleasant place to be and she sang to herself quietly, a song her mother had taught her about a heartbroken lover and a winding shroud. It added a note of melancholy to her mood but she hummed the tune nonetheless. When the hips had softened, she strained them into the mortar that had once been her mother's, and pounded them to a pulp before returning them to the liquid. The mortar was little more than a hollowed stone, with a long rounded rock as a pestle, but Rowan liked to believe that it still held some of her mother's power.

When she deemed it time, she decanted the mixture into a beaker and set it aside on the windowsill to cool. Later she would stopper it with a cork that she had taken from one of the master's empty port bottles. It was a small thing to make a soothing draught for Prudence, but as she worked she felt the connection to the women of her family who had gone before her, that they too had made such remedies, and it gave her great comfort.

~

One afternoon, Tommy Dean appeared again at the back door and displayed his leg for the women to inspect. 'Look!' he said, with a triumphant expression. The wound had completely healed over, only a faint scar now visible. ''Tis almost as if it never happened.'

Rowan grinned back at him, pleased that he was well and happier still to see him, for in idle moments she had found herself recalling the warmth of his smile and wondering if she might see him again. Though it had been only a matter of weeks since their first encounter, Tommy looked as though he had filled out in that short time, becoming broader in the chest. His voice had deepened and he was noticeably taller. She was reminded that her brothers would be changing too and it made her momentarily sad that she was so far away from them. 'You'll steer a wide path away from the horses in future, I'm sure,' she said.

'I'll certainly be quicker on my feet,' he laughed.

Prudence nodded approvingly at her. 'You've a rare talent there, Rowan,' the cook admitted.

'What's that?' Alice asked, looking up from the sock she was darning.

'She has a healing gift,' said Prudence. 'I have seen it myself, for my cough is already improved.'

Alice buried her head in her mending but not before Rowan had seen a sneer of contempt mar her features. 'You disagree, Alice?' she asked boldly.

'I am not certain I have an opinion one way or the other,' she replied, though her tone was at odds with her words. 'Best the master not hear of such a thing,' she added. 'If there is the slightest breath of magic or witchcraft under his roof . . .'

'Hush, I say!' cried Prudence, making the sign against evil spirits. 'Do not use that word inside of these walls. We are talking of a healing talent, nothing more.'

'Remember what happened to Widow Spanswick,' said Alice darkly.

'What?' Rowan asked.

'She used to offer syrups, balms and the like,' said Alice. 'Came into town on market days. Then, last harvest time, the baker's daughter took ill. The pox. He begged her for a tincture, and then gave it to his wife, but the wife and child were both dead 'ere the week was out. Cold as marble.'

'And then what happened?' Rowan asked, concern blooming in her chest.

'The widow was driven from the town,' said Alice, obviously relishing the story. 'Some of the men – our master included – confronted her at the next market day and told her that if she ever showed her face in Oxleigh again, she would be brought before the magistrate. It was only due to the fact of her late husband having been so well thought of that she wasn't thrown in the town lock-up and accused of poisoning.' She locked eyes with Rowan.

'Stop frightening the girl,' Prudence scolded. 'Rowan would never be so foolish as to try to treat someone with the pox.'

Alice shrugged and returned to her mending, a sceptical expression on her face, and Rowan felt a chill of unease snake down her spine.

~

Most of the time, Alice saw to Caroline, but one afternoon when Alice was out on an errand, two women came to call. As Rowan served them tea and sweetmeats prepared by Prudence, she snuck fascinated glances at their fine clothes and elegantly dressed hair. One had a swollen belly, and as Rowan overheard excited chatter about a growing family, she saw her mistress's serene expression slip for a moment.

After they had departed, Caroline pulled her aside and led her into the shop at the front of the house. There, Rowan looked on in open-mouthed awe at the bolts of fine cloth spread out on the long, wide countertop, so fine and fluid that they spilled over the edges like water from a dam. Her fingers itched to touch them, to feel the softness for herself.

'We're here to choose the fabric for a new gown, for I cannot have you serving my friends again in *that*,' Caroline said, running her eyes over Rowan's coarse chemise and the patched flax of her dress. 'Heaven only knows what they will think of us if we cannot even keep our maids properly clothed.'

Rowan was like a ravenous man at a feast of delicacies as she stared at the fabrics. Which might she be permitted to choose? Indeed, would she be allowed to choose or must she accept what she was given? Alice's garments, though of course not as fine as their mistress's, were still well fitting and fashionable.

Several heavy leather-bound pattern books sat on the counter, but she could not confess to her mistress that she had already snatched glances at the swatches of vibrant fabrics contained therein as she swept the floors every morning. She remembered one with a soft pink stripe and another woven with posies of tiny blue and yellow flowers and allowed herself a small dream of a beautiful gown with a full skirt, matching sleeves and a fitted bodice sitting neatly over her stays.

Jeremiah, the pinch-faced, bewigged man who served in the shop, pulled out a bolt of plain broadcloth, the colour like that left in the trough after Prudence had washed the dinner dishes, a kind of murky grey–brown. 'This is most serviceable,' he said, his gaze travelling the length of Rowan's shabby dress.

Dishwater grey. Rowan's hopes were dashed. It had been too much to wish for a prettier colour, and she struggled to hide her disappointment.

Caroline nodded in agreement. 'She will need a new cap too. Perhaps some ribbon as well, for even a maid might dream of dressing like a duchess. You may have a trim of your own choosing, Rowan.'

'Yes, mistress. Thank you.' It was a small kindness, she supposed.

'I wonder if I might ask something of you?' Caroline said as they left the shop and entered the parlour. A curious expression coloured her pretty features, one of hope and anxiety combined.

'Yes, mistress?'

'I understand you have a gift with herbal tonics and the like.'

Rowan thought carefully before answering. 'They . . . they are but commonplace remedies,' she stammered, remembering Alice's tale of Widow Spanswick. 'Simple infusions and tinctures, no more'n that.'

'I see,' Caroline said. 'Nothing stronger?'

Margaret Gyngell, Mistress Anne Bodenham, the Handsel sisters: her mother had whispered their names to Rowan, warning her of their fates. Even now, a person could still be fined or imprisoned for claiming to be a witch. Rowan hesitated, for she did not know how best to reply, but she was saved from answering as her mistress continued.

'This is rather a delicate matter, you understand. Not one I would generally discuss with a serving maid. I trust you will be discreet.'

Rowan nodded, aware as they stood side by side of how slight her mistress was, the handspan of her waist.

'Then I will speak plainly. My husband and I have been married five years, but are yet to be blessed with children. I have prayed daily, until my knees are quite bruised, but to no avail. I have to confess it is a great sadness to me. I worry that my marriage has a sickness and that my inability to produce an heir is the cause of it.'

Caroline tapped her fingers against her skirts, seemingly unaware of the rhythm she played. Rowan recalled the tarnished rattle she had found on her first day at the house and not seen since.

'I am compelled to ask if you know of a nostrum that might . . .' She cleared her throat, a rising pinkness in her complexion indicating her embarrassment with the subject. 'Assist in such matters.'

Rowan weighed up the wisdom of revealing the extent of her knowledge. If she agreed, then might her mistress come to suspect her of unnatural powers, especially if she was not successful? And if her master were to find out? She shuddered, for she now knew what might happen then. But if she were to refuse, then Caroline might take against her. She wanted to help if she could, for to be a wife but not a mother was surely a sad state to be in.

There was trouble in either course of action.

'I have heard of one such receipt,' she said carefully. 'But it can be dangerous, if ill used. And I am not certain that I will be able to find all that I need.'

A look of relief came over Caroline, and Rowan saw once more the sweetness in her mistress's face when she smiled. 'I shall let Prudence know that you may have extra time to search for all that you require. The forest to the north of the town yields all manner of plants that are not found elsewhere, so I am told. However, if you cannot find all that you seek growing nearby, you may visit the apothecary. Be sure to instruct him to send the account to me directly and not my husband.'

'Some of the ingredients might prove costly,' Rowan cautioned.

Caroline waved away her concerns. 'Do not trouble yourself with that.' She also didn't seem to have heard Rowan's doubt that she might not be able to concoct the draught. Rowan knew plenty about the birthing of babies, having watched and once even helped her mother bring them into the world, but the making of them – how to bring about the kernel of a new life beyond what she had observed in the paddock and the stable – well, that was something else entirely.

Rowan's mind went back to a time when she had watched her mother scour the hedgerows and pound herbs by the full moon's light. She was thankful that she had paid close attention, that her mother had made her repeat the ingredients and method of combining them back to her until she was satisfied Rowan could recite all of them without error. Perhaps she would be able to find the nettles, dandelion, orris root and other ingredients that she needed hereabouts. 'It may take me some weeks to gather the herbs. I shall need until early spring at least,' she said.

Caroline sighed impatiently. 'Are you sure it cannot be done sooner?'

Rowan shook her head. 'Some will not yet be in bloom.'

'Very well, what is a few months more, I suppose,' she said, sighing again. 'But say nothing at all to my husband.'

'Of course not, mistress.' Rowan caught a flash of the shape of a baby in her mind's eye. But it did not fill her with warmth, for its face was as pale as candlewax, the eyes closed. She shooed the image away.

'I understand you are an orphan, but have four brothers.'

Rowan was surprised that Caroline had taken note of this. Prudence must have informed her, for she was certain she had not mentioned it to anyone else. She nodded. 'They are all younger than I.'

'You must miss them, for family is a comfort. If you are successful, then I will perhaps manage to persuade my husband to grant you a week's leave, that you may go and see them.'

'Thank you, thank you indeed.' Rowan turned to leave.

'Oh, and Rowan?'

'Yes, mistress?'

Caroline produced a small folded paper from the pocket of her frock coat and held it out.

For a moment, Rowan didn't understand what it was.

'Your wage,' Caroline said.

Rowan took the packet and felt its weight in her hand, tangible evidence of her months of hard work. 'I am much obliged, mistress,' she said, bobbing a curtsey. Caroline dismissed her and Rowan left the room with her mind awhirl. She had been right to offer assistance. The thought of perhaps seeing her brothers in the months to come and being able to give her aunt and uncle money she had earned to help with their keep, was more than she had allowed herself to hope for.

TWELVE

December 1768, London

After waiting a respectable half-hour following the departure of the silk merchant, Mary left the house. She clutched a handful of the coins he had given her as an advance and went immediately to the butcher on the corner of Spital Square. 'Your finest pullet,' she said, feeling a thrill of pride rush through her. 'And a pound of lamb's fry, if you please.' She and Frances would feast that night, and the ones to come.

When she returned home again, cheeks flushed with the cool air and the astonishing turnaround in their fortunes, she found her sister sitting in the drawing room. Mary's sketchbook was in her hands.

'Is anything amiss?' she asked, for Frances wore a most serious expression. On the table by her side, in a short, stacked tower, were the remaining coins that he had left them.

Frances glanced up. 'All your eggs in one basket? Is that wise? And does he really know what he is doing, to promise you work for a year or more? I know your designs are unique, sister, and please do not misunderstand me when I say this, but not one is yet woven into fabric. Can you trust him?'

'I believe so. Why do you doubt him?'

Frances picked up one of the coins and held it to the light as if testing whether it were real. 'There is something . . .' Her voice trailed off.

'Something? What, exactly?' Mary was put out. She didn't want her sister to prick the bubble of goodwill that Mr Hollander's proposal had brought, but on the other hand, she respected her judgment.

'Nothing, I suppose,' Frances waved her away. 'In any case, beggars cannot be choosers.'

'Well, tonight we are not beggars. We have a fowl for supper, and more, and I for one will be glad not to be hungry for a change,' Mary said firmly.

~

Mary had a month to create three new designs. Before Mr Hollander had left, they had gone over her sketchbook and he indicated a couple that might be suitable but that would need more work. 'They are beautiful, but rather spare,' he advised. 'Add more detail. Your sense of geometry and proportion is most pleasing, but give me more.'

She wasn't entirely certain of his meaning, but she would do her best. The following afternoon, with a belly full of a chicken dinner, she went to work.

When she was convinced she had a design she was happy with, she began to make notes she hoped would assist the weaver when it came to mounting the design. She painstakingly copied the design onto point paper, but then had a further idea. What would the design look like when it was made into a gown? A waistcoat? The wide planes of a man's chest were easy to imagine and presented less of a conundrum. But when it was pleated and shaped to the curves of a woman's body? She knew she would have to think carefully about that, for it would be too late once the fabric was woven.

As she hunched over the paper she saw in her mind's eye the figure of Mr Hollander, could not help herself from imagining one of her designs as a waistcoat to fit those broad shoulders. How fine he would look. She hummed to herself as she worked.

Over the following weeks she found herself painting by lamplight and sacrificing sleep to complete the first few designs, worrying over the contrasts of light and shade, the exact proportions of the meandering, serpentine curve of a stem and how to transfer that to the paper, which colours to choose. Time and again she found herself returning to the plants before her, aiming to capture their exact form, to demonstrate what made them distinctive.

Guy had told her of a three-dimensional shading technique. '*Points rentrées*,' he said. 'It will make the flowers come alive on the cloth.' She returned to the weaver's loft, asking questions of the journeyman, learning exactly how he worked in order to achieve the effect she was after. He received her graciously, and patiently explained the process, but still the task was arduous and the standards she set herself exacting.

'I don't know why I ever thought I could do this!' she cried one evening, throwing another discarded design on the fire. 'It is impossible.'

'You *can* do it,' Frances soothed. 'Nothing worthwhile ever comes easily. Sleep on the matter and then start again in the morning.'

'Oh, I suppose,' said Mary, tiredly rubbing her arm across her forehead. 'But I wish to create something different, something new, a design of the like that people have never before seen. That is the hard part.'

'I might know of something to help,' said Frances. 'A particular book.'

The next afternoon, her sister returned from the hospital with a large volume under her arm, and watched in anticipation as Mary studied the frontispiece. '*A Curious Herbal*,' she read, 'by Elizabeth Blackwell.'

'I thought it might prove useful,' Frances said, a hopeful expression on her face.

'But where did you find it?' Mary asked.

Her sister put a finger to her lips. 'Do not ask, but I must return it in a few days' time, before anyone notices that it is missing.'

The book contained illustrations of medicinal plants, marigold, lady's mantle, frothy elderflower, lavender and chamomile, melissa, evening primrose and feverfew, senna and rhubarb, as well as marsh mallow, hollyhock and horse chestnut, blessed thistle, hawthorn, witch hazel, dandelion and burdock. Some of these Mary had encountered on her walks, but many were unknown to her. She found herself drawn to the chapters that described the deadliest plants, for they were among the most alluring:

nightshade, the pretty flowers of monkshood, the red fruits of laurel, the purple of belladonna, the freckle-throated foxglove, the orange berries of cuckoo pint and the delicate crumpled-silk petals of scarlet poppies.

As she turned the pages, a design began to appear in her mind's eye and a sharp fizz in her stomach told her that she was on the trail of something new, something dazzling and original, work that would have the fine ladies of the city clamouring for her designs. She could not wait to begin. She imagined combining the flowers and berries of some of the most poisonous plants, for not only were they beautiful on the surface but, she felt sure, a bold woman would appreciate that behind the pattern of their curling stems and bell-like flowers lay a darker message.

~

Finally, some three weeks later, Mary had four drawings, together with a carefully annotated, detailed paper pattern for each.

As well as the poisonous plant design, she had devised three that included not only the more traditional flowers of columbine, cornflower and campion, stitchwort and traveller's joy, sweet peas and roses, morning glory and lily, but also insects: the wasp and the beetle, and as well as the common butterfly she included the caterpillar, fat and green, in the hope that these would set her work apart.

She took them to Guy, who raised his eyebrows as he studied them, but agreed that he could weave them. 'Though they are unlike anything I have hereto seen.'

Despite Guy's dour tone, Mary was pleased by the comment, for she did not wish to copy the work of the male designers.

Patrick Hollander had wanted something new and arresting to the eye, and that was what she would give him.

She had made a careful copy of each and so sent a set of the designs to Oxleigh by the morning mail, barely able to contain her impatience for a response.

THIRTEEN

December 1768, Oxleigh

Rowan lay in bed, pinching herself to stay awake, certain that her arms would be blue with bruises by the morning. It was the night of the cold moon, the last of the old year, and she planned to gather the leaves of the witch hazel, for they would make a potent skin tonic. There was a fine tree on the common about half a mile beyond the town's main street, and leaves struck by the light of the full moon were said to be the most potent, but she had to gather them before dawn. She was also anxious to explore further afield to see if she could find red clover for the draught her mistress required.

She yawned, trying not to disturb Alice, who snored beside her, and surrendered to the tiredness that had threatened to wash over her many hours before. A moment later, she jerked awake again and, determined not to miss her chance, she slid out of bed.

Once on the main street, her way was lit by the moon, which hung large and low against a cloudless sky. Not a soul was about. A thick frost had coated the cobbles and Rowan shivered, gathering her cloak about her for warmth and walking as fast as she dared on their slippery surface.

As she approached the common, she came towards the long, low barn that stood at its edge. To her surprise, light spilled out of the doorway, and as she drew closer she heard a low rumble of voices, jeers, and occasionally the clash of metal, the screech of an animal in pain.

Drawn by the sound, she crept along the flint wall of the barn, keeping to the shadows. The door was open a crack and she stood behind it, craning her neck to see around. The smell of ale and of sweat rolled towards her as a warm fug, the noise almost deafening, and what she saw nearly caused her to cry out. A swarm of men, plenty of whom she recognised – the butcher, the man who sold his cheeses at the market, the chandler, the saddler and more – were gathered in a circle, shouting and calling, chanting, occasionally gesticulating and grunting, spitting and swigging from flagons, intent on the spectacle before them. No one noticed the young woman watching from the doorway.

At the centre of the circle, the chaff swept clear, was the bloodiest thing she had ever observed.

A cockpit.

Two birds faced each other, leaping and scratching, wings flapping, their neck feathers fluffed out like a ruff, their crows almost drowned out by the shouts of the men. Rowan saw the glint of metal spurs attached to their claws, a gash in the eye of one of the birds.

A cockfight.

She had seen her father slaughter a pig, watched as the blood streamed out from the gash in its neck, observed her mother wring the neck of a chicken, and had heard of those who laid wagers on the outcome of a fight, but this was different. This baiting of animals – how could it be enjoyed as a sport?

Then, as she inched further around the door, she gasped as she caught sight of her master, rusty marks on his snowy breeches, a leer on his face. He stood almost inside the circle, using a stick to thrust the cocks back to the centre of the pit. She recoiled as disgust and fear ran an icy trail through her veins. Rowan had believed him to be a gentleman, but in that moment he more closely resembled a savage.

~

The next morning, as she lit the fire in the drawing room, her master entered, bringing with him the smell of sour ale. His fine waistcoat was awry, his hair mussed and the insides of his pockets hung out, as if he had been in a hurry to empty them. He squinted at her, red-eyed, as if surprised to see her there, before collapsing on the chaise. 'Lady luck has not smiled upon me of late,' he said with a sigh.

'No, sir,' said Rowan quietly. When she had returned to the house in the early hours – with the leaves she needed tucked carefully into a pocket – she had lain awake until dawn as the scene she had witnessed played through her mind, and she now found it hard to regard her master with the respect she once had for him.

Later, as she returned to clear the breakfast dishes, she heard the rising sound of an argument, Patrick's voice placating, Caroline's loud and furious. She stopped a few inches from the door, uncertain whether to enter.

'Do not think I am unaware of what happens under this roof,' Caroline said. 'The maid must go.'

Rowan froze. What could she have done to offend her mistress? Had she taken too long to prepare the draught Caroline wanted? Or had Patrick spotted her peering into the barn?

'As I have told you before, you are seeing things that simply do not exist,' Patrick replied wearily. 'As if a respected merchant would concern himself with a lowborn maid. There is absolutely no reason to dismiss Alice. Besides, she is good at her job, you've said it yourself, and in case you hadn't noticed, there is a lack of suitable servants until next year's hiring.'

Rowan was able to move again as she heard Alice's name, not hers. The memories surfaced: Alice's absences from the house with no explanation; Alice outside the master's bedchamber; Alice and the master in the back recesses of the garden, their heads inclined towards each other, his hand on her elbow almost a caress. It seemed the mistress was not unaware of such things either.

'Well, this cannot possibly continue,' Caroline said, changing tack. 'You are out until all hours and then incapable of doing an honest day's work. You spend more than we have. Do not think that I am incapable of understanding the ledgers.'

'They are nothing to be troubling yourself with,' Patrick said. 'There is ebb and flow in every business. If I am not overly concerned, you should not be. Trust me, my dear.'

'Do not take me for a fool,' her voice rose. 'You traipse about the country doing who-knows-what and are almost never here. I fail to see that business calls you away quite so often.'

'If there were more to keep me here, I might be more inclined to stay,' he said coldly.

'What exactly do you mean by that?' Rowan could almost taste the bitterness in her mistress's voice.

'I wonder if I have married a barren woman. There are those in the town who mock me for this, I am sure of it.'

Rowan stifled a gasp at her master's cruelty, though in truth she was no longer shocked by it.

'Well, perhaps, husband, if you were at home more often . . .' Caroline bit back.

Rowan knew she must redouble her efforts to make the draught her mistress so desperately desired. Caroline Hollander had shown kindness to her, and she could not bear to see the master treat her so ill. Besides, Rowan knew, a settled household was a far better prospect for her own continued employment than a troubled one.

~

On a Sunday afternoon early in the new year, when her work was done, Rowan wandered along the path that ran alongside the river and edged the town like a ribbon. She wrapped her mother's red cloak around her and took a deep lungful of the crisp, sweet air then raised her face to the pale sun. It was bitterly cold, and her breath came in clouds as she walked, but she had been indoors for too long, knew herself to be far happier outside among meadows and barley fields and under a great canopy of sky. As she followed the riverbank she searched for the herbs she might need. She spied chickweed, hawthorn, coltsfoot and elderberry, making a note of their locations, planning to return and collect them in spring, when the hawthorn would flower, and late summer when there would be elderberries to make into a syrup for winter sore throats and chills. But of the red clover and henbane she required, there was no sign.

She was deeply absorbed in her search when, from the corner of her eye she saw a sudden, swift flash of rust. There it was, on the path up ahead of her. A thick brush waving in the air, a pale muzzle coming towards her. Now it was in front of her. She stopped and they watched each other, the animal's yellow eyes staring directly into her own. She stayed completely still, felt her blood thrum in her ears. She prayed that it would not make a sound and held her breath, only letting it out as, with a twitch of its tail, the fox trotted past her. A fox's call was commonly believed to be a harbinger of death, and such superstition bit hard among country people, herself included.

Relieved at its silence, she continued on her way until she came to a watermill, where a large paddlewheel churned the water into frothing whiteness. Fascinated but unnerved by the roar of the thing, she drew as close as she dared to the deep pool of water. She was quickly chilled by the icy spray that landed on her face and arms, and withdrew a safe distance away.

The slippery quality of water had always unsettled her. She frequently dreamed of being carried away on a fast-moving stream and couldn't comprehend how something fluid could have such power. Even in the heat of summer she had to be cajoled by her younger brothers to wade into the river's murky green depths, scared and thrilled in equal parts by the pull of the current as it flowed between her legs and pulsed through her outstretched fingers. She had never been more than waist-deep in water, had never the courage to immerse herself, could not imagine how one could possibly move against such a current without one's feet firmly on the ground. Her brothers hadn't shared her fear; diving, disappearing and then reappearing from beneath the water's opaque surface. They jeered encouragement at her, but she would not let her body rise up and float, nor untether her feet, lest she be carried away from the safety of the bank.

As she lingered on the memory of summer days gone by, she watched the figure of a young man up ahead. As she drew closer she saw that it was Tommy and she hurried to catch up, breathless by the time she reached him, wincing as her stays pinched her tender skin.

'Rowan!' he cried, a smile lighting up his face. 'Good day to you. What brings you here?'

'A stroll,' she said, for even though he had witnessed a little of her skill with herbs, she dared not reveal her purpose in this instance. 'And you?'

'I was on my way back from a delivery. Don't tell anyone but I took the long way – I like to walk by the river whenever I get the chance.'

She smiled back at him, feeling a thrill of pleasure at coming upon him so unexpectedly, for he was the closest thing to a friend that she had in the town. 'Even when it's so cold out?' she asked, noticing the thinness of his smock.

'Don't even feel it,' he said, throwing his arms wide. 'And I can breathe here.'

'I know what you mean,' she said. 'Sometimes I think I might suffocate inside, especially when the fire smokes so.'

'Give me the sky above my head, the fields beneath my feet and the river beside me, and I'm a happy lad.'

'If that's the case, shouldn't you have been a farmer?' She snuck a glance at his merry face, liking this boy who was as fond of nature as she.

'Labourer is about the best I could hope to be, and there's no future there. No, it's fortunate that I've a trade to learn. There's money in meat, so my guv'nor says. And I intend to have the best butchery in Oxleigh one day, you'll see.'

Rowan laughed at his bold statement, but was secretly pleased that he had ambition. It was most agreeable to be around someone who had a thought to better themselves.

'You think that is funny?' he asked, a hurt expression clouding his normally sunny features.

'No, no,' she rushed to reassure him. 'If anything, it is that I am impressed at your vision for the future.'

'And what is yours, then?'

Rowan paused. She had given little thought to such matters. 'I don't know. I suppose I hope to remain in Oxleigh. Help those who need it.'

'You mean like you helped me when I was hurt?'

'Exactly. Perhaps one day to be more than a maid,' she dared to admit.

He smiled broadly at her. 'I, too, am impressed by your ambition,' he said. 'You are not like most other girls, for you are not concerned with trifling, empty-headed notions. You are a grand person to associate with, Rowan.'

She put a hand to her cheek, feeling the scarred ridges extending from her eye, suddenly bashful at the roses that bloomed there at his words.

FOURTEEN

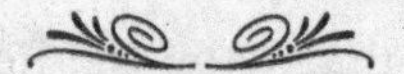

Now

'Hey, custard guts!' a boy called out.

'We heard they only let you in 'cause your father's the headmaster,' said another.

'Yeah, and they put you in Silk House 'cause they didn't want you any closer to the school in case you infect the place.'

Thea, on her way to the hockey pitches at the end of the day, her favourite stick tucked under her arm, rounded a corner and spotted a group of younger boys and three of the new girls several yards ahead.

'Ah bless,' she heard Sabrina reply, saccharine-sweet. 'Is that the best you've got? You really will have to try harder.' She laughed in their faces and turned to the others. 'Come on, girls, we'll be late for practice.'

The boys scattered, and Thea allowed herself a smile. They could easily hold their own. She looked further ahead and caught sight of the playing fields: fourteen hockey pitches, several all-weather and the rest grass, spread out next to the same number for rugby, two football pitches, as well as countless netball and tennis courts and she exhaled. Thought about how good it would be to play again, to feel the sweet thwack of her stick against the ball. It had been months. Then she remembered that her father had played on these same fields and gulped down a sudden piercing sadness.

Gareth Pope was already on the fields, setting up a series of cones and balls. He glanced pointedly at his watch when she arrived. 'Understand you're helping out with the new mixed team,' he said, not sounding entirely pleased about it.

'I've played a bit,' she admitted.

'The school has hardly lost a match in ten years, but we're not about to rest on our laurels. We'll take the best of the boys for the First Eleven but we should be able to summon a mixed senior team as well – that's if the girls are up to it.'

'I'm sure they will be,' she said, her tone as dry as the pitch she stood on.

'Come on then, boys and girls,' he called out, as the players straggled out from the changing rooms. 'Give me three laps of the playing fields as a warm-up.'

There was a muffled groan, and Thea noticed Fenella, Sabrina, Joy and Aradia among the boys who began a slow clockwise run. Standing across from her, Gareth picked up a stick and began bouncing a ball on its flat surface.

Showing off.

Thea ignored him and ran after the students with an easy, fluid gait. She caught up with them after half a lap and then slowed as she drew alongside them.

'Hi Miss,' said Fenella between breaths.

'How was your first day?' Thea asked.

Fenella was about to reply when a couple of the boys picked up the pace and the rest of them were hard pressed to keep up. The final lap was almost a sprint to the finish and Thea could tell they had something to prove. She worked a little harder, staying with the fastest pair and was pleased to see that they didn't gain much ground on the girls either.

When they had finished their warm-up, Gareth divided them into groups and set them to a number of drills, all the while bouncing the ball on his stick. It was beginning to get on Thea's nerves, so she went to supervise the group furthest away from him.

After half an hour or so of drills, he called them over and formed the players into two teams. Thea watched without comment as he put all of the girls on one team, together with a handful of the weaker boys.

So, that's how it's going to be.

He threw a bib at her and she caught it deftly in one hand.

'Let's have a knock around to finish. You can join the girls; we won't bother with goalies.'

'Sure.' Thea swiftly directed her players into position, putting Fenella at centre forward, and taking left back for herself, where she could keep an eye on things and give encouragement if needed.

Gareth had taken up an attacking position on the opposite side.

He blew the whistle to start the game. His team gained possession of the ball and came thundering down the pitch towards Joy, who put her head down and tackled the player, easily relieving him of the ball and flicking it across to Sabrina.

The boy whipped his head around, astonished to see one of the girls flying to the other end of the pitch with the ball.

Sabrina dribbled the ball up the pitch, dodging two more players before being tackled.

The boy who had now taken the ball passed it out to his wing, who collected it and passed it on to the centre forward, who dodged Aradia in defence and whacked the ball into the back of the net.

'One–nil,' called Gareth, not hiding his smirk.

Thea ignored it. They were only just getting started.

The game continued, with the boys scoring again, and then Gareth had the ball and was coming right for her. As he was about to flick the ball beyond her, Thea hooked her stick around it and ducked to avoid colliding with him, before passing the ball with an almighty thwack halfway up the pitch to where Fenella was waiting, just on side. From there it was an easy job for her to send the ball to the waiting wing and for him to cross it into the goal.

The game continued for another twenty minutes, with the girls on Thea's team scoring twice more.

Red in the face, Gareth blew the final whistle and they jogged back to the practice equipment. He gave her the faintest of nods as she reached him.

He hadn't called out the final score, but that didn't matter. He had not only miscalculated her ability, but the girls' too and although she knew it was probably childish, she allowed herself a private moment of smugness at the victory.

'That's all we've got time for today,' Gareth said when everyone had gathered around. 'I can see there's plenty we need to work on before our first interschool match, and we'll need to improve all of your fitness as well. Off you go now, back to your houses and I'll see you at practice on Thursday.'

Thea began to gather up the equipment, picking up an armful of cones. 'Give me a sec,' she called to the girls as they were leaving, 'and I'll come back to the house with you.'

'Good play, girls,' Gareth said as they left. Thea knew it had cost him to say that, heard the barely concealed grudging tone.

'Don't worry, Miss,' said Fenella once they were out of earshot. 'They hate it when we're better than them.'

Thea laughed. 'They're going to have to get used to it, aren't they?'

'It'll make them better players too,' said Fenella. 'Though some of them might not see that to start with.'

'Nothing like a little healthy competition from where you least expect it, hey?' she replied with a smile. 'By the way, Sabrina, I overheard what some of the junior boys were saying to you before practice. You let me know if any of them bother you again and I'll report it.'

'It was nothing,' said Sabrina. 'They'll get over themselves. Besides, I really don't want the reputation of running to Daddy every time something like that happens.'

'Fair enough,' agreed Thea.

'The other boys, the ones in our year,' said Fenella, 'they've been really nice.'

'Ooh,' said Aradia and Sabrina in unison as she blushed tomato-red. 'Someone's keen.'

'Not like *that*,' she protested.

~

'May I have a word, Miss Rust?'

Thea suppressed a sigh as the Dame appeared behind her. After supervising the girls' supper and sending them up to their rooms to begin their homework, she had stayed behind to make herself a cup of tea and was about to go up to her study to work on her lessons for the rest of the week.

'Shall we go into the small sitting room?'

Thea picked up her mug and followed her across the hallway into the room at the front of the house. There were a couple of large sofas, several beanbags and an upright piano in one corner, and a bow-fronted window that overlooked the street. It was to be used as a space for the girls to relax in, though Thea had begun to wonder when they might ever be allowed free time. Their lives were heavily scheduled, with barely ten minutes between activities. Perhaps the weekends would be quieter, though for those playing sport there were Saturday matches and for those not, extra homework and music practice.

'How was your first day?'

Thea was taken aback that the Dame would bother to ask, given her previous dour demeanour, but she hid her surprise. 'Fine, thank you. Nothing that I can't handle. The girls all seem remarkably well adjusted.'

'Well, they have all been specially selected,' she said.

Thea raised her eyebrows. The Dame made it sound almost ominous. 'They do come with the highest reports,' she agreed. 'But they are still teenage girls. They will doubtless face challenges, no matter how privileged their background.'

'And how about the other staff?'

'Just fine.' Thea was hardly going to report that Mr Battle had been openly dismissive on their first encounter nor that Gareth Pope had tried to show up her and the girls. She could more than cope with both of them.

'I wanted to warn you.'

'Warn me?'

'Things in this house might not always be exactly what they seem.'

Thea watched the Dame, waiting for her to continue, to elaborate, for she hadn't the faintest idea what the woman was on about.

'You might . . . hear things. At night.'

'Actually, I did hear something, last night,' she replied. 'But it turned out to be Fenella, getting some water from the kitchen.'

'It's an old house, dates back to the mid-eighteenth century. Sometimes it creaks and groans as if it has a life of its own.'

'Like an old lady,' said Thea with a quick smile.

'Yes, a very old lady. There's bound to be a book or two about its history in the local library, possibly even in the school library if you're interested.'

Thea glanced around the room, noting the high, coffered ceiling, the age of the worn timbers, blackened by smoke, soot and time. Just how many lives had these walls contained? 'Yes, I would be, actually,' she said, deciding in that moment that she definitely wanted to find out if there was any foundation for the eerie feeling the house gave her, especially at night.

'I'll get you something for that.' The Dame stood up and glided out of the room, leaving Thea blinking at how fast she had disappeared. She felt a twinge in her thumb and regarded the plaster covering the paper cut. How had the Dame known that it was sore?

She reappeared and placed a small glass pot on the table in front of Thea. 'Balsam. My mother's recipe, passed down from her grandmother. Take off the plaster.'

Thea did as she was told, noticing that the cut had taken on a green tinge. 'Ugh, how did that happen?'

The Dame said nothing, but indicated that Thea should smear some of the ointment on her thumb. As she unscrewed the lid a flowery aroma wafted into the room, reminding Thea of the smell in her bedroom the night before. Nevertheless, Thea looked unenthusiastically at the thick green paste.

'Really?'

'Yes, really.'

Thea gingerly dabbed a little of the paste on her cut finger.

'That should do it,' said the Dame, getting up to leave the room. 'I can't have my girls injured.'

Thea was left wondering as she sat alone in the room staring at the pot of salve. What had the Dame wanted to talk to her about, anyway? Was it only to warn her about strange noises in the night? She wiggled her thumb. It had stopped throbbing quite so much; indeed it felt a little better already.

FIFTEEN

January 1769, Oxleigh

Thanks in part to Prudence and Tommy, word had spread of Rowan's talent among the servants of the town and several had come calling. A soft knock on the back door late at night often heralded requests for tinctures and salves, draughts and poultices. A sprained ankle, several coughs that had settled on the chest, a young child with quinsy, an aching tooth and a cut to the head all required Rowan's medicines. She had taken to mixing up the most oft called-for ointments and salves and keeping them – as well as numerous bunches of herbs – in the scullery in advance of when they were needed. She refused, however, to see anyone with the flux or a pox, for she knew the limits of her skills, and heeded Alice's tale of the Widow Spanswick. While Prudence sang her praises and happily accepted payments in kind, perhaps a clutch of eggs or a small cheese, Alice looked on with barely disguised ill humour.

Patrick had once again departed for London, and Caroline was about to visit cousins in Salisbury. Before the mistress left, Rowan was called on to help Alice prepare the travelling trunks, but her initial delight at handling the luxurious silks, finely woven wool and plush velvets turned to frustration – she thought she might snap from the effort of holding it in – as Caroline chose first one gown and then another before discarding them all and calling for more to be brought for her consideration. The process of packing took several days, leaving Rowan behind with her other tasks. She tried not to sigh at their mistress's indecision, nor to feel ill will towards her, but her good heart was sorely tested. Rowan could not understand how a person could be so spoiled as to not be satisfied with even one of the beautiful gowns that Caroline possessed, let alone the dozens she owned.

She caught Alice's eye as they brought forth gown after gown, and they shared a look of understanding at their shared plight. It was the first time Alice had done anything other than ignore or sneer at her, and it heartened Rowan immensely.

As they packed the rejected gowns away, Rowan could not help running her fingers along the silk, wondering what it might feel like to wear such a gown, to feel its softness against her skin, the weight of the skirts as they fell from her waist, the whisper of it as she walked.

'Beauties, aren't they,' sighed Alice. 'I'd choose the pearly grey one. No one would be able to take their eyes off me in such finery.'

'It would indeed set off your colouring,' Rowan agreed. 'But a girl as pretty as you does not need a fine gown to be noticed.'

She was rewarded for her kind words with a rare, and fleeting, smile.

~

Before she departed, Caroline summoned Rowan to the drawing room. 'Is it ready yet?' she asked.

'Soon, mistress,' Rowan promised, knowing exactly what it was that she referred to. 'I need a few more weeks.'

'It will be ready on my return.' Caroline's words were a command, not a question.

Rowan nodded. 'But a few more plants to come into flower. I wait only for the first signs of spring.'

As she left the room, she saw Alice retreating along the corridor and got the distinct feeling that she had been eavesdropping. It did not surprise her in the slightest.

~

The morning after Caroline's departure, Rowan put down the brush she was using to scour the pewter and wiped the sweat from her forehead with the back of her arm. Her muscles quivered from the effort of cleaning. Not for the first time, she cursed the slovenliness of the maid before her, for the pewter Prudence had directed her to clean that day had been discovered at the back of a cupboard and had been as tarnished as if it had been smeared with the soot from a fireplace. She held the jug in front of her, turned it this way and that, and reckoned it shone as brightly as it was ever going to. She inclined her head, listening as the church bell sounded twice. If she was quick, she would have enough time to search for the herbs she needed before darkness fell.

Although spring yet waited in the wings and dandelion root grew in profusion along the muddy paths in the outer reaches of the town, fresh leaves of raspberry, red clover and peppermint had so far proved impossible to find. On leaving the house, she walked the length of the high street before following the path that led to the mill, remembering the coltsfoot she had seen there, and hopeful of perhaps also finding a clump of iris, as well as searching for the herbs she more urgently needed.

As she walked, her cloak brushing the verge, there was a movement ahead of her, a shadow in the gloomy light. Was it her imagination, or was someone or some creature there? She didn't particularly want to come across the fox again. As she rounded the bend hesitantly she saw that it was Tommy. He turned, waiting for her with a lopsided grin on his face.

'Rowan,' he called out as she drew near.

'Did you imagine that I might be here?' she asked.

His answering blush told her all she needed to know. 'Finished all the orders early,' he said with a smile that dimpled his cheeks. 'And this *is* my favourite place to come,' he added, nodding to the fishing rod he carried, a hazel stick affixed with a line of braided horsehair and a small bent hook at the end of it. 'The trout are good along here, near the pond. They start biting as the sun goes down.'

'Isn't that poaching?' she asked warily.

'If it is, you didn't see me,' he replied, giving her a sideways glance. 'You're heading that way too?'

'Aye.'

'Shall we walk together, then?'

They fell into an easy pace, climbing the small rise before the mill appeared. The paddlewheel was still, the millrace closed, for the grinding of wheat into flour was finished for the day.

The air held February's bitter chill, but overhead tiny wrens and chaffinches came in to roost, wheeling and chirruping, and in the west the sun was a pale orb of light. Rowan felt the calm of the landscape descend upon them, enjoyed the feeling of walking comfortably in step with someone, no need to converse.

When they reached the mill, Tommy sat at the foot of the riverbank, retrieved a wriggling knot of worms from his pocket, hooked one and then cast his line.

Rowan wandered further, towards the pond, and before long became absorbed in her task, finding common groundsel, wild garlic, even a patch of elder. Finally, in the lee of a tall oak she came across it: fresh red clover, in flower far earlier than she had expected. As she gathered the herbs, the distant sound of the church clock chiming the half-hour rang across the meadow. She returned to where Tommy was fishing, the light now grown dimmer.

'What have you got there?' he asked as she sat beside him.

'Just a few leaves and whatnot,' she said dismissing her haul. 'Any fish?'

He nodded, indicating three glistening brown trout on the grass beside him. 'Care for one for your supper?' he asked.

'But what would Prudence say?'

He laughed. 'She'd surely know who caught 'em.'

'All right then, Tommy Dean. But we should go soon,' she said, seeing the darkening sky.

'Aye. A few more minutes.'

They sat in silence for a moment, both watching the line as it dropped into the water, as a ripple grew from where it entered, ruffling the glassy surface.

'How do you like the merchant's house?' he asked.

'Well enough,' she replied. 'Prudence, of course, has been kind. And my mistress too, though I fear she is not entirely happy.' Though Rowan knew better than to gossip about her employers, she trusted Tommy. 'But Alice . . .' She didn't know how to explain the maid's countenance without sounding mean-spirited. Besides, Alice had begun to warm to her in recent days, particularly since their mistress's departure.

'The master likes her, so I hear,' Tommy said.

Rowan didn't have time to ask him how he knew this, for, as she glanced at him she had a flash of a vision. Saw Tommy kissing her, his lips pressing on hers. She had never been kissed, not like the image that appeared in her mind anyway, and the feeling it gave her, like a shiver and a scorching heat all at the same time, was an entirely new one.

He noticed her looking at him and turned to face her.

'It – it doesn't bother you? My eye, I mean?' she asked suddenly.

'Nothing to be bothered by,' he said.

She smiled. An encouragement.

And so he leaned towards her and gently rested his lips on hers. She pressed back, enjoying the softness of him, the sweetness like a warm strawberry. She found she didn't mind it, that tremor and the fire that rose between them. Didn't mind it at all.

His lips reluctantly left hers.

Her first kiss. She would remember the moment always.

'We should get back,' he said reluctantly.

She grinned at him, holding the newness of the feeling to herself, basking in the glow it gave her, as they retraced their steps along the bridleway to the town. A breeze blew from the east and she fancied the sound of it in the branches sang his name.

When Rowan returned to the kitchen, Prudence eyed the trout with suspicion. 'I know who that's come from,' she said, taking it from her nonetheless.

'We met near the millpond,' said Rowan as innocently as she could. 'I was collecting herbs.'

'I'll bet you did,' the cook replied. 'Don't you go getting into any mischief, now.'

Rowan was indignant. 'I'm no foolish country girl anymore,' she said. 'I have my wits about me. At all times.'

It was true. Outwardly she appeared as a hard-working maid from a respectable family and indeed, she could hardly recall the simple girl she had been but a few months before. The grey broadcloth had been fashioned into a well-fitting gown and despite its ordinary colour was most pleasant to wear and a definite improvement on the patched and worn clothing she had brought with her. For her cap, she had chosen a cherry-red ribbon that lifted her spirits simply to look at it. She was able to complete her work with efficacy, to navigate the busy market with ease, bargaining with the stallholders and conducting herself with newly acquired confidence. Not for the first time, she wished her mother and father were alive to see the capable young woman she had become. Even her hard-to-please aunt would have been satisfied.

Prudence tipped her head back and laughed loud and long, until Rowan worried that any passer-by might hear the sound coming from the house. 'Yes, I suppose you do,' she said, wiping tears from her eyes.

~

The next afternoon, she ventured to the apothecary, which lay at the opposite end of the high street to the church, not far from where the cobbles ended and the street became a beaten dirt path. She hoped he might stock the dried versions of the herbs she needed for her mistress, for she was running out of time to find them growing wild. She would need pennyroyal and dittany, black hellebore too. The latter she had only ever been told about, had never seen it with her own eyes, for it did not grow near Inkpen, but her mother had described it to her in such detail that she felt as though she would know it the instant she saw it.

The shop was gloomy and dank, with only a little light coming in through a small low-set front window. It was at the less prosperous end of the town, where mangy dogs skulked in packs and rats ran boldly across the mud right in front of a person, but as soon as she stepped inside, Rowan felt at home, as if this were a place she had been to before. Even the smells were recognisable: aromas of rosemary and licorice, bitter aloe and ginger root wafted towards her as she surveyed the narrow shelves, the amber and green glass bottles aligned upon them, and at the numerous drawers beneath that surely contained all manner of powerful substances. A counter ran the length of the shop and on it sat a large, heavy-looking stone mortar and pestle, as well as a number of small copper bowls and a fat leather-bound book. It was both strange and familiar all at once; some of the items in the jars were similar to ones her mother used, others unfathomable.

Rowan was alone in the room. She cleared her throat lustily, and after a moment she heard the sound of a door at the back of the building thudding shut and slow, dragging footsteps upon the stone floor.

'And who have we here? For I am certain I haven't seen the likes of you before,' said the man who appeared from the passageway. 'I would surely remember one with hair so fair.'

'Oh,' said Rowan, putting her hand to the crown of her head and realising that the hood of her cloak had slipped to her shoulders.

The man was tiny, scarcely taller than her, and his hair was almost as white as hers, though that was likely the effect of age, for the skin on his face was coarse and lined and hung in great folds from a jaw that flapped softly as he spoke. His coat was a rich mossy green, as might be expected in a grotto, and extended well past his knees. Indeed, it seemed to have been made for a far larger man, though his waistcoat stretched tightly over a rounded belly.

Rowan couldn't help but stare at him, for he seemed so very peculiar. 'No, we have not made each other's acquaintance,' she said. 'I am come from the merchant's house. Mistress Hollander bade me fetch some herbs. Rowan Caswell, maid-of-all-work, sir.'

'Very well. What is it that you desire?'

Rowan listed the ingredients she needed, and he pulled down canisters and bottles from the shelves, rummaged in drawers and then balanced the ingredients one by one on a set of brass pans. When he had assembled most of what she required and wrapped each one carefully in a twist of paper, he regarded her again, his eyes seeming to bore into her. 'You said this was for Mistress

Hollander?' he asked, tipping a fine powder from one of the jars onto the pan balance. 'I hope you know what you are doing.'

She nodded. 'I have some of what I need already.'

'Dandelion root? Nettles? Red clover?'

She nodded.

'And exactly how did you become knowledgeable in such matters?' he asked, his hands stilling and a frown of suspicion further deepening the creases that lined his face.

Rowan had no choice but to reveal a little of her past. 'My mother instructed me in the necessary healing tinctures and poultices.'

'This is more than a mere healing poultice.'

'Is it, sir?' she asked, pretending innocence.

'This is a strong remedy. I hope she instructed you well.'

'She did,' Rowan said, quaking a little at his intense regard.

'She was not from these parts then, for I surely would be acquainted with her.' He opened the book on the counter and flipped through its pages. Rowan could see the closely written script, with measurements and drawings, and craned to get a better view, though she was a poor reader. The apothecary did not seem bothered by her interest and continued to run a finger down one of the pages, muttering to himself.

When he had finished measuring out all of the herbs she required and made notations in his ledger, she packed them carefully into the basket she had brought with her and bade him farewell, instructing him to send the account for the attention of her mistress.

Her satisfaction at finally having the required ingredients, however, was soon extinguished. As she emerged from the apothecary, a stranger approached, mouthing the word 'witch' at her before crossing to the other side of the street. Shaken, she hurried back towards the merchant's house, chasing the sun as it set over the hills beyond the town, all the while cursing herself for not being more circumspect in her activities and in whom she assisted with her concoctions. She could not risk being tainted with that word. Indeed, was she doing the right thing this day? The potion for her mistress was a far more powerful medicine than a simple ointment or poultice. To conjure new life, that was surely closer to witchcraft?

As she reached the house she pushed the worry down, as if banking the embers of a fire. The shop was shuttered and the door that connected it to the rest of the building was locked. She had been away longer than she had realised.

She entered the kitchen from the back of the house to find Alice sitting at the table, polishing a number of small items of jewellery – their mistress's, she presumed – and Prudence reclining in a chair next to the range with her feet resting on a scuttle and her eyes firmly shut. A gentle snore emanated from her. Alice barely acknowledged her, but Prudence stirred as Rowan drew near. 'You were gone a good while,' she said, rousing herself and yawning widely.

'I'm sorry if you missed me,' Rowan answered. 'Mistress gave me instructions to visit the apothecary. She asked for an ointment for her chilblains.'

Alice's eyebrows rose at the lie but she said nothing.

Rowan knew that Alice likely had a better idea of her true intentions, but the less said about the real nature of the draught the better. She noticed Alice's fingers work faster with the cloth and the brooch she held, as if she wanted to buff something out of existence, but as ever, she was inscrutable.

'She has sent word that she will be back a week hence,' said Prudence. 'The master is delayed a while longer.'

Rowan set her basket on the table. 'Then I have little time to waste.'

SIXTEEN

Now

The fog wrapped the hills like a blanket, swirling around Thea as she ran along the path that led out of the town, and obscuring everything around her. She could barely see a few feet ahead, had to force herself to slow down to avoid tripping on an unseen rock and risking a sprained ankle. Claire had mentioned in the staffroom the day before that the path was one of her favourite running tracks. 'It'll take you all the way to Summerbourne, the nearest village to Oxleigh,' she said. 'It's only a couple of miles there and back, but it's very pretty. Good pub too.'

Dawn was the faintest glimmer when Thea set out, and it was cold, pinching the tips of her ears and nose, but she soon warmed up as she flew along the lane, spooking an early-rising rabbit and causing a trio of birds to startle as a branch snagged the sleeve of her sweatshirt. The path ran alongside a stream, though the fog was so thick she could hear but not see the rush of water as she passed. By the time she reached Summerbourne she was breathing heavily and her lungs were burning, so she slowed to take in the old red-brick, moss-covered buildings that lined the road: a handful of houses, some freestanding, and others conjoined in rows of three and four, a village hall and, as Claire had promised, a lovely-looking pub with a thatched roof and whitewashed walls. Though lights shone from a couple of the houses she passed, it was eerily quiet, too early for anyone else to be out and about. A little way further along she came across a flint-walled church with a steep spire, stained-glass windows along the nave and gravestones peppering the churchyard. Save for the cars parked at intervals along the narrow road, the village looked as it must have done for centuries, and she could easily imagine what it must have been like to live in such a place in a time long past. A person's knowledge of the world would have been so limited; likely they never travelled more than a few miles from their home their entire life. Seeing the past coexist with the present like this was one of the things that had drawn her to study and teach history, to try and tease out what had happened in centuries gone by.

Thea reached the far end of the village, where the lane joined the main road, and then turned around and headed back to the boarding house. As she plunged into the misty valley once more, the clouds of her breath shrouded the already poor visibility and she felt almost as if she were running in a ghost world. As the path drew closer to the river again, the fog thickened and she had to strain to see the way ahead. She heard the race of the water over rocks, could imagine it frothing below.

Had her father ever walked or run this path as a schoolboy? She imagined him coming this way on a sunny summer's day, perhaps stopping for a dip in the river after a match at the school's tennis courts that backed on to this path. She pictured the framed black-and-white photographs of him in his whites, doubles and singles champion, that had decorated the walls of his study at home, and felt a sudden wave of sadness wash over her.

Lost in her thoughts and the fog, she didn't see the figure coming towards her until it was almost upon her. It nearly caused her to veer into the ditch, a flash of red as it shouldered its way past.

'Hey!' she called out, but as she turned, shaken, it was only to see the stranger disappear out of sight. It took her a moment to work it out, but judging by his build, she thought she knew who it was. Why hadn't he bothered to stop? Granted it was foggy, but he should have seen her, or was he really that self-absorbed? Such behaviour added weight to the opinion she was forming of the arrogant PE teacher. One way or another, she'd get to the bottom of it.

~

The mist had begun to clear by the time Thea reached the boarding house. She heard the sounds of the kitchen staff preparing breakfast, the distant babble of a radio, the splash of running water and the occasional high-pitched laugh as the girls got ready for the day.

She peeled off her sweatshirt and made her way to her room, only to find the door swinging open. She checked the mechanism, certain she had closed it as she left for her run. It seemed to be working, clicking shut and holding firmly against the jamb when she closed it again. A small worry began to form in the back of her mind; did someone else have a key?

She stepped quickly into her study, looking for anything amiss there, spotting straightaway several small piles of dirt, like miniature pyramids, in the seam between the floorboards at the edge of the room where the rug ended. It reminded her of the pavements of her childhood, where ants burrowed between the cracks, excavating mounds of sand and dirt; but there were no signs of anything similar here. Were there borers in England? She looked more closely, discovering another smaller pile further along. Could it be white ant or dry rot – or whatever they did have here? And if so, were they at risk of the whole house collapsing around their ears? She leaned against the wall and felt it bow beneath her weight, almost making her stumble. She recovered herself and probed more carefully, noticing for the first time what appeared to be a faint shadow running up the corner and along near where the moulding met the ceiling. She tested the wall again, feeling it move a couple of millimetres.

She was about to investigate further when the alarm sounded, signalling twenty minutes until breakfast. It would have to wait.

As she ran the water for a shower in her tiny bathroom, she reminded herself that the house had stood for several centuries, so was unlikely to crumble beneath her now.

SEVENTEEN

Now

It was all Thea could do not to gasp aloud as she pulled open the door to the library and stepped inside. The building was cavernous, with high ceilings and shadowed shelves that seemed like they might make excellent hiding places. Wall-to-wall books, some leather-bound, their spines cracked and worn, looked as old as the school itself. There were a number of long tables with old-fashioned green reading lamps at each place, though on this sunny morning light streamed in from a large arched window at the end of the room, rendering them unnecessary. The only nod to the twenty-first century was a series of charging stations at intervals along the tables. The library was empty now, for all of the students were at their classes, and Thea planned to use her additional free hours constructively before she was required in the classroom after lunch.

She wasn't going to spend it entirely on school matters, however. Though she needed to assess the resources for her A-Level classes, she was also keen to search the shelves for anything that might give a clue to the history of Silk House. The Dame's mention of the age of the house the evening before had stuck with Thea, sparking her historian's curiosity and she couldn't help but wonder as to who had built it, and who had lived, loved, possibly given birth or died, celebrated and cried within its centuries-old walls.

'You must be Miss Rust.' A voice as rich as fruitcake floated towards her and she turned in surprise as an elderly man materialised from behind a set of shelves. A sprig of lavender in the buttonhole of his jacket drew Thea's attention; she didn't think anyone wore such things anymore, apart from at weddings.

'That's impressive,' she said, holding out her hand. 'I am afraid I haven't had the pleasure . . .'

'Dickens. Barnaby. No relation to the writer, more's the pity,' he said, taking her hand in his. 'And not especially impressive. Details of all new staff are circulated before the start of term.'

'Oh, I see.' Thea felt slightly foolish.

'How may I help you?' he asked, and listened intently as she explained the reason for her visit, adding that she had a particular interest in the history of the area, as it pertained to the treatment of women.

'Accusations of witchcraft specifically,' she said. 'In the Tudor and Stuart eras.'

'Very interesting,' he tapped a finger to his lips. 'Now about Silk House: it's been through more hands and incarnations than almost any other building in the high street, I believe. Before the college took it over, it was a boutique hotel, a bed and breakfast, a family home . . . It was derelict for a number of years. There was a bit of a stoush between the college and a local society for the protection of old buildings when they wanted to buy it, but the college won. It usually does – it's too important to the town you see, even today. They got it for a song, if local gossip is to be believed. Now, let me see . . .' He scuttled off towards the back of the library, disappearing around a corner. After a moment, Thea followed. 'Here we are.' He was standing on a ladder that stretched almost to the ceiling and pulled a small, slim volume bound in green leather from the top shelf, handing it to her. 'This should shed some light on its early history.'

Thea turned the book over to read the words stamped in faded gold leaf on the spine: *The Silk Merchant's House.*

'Oh fantastic, thank you.'

'You'll have to read it here. Rare books can't leave the library. School rules I'm afraid.'

'Of course,' said Thea, glancing at her watch; she had another hour or so of free time left before lunch and then her afternoon classes. She opened the book to the first page. It was only a small book but the paper was wafer-thin and the type close-set and dense.

'But I can put it aside for you – if you should need to consult it again.'

'I almost certainly will.'

Mr Dickens withdrew with a friendly nod, and Thea made herself comfortable at a desk. She carefully leafed through the book, and at the back she discovered a folded piece of coarse cloth had been tucked between the final pages and the binding. It was yellowed with age and foxed with mildew, and she unfolded it, intrigued. An old bookmark perhaps?

Tucked within the folds of the cloth was another piece of fabric, a narrow strip a few centimetres wide of something that was almost certainly silk, probably once white, and woven with a pattern of purple flower heads, a silver web and the edge of what appeared to be a number of black insect legs. She ran her fingers over the flowers. Could it be an example of the silk merchant's wares? Would it really have survived that long? Perhaps, she supposed, especially if the book was rarely used. She felt a small thrill of excitement: this was when history came alive for her, not treaties, coronations or battles, but mundane objects that had been made by another's hands, someone now long gone from this earth but their work remaining for others to wonder at.

She reluctantly set it aside and turned to the front of the book. The next hour flew by as Thea picked her way through the first chapter. It started with the head of the family, Patrick Hollander, who was, by this account, a prosperous silk merchant. After a brief scan of his early life – she read that he came to Oxleigh upon his marriage to Caroline – the chapter concerned itself with the building of the house, going into great detail as to its construction. There were orders for bricks, the names of the master craftsmen hired from London to lay the floors and fix the slate tiles – quarried in Wales – to the roof, the crafting of the timber-lined drawing room . . . the delivery of the town's first pianoforte . . . the list went on.

As time ticked away, she flicked towards the middle of the book, reading of a fire that had destroyed the back part of the house, nearly two decades after it had been built. A young woman – a maidservant – had died in the blaze. As she moved on, she was interrupted by a slight cough next to her, and she glanced up to see that the librarian had returned. 'It occurred to me. The local records office might also have papers that relate to the house's history. That is if you are interested.'

Thea knew she would be. 'Oh heavens,' she said, glancing at her watch, 'I'd better run. I can't be late for lunch.' She handed the book to Mr Dickens, and gathered her notes. 'Thanks again,' she said as the door closed behind her and she flew out of the room.

According to the school calendar, the staff ate together every other Tuesday of term, beginning in the first week, and punctuality was expected. Thea got lost on the way to the staff dining room, though, going first to the main school dining room, which was already full of students. As she poked her head around the door she noticed that the girls were all sitting together on a table separate from the boys, and she made a mental note to see if something might be done about that in the future. It was important that they mix with the boys.

When she eventually reached the smaller dining room, at the other end of a long corridor, she was the last to arrive. There was only one seat left and she grimaced inwardly as she saw that it was next to Gareth Pope. At least Claire, a beacon in a purple silk top, was sitting opposite, a couple of places down the table. She slid into the empty chair as the headmaster cleared his throat to say grace.

As the meal was served, Thea turned to her left. 'Early start this morning?' she asked.

Gareth Pope looked at her as if she'd said something impolite, and Thea couldn't shake the feeling that she'd made an enemy of him, although on what grounds she had no idea.

'That was me you nearly bowled over on the lane to Summerbourne,' she explained.

'I'm sorry,' he said as he passed her a bowl of green beans. 'You must have me confused with someone else. Trust me, I wasn't anywhere near Summerbourne this morning. It was pretty foggy, though, could have been anyone.'

'My mistake,' said Thea, reddening as she helped herself to the vegetables. God, was she losing it? She kicked herself for having accused him. She'd been convinced at the time that it was him, but the more she thought about it, the more she realised that she hadn't actually seen the person particularly clearly. And he was right, it *had* been foggy.

She turned to the teacher on the other side of her and introduced herself, becoming embroiled in a spirited discussion about the merits of the English cricket team set to play in Australia for the Ashes in a few months' time. She noted the eyebrows raised in surprise as she held her own, familiar with not only the Australian but also the English players selected for the team.

The background sound of Thea's childhood was Richie Benaud commentating summer matches, the thwack of the ball and waves of applause when a batsman scored a six; backyard and beach games with her mum as wicketkeeper, Pip in the outfield; the whole family sweltering at the MCG for the Boxing Day Test. Every. Single. Year. She suspected that her father wished that he had had sons instead of daughters. Their nicknames alone were telling: Theo for her and Mr Pip for her sister.

'Ooh, dead baby!' came the murmurs from further along the table. Thea turned to see in the middle of the table a long rectangular tin containing a pale, lumpy mass and leaking a bubbling red substance, like Hammer-horror blood, at the edges.

'The oldies go nuts for a proper pud. Jam roly-poly: suet sponge with jam. Stodge. Your basic heart attack on a plate,' said Gareth, seeing her horrified expression. 'Fancy some?'

Thea shook her head. 'I'll pass, thanks.'

EIGHTEEN

Now

'Wait for me!'

No one could miss the brightly attired woman. Thea was reminded of a tree in autumn when the leaves were turning, and the sight of Claire's swirling mulberry and saffron dress and coppery bracelets was a cheering one. She watched as Claire jogged over, bangles jangling like a wind chime, to where she stood at the entrance to the school. For a change, Thea wasn't the one who was late. The combined effect of the constant alarms – she had considered throwing the grey pebble across the room like a frisbee on several occasions – and having to walk the girls across to school every morning meant that she was where she should be, several minutes before she should be, for possibly the first time in her life.

Her father, of course, had been a stickler for timekeeping, and Thea's tardiness a constant source of frustration to him. She had tried her best, she'd had her watch set ten minutes early for years now, but somehow she could never measure up to his strict standards of punctuality. It would doubtless have amused him no end that Oxleigh was responsible for her finally managing to arrive promptly.

'You're free on Saturday night, right?' Claire asked once she had reached her.

'I was thinking of a quiet one, actually; it's been a big week. Why?'

'The beginning of the first term is always shattering, especially when you're new, but there's no way I'm going to let you stay in. There's a party over past Little Coldwell.'

'Where?'

'I keep forgetting you don't know this area. It's about ten miles north of Oxleigh. Anyway, it should be good. A friend of a friend lives over that way. It'll do you good to get out of the college for a while. Realise there's more to this place than textbooks and pimply schoolboys – and girls – and pugnacious PE teachers.' Claire grinned.

'So, you'd noticed?'

'He's got the wind up because you showed him up on the hockey fields this week – so the staffroom scuttlebutt has it, anyway.'

They shared a smile and Claire headed to her first class of the day, Thea to the library. She kicked through the leaves that carpeted the gravel pathway, feeling the bracing nip of autumn, relishing the cool air on her face. She'd been so caught up in the unfamiliarity of everything, of finding not only her way around the school but also getting to know the girls in her care, that she'd forgotten to enjoy something as simple as the change of a season. All that she'd left behind in Australia seemed a long way away. She still carried something with her, though, and it was weighing her down more than she cared to admit.

Barnaby Dickens, the librarian, seemed surprised to see her. 'Back so soon?' he asked, his unruly eyebrows beetling at her from behind his thick glasses. This time the flower in his buttonhole was a deep purply-black. 'Hellebore,' he said as he noticed her looking at it. 'Beautiful, are they not? Poisonous, though.'

Thea nodded. 'I thought I'd take another look at that book on the house.'

'Yes, of course.' He hurried off to fetch it and Thea glanced around the beautiful room, noticing the shafts of light that shone through the windows, illuminating some shelves and casting shadows on others. So much history. Her father's, and now she was creating some of hers.

'That's most odd,' Mr Dickens said as he returned. 'Most odd indeed.'

'What's that?'

'It's not there. The book. I could have sworn I replaced it yesterday.'

'I'm afraid I don't understand: how could it have disappeared?' She tried not to let her frustration show.

'Damned if I know. I'll have to check with the assistant librarian. She was the only other person here aside from myself.'

'Do you have a digitised system?' Thea asked, looking pointedly at the computer that sat on his desk. 'That might tell us.'

'Yes, yes of course. Give me a minute.'

He went around to the front of the desk and tapped a few keys. Waited. 'Now, let me see . . . Oh. It says here that the book has been checked out.'

'But I thought you said it wasn't to be removed,' said Thea.

'I shall have to make enquiries.'

'So, who *has* borrowed it?'

'I am afraid I am not at liberty to say.'

Thea sighed. 'Is there anything else on the house?'

He shook his head. 'You might try the town library. And the records office, as I mentioned earlier in the week.'

'All right, thank you, I will.'

'I'll be sure to let you know as soon as it is returned.'

Frustrated, Thea spent a while among the shelves of books on Tudor England. She was impressed by the depth of material and pleased to see a couple of the texts that she considered to be essential among the selection. Wandering further into the library, she climbed a stepladder to the higher shelves, where some of the oldest books were housed. She was about to reach for one that looked interesting when Mr Dickens materialised below her, a book in his hands. 'Miss Rust, I thought you might find this interesting,' he said, holding it out to her, as if it were a peace offering. 'Given your area of study. Witchcraft and persecution, isn't it? Sixteenth- and seventeenth-century England?'

Intrigued, she climbed down the ladder and took the small leather-bound volume from him. *The Legend of the Handsel Sisters*. 'Thank you,' she said, turning to the frontispiece and seeing a linocut illustration of four gnarled trees. 'Thank you, Mr Dickens.'

She found a seat and quickly became absorbed in a story that, she realised with growing excitement, could potentially prove extremely valuable to her studies. When she turned towards the back of the book, the addendum for further reading caused her heart to race. It listed the names of a dozen or so women, followed by dates – spanning nearly three hundred years, from the early sixteenth century to the late eighteenth century – and locations. All the women were from Wiltshire, and one was from Oxleigh: *Rowan Caswell, maid, silk merchant's house.* She stared at the page, still not quite believing her eyes. Just a handful of years after the house was built.

Though the list didn't specifically say so, Thea presumed these were other women in the county who had been accused or found guilty of witchcraft. She gave an involuntary shiver as her imagination spun any number of wild theories, and she had to take a few deep breaths to calm herself down. Could this be a clue to some of the happenings in the house? To the unease she felt when she was there alone? She looked back at the list and was still pondering this when she heard a discreet cough at her shoulder. 'Miss Rust?'

'Yes?'

'I taught your father, you know,' the librarian said.

She paused. 'I didn't think there were any teachers left from his time.'

'A couple, actually. We were all so sorry to hear the news –' he began, then cleared his throat. 'He was an excellent student.'

'It's nice to hear that,' said Thea. 'He spoke so fondly of his days at Oxleigh.'

'I took the liberty of getting out a couple of the old photographs.' He held out a large leather volume. 'From your father's time.'

Thea saw that he had marked a few of the pages.

'He was in nearly all the teams – a talented sportsman.'

Thea opened the book to the first marked page and drew in a quick breath as she leaned in. A cricket team, arms folded, arranged in rows, wearing baggy whites and banded V-necked sweaters. A pair of bats crossed at the front. She recognised her father instantly, standing in the back row: the wavy hair, strong chin and curving mouth. Was it Oxleigh College that had given him such rock-solid self-belief? She wished that she'd tried harder to understand him, that she might have just one more day to spend with him.

NINETEEN

February 1769, London

A long fortnight after sending her designs, Mary began to fret. She had expected a reply, some indication from her sponsor by then, and she began to think the worst, that Patrick Hollander had changed his mind and no longer believed her to be a 'natural genius' (for it was true, those words had echoed in her head as she worked, helping to keep her spirit strong).

The bitterest month of the year brought flurries of snow and freezing rain; each morning the chamber-pots were iced over, and coal for the fire to keep them warm was hard to come by. Mary began to increasingly despair of the situation. She felt sick at her presumption for having imagined their troubles might soon be eased. She could not bear to speak of it with her sister.

Once, on her way to the market, she caught the flash of a peacock-blue coat, the curl of hair gathered at the nape of a neck. She hastened towards the man but lost sight of him as he disappeared into the market's throng. She told herself later she had imagined the likeness.

At the end of the month, Mary walked around to the house on Spital Square, climbed the stairs to the attic weaving room to see if Guy Le Maître had perhaps received word. 'But you have worked with him before, no?' she asked, speaking loudly to be heard over the clamour of the shuttle and the clack of the loom.

Guy shrugged with Gallic nonchalance. 'Do not be concerned. There may be a delay in the mails, perhaps.' He raised his eyes to the sky through the window. 'The weather . . .'

It was true; after the snow, heavy rains had washed through the streets for more than a month, torrents that left drowned rats in their wake and formed deep puddles to catch out the unwary. Perhaps it was raining throughout the country, not only in London? Mary tried to believe that was the reason for the delay. She pulled the hood of her cloak over her head and returned to her home. To wait some more.

On the walk home, her disappointment and frustration turned to anger. How dare Patrick Hollander raise her hopes and then simply disappear? It was as if he had become a ghost: as insubstantial as the morning mist, a figment of her imagination. As she walked, hearing the rhythmic clatter of the looms from attic windows in almost all the dwellings in Spitalfields, she cursed the fact that not one loom had her design on it; of the yards of silk that were being woven, none were her patterns and colours.

The next day brought the long-awaited reply.

Mary was finishing her breakfast when there was a loud rap on the door. Moments later her mouth hung open in shock; Patrick

Hollander stood before her, exactly as she had remembered him. He wore the ready smile of a man certain of a warm welcome wherever he went.

'I had imagined you a spectre, for I have heard nothing from you since our meeting of last year,' she said coolly. 'Tell me that this is not how you generally conduct your business?' She fixed him with a steely glare and prepared to launch into her grievances, for she had had many long, cold nights to rehearse them.

He held up a hand to still her. 'Madam,' he interrupted, 'I am *most* sincerely apologetic. I have been occupied with other matters and unable to get word to you until now. My own poor mother has been taken ill and I have been unable to leave her side for fear of her expiring in my absence.' He regarded her with a sorrowful expression. 'I fear I have neglected my business terribly, but I do hope you can forgive my circumstances.'

Some of Mary's indignation left her. She could hardly argue against a man who had been looking after his mother. 'I trust she is in better health now?' she enquired, swallowing the remains of her anger.

'I confess that we buried her a fortnight past.' Mary observed the clench of his jaw, and her heart softened towards him.

'My sincere condolences to you, Mr Hollander.'

'She went peacefully at the end.' He looked about the street, as if someone might be eavesdropping. 'Perhaps we might continue our discussion indoors? As I have said before, Miss Stephenson, I am very much enamoured of your designs, and I only hope that you will agree to work for me despite the unforeseen hold-up.'

Mary regarded him carefully. Was she right to believe him?

~

On Frances's return later that day, Mary held out a note. 'Go on, read it,' she said.

'Two patterns of meadow flowers received and approved. I hereby authorise Mary-Louise Stephenson to instruct Mr Guy Le Maître in the weaving of fifty ells of each. Faithfully yours, Patrick Hollander.'

'I was wrong to doubt him,' Mary cried with relief. 'For he called upon me this very morning.'

Frances raised her eyebrows but said nothing as Mary explained the reason for Mr Hollander's absence. She frowned at the letter. 'Why has he not commissioned Mr Le Maître himself?'

'He was to take the stage to Oxleigh not moments after our meeting. He has been most caught up in resurrecting his business, and did not have time for that visit.'

'It is but a ten-minute walk away.'

Mary sighed. 'I shall take them now.' Gathering the original patterns she had kept, she walked to the weaver's loft, full of excitement. But Guy frowned at her even as she showed him the letter. 'I have a family to feed, apprentices to pay. How do you propose I do that if I am working without coin myself?'

'Surely Mr Hollander will see to that?'

'Ah,' sighed Guy. 'He has not paid his last account, nor the one before that. I cannot continue to work for him until he settles upon me the money he owes. I must have the money first. And that which I am owed.' Guy was immovable.

'How much?'

When he named the sum, all of Mary's hopes dissolved.

~

She could hardly bear to report on the delay to her sister. 'It is so unbearably frustrating,' she raged. 'Why, only last spring a pattern of snowdrops and curling ivy was chosen by the Duchess of Portland. I am certain that this fabric will be desired by such grand ladies and gentlemen.'

Her sister regarded her sadly, then became thoughtful. 'Perhaps there is another way.'

'How so?'

'Connor O'Neill.'

Mary had never heard the name.

'He is a journeyman that Samuel once knew. He was suspected of being a cutter.'

'A cutter?'

'A few years ago, before you came to live here, a group of journeymen cut the silk from their master weavers' looms, destroying weeks of work. To protest about unfair wages. In one night alone they cut the silk from fifty looms. The air rang with the sound of pistol shots and we were forced to barricade ourselves inside the house. I feared for our lives. If what I hear is true, it is likely that such a thing may happen again.'

Mary stared in disbelief. 'So, what happened to Connor O'Neill?'

'He disappeared.'

'Well, I don't see how that will help us, then,' she sighed. Her sister was talking in riddles. 'In any case, how can we expect a weaver to work for free?' Mary asked. That was the stumbling block – they had no spare money to fund such an enterprise themselves.

'If we can locate him, I believe he will undertake the work for a better than fair price.'

'How so?'

'After the company blacklisted him, he struggled to find work. But Samuel believed him to be falsely accused and took pity on him, passed him work from time to time, enough to save him and his wife from the poorhouse and their children from an orphanage.'

'That still doesn't change the fact that we have almost no coin, and certainly none to spare for silk,' Mary protested.

'Oh, but you are mistaken, sister,' Frances said with a secretive smile. 'For I have the money needed to weave about twenty yards of silk at a price that I believe Mr O'Neill will agree to.'

'What? How?'

Frances hesitated. 'Mother's necklace.'

'No!' Mary was shocked at the suggestion. 'You cannot sell that.'

'Too late. I have already done so.' Frances held up a handful of paper notes. 'The pawnbroker was glad of it.'

Mary gasped. 'But how did you know that Mr Le Maître had not been paid?'

'I confess, that I was unaware of. I had already arranged the sale. How do you think we have survived these past months? He already has my watch and wedding ring.'

'Oh no,' said Mary glancing at her sister's hand and noticing for the first time that it was bare. 'Why did you not tell me of this sooner?'

'Would it have made any difference? Do not worry yourself over it. If all goes well, we will be able to buy them back before long.'

'Then we must proceed apace.' Mary was decisive. 'Where do we find this Mr O'Neill?'

'I shall have to make discreet enquiries. Leave it with me.'

~

There was a fingernail of moon still high in the sky, a handful of fading stars gathered around it, when Mary and Frances ventured out before dawn the next morning. Their route took them past the Brick Lane market, north along the newly paved thoroughfare until its confluence with Great Bacon Street. From there, Mary followed her sister along a series of narrow lanes until they reached the back of a huddle of squat brick houses. The way was slippery with clay and the area appeared all but abandoned, desolate in the grey of the early morning.

'I believe this is the one,' said Frances, lifting her skirts clear of the mud and stepping over the rough ground towards the furthest building.

Mary followed close behind, wincing as her boots sank deep in the clay and glancing about her to be sure no one was approaching. This was not an area to which she had ventured before and the quietness after the clack and clatter of Spitalfields was unnerving. 'I hope you are right,' she said, spotting two urchins sitting on a brick wall at the end of one of the houses. Their feet were bare and black with filth, their hair did not look like it ever came within arm's reach of a comb and their clothes were the indeterminate grey of unwashed cloth. As Mary and Frances approached, they hopped off the wall and disappeared into the house, shutting the back door with a bang.

Mary startled at the sound, nearly dropping her bag containing the sketches and patterns. As she fumbled with her belongings, the door opened again and from somewhere inside the house came the sweet chirrup of a bird. A linnet, she fancied. Several of the weavers kept them in cages in their attics, but she rarely heard their song over the noise of the looms in Spital Square and thereabouts. Here, it was quieter, for there was not the rhythmic clack of a single shuttle.

'Who's there?' A woman's voice called from beyond the door.

'It's Frances Wycroft. Samuel's widow. I'm here with my sister, Mary Stephenson.'

There was a pause, then the woman spoke again, quietly this time and Mary had to strain to hear her words. 'Best you come in, then, and stop drawing attention to yourselves. Be quick about it.'

They hastened towards the door, entering the house and finding themselves in a narrow passage that brought them into a small, dim kitchen. There were old rushes on the floor, grey with dried mud, and the hearth smouldered. A smell of boiled cabbage filled the room. The woman seemed old, with sunken cheeks and thinning hair, but she had a baby slung against one hip, a toddler hanging from her skirts. The older children sat in the corner of the room, watching them with wide eyes. 'We were hopeful of speaking with Mr O'Neill,' Frances said.

The woman sneered. 'You're sore out of luck, for he's not seen fit to show his face here for months. He's a wanted man, didn't you know?' She laughed mirthlessly, picking up a clout from the table and wiping a thick river of snot from the infant's nose.

'And I take it you have no idea as to his whereabouts?' Mary asked, her spirits sinking. It appeared as though this was to be a hopeless errand.

The woman looked at her like she was the village idiot, and Mary shifted uncomfortably. 'Of course not,' she murmured. 'I'm so sorry for your . . .' her voice trailed off. She did not know what to say in such circumstances. 'We were hoping to offer him a commission.'

'Aye?' Her voice became more accommodating. 'Well, he's not the only weaver in the house.'

It took a moment before Mary cottoned on to her meaning. 'Oh, I see. Of course, Mrs O'Neill.' Several of the journeymen weavers taught their wives to weave, mostly the simpler designs, and often set up two or three looms in their attics, for the older children could also be pressed into service when need be.

'Why've you come here? Why not go to one of the journeymen in Spital Square?'

'We find ourselves in a bind,' Mary admitted, before explaining the situation.

The woman nodded. 'Call me Bridget. Well, then . . .' She handed the baby to one of the older children and cleared a space on the table. 'Let me see the pattern.'

Mary pulled out the papers from her bag and laid them flat, standing back so Bridget could see them.

She pursed her lips, peered more closely, muttered something to herself and then addressed Mary, who was watching her anxiously. 'Can't exactly say I've seen anything like this before. Seems like a garden of death,' she said, pointing to the pattern.

Bridget's breath whistled as she sucked it in through the gaps in her teeth.

'Belladonna,' Mary replied, in a matter-of-fact tone.

'So it is,' said the woman as she returned to her study of the dot paper. Mary waited for her to point out a novice's mistake, an error in the design, for though she had gone over it several times, she feared she might have missed something obvious to a more trained eye.

'This pattern is of your devising?' Bridget asked, her gaze narrowing.

'Of course,' said Mary. 'But it was commissioned by a mercer. Patrick Hollander of Oxleigh. I shall be sending the cloth to him when it is completed.'

The woman startled as she heard the name.

'Perhaps you know of him?' Mary asked.

'I do believe my husband mentioned his name once or twice,' Bridget replied quickly. 'No more than that.'

Mary glanced at her sister. Did she too imagine Bridget O'Neill knew more than she was letting on?

'It is rather unusual for the pattern-drawer to come directly to the weaver, is it not?' Bridget asked, interrupting her thoughts, but the baby began to grizzle and Mary was saved from an explanation. Bridget took the infant from her daughter, rocking and shushing the child but never taking her eyes from the paper. Eventually she returned her gaze to the two women. 'It can be done,' she said. 'And as luck would have it –' She broke off with a laugh that turned into a hacking cough. 'I can get to it right away. Thomas here is as good a draw boy as you'll find.'

The taller of the two boys nodded solemnly.

Mary couldn't believe the words she was hearing. Someone was actually going to weave cloth from her design. The thought almost overwhelmed her. She ignored the fact that it was in such ignominious, and far from clean, surroundings, for it wasn't as if she had any other options. 'Oh, thank you, thank you,' she said. 'Here –' She held out a sheet of paper. 'I made some notes – to help with the weaving of it.'

Bridget took the paper and squinted at it. After a while she raised her face to meet the two women's gazes and said, ''Tis I who should be thanking you. From the look of this design, the mercer will get what he deserves.'

'What do you mean?' Frances asked.

'Oh, I think Mistress Stephenson knows what I mean,' said Bridget, with a sly grin. 'Now we have only to agree on a price.'

'There's another, too,' said Mary, handing her the second pattern.

'What was that about?' Frances asked once she and Mary left the house. 'That Mr Hollander will get what he deserves?'

'I have no idea. But if she is as talented a weaver as you say her husband was, then I must be grateful for that.'

TWENTY

March 1769, Oxleigh

The anticipated return of Caroline Hollander caused a flurry of activity that roused the house from its wintry slumber. Delivery boys deposited their wares, and Prudence prepared all manner of food. When Tommy came with a haunch of venison, a buttock of beef and a ham, he flushed and then grinned as he caught sight of Rowan. They'd taken to meeting by the river in the afternoons after Tommy finished at the butcher's, Tommy fishing while Rowan gathered herbs, and she had come to look forward to their hours together, urging the clock to advance so that they might meet again. This time, however, there was no time for an exchange of words, and he slipped away down the back lane before Rowan could think of a reason to delay him.

She lit fires in the downstairs rooms and aired the upstairs ones, opening the shutters wide and raising the window sashes.

Much of the house had been unused for nearly a month and a creeping damp had invaded the rooms. Even though the bedding had been seen to weeks before, she aired the counterpanes and beat and fluffed the goose-down quilts until they lay lightly on the beds once more.

Prudence set about boiling the beef, preparing sweetmeats and pies. She was standing at the kitchen table, her forearms covered in flour, when Rowan appeared. A conical loaf of sugar sparkled in the light that shone through the window, a bowl of damsons like dark jewels beside it.

'I don't wish to get in your way, but perhaps I might complete a dra— ointment?' Rowan asked, catching herself in time. 'I only need a small space.'

'You'd best get on with it in the scullery,' Prudence replied, pounding the pastry into submission. 'For there is no room here.' The normally agreeable cook was short with her, all her attention on the piecrust.

'Of course. I shan't trouble you any further.' Rowan slipped out of the room.

She began by sluicing her hands and face with cold water, for they had become blackened with smuts from the fire as she fanned the flames. Then she cleared a space on the wide scullery counter that overlooked the garden, and thought back to the day her mother had instructed her in the mixing of this particular draught. It was important that it was made as close to the drinking of it as possible. There weren't many married women in the village who had need of such things, but she remembered the day the lady of the manor's maid came to call. Rowan also hadn't forgotten how handsomely her mother was paid for her efforts, but try as she might, she could not recall whether or not the draught had had the intended effect.

As her mother had done, she had already soaked the nettles, red clover buds and dandelion root in vinegar over several nights, and now she gathered a scrap of muslin through which to strain the liquid into a glass bottle. To this she added the other herbs and powders from the apothecary in careful amounts, before pressing a stopper upon the bottle to seal it. She thought to taste it herself, but a shout from the kitchen put paid to that and she placed the bottle carefully out of harm's way on the windowsill. She was about to leave the scullery when Alice pushed her way inside.

'Don't think that I don't know what you are about,' she said.

'Begging your pardon?'

'That's no chilblain ointment. I wonder what the master might have to say about such a thing?' Alice crossed her arms and regarded her suspiciously. 'You well know his thoughts about witchery and the like.'

Rowan had had enough. She refused to be cowed any longer. 'Witchery, you say?' she stepped towards Alice, filling the narrow space. 'I wonder what the mistress might say if she were to find out about your . . . your *closeness* to the master? She already has her doubts. Perhaps *you* might be the one accused of bewitchment?'

Alice's eyes widened and Rowan took advantage of her hesitation, reaching for the bottle then concealing it among her skirts as she slipped past her and along the passage to the kitchen. Her heart still pounded at the unexpected confrontation, and she drew a few deep breaths to calm herself.

'The mistress is returned,' said Prudence, pausing as she rolled out the pastry, 'and asking for you. Can you take her this? Alice is seeing to the unloading of her luggage.' She indicated the table, where a teapot and china cup and saucer had been assembled on an oval tray. 'Is anything amiss?' Prudence glanced at her.

'No, no, everything is perfectly fine,' Rowan assured her as she smoothed her apron and tucked a stray strand of hair under her cap, her heart returning to its regular, steady beat.

When she entered the room, her mistress was seated on the chaise in front of the fire. Rowan went towards her and placed the tray on a table beside her.

'I trust your stay was an enjoyable one, mistress?' she ventured.

'Thank you, Rowan, it was. You have the draught?' Caroline asked, showing what had clearly been uppermost in her mind during her absence.

Rowan was relieved to give her the answer she desired. 'Aye, mistress.'

'Very good.'

'You will need to take but a small spoonful twice a day. No more than that,' Rowan warned, handing her the bottle. 'And continue to do so until the bottle is empty.'

'Don't forget a spoon, then.'

Rowan turned to leave. 'I will make certain of it.'

As Caroline turned to face her, there was a familiar bleakness to her expression. 'Let us hope it works.'

~

A week later, with a loud 'Whoa!', the clop of hooves and jangle of brass, a coach and six drew up outside the house. Alerted by Prudence, Rowan hurried to the door to let in her master, holding it wide and standing back as he brushed past her and went straight to the shop.

She was oft treated by those she served as if she were invisible, for servants, she had learned, must contrive to be where their betters are not, until the point of being called upon. Then they were required to appear as if by magic, undertaking their master's or mistress's bidding without delay. Nevertheless, she was surprised not to receive even a greeting upon his return after so long away. Even Alice, who had hastened to the front door with Rowan, got little acknowledgment beyond a fleeting smile. Rowan saw the other maid's face fall as she turned away, retreating to the shadows at the back of the house.

Patrick Hollander had other matters on his mind, however, for once in the shop he began pulling the cloth off the shelves and holding it up to the light as if he were searching for something, discarding the precious fabric as he went, not caring that it fell off the counter and spilled on the floor. Jeremiah, who had been serving a customer, appeared to be frozen in fright at first, but then began hastily retrieving the bolts, brushing them off where dust had collected and attempting to return them to the shelves. The woman he had been serving hurried past Rowan and out of the door, glancing behind her, an aggrieved expression on her face. Rowan ventured closer to the shop doorway, for she was curious as to what had brought on her master's volatile mood.

'Do not bother with that, Jeremiah,' said Patrick. 'Out with the old, for we are starting afresh.'

Then Caroline appeared in the passageway and she too barely seemed to register Rowan, sweeping past her and into the shop.

'Have you taken leave of your senses, husband?' she demanded. 'What is this commotion?'

'On the contrary, my dear, I have never seen the world so clearly. We are no longer going to sell the same designs as every other merchant from here to the southern shores, for I have engaged a designer who will bring forth a new style. Our fabrics will be sought after by the entire country. The ladies at Bath will promenade in gay colours and uncommon patterns that will dazzle the eyes of all who see them.'

'That is all very well and I am most pleased to hear that your business in London was successful,' Caroline said, placing a hand on his arm to calm him. 'But until we have these new fabrics, what do you suppose we might sell? People will still require cotton and muslin, broadcloth and linen, you know.'

A maniacal light danced in his eyes. 'Forgive me my enthusiasm,' he said, shaking off her hand. 'It appears you do not see things as clearly as I do.'

'Come now, that is not what I meant at all,' she said. 'Merely that it might be unwise to cease business so abruptly. For if we were to do so, our customers – and I am relieved that there is not one here at present to witness this – would perhaps not return when we do have material to sell them. We should not want them to take their business elsewhere, should we? What are your thoughts on this, Jeremiah?'

'It is not fair to involve him, my dear. I suppose you talk sense,' Patrick said sulkily. 'But I have found a designer of whom there is no equal. And all of London is too blind to see it. I am the only one with the vision, the only one who knows her worth. We shall make a fortune with her designs.'

'*Her* worth?' Caroline repeated.

'Have you a head made of wood?' He was exasperated now. 'Yes, I said *her* worth.'

Rowan caught Jeremiah's eye as her master and mistress faced each other. He appeared bewildered, and as if he wanted to say something but feared to. Did he know more about the state of the merchant's finances than their master was prepared to reveal? Rowan thought it likely.

'I hope you know what you are about,' Caroline said eventually.

'For goodness' sake, mistress. Leave me be to conduct *my* business,' he said. 'It is nothing for you to concern yourself with.'

'Very well.' Rowan heard the bitterness in her mistress's voice.

But the next time Rowan passed the doorway to the shop, she saw that the bolts of cloth had been returned to their rightful places and any sign of her master's wild interference had been cleared away.

~

One cold, bright morning a few weeks after her mistress's return, Rowan entered the dining room, to see Caroline sitting alone, her chair pushed away from the table, her plate of bacon and bread untouched and her hands resting on the embroidery of her stomacher.

'Was it not to your liking, mistress?' Rowan asked as she gathered up the plates.

Caroline shook her head, and Rowan regarded her more closely, seeing that her skin was paler than usual and her face had a drawn look about it. 'Are you quite well?' she asked.

Caroline went to reply, her lips moving soundlessly, but then her face blanched whiter than whey, and she slid off the chair and crumpled into a heap on the floor, her skirts billowing about her like a puffball fungus.

'Alice!' Rowan cried as she grasped her mistress by the shoulders and did her best to raise her to an upright position, 'Alice! Come at once!'

She dared to slap her mistress's face to try to wake her – gently, mind – but there was no response. After what seemed like an age, but must have only been minutes, she heard someone coming towards her.

'What?' Alice appeared, the broom she had been holding clattering to the floor as she took in the scene. 'What strange spell have you cast upon her? Is it the draught? I knew it was bad medicine,' she cried. 'You have poisoned her. You've killed her!'

'Oh, don't be ridiculous,' Rowan scolded Alice as if she were one of her brothers. 'She has fainted clean away, can you not see that?' She hoped she was right in her assumption. 'Help me get her to the parlour where we can lie her upon the chaise and loosen her clothing. Take her feet, won't you?'

Together they half-carried, half-dragged their mistress across the passageway and into the parlour. 'I should go for the master,' Rowan said once they had arranged her on the chaise longue and placed a small pillow under her head. Alice began to loosen Caroline's bodice and unlace the ribbons of her stays, but she was interrupted by the arrival of Patrick, thundering up the stairs.

'What is this? I heard the commotion all the way in the shop! Must you make so much noise? Caroline? Rowan? Alice?'

The two maids kept their gaze fixed firmly to their boots.

TWENTY-ONE

Now

As Thea lay on her bed reading early on Saturday evening, she could hear the faint noises made by the girls below, music playing in some rooms, piano and violin practice in others, laughter, indefinable thumps and thuds, squeals and hurrying footsteps as they came and went. They had adjusted well – in fact, she could hardly believe they'd only been at the school a week. She had been pleased to see almost all of their names on the sign-up sheet for the hike she had planned for the next day.

When Thea was growing up, Sundays in her family were always, even in driving wind and rain, reserved for long walks along the Mornington Peninsula coastline or the windy bluffs of the Macedon Ranges. Her mother would pack food, a Thermos of hot chocolate in winter, orange cordial in summer, and they'd hike for miles, her father often a speck in the distance as the rest of the family struggled to keep up with his cracking pace. When they were older, she and Pip grumbled and had to be dragged into the car when they would have preferred to spend their Sundays absorbed in a film or a book or out with their friends. Now, those memories had softened with time and she could think of them almost fondly. She remembered her mother's call for lunch, her father's insistence not to stop until well after noon. Looking out to sea or on the spine of a ridgeline, always ravenous, unwrapping squashed ham-and-tomato sandwiches from their daypacks. Even now, the smell of tomatoes took her straight back there.

Thea became so engrossed in her book that she was barely aware of darkness falling. It was only when the alarm trilled for dinner – unlike during the week, the girls ate all of their meals in the boarding house at the weekends – that she leapt up and flew into the shower. Claire was coming to pick her up at seven-thirty and she had less than half an hour to get ready.

She had finished drying her hair and was running her fingers through it to give it some semblance of style, when the honk of a horn sounded through her open window. She glanced at her watch. Claire. Right on time.

She grabbed her coat and bag and wound a scarf around her neck. Shoving her feet into boots, she glanced around the room, checking that she hadn't forgotten anything. Wine. Yes, the wine. She picked up the bottle she'd bought that afternoon and ran down the stairs. When she reached the bottom she stopped at the dining room, where the girls were eating pizza. She flashed them a brief smile and raced along the passage to open the front door, knowing the Dame would be there in case they needed anything.

'Only five minutes late,' said Claire, as Thea climbed into the passenger seat and drew the belt across herself, clipping it in place.

'Sorry. Must do better.' She made a face.

'Teasing,' said Claire with a quick grin.

Thea did a double-take as she noted Claire's outfit: a wide scarf embroidered with multicoloured flowers across her shoulders thick gold hoop earrings, hair pulled back in a middle parting and heavily pencilled eyebrows.

'Come as your favourite feminist icon,' said Claire.

'Wait, what? Who?'

'Frida Kahlo. Don't worry, if you keep your glasses on you'll be the spit of Ruth Bader Ginsburg.'

'Thanks, I think,' she answered, pushing them up onto the bridge of her nose.

Claire smirked and pulled away from the kerb, 'I'm kidding about the fancy dress, by the way.'

'Just promise me there won't be karaoke.'

They headed towards the roundabout at the top end of the town. Thea had seen the church on her first morning in Oxleigh, but at night it was spot lit, the beams trained on the tall spire, and looked rather magnificent.

'You can go up there if you like,' said Claire, seeing her glance skywards. 'There are tours. Great view of the town.'

'How long have you lived here?' Thea asked.

'Five years. Can you believe it? Still, there are plenty worse places to be. I'm pleased there are girls at the college now – it can only be a good thing; give the place some balance.'

'I don't think all of the teachers share your view.'

Claire laughed. 'That'd be the dinosaurs. I overheard one of them calling the girls' house "The Coven"!'

'What the bloody hell?' Thea was outraged. 'Shouldn't someone say something? To the headmaster, I mean?'

'They'll get used to it. They don't have a choice, not if they want to keep their jobs anyway.'

'What are they so afraid of?'

'The unknown, most likely. Change, quite possibly.'

They carried on along the road out of town, each lost in their own thoughts.

'Have you noticed anything unusual about Silk House?' Claire asked, breaking the silence.

'Should I have?' Thea wasn't ready to admit to her own concerns just yet.

Claire hesitated, flicking on her indicator and turning left off the main road. 'There was some gossip, several years ago, that it was haunted.'

Thea forced a brittle laugh. 'No one believes in ghosts these days, surely? Besides, I'm sure there would be rumours about any house that old.'

'But it's odd that it's never been held by any one owner for long.'

'How do you know that?'

Claire shrugged. 'Common knowledge.'

'That could be for any number of reasons. Anyway, who's this ghost supposed to be? Or is it ghosts?'

'A white-haired woman, according to some. Wearing a red cloak. Although others claim she has dark hair.'

'Well, that's a cliché if ever I heard one. Who told you about it?'

'Someone in the pub, I think. I didn't pay too much attention, and there was talk about several houses in the town being haunted, not to mention the mill.'

'The mill?'

'The one on the way to Summerbourne.'

'I ran there the other morning. Didn't see a mill. Mind you, it was thick with fog. Although, come to think of it, I did hear the water. And who's the ghost there?'

'Well, that's the odd thing. From what I can gather, it's very similar to the woman that's supposed to appear at Silk House.'

'You know, I found a very odd thing in the library,' Thea said after a pause. 'At the end of a book on four local sisters murdered for suspected witchcraft in the eighteenth century.'

'Go on,' Claire flicked a glance towards her then returned her focus to the road.

'There was a list of names – and one of them, a woman by the name of Rowan Caswell – was once a maid at the silk merchant's house, now known as Silk House.'

'Do you think . . .' Claire turned briefly towards her, her eyes round.

Thea scoffed. 'I think my imagination is getting the better of me right now. So, thanks for inviting me to the party – I could use the distraction.'

'You're probably right,' Claire agreed. 'It does seem rather far-fetched. Interesting, though . . .'

They had been driving for about twenty minutes when Claire indicated a second time and turned off onto a dirt track. Headlights showed the way, which was overgrown with trees, their branches almost meeting overhead, forming a dark tunnel.

The lane was narrow, hardly wide enough for Claire's car. Thea instinctively grabbed the sides of her seat and held her breath, hoping they wouldn't meet anyone coming the other way, especially as they were still rocketing along; clearly Claire was more used to these roads and felt no need to reduce their speed once off the tarmac.

'Not likely to have a collision,' said Claire, apparently reading her thoughts. 'Everyone will be going in our direction – there's only one cottage at the end of this lane.'

Thea was only slightly reassured.

About a mile later, they came towards a dozen or so cars parked at haphazard angles at the end of the lane, but there was no house in sight. Claire drew up behind one of the cars, a little hatchback well suited to country lanes, and turned off the engine. 'Hope you don't mind a bit of a walk,' she said. 'It's over the stile and through that meadow.' She reached across Thea into the glovebox and retrieved a heavy torch that, Thea imagined, would make a good weapon as well as light their way. 'Don't want to risk a sprained ankle. The ground's pretty uneven.'

Thea shivered at the change in temperature as they got out of the car, and pulled her jacket tighter around herself. Coming from a city, she was unnerved by the pitch black of the night: a slender sickle of moon hung low in the sky and gave only a faint glow. Thankfully, Claire's torch threw a strong beam ahead of them, though outside of that everything was as black as soot. Mist lay on the ground and it seemed as if they were walking on clouds as they made their way across the rough paddock that Claire had so quaintly referred to as a meadow.

'Well, this is one way to get to a party,' Thea said, amused. As they walked, the faint sounds of music, the thump of bass and then lights in the distance drifted towards them.

Claire's torch flickered and then went out, casting everything into sudden darkness. 'Bloody hell,' she cursed. 'Battery's flat. I only replaced it last week.' She shook it, attempting to revive the thing. 'Must've been a dud.'

'Doesn't matter too much,' said Thea. 'We're here now.'

A long, low house with tiny square windows, whitewashed walls and a shaggy thatched roof that looked in need of a good haircut was in front of them, a path winding to the front door.

As they approached, the door opened and Claire stepped forward to embrace the man standing there. Thea hovered behind her, pleased to see that he was wearing jeans and an old rugby jersey and that Claire had only been teasing her about the dress code.

The thought that she probably wouldn't know a soul there apart from Claire turned out to be a false assumption. No sooner had she crossed the threshold than she came face to face with Gareth Pope, leaning against a door frame. She smiled in recognition, but he gave her a curt nod and turned back to the woman he had been talking to.

Well, two can play at that game, she thought as she and Claire were swept towards the kitchen, where a warm fug filled the air, steaming up the windows. The smell of spices, cloves and cinnamon wafted through the room and Thea found a warm glass of red wine with orange slices floating in it pressed into her hand.

'Come on, let's dance,' said Claire, after introducing her to a few people. She pulled Thea towards a long, dim living room where a few other guests were enthusiastically flinging themselves about, some more in time to the music than others. Thea took a swig of her drink before setting it on a bookcase and following Claire. She gave herself up to the beat, letting it pulse through her. Losing herself in the music and the darkness was easier than trying to talk to people she didn't know. It also made it easier to avoid Gareth Pope.

In between bouts of dancing, Thea sank into one of the battered old couches that had been pushed back against the walls. She smiled at a few people, but the music was too loud for anything but the most superficial conversation.

At one point, Gareth came into the room, noticed her and then ducked out again. It seemed he was no more eager to talk to her than she was to him.

Sometime later, as the crowd thinned a little, Thea went in search of the bathroom. She was a little dizzy from the wine, the warm room and the incessant music. As she climbed the stairs, she stopped to look out of the window on the landing, noticing straggling shadows moving across the field. It was later than she realised, and people were leaving, which also didn't seem like a bad idea to her.

When she returned downstairs, there was no sign of Claire. She searched in vain for her friend but found Gareth instead, who shook his head when she asked if he had seen her. 'Not for at least an hour, but don't sweat it, she'll be here somewhere,' he said taking a swig of his beer.

Thea searched the kitchen and then another room that appeared to be a study, but with no luck. The possibility that Claire might have abandoned her in the middle of nowhere began to dawn on her. As she was cursing under her breath while trying to see if she had any mobile coverage to call a taxi – the thought that she might be forced to beg Gareth for a lift back to Oxleigh was too much to contemplate – Claire suddenly materialised.

'Ready to go?' she asked and Thea gave a relieved nod.

'Where were you? I looked everywhere.' Thea hated the neediness in her voice, but she'd been worried.

'Oh, sorry,' Claire said. 'There's an old stables out the back that's been fixed up as a studio. A few of us were in there; it was a bit quieter.'

Most people had already left and they were alone as they walked across the field, Thea's boots becoming soaked by a heavy dew that had fallen in the hours they'd been at the party. She shivered. The temperature had dropped by several degrees too.

They walked on, mostly in silence, both tired now, Thea thinking longingly of her bed at Silk House.

Then, as they were about halfway across the field, a high-pitched shriek sounded from somewhere out in the darkness.

There are certain sounds that carry: a soprano hitting high C, a hammer drilling into rock . . . and the piercing scream of someone frightened out of their wits. Thea stopped abruptly, all of her senses alert, fearing what might be ahead, beside or behind them. 'What the bloody hell was that?' she whispered.

'Ouch!' said Claire, not realising that Thea had come to a halt as she stumbled into her. 'Probably a fox,' she said, dismissing her concerns. 'A vixen scream.'

'A vixen? It sounded human to me.' Thea was not even slightly reassured.

'Nah,' Claire replied. 'I forgot that you're not used to our wildlife. They're fairly common here, don't worry.'

Only partly convinced that it was nothing malevolent, Thea walked on. 'Can I ask you something?'

'Sure, what?'

'How well do you know Gareth?'

'Not particularly. He's only been at the school for a couple of years, but he's well liked. Why?'

'Only, he doesn't seem to like me very much. He seemed annoyed at our first hockey practice, and barely acknowledged me tonight.'

'He was the coach of the First Eleven last year. That's probably why his nose is out of joint. Seeing as how you're here now, and you've played – and coached – at a much higher level than him.'

'Ugh,' said Thea. 'I'm only helping out, it's not as if I'm going to take his place. I've got enough on my plate with Mrs Jackson away to want that.'

'Mrs Jackson?'

'The woman who was supposed to be the housemistress at Silk House.'

'Oh, right.'

It was dark without the torch, but they had the advantage of knowing their way and reached the car without further mishap.

As Claire started the engine, the beam of the headlights barely penetrated the mist. If anything, it was thicker than when they had arrived. Thea tried not to let the dark and the mist and the silence get to her, but the hairs on the back of her neck prickled and she felt a rivulet of sweat work its way down her spine.

They had almost reached the turn onto the main road when, out of nowhere, a shape loomed in front of them, coming directly towards the car.

Claire screamed and spun the wheel to avoid it.

'What the *fuck*?' cried Thea.

With a screech of brakes, the car came to a slithering halt, slewing sideways across the narrow lane.

They stared at each other for a moment, the whites of their eyes showing in the greenish glow from the instrument panel. Seconds ticked away as Thea tried to decide whether or not to look behind her. 'Do you – do you think there's something, or someone, out there?' she asked shakily.

'How do I know?' There was a definite waver to Claire's normally confident voice. 'I'm too scared to check.'

'So am I.' Despite her words, Thea slowly turned around. She craned her neck but there was nothing but swirling mist in the car's rear lights. 'Whatever it was, I don't think we hit it; I didn't feel any impact.'

Claire turned and followed her gaze. 'Shit. We're lucky I didn't drive into the ditch.'

'Should we get out and take a look?' Thea asked.

'Are you crazy?' Claire sounded rattled.

'It might have been –'

Thea's words were cut off by the radio, which decided at that moment to crackle into life and they both jolted back in their seats at the unexpected noise.

'Christ!' said Thea. 'What's going on?' She reached to turn the dial down, reducing the blaring sound to a burble.

'Might have been what?' Claire asked.

'I don't know . . . a deer?' But in the split-second before they drove through it, Thea thought she had seen the shape of a woman. With a pale face and fair hair, wearing a gown that trailed along the road. Much like the one Claire had told her about earlier.

But that's ridiculous, she scolded herself. If anything, it said more about the power of suggestion than anything real. Nevertheless, she braced herself, then wound down the window and leaned out. The mist almost seemed to invade the car, curling against her face, and she couldn't see a thing in the pitch black. She quickly wound it up again.

'I'm too scared to move,' said Claire.

'Come on,' said Thea, her voice still wobbly. 'There can't really be anything out there.'

'I'm sure you're right.' Claire didn't sound convinced.

'Would you like me to drive?' Thea asked.

Claire shook her head. 'That would mean we'd have to get out of the car to swap places.' She turned the key and started the engine again. 'And I'm not game for that.' As she revved the engine and put it into gear, the car's tyres slipped and spun on the muddy road, eventually gaining traction. 'Let's get the hell out of here,' she said and pressed her foot down hard on the accelerator. 'Before anything else tries to jump in front of us.'

TWENTY-TWO

Now

When Thea woke on Sunday morning, she wondered for a minute if she had imagined the near-miss the night before. It hadn't been real, had it? If not, what was it? An apparition? The result of an overwrought imagination? Tiredness? Spiked wine? All of the above? It couldn't have been the drinks, because Claire had seen it too and she had stuck to a couple of beers. In the daylight it all seemed rather foolish to have been so badly frightened and she was sure there was a reasonable, logical explanation.

The hum of breakfast and the restorative power of waffles and pancakes dispelled Thea's lingering uneasiness. The weather was looking fine, she was pleased to see, and she was looking forward to the day's hike.

As an idea occurred to her, she got up from where she'd been sitting and went back to the kitchen. Three women were at work there, one loading a dishwasher, another cleaning pots and a third standing by the bank of refrigerators.

Thea approached the one at the fridges, the one she remembered serving her earlier in the week. 'I was wondering if I might get the girls to help make some lunch that we can take with us on our walk? Just some sandwiches, fruit . . .'

'That shouldn't be a problem,' she replied. 'Where are you thinking of going?'

'Grovely Wood.'

The three women stilled.

'Don't be getting lost,' said the one who was washing pots, her scrubbing brush suspended in mid-air.

'It can be treacherous,' warned the other.

'As long as you can read a compass,' said the first woman she'd spoken to, closing the fridge and turning to her. 'And make sure you're back well before dark.'

'Of course,' she reassured them as she left the kitchen and went to speak to the girls, all the while trying not to roll her eyes. It wasn't as if there were any dangerous creatures to be worried about – no deadly spiders, snakes or crocs in the English countryside.

~

They set off later that morning, each carrying their lunch and drink bottles in their backpack. They were dressed in shorts and long-sleeved T-shirts, for it was a bright, sunny autumn morning, and walked along in groups of twos and threes. Thea brought up the rear of the group as they entered the woods, falling into step next to Fenella, content for the moment to enjoy the scent of the pine trees, the cushiony softness of the needles underfoot and the chatter of the girls ahead – they were bright, sparky individuals, nothing like the spoiled princesses she had feared they might be, and she was fast becoming fond of each of them as she got to know them a little better.

They came to a long avenue of oak trees, their heavy branches causing the sunlight to dapple and fracture on the path in front of them. Crisp brown leaves collected around their ankles and crackled underfoot. There was no sign of anyone having walked this path for days. At the end of the avenue, Thea stopped and suggested a break. Everyone went quiet as they drank from their water bottles and she became aware for the first time of the stillness of the forest; even the birdsong had grown distant. In that moment she couldn't shake the feeling that someone or something was watching them. She took out her phone, telling herself that it was likely the result of the scare on the road the night before and a lack of sleep, perhaps even what she'd read about the Handsel sisters, rather than anything concrete. They were so deep into the forest now that there was no signal, but before leaving the house that morning she'd taken a screenshot of a rough map she'd found online. She showed the phone to Fenella. 'Tell me where you think we are,' she encouraged.

Fenella squinted at the image on the screen and moved it a fraction to the left then zoomed in. 'I suppose this could be it – if those are the oaks,' she said, pointing towards a path that cut through the green shading on the map.

'Excellent.' Thea noticed her colour at the praise. 'Trust your judgment.'

'Miss, what are these?' Joy, who was standing next to a fallen log, pointed to something growing on it. It seemed to glow in the dim light, as if it were phosphorescent.

'Don't touch!' Aradia called, coming closer. She knelt down and peered at the log. 'Ghost mushrooms. Poisonous. To humans and some animals.'

'Are they common in English woods?' Thea asked.

Aradia shook her head. 'Rather rare, actually. It's a surprise to see them here.' She got out her phone and took a few photos. 'What?' she asked as she noticed the rest of them looking at her curiously. 'Mycology's an interest of mine.'

'Miss . . .'

Thea turned to see Sabrina limping towards her. 'Blister?' she guessed.

The girl nodded.

'No worries.' Thea reached into her daypack. 'I've got some Band-Aids here somewhere.'

Sabrina unlaced her shoe, leaning on Aradia for support and wincing as the sock came off.

'You should have said something earlier.' Thea inspected the blister, which was raw and bloody. 'No point in suffering in silence.'

'Sorry, Miss. I didn't want to cause a fuss.'

'We'll have you patched up in no time.' She unzipped the first-aid kit.

'Miss?' Aradia asked. 'I heard one of the boys saying that this wood is haunted. It's not true is it?'

'Well, there is a story . . .' Thea began to tell the girls. 'There were four of them,' she said. 'The Handsel sisters. They were originally from Denmark. In 1737 there was a smallpox outbreak in the villages on the edge of this wood. No one knows exactly why, but the surviving villagers became convinced that the sisters were responsible – perhaps because they were foreign – and accused them of consorting with the devil.'

'Witchcraft, you mean?' Sabrina asked, wincing as Thea applied the sticking plaster.

Thea nodded. 'Before they could be properly tried, they were brought to the wood and bludgeoned to death. Their bodies were buried here, far enough apart that they couldn't arise and conspire against the villagers.'

'Really, Miss?' Aradia asked. 'That's kind of unbelievable.'

Thea smiled. This was just the kind of story that teenage girls lapped up. 'Somewhere near here are four old beech trees, and local legend has it that they mark the burial place of the dead sisters. But I'm not sure it means that the wood is actually haunted. There you go,' she said to Sabrina, handing her her shoe. 'That should make walking easier.'

'Thanks, Miss.'

'You mean like those over there?' Joy asked.

They all looked to where she was pointing, and Thea stared. How could she have missed them? About thirty metres away stood four trees, as if at four points of the compass, their thick gnarled trunks topped by a cascade of copper and crimson leaves, dead leaves and shadows darkening the ground around them.

Thea held her breath. 'I think so,' she said, leaving the girls and going over to the trees. When she reached them, she placed a hand on each of the trunks in turn, feeling connected to the story despite the centuries that had passed. A shiver went through her. This could definitely be a starting point for her study.

'It happened a lot in those days, didn't it?' Fenella asked, drawing close.

'If you mean to women – especially those who were a little different, or who appeared to have some medicinal or herbal knowledge – then yes, I'm afraid it did. Superstition, ignorance and a fear of what could not be readily explained or understood, was rife. Don't forget, most people had little education. And those who did – well, they were just as ready to lay the blame on women, especially those who couldn't properly defend themselves.'

'It still happens now,' said Joy quietly. All of the girls had joined her.

'Unfortunately, it does, albeit sometimes in subtler ways,' agreed Thea, impressed at her insight. 'But we are getting better at raising our voices, at calling it out.' She almost mentioned the list she'd found at the back of the book – that there'd been the name of a former maid at the house, but thought better of it, for she didn't know them well enough yet to determine how they might react. *And they're only sixteen and seventeen*, she reminded herself.

In the time since they had stopped, the wind had begun to gust, bringing with it scudding grey clouds, the smell of rain, a distant rumble of thunder and a sky that looked like trouble. Thea calculated they had another hour's walk until they reached the lookout, and then a couple of hours more to get back to the house. She really didn't want to turn back before they reached their objective. 'All right, then,' Thea said a little doubtfully. 'Let's push on until we get to the landmark – it's only a couple of miles away.'

They stowed their bottles and began to walk deeper into the woods. Crossing her fingers that it would only be a brief shower at worst, Thea led the girls onwards.

The way became sharply steeper, and after a steady climb that left Thea's thighs burning, they reached the summit and stopped to catch their breath. Though the rain so far had held off, in the distance the sky was ominously dark, clouds now massing towards them.

At the top of the lookout was a tall stone spire, at the base of which was a partly obscured symbol. Thea pulled aside a clump of weeds to reveal a carving of a quiver of arrows.

'What's that, Miss?'

'It's a monument to Artemis,' said Fenella, reaching them. 'Goddess of the hunt. It was erected in the 1900s by a local landowner, in tribute to his sister.' She pulled her phone from her pocket and took a quick snap.

Thea blinked at her. 'Very impressive.' The girls were sharp, there was no doubt of that.

'I did some research the other day, after I saw the patterns on the house keys,' Fenella shrugged. 'It's also a secret symbol of female empowerment,' she added, raising her eyebrows in wry amusement.

Thea took a long pull from her water bottle, her mind flashing back to the symbol on the underside of the kitchenhand's wrist. She ignored the nagging feeling that she was missing something, that there was some kind of connection, and instead suggested they stop for lunch. The hill was exposed, the wind whipped their hair about their faces and cut through the sweatshirts that most of the girls were now wearing, but no one complained, though they were quieter than they had been earlier on the hike.

A rumble of thunder caused Thea to look up from her sandwich. Rain blurred the horizon and the wind had increased its strength. Joy pulled her hands into her sleeves and Thea realised that her own fingers were numb. She didn't want to risk any of them getting hypothermia, which was a possibility if they stayed much longer, especially if they were hit with the freezing rain that was now undoubtedly on its way to them.

They packed up and scrambled down the narrow track that led away from the lookout. Walking in single file, they maintained a steady pace, the wind at their backs driving them along. It was some time later that Thea stopped and did a quick headcount. She scanned the group of girls strung out behind her. 'Has anyone seen Sabrina?' she called.

'She was trailing me,' said Aradia.

'I think her feet were hurting again,' said Fenella.

'Perhaps she stopped to rest?' Joy suggested.

Thea ground her teeth. 'Well, she should have told someone. Come on. We'll have to retrace our steps. Hopefully she's not too far back.'

There was some grumbling at this – 'Can't we wait here for her, Miss?' – but Thea was adamant. 'We can't lose her.' *Not the headmaster's daughter*, she said to herself, feeling the cold slice through to her bones.

As they began to walk back uphill, the rain started to fall, softly at first, but soon in sheets that soaked them through. Thea cursed herself for not insisting they all bring waterproof jackets despite the extra bulk that it would have entailed.

When they'd walked about half a mile, she noticed a flattened section of bracken; the dry, rusty fronds to one side of the path had been trampled. The terrain sloped steeply here and was thick with trees, but she stopped and peered downhill. Far below she could just make out a bright flash of colour among the undergrowth.

'What's that down there?' she asked, pointing towards it as her stomach tightened. 'Is that a water bottle?'

'Yeah,' replied Fenella. 'It's Sabrina's.'

TWENTY-THREE

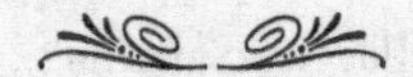

March 1769, Oxleigh

'There is no need for the doctor.' Patrick Hollander stood in front of his wife regarding her with curiosity but not concern. Her breathing, although shallow, had steadied and her eyelids fluttered like a moth before a lamp. 'Let us spare that expense for the moment.'

Though her mistress had cause to mention money from time to time, it was the first instance Rowan could remember that her master had shown the slightest concern for their finances. Perhaps things were worse than they appeared?

Patrick reached into the pocket of his waistcoat and withdrew an enamelled snuffbox. He tapped a small amount of the yellowy-brown powder onto his hand and raised it to his nose before sniffing deeply. 'Caroline is perhaps overtired.'

Rowan was taken aback by his lack of concern, and in any case, how could her mistress possibly be overtired? She had only just risen from her bedchamber, and her days consisted of reading – usually a prayerbook – by the fireside, playing her pianoforte or taking tea with her friends. But Rowan knew her place and so held her tongue, for fear of reprimand or worse. Perhaps Caroline was no stranger to fainting, though Rowan had not seen evidence of it in the months she had been at the merchant's house. 'I'll fetch some water,' she said, wanting to do something other than stand idly by. As she left the room, she caught sight of Alice, who was as pale as her mistress, and registered the glance that flew between her master and the lady's maid.

When she returned with the water, her mistress had revived somewhat, her eyes were open and a little colour had returned to her cheeks. 'Perhaps you can help me to sit up?' Caroline asked. Alice lifted her mistress as Rowan placed pillows behind her back until she was comfortable. 'I have a vinaigrette.' She reached into a pocket in her skirts and produced a pretty little silver box, opened a catch and inhaled. Rowan had seen one of these once before, when the lady of the manor had been overcome by the ordure on the path between the cottages of Inkpen. When she had asked later what it was, her mother had told her that it contained a small sponge that had been soaked in vinegar. Though her mistress grimaced as she inhaled and her eyes watered, it seemed to revive her a little.

'I am feeling slightly better,' Caroline said. 'I confess I did not feel much like eating breakfast earlier, but perhaps some bread now?'

'Of course,' said Rowan, taking the vinaigrette from her and placing it on a nearby table. She was relieved to see that her mistress's eyes had lost the glazed, vacant expression that had so frightened her earlier.

'Well, if there's nothing more I can do,' said Patrick distractedly. 'I must return to the shop.'

Rowan bit her lip, for she wanted to say that he hadn't actually done *anything* to assist his wife. She remembered the look she had seen on her master's face when she had stumbled upon the cockfight, the same expression she had seen as he threw the bolts of fabric on the floor in the shop, the argument she had overheard . . . There was no longer any doubt in her mind: he was an unpredictable and sometimes cruel man and she needed to remember that.

When Patrick had left the room, Rowan turned and closed the door. 'Are you certain you are quite well now?' she asked. Then, when Caroline did not answer, 'Have you been taking the draught, as I advised?'

Caroline nodded and sudden knowledge lit up her eyes. 'Do you think . . .' she began.

'I am not certain it could have taken effect so quickly,' Rowan replied.

'You have not had your courses for quite some months now,' Alice said quietly.

'Yes, but they have never been regular,' Caroline said.

'You must rest,' said Rowan. 'I shall make up a tonic, to strengthen the blood. Perhaps you should return to your bedchamber after a little breakfast,' she suggested.

'Indeed,' Caroline agreed. 'Alice, please go and see that it is ready.'

Rowan noticed the expression on Alice's face as her mistress gave her orders. A flash of disdain, or was it envy?

She had a feeling that Alice had her sights set on a far grander life than that of a maidservant. Once, when Caroline was in Salisbury, she'd caught a glimpse of Alice turning in front of the looking glass in her mistress's chamber. She had been dressed in one of Caroline's most sumptuous silk gowns. Rowan had said nothing at the time, for she could hardly blame her: had she not herself imagined the feeling of fine silk against her skin?

The mistress spent several more days lying in bed and Prudence prepared her breakfast for her on a tray that Rowan or Alice carried from the kitchen up several flights of stairs. Rowan remained silent as her mistress complained of cold toast and bitter chocolate.

One morning, as Rowan was carrying the slops down the back stairs, she almost collided with Alice. The maid recoiled from her, a hand clamped over her mouth. Rowan stood back just in time, watching as she crashed through the back door. Curious, she followed her, seeing her retch in the gutter that ran along the side of the garden.

'Are you unwell?' Rowan asked when Alice had finished.

Alice straightened and wiped her mouth with the back of her hand. 'Must've been summat I ate,' she said, a scowl marring her pretty features. 'Don't trouble yourself. 'Twas nothing.'

They had both partaken of the same meal the night before – cold tongue and barley bread, washed down with small beer – and Rowan had not felt any ill effects. 'Are you sure?' she asked, searching her face, which, she saw, was drained of colour, just as her mistress's had been before she fainted.

Alice's hand went involuntarily to her belly and she would not look Rowan in the eye.

In that instant, Rowan knew without having to be told what it meant.

'Who?' she asked quietly. 'Surely not the master?'

Alice shook her head violently. 'Tommy Dean,' she replied, a calculating expression on her pretty face.

Rowan's heart stuttered. They had shared one kiss, but she had become very fond of the butcher's boy, even imagined – a flight of fancy, mind – a future with him one day. She knew him to be a good and kind young man and had believed that he had a care for her. Had he so readily transferred his affections? That it was to Alice knocked the breath clean from her lungs.

'Tell me why I should take you at your word,' she demanded. 'Do you wish to hurt me that much?'

'Believe me when I say that it has absolutely nothing to do with you,' said Alice.

Rowan couldn't say exactly why, but something in Alice's voice chilled her to her marrow.

~

'I must hence to Bath,' Patrick declared as he sat with his wife taking their breakfast a week later. 'For I am convinced the time is ripe to increase our business. I believe there is a growing need for merchants of fine silk in the town. We saw it ourselves when we last visited, did we not?'

Rowan, who had entered the room with a pot of chocolate and placed it next to her mistress, gave, as she always must, the appearance of being oblivious to their conversation, disappearing into the background, though the truth was she listened carefully to whatever was said, her mind hungry for information of any kind.

It seemed to her that the Hollanders' finances ebbed and flowed like the stream at the bottom of the garden: sometimes in full flood, at others no more than a thin trickle. She supposed it must be the way of doing business. Indeed, there were similar times in her village, good seasons and bad, bounty and scarcity. She had learned to live with such uncertainty, but she could not help but be interested in her employers' fortunes, for they surely affected her as well. She was still reeling from Alice's allegation, but had not been able to find Tommy to ask for the truth from him. Time and again she had returned to the riverbank, but he had failed to appear, his absence only serving to lend weight to Alice's words.

'I wager that you make a good point,' Caroline said, taking a sip of chocolate. 'But I am anxious for you not to extend yourself to the point of fraying, husband dear.'

Patrick laughed as if she had made a good joke. 'Do not fuss, especially about the complications of business. A wife should not have to bear that burden.'

'I am no simpleton, husband,' she replied.

'Of course not, but 'tis better that you fill your head with the concerns of our household, our growing family.'

'Will you be gone for long?' she asked.

'No more than a month, I imagine,' he replied. 'I am to see about a lease on a property on the Westgate. In any case, I do not wish to leave you for long, not in your condition.' He placed a hand on hers and regarded her with affection, the first time in many months that Rowan had seen him look at his wife that way.

It was confirmed, then. That it was so soon after giving her mistress the draught led her to believe that the seed must have already been planted before her mistress's departure.

Rowan supposed she should not have been surprised to see her master treat his wife rather differently now. He was most solicitous, speaking to her with a new gentleness and reverence.

As she checked the dishes to determine if they required replenishment, an idea began to form. Could she perhaps take advantage of her master's absence to absent herself? To return to Inkpen and her brothers, even if only for a few days? She missed them so terribly, and wondered often if they were well, if Albie was in good health, if Will was being a help to his uncle, if Joseph and Elias were less mischievous. Anything could have happened to them in the months she had been away and it gnawed at her not to be able to see them, to feel them close to her once again. Their company would surely be a salve to her bruised heart.

When Rowan came across Patrick later that afternoon, she put the question to him. 'My mistress hinted that I might soon have leave to visit my family,' she said. 'I believe she was to raise the matter with you.'

'She has not. However, I am not at all certain that I can spare you.' Patrick Hollander was dismissive. 'With Alice unwell, your mistress may have need of you.'

It was true that Alice had been recently confined to her bed, and even that day Rowan was attending to both her master and mistress, ascending and descending the steep back stairs so many times that she was almost dizzy with the effort. She held her tongue, frustrated that she had no argument to refute this, and that there was no choice but to accept her master's dictates. Rowan's amenable nature deserted her for once: in that moment, she disliked her master intensely, Alice even more so.

TWENTY-FOUR

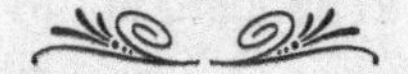

Now

'Perhaps you might explain how it was that my daughter came to be halfway down a sheer hillside on her own this afternoon, Miss Rust?' The headmaster's voice was calm, but Thea could feel the ice in his tone.

'I take full responsibility. She was in my care and I failed to keep her safe. She became separated from the rest of the group and stumbled in a steep part of the woods.' There was no point in making excuses. She and Fenella had scrambled down the sheer side of the track, finding Sabrina in a crumpled heap, and between them had managed to help her back up to rejoin the others. She had some cuts and bruises and a sore ankle but appeared not to have sustained more serious injuries. She was pale and shaken, but with the assistance of two of the girls, had been able to walk the remainder of the way out of the woods.

As soon as they returned to Oxleigh, Thea had seen the girls safely back to the boarding house and then hurried over to the headmaster's house to inform him of the incident.

'I see,' he said, making a bridge of his fingers. 'I have to say that – aside from the fact that she is my daughter – your supervision of the girls was careless. Some might argue it was negligent, Miss Rust. For such a thing to happen, not to mention that the girls have been here scarcely a week . . . I shall have to think carefully about whether more serious action is required.' He peered at her over his glasses. 'For now, it's probably best that you go and get yourself dry. You've doubtless had a shock yourself.' There was a slight note of kindness in his voice now.

When Thea returned to Silk House, she went straight to her bathroom and stripped off her wet clothes, shivering with cold until she thawed out under a scalding shower. It was not until later, when she went to her study to fetch some marking, that she noticed the small piles of earth on the floor again. She had left her hiking boots in the cloakroom at the back of the house – everyone had – meaning that she couldn't have brought it upstairs with her. So, what was the origin? She knelt down to take a closer look. It seemed to have come up from the joins in the floorboards, where there was a slight gap. She prodded the wood, finding a softer spot where the board crumbled beneath her touch. She stood up and glanced around for something to dig at them with when her eyes fell on the bookshelves. Something was missing.

The tin. The one she'd brought with her from Melbourne.

It had been on the shelf in her study when she left that morning.

Frantically, she scoured the other surfaces, her eyes travelling up and down the small bookshelf, and then across to the desk.

Ah. There it was. She was sure she had not moved it, and no one came in to clean, certainly not on a Sunday. She left the floorboards and went across to the desk, resting her fingertips on the lid of the tin as if to reassure herself that it was still there.

The warmth from her shower was fast leaving her and so she returned to her bedroom, flopping back on the duvet, closing her eyes and promising herself a few minutes' rest. She was asleep within moments, and dreamed she was back in the forest clearing, sitting in the centre of the beech trees. The branches were thin and snaky, reaching out to her and catching on her T-shirt, scratching her arms, but she couldn't move away from them, was as frozen as a statue . . .

The bright, brassy sound of trumpets rudely cut through Thea's dream, causing her to jolt awake. She still had no idea who set the alarm music – or quite possibly it was randomly generated – but she appreciated violins or the flute more than the trumpets. The room was dark and she reached for her phone, looking blearily at the figures. Eight-thirty. For a moment she didn't know if it was morning or night. She lay and listened to the thunder of footsteps on the stairs, the snatches of conversation, and guessed that it was suppertime. She felt around for a pair of shoes, pushed her feet into them and left to join the girls.

The dining room was warm, but Thea couldn't seem to stop herself from shivering. She glanced around the room to see if anyone else was similarly affected, but the girls all looked bright-eyed and animated as they chatted away. Sabrina was the focus of attention, as they fussed over her, helping her rest her sore ankle on a cushion.

'You are unwell,' the Dame said after the meal was over and the girls had left.

'A chill. Really, it's nothing,' Thea protested, though beads of sweat had broken out on her forehead and it hurt her throat to swallow.

The Dame produced a small paper bag and handed it to her. 'Brew a teaspoon of this in some hot water and add some honey and lemon. Keep taking it until it's finished.'

'That's very thoughtful.' Thea was touched by her concern. 'Dame Hicks . . .'

'Yes?'

'I meant to mention it earlier, but I've noticed that there are often piles of dirt on the floor in my study. I'm worried there might be termites.'

'It's probably best to speak to the porter. He can organise an inspection,' she replied tersely.

'Okay, will do.' She forced a smile. Surely the Dame could handle it, couldn't she? Though the older woman knew more about school protocol than Thea did, so she let it be.

'And how is your thumb?'

'Oh,' she said in surprise, raising it to check. 'I had forgotten all about it. It's completely healed.'

'Good,' said the Dame. 'We must make sure you stay safe. A couple of aspirin wouldn't be a bad idea, either.'

It seemed the Dame wasn't entirely about herbal remedies. But what did she mean by making sure Thea was safe? If she said it about one of the girls Thea could understand it, but herself?

Thea took the bag to the kitchen and found a mug, putting the kettle on to boil. The kitchen staff had finished clearing up and only one was left, wiping down the benches. Thea recognised her as the woman with the tattoo; indeed, she saw it again on the inside of her wrist as she came closer and wiped the surface next to her.

'We haven't met properly,' said Thea, introducing herself.

The woman started, as if surprised at being spoken to. 'Moira,' she answered.

'Do you mind me asking why you got that?' Thea indicated her wrist.

'It's supposed to protect a person from harm,' she shrugged.

The kettle boiled, beeping an interruption and the woman moved away. Thea's head was thick with fever and she was too tired to think more about it. For now, anyway. She stumbled up the stairs, sipped her drink, wincing at its bitter taste. Minutes later, she was sound asleep.

~

A woman sat on the end of Thea's bed, curling tendrils of jet-black hair escaping a hooded cape. Her eyes as dark as pansies. Thea willed herself to move, but it was as though a weight sat on her chest and try as she might, she could not.

'What?' she finally whispered, her breath coming in quick gasps. 'It's not real. It's not real,' she repeated to herself. 'It's all in your head.' But a creeping sense of dread filled her, pressing her down into the mattress. She had the distinct feeling that the woman did not want her there.

A blaring beep went off and she jerked awake. She blinked and looked towards the end of the bed, but the woman had vanished. The powder that the Dame had given her; had that been the cause of such a bizarre dream? Whatever had been in it had certainly worked on her cold – she felt much better and even her sore throat had eased. Thea closed her eyes again. She was so very tired . . .

Seconds later the bedroom lights flashed on and then off again and the beeping continued without stopping, growing even louder. It had to be a fire alarm, for there could surely be no other reason for the infernal racket. She reached for her glasses, stumbled out of bed and stepped out into the corridor, where she found Fenella, a small white face showing in the glow from her torch. 'It's all right, Fen, it's all right,' she said, trying to keep her voice as calm as possible. 'Just a fire drill, so we all need to leave the house. The assembly point is in the street, two doors down, outside the Lamb and Flag.'

Fenella nodded, wrapped her dressing gown about her and quickly found her slippers while Thea waited.

They went down the stairs together and she ushered Fenella in the direction of the ground floor before going along the corridor to make sure the other girls were up.

The alarm was still incessantly beeping.

All of the girls had by now been woken by the loud noise, and when she was certain they were all safely out of the house, Thea hurried after them. When she reached the front door, she realised that she had not seen the Dame. She ran to the back of the house and knocked on the Dame's door but there was no answer. She rattled the doorknob, calling out to her. Finally, she opened the door and peered in. The room was in darkness, but she could see the bed. It was empty. And unslept in. There was no time to be annoyed that she hadn't stayed to ensure the girls' safety.

When Thea stepped out into the high street, she noticed lights on in a number of neighbouring windows. As a siren wailed, she turned to look back at the house. There was no sign of fire, no obvious smell of smoke. She saw the Dame, standing at the back of the group of girls, and waved, but the Dame gave no indication of having seen her.

After calming the girls down and ensuring that everyone was accounted for, Thea went to speak to the firemen, who had climbed down from their truck and begun to investigate. 'The power's out,' said one of them. 'A surge and then an outage might be what triggered the alarm.'

'Is it only out in the house, not the street?' she asked.

'It seems that way.'

'There's nothing wrong with the fuses,' said another. 'But you might want to call an electrician in the morning, in any case.'

She nodded and noticed that dawn had begun to lighten the sky.

'It's safe to go back in now anyway,' he added.

'Thank you. Come on girls,' she said, ushering them back to the house. 'I don't think any of us will manage to get back to sleep after all that kerfuffle, but you can at least go and rest until it's breakfast time.'

As she stepped through the door after the girls, her mind swam with thoughts. Dodgy electrics, doors unlocking themselves and a possible infestation, not to mention the strange dream: Thea began to worry that something was very wrong with the house.

TWENTY-FIVE

Now

'Cappuccino, please. Extra strong.' Thea needed something to wake herself up after the night's broken sleep. The power was still off and she'd been able to arrange for the girls to have breakfast at one of the boys' boarding houses before school. She'd invited the Dame to join her at the cafe a few doors down from the house, but the older woman had declined, saying she would wait in for the electrician. 'You know how it is. The moment you turn your back, they arrive.'

Thea had suggested that the electrician had her number and they could return to the house with a minute's notice, but the Dame would not be persuaded, and as ever her countenance did not invite argument. Nor was Thea game to raise the matter of the Dame leaving the house in advance of the girls during the false alarm the night before. The last thing she needed was to get the Dame offside; the headmaster already thought she was incompetent, and she needed all the allies she could muster.

As she reached into her bag for her wallet to pay for the coffee, Thea's fingers encountered something soft. She pulled it out, staring in confusion as she realised that it was the fabric from the book in the school library. How on earth had that ended up in her bag? A flush of shame rose within her that she might have stolen it, even unwittingly.

She gathered it up, glancing furtively around to make sure that no one had seen her, though the other occupants of the cafe – two elderly ladies, one of whom was feeding bits of muffin to a small Pomeranian partly concealed in a shopping bag – paid her scant attention. She refolded the fabric and placed it between the pages of a notebook, the best way she could think to keep it safe, and promised herself she would return it to the library as soon as she got the chance.

After she paid, she left the cafe, glancing at her watch and hurrying as she saw the time. Lessons started in fifteen minutes and she had another job to do first. Clasping her bag tightly, she started to run.

She went to the school's main entrance and found the porter scowling at a piece of paper on the desk in front of him. She had to cough to get his attention, though she was certain he'd heard her come in. 'Mr Battle, have you got a moment?' she asked.

'A moment? I believe I can spare one, Miss Rust.' His voice dripped acid.

'You are doubtless aware of last night's fire alarm at Silk House,' she said. 'An electrician is on his way there this morning.'

'Indeed, Miss Rust.'

'Well, there's another problem, and the Dame suggested I take it up with you. The floor in my study is covered with piles of dirt. No sooner do I clean it up than more take its place. It's been going on since I arrived. I'm not sure whether we need pest control or a structural engineer.'

'I see. Are you certain it is not merely mud from your shoes?'

She looked at him mulishly.

'Well, a structural engineer sounds a little excessive, wouldn't you say?'

'I don't know; does it?' Thea stood her ground.

'Very well,' he sighed heavily. 'I shall arrange an inspection.'

'Thank you, Mr Battle.' It was a start.

'I really have nothing better to do.'

She refused to rise to the jibe, letting his sarcasm wash over her. They arranged to meet at the boarding house later that day.

On her way to class, Thea found the address of the local records office and calculated that she had just enough time after lunch and before meeting Mr Battle to spend a couple of hours there trying to find out more about the history of the house. She also wanted to do some more research on the Handsel sisters and see if there were any other stories about local witches that could tie in with theirs. She rang the number listed and gave Helen, the woman who answered the phone, a few brief details of the area of her research.

Before lunch, Thea ducked into the staffroom to collect the keys to Claire's car; she found them in her pigeonhole together with a note giving directions to where the car was parked. She nodded hello to a few of the teachers whom she'd begun to recognise, and breathed relief that Gareth Pope seemed to be nowhere in the vicinity.

She slid into a parking space near the records office as the church bell sounded twelve. She was greeted with recognition by Helen when she gave her name. 'I've retrieved everything we've got on the house,' she said. 'There are a number of folders.' The woman's eyes lit up and Thea felt an answering excitement rise within herself. She was anxious as to what had happened within its walls, wanted to know more about the man who had the vision to build it and the families who had lived there over the centuries.

Helen asked for her bag. 'Nothing allowed except paper and a pencil,' she explained, taking it from her and handing her the writing tools. She ushered Thea into a small room furnished with a wide table and an office chair. The only items on the desk were a number of small white silk-covered beanbags. Helen held out a pair of pale cotton gloves. 'Some of the material is rather fragile,' she said. 'It can be damaged by the oils on your skin.'

'Of course,' said Thea. 'Thank you.'

'I'll be back in a jiffy.' She left the room, then returned a few minutes later with several bulging foolscap folders and a cardboard tube.

'There's a copy of the house plans in the tube,' she said as she placed the folders on the table. 'They weren't listed as part of the archive, but I acted on a hunch and managed to find them among a number of other plans for houses on the high street.'

Thea's eyes widened. This was more than she had been expecting.

'I'll get it out for you.' She opened the end of the tube and gently removed the paper from within it, weighting the curled ends down with the beanbags to hold them flat on the table. 'I took the liberty of doing a little preliminary research,' she said. 'It was one of the town's grandest residences in its day. Commissioned by Thomas Bayly and completed in 1763. He was a local landowner, I believe. It was a wedding present to his daughter, Caroline, and her new husband. Well, more to her husband because women weren't allowed to own property in their own right then.'

A bell pinged from the reception area.

'I'll leave you to it.' Thea could hear the reluctance in her voice as Helen went to see what was needed outside.

Thea leaned forward and peered at the paper in front of her. It might have been a copy, but it seemed almost as old as the original, yellowed and speckled with age. The ink had faded to a pale sepia and the writing was looped and scrawled across the page, but it was possible to make out the different floors, each of which had been drawn separately. She found the kitchen, the drawing room, which was now the girls' dining room. The Dame's room was once the scullery, she noted. And there had been a shop on the ground floor, she saw, now the sitting room. There was the narrow back staircase that went all the way from the kitchen to the attic – used by the servants, as the Dame had explained.

On the second floor were a number of large rooms, and she guessed that they must have been later divided into the smaller bedrooms and bathrooms that now existed.

On the attic floor was Fenella's room, and Thea's too, and then another room, now her study she guessed. She looked closer to see another doorway off that room that led to what appeared to be a small cupboard. If Thea was right, this was where she had felt the plaster give way when she leaned on it. But why had this space since been blocked off?

The plans showed the gardens, including a sketch of the parterre garden in the shape of a pentacle. A pentacle, she was well aware, was a shape linked with witchcraft, a symbol alleged to be employed in magical evocation, to foretell the future, or to have power over the devil, though it was also often associated with the element of earth. So, it had been there from the very beginning. She felt her stomach twist; her instincts told her that this was significant, though she wasn't sure exactly how yet.

Thea had kept her phone on silent in her pocket, and she now pulled it out and surreptitiously snapped a couple of pictures of the plans before moving further along the table to where the archivist had left the folders. She checked her watch as she opened the first page. Twelve-thirty. An hour before she would have to leave.

The first folder showed more recent artefacts: newspaper advertisements from a couple of decades ago for 'Silk House Hotel' as it had once been known, a poster for a dance to be held there, a bill of sale. A listing taken from a local estate agency described it as a 'Grade II listed house of historic importance and note'. There was a 1980s magazine feature, its faded colour photographs showing a grand room laid for dinner and a bedroom decorated with swags and festoons of fabric. She hardly recognised the place.

Then, a black-and-white print of the exterior, dated 1931. It showed the same gable roofline and wide front door. Little had changed, on the outside at least, in the following eighty-something years.

As she leafed through the first folder, it seemed that not much of note had taken place there in the past century. But she was more interested in going back further, though she knew there was likely to be far less material that related to the house's early days.

There was a knock on the door and Helen popped her head around it. 'You've got everything you need?'

Thea nodded, conscious that time was running short and she still had a great deal to read through.

Helen left her in peace again and Thea opened the second folder. It seemed more promising. But it was also much slower going, as there were handwritten pages from a ledger, letters, and then, as she turned the page, a wadded piece of plain white cotton. She hesitated, then unfolded it. Placed between the folds was a strip of silk fabric.

Her heart skipped a beat.

It was exactly the same design as the one she had in her notebook. The colours were brighter, the silk whiter, but the pattern was identical. She took a quick snap of that too, to compare it to the other piece of fabric that was still hidden in her handbag.

Then, a church bell began to chime again. She had to leave right away if she was to make it back to the house to meet Mr Battle.

~

'That's it?' The porter knelt down awkwardly near where Thea was pointing. In the time she'd been away from the house the piles had grown larger, until they were now several inches high. He'd brought a pest inspector with him, a tall, unsmiling man wearing khaki overalls and safety glasses.

'What do you think, Jim?' Battle asked.

The inspector bent down next to him and rubbed the dust between his thumb and forefinger. 'Hmm,' he said. 'It's extremely fine, almost a powder.' He looked back up at Thea. 'Unlikely to be rodents,' he said, pressing the wooden floor with his hands experimentally. 'Looks as though it's coming up between the floorboards.'

'And next to this wall,' said Thea. 'Do you think there are borers or something under the floor?'

The inspector straightened up. 'Whatever it is, it's not dry rot, so that's good news. I'll need to inspect the outside of the building as well, and take some samples.' He got out a couple of small clear plastic cylinders and scooped some of the dirt into each one, before screwing the lids on tightly. 'Is it only in this spot that you've noticed it?' he asked, scrawling details on a couple of labels and affixing them to the cylinders.

Thea nodded.

'We'll run some tests and get back to you if there's anything to worry about. It could just be general dust, or mud from your shoes? Perhaps a breeze sweeping it into piles.'

Thea didn't believe that explanation for a second. 'But the piles are getting larger,' she said, frustrated at his apparent lack of concern. 'And I nearly always leave my outdoor shoes downstairs.'

'D'you know, the last time I saw dirt like this was at my grandfather's funeral,' Battle mused. 'They don't really go in for it anymore. It's all cremations and memorial services these days, no respect for tradition.'

'What?' Thea had no idea what he was on about.

'Ashes to ashes, dust to dust . . . it looks almost exactly like the fine dirt that moles throw up when they are digging; it was traditionally gathered and used at funerals.'

'But that's impossible here; we're three floors up,' said Thea.

'We'll get to the bottom of it, don't you worry,' the inspector reassured her. 'A good spraying will likely do the trick, if it's needed at all. But don't worry about the house – it'll outlast all of us.' He gave a dry bark of laughter that did little to alleviate her growing anxiety.

~

When Mr Battle and the pest inspector had gone, Thea went in search of a drink. There was a kettle at one end of the dining room, and she grabbed a teabag from the canister next to it while she waited for the water to boil. As she poured the hot water into the mug, several black specks rose up from it. Annoyed that she must have ripped the bag, she went to tip it out and start again, but just before she did, movement in the water caught her eye. She took a closer look. The black specks weren't tea leaves. They were tiny beetles. She flinched. *Ugh.* What had got into the tea?

She checked. The whole thing was crawling with them.

Thea wasn't especially squeamish, but the sight of the moving mass of tiny insect bodies turned her stomach and she gagged at the thought she might have unwittingly drunk them. As she went to the kitchen and tipped the lot into the bin, she wondered briefly if someone was playing a trick on her and the girls. *Oh, stop being paranoid*, she scolded herself as she set about brewing a pot of coffee instead. *Who would do something like that?* She knew that infestations were a fact of life, particularly in old houses, and not something to read anything untoward into. She could only hope that a proper fumigation would get rid of *all* the unwelcome creatures inhabiting the place.

The coffee was hot and strong and thankfully unaffected, and so she sat at one of the dining tables, placing her mug to one side before taking out the strip of fabric to compare it to the one she had photographed in the records office.

She set the fabric down and turned to the photos on her phone. There was no doubt: it was from the same weaving. There was even a tiny notch on her piece of cloth that was missing from the one she had photographed. She clicked her phone off.

'Where did you get that?'

Thea jumped.

'Get what?' she asked, sounding foolish as she turned to see Dame Hicks standing behind her. Sometimes the woman made her feel twelve years old and as if she were about to be told off. And how did she always manage to move so silently? *Please at least cough as you sneak up on me*, Thea wanted to say but didn't dare.

The Dame pointed to the cloth, her eyes alight with curiosity.

'Er . . .' Thea decided to come clean. 'Actually, in the school library.'

The Dame pinched her lips together, as if trying to decide whether or not Thea was being straight with her. 'Witches' weeds,' she crooned to herself, reaching out a gnarled finger and gently stroking the fabric.

'What?'

'Poisonous plants. Henbane. Or nightshade as it's more commonly known. And that's a black lace-weaver spider, or something similar. *Amaurobius ferox.* The young devour the mother after hatching,' she said, a smile playing about her thin lips.

'Nice.' Thea shuddered.

'What was it doing in the school library?'

'I have no idea. I didn't mean to take it, really I didn't.' Thea felt herself squirm like a schoolgirl caught in a lie. 'I found it between the pages of a book. A book on the history of this house, actually. I must have gathered it up with my diary and notebooks when I left. Do you think it might have been sold by the silk merchant who lived here? Could it really be that old?'

'That is of course possible, perhaps even likely,' the Dame said. 'Would you mind if I borrowed it?' she asked.

Did she imagine it, or did Thea see a look of avarice flit across the woman's face?

'But shouldn't we return it? Won't it have some value, if that's the case?'

'Oh, I don't think they're likely to miss a tiny scrap of fabric, do you? I'll see that no harm comes to it. I only want it for a little while.'

'I suppose,' said Thea. She was reluctant to hand it over but couldn't think of a good reason not to. Indeed, it might help get the Dame on side. 'But what do you want it for?' She held off from mentioning finding more of the same fabric in the records office earlier that day, that it was a match to this piece.

'My mother was a herbologist. She left me some of her recipes, as I believe I mentioned. She's in a nursing home now, pushing ninety. There's not much excitement in her life any more, but I think she would enjoy seeing this.'

In the face of that explanation, Thea could hardly refuse.

TWENTY-SIX

Now

Thea had been having trouble sleeping, waking in the early hours ever since she'd moved into Silk House. Sometimes, in the moments before she dropped off the edge of consciousness, she imagined that the house was trying to talk to her, that the groans and rumbles were more than simply those of an old building settling into itself.

Once again, her eyes snapped open and in the pitch dark all she could see were the lights of the wretched alarm. But it hadn't gone off. Something else had woken her, she was sure of it.

She definitely heard a noise. *That* was what had roused her. A scrape of furniture, then a muffled laugh. She checked her watch. After midnight. The girls should be fast asleep. Then she heard the noise for a third time. She lay there for a moment, pretending she hadn't heard anything. She really didn't want to leave her warm bed to go and investigate, but knew she probably had to. Besides, if she didn't she'd never get back to sleep, that she was sure of.

Shoving her feet into her slippers and shivering as she pulled on her dressing gown, she grabbed her glasses, found her phone and switched on the torch. She opened her door, peering along the corridor. More noise, and a faint light coming from under Fenella's door. She was surprised, wouldn't have imagined it of the quiet, bookish girl. She tiptoed along the corridor and listened outside the door. Another giggle; two different voices. A hastily stifled scream.

The scene when she opened the door was not one she had wanted to see – a group of girls gathered around a circle of letters. She knew straightaway what they were up to. As she breathed in the fug of scented hand sanitiser (all of the girls, without exception, seemed addicted to the stuff: she remembered the sticky cherry lip gloss of her teenage years as a similar passionate adherence), she shone her torch at them. 'Really?' she snapped as they scrambled to cover up the letters on the Ouija board in the middle of their circle. 'Summoning spirits? Do you have *any* idea of the trouble you'll get yourselves into?' Sudden fury gripped her and her tone was harsher than it probably should have been.

She remembered another time, years before. A trip to Sydney and a visit to the Quarantine Station in Manly. Standing in the small bathroom of one of the guard houses. Fear creeping up the back of her neck, a sudden urge to flee. She had stumbled through the crowd and out of the front door; gulped in air.

Something terrible, something evil, had happened in that room, she had known it. The house was starting to give her a similar feeling and it was seriously beginning to play on her nerves.

'Oh Christ,' murmured Morgan.

'Sorry, Miss,' Fenella apologised.

'I have to say I thought more highly of all of you.'

'It was just a bit of fun,' said Sabrina.

'This is hardly the time or the place, now, is it?' She glared at them.

Aradia, who had hastily scooped up the letters, began to speak but Thea silenced her with a hand. 'No explanations. I want you to return to your rooms and go straight to sleep. If I so much as hear a peep out of you before morning you will have the headmaster to answer to. We will discuss this further tomorrow.' She held the door open and the four girls who didn't belong there scurried out of the room and down the stairs, nearly tripping over themselves in their haste to leave.

~

The next evening, the girls who had been involved in the shenanigans were waiting for her in the dining room. Before they had left for school in the morning, Thea had asked them to meet her there after supper, opting to let them sweat on their fate for the entire day. She knew that was likely to be punishment enough and, she hoped, a deterrent to prevent them getting up to mischief again in a hurry.

'So,' she said. 'Who's going to tell me what you were doing last night?'

The girls reddened, fidgeted, looked at their hands, their shoes, the floor, anywhere but at her. The silence stretched. Only Fenella met her eye.

Eventually she spoke. 'We were only mucking about. I know it was wrong, but it was honestly nothing more than a bit of a lark.'

'Yes, Miss,' Sabrina added. 'We're ever so sorry.' She sounded contrite. Either that or she was putting on a good show. Thea was not yet convinced.

'We really are,' added Morgan. 'Obviously.'

'Obviously,' echoed Fenella, and all the girls nodded, murmuring their agreement. 'It's just that after what the boys said . . . we thought there might be a . . .'

'A what?'

'A spirit, Miss.'

Thea immediately thought of Claire's story of the young woman rumoured to haunt Silk House, the visions she herself had experienced, the unease that had been building within her – but she wasn't about to relay any of that to the girls. 'Come on, now; you're all sensible enough to know that's absurd, right? You probably frightened yourselves silly,' Thea said, relenting a fraction. 'If Joy's scream was anything to go by.'

'That was because of Isis, Miss,' Joy said. 'I thought she was a ghost.' Her face reddened.

'Well, I'm not going to lecture you on the importance of sleep for your schoolwork and general wellbeing. But I will say this: you are all doubtless well aware that you've been specially selected for your abilities and intelligence, but that does not mean you don't have to work hard for your results. You won't get there on natural talent alone. Ignore silly distractions and don't let yourselves down, girls,' she said, a gentler note entering her voice.

They shuffled uneasily and Thea could see that they had taken in what she was saying. They were conscientious girls, wouldn't have been enrolled at the school if they weren't, even Sabrina, who had shown herself to be more likely to push the boundaries than the others. 'I'm surprised to have to remind you of that; as the first intake of girls to the school, you are going to be subject to more scrutiny than the rest of the pupils. The slightest step out of line will have consequences, no matter how unfair that might seem.' Her words hit home, judging by the remorseful expressions on the girls' faces. 'I'm not going to ask whose idea it was,' she added, 'for as far as I'm concerned you are all responsible. But . . .' She paused, letting them feel the weight of her words. 'As it is a first misdemeanour I will let it go this time.' The girls exchanged looks of relief. 'Any further misbehaviour, however, and I will have no choice but to refer the matter to the headmaster.'

'Yes, Miss,' they chorused, relief evident on all of their faces. 'We promise.'

'I also do not want you to speak of this to any of the other girls. I certainly don't want anyone else getting any foolish ideas.'

They all nodded, meeting her eyes now.

She was about to dismiss them when Fenella spoke up. 'There's something that we haven't told you about last night.' She hesitated. 'It's pretty intense, Miss.'

'Well, go on, then,' Thea said.

'It did spell out something. To begin with, I thought it was a word: *trust*. But then I realised it was your name, literally – *T Rust*.'

'*Literally*,' echoed the other girls.

Thea ignored a sudden chill that ran down her spine. 'Well, I think we should take that with a pinch of salt, don't you?' Her tone was brisk. 'Any one of you could have been manipulating things.' She refused to countenance the thought that there was anything more to it than the girls' hijinks.

TWENTY-SEVEN

April 1769, London

When the patterns emerged from the loom, Mary caught her breath at their beauty, for they were even more alluring than she had dared to imagine. She had returned to the weaver's house after a fortnight, unable to wait a moment longer to see the progress that Bridget had made.

The lustre of the silk and the delicate colours made the flowers seem almost as real as the blooms she had picked from the hedgerows to inspire her. The fabric on the loom had a pale green background, as if it had taken its tone from the first fuzz of spring on a willow tree. Woven into this were columbine, cornflower and campion, stitchwort and traveller's joy, with the occasional fat caterpillar caught in the act of nibbling on a leaf, the scarlet carapace of a ladybird resting on the curl of a flower petal, the yellow-and-black body and translucent wings of a bee gathering pollen.

''Tis unlike anything I've seen before,' said Bridget. 'Though I admit you have achieved a lifelike design. But insects?' she shuddered. 'Who might desire to wear a gown or waistcoat with those common creatures upon them?'

Mary kept her counsel. 'Thank you, Bridget. It is indeed remarkable to see the design emerge so. I am much obliged for your skill and dedication.'

The woman grunted and bent over the loom once more, 'Come back in a week; I should have the work completed by then.'

Dismissed, Mary gathered her things and reluctantly returned home. The days would pass slowly, for though she had new designs to work on, she could scarcely contain herself until the fabric was ready.

When she saw the second design, which featured the witches' weeds she had become so enamoured by, she was left speechless. The purple belladonna and freckled foxglove woven on a rich cream background seemed to glow in the dim light of the cottage. 'A fabric designed to be seen by the light of a thousand candles,' Frances said as Mary showed it to her later, for Mary had bargained with Bridget for a small amount of silver thread to be woven through the cloth and it glittered as it caught the sunlight filtering through the window.

'And see this?' Mary said proudly. Tucked away in a corner of the pattern was a tiny lace-weaving spider – her own private joke – spinning its silvery web.

Pretty but deadly. 'Did you know that in ancient Egypt spiders were associated with the goddess Neith? That they were seen as spinners and weavers of destiny?'

Frances narrowed her eyes. 'I trust you are right in this, sister.'

Mary refused to countenance any doubt. She imagined a lady with perhaps a profane sense of humour and a sharp intelligence who might be delighted by such an unconventional pattern and desire it for a gown. There would not be another like it in all of England, she was certain.

'I shall send one to Mr Hollander by the next stage. With an account for the weaving.' She stroked both fabrics, unable to tear her gaze away from them. 'Which of you beauties should I let go first?'

'The belladonna,' said Frances firmly. 'For it unsettles me to have it here.'

Mary gave her a puzzled look. 'Bridget O'Neill said something similar when I collected it from her. Said she had troubled dreams almost every night after working on it, barely slept, so she claimed. 'Twas why it was ready so soon – said she could not wait to get it out of the house. Though I never would have credited you with such superstitions, Frances?'

'In truth, I cannot explain the reason for it, but I would rather you send that one first,' her sister replied.

'Of course, then, it is decided.' Mary wrapped it carefully in a layer of rough cotton, and then in several layers of brown paper, securing the parcel with string after she had written the account and tucked it inside.

'Let us hope that payment is soon forthcoming,' Frances said.

TWENTY-EIGHT

Now

The next afternoon, once lessons had finished for the day but the girls were still in the prep room at the main school doing their homework, Thea sat at the desk in her study. The house was quiet, the staff who prepared the girls' supper had yet to arrive and Thea had seen no evidence of the Dame, though she knew she was likely to be somewhere in the house. She worked away steadily, making notes and flipping through the textbooks that lay scattered across her desk.

Her students had whipped through the first topic much faster than she had anticipated, and she had some catching up to do if she was to stay ahead of them. She planned to speak to her head of department about it; she didn't want them working so quickly that they missed the detail and nuance of the subject. It was exhilarating to teach such bright kids, if rather exacting.

Then came the distant sound of a piano. She listened for a moment, soothed by the sound, then it occurred to her to wonder who was playing, for the girls were all at school. Something soft brushed up against her ankles. Isis. The cat curled around her and Thea bent down to ruffle its fur, was rewarded with a plaintive meow. She straightened, then listened again, hearing a door slam at the back of the house. The music had stopped. It was time for a break, so she made her way down the stairs to investigate.

'Hello,' she called. 'Is that you, Dame Hicks?'

A muffled sob or perhaps a cough. Slow footsteps. A dry rustle, like reeds in the wind.

'Hello,' Thea called again, louder this time.

The Dame emerged from the gloom, her skirt caught up with leaves and twigs trailing behind her.

'Is everything okay?' Thea asked.

The Dame turned to Thea. 'Dead,' she said flatly. 'All dead.'

Arctic air from outside blasted down the passageway. 'What? Who's dead?' she asked.

'The fish. The goldfish. Every last one. Poisoned.'

'Are you sure? Perhaps the cold weather got them?'

'Don't be silly. They'd survive even if the pond was frozen over. No. They were poisoned. Go and see for yourself.'

When Thea reached the pond she shone the beam from the torch on her phone towards the water. The Dame had been right. The bloated corpses of the fish floated there, white bellies glowing in the light. She knelt down. It was hard to see, but she thought their gills had a green tinge. It did indeed look very much like poison.

Then something else caught her eye. Glowing iridescently in the light from her torch. She didn't have to get any closer to work out what it was. Ghost mushrooms. Exactly the same as the ones she and the girls had seen in the woods. Could someone have used them to deliberately poison the fish? As she returned to the house, she shone a light on the garden bed. The plants were shrivelled and brown, even the rosemary. Not two days ago, they had been glossy and upright, the winter herbs thriving.

'The plants too,' Thea said as she saw the Dame waiting in the doorway. 'Even the rosemary. And that's almost impossible to kill.'

The Dame was agitated now, rubbing her hands together over and over. 'Tell the girls not to go out there, that it's out of bounds for the time being. We don't know if it's harmful to humans as well.'

Who would do this? And why? Was it a stupid prank by one of the girls, or were some of the college staff so fearful of their presence that they were doing their best to scare them away? Was it linked to the beetles in the tea canister, the piles of dirt in her study? Was there some kind of poison in the house itself? The thought was ridiculous, but try as she might, Thea couldn't shake it.

She knew she would have to speak to the girls at supper about the garden and what the Dame had discovered there. She didn't want to alarm them – heaven knew how suggestible a group of teenage girls were, especially after the Ouija nonsense – but they were clever enough not to be fobbed off with excuses as to why the back garden was now out of bounds. The truth – or a sanitised version of it at least – was the best way to proceed.

After the supper plates had been laid out – piles of toasted sandwiches and jugs of milk – Thea clapped for quiet. Without going into detail, she asked the girls not to use the garden until the pond had been drained. 'It appears that something has happened to cause the fish to die,' she said. 'There's probably a simple explanation, but until we know what it is, I would ask you not to go out there.'

There was a hubbub of voices, some worried, some indignant, most asking to know more.

'Miss?' Joy had put up her hand. 'I didn't think much of it at the time, but after hockey practice last week I overheard Mr Pope and Mr Battle discussing whether or not us girls would last the year. Mr Battle said he'd be surprised if we did. Do you think that's got anything to do with this? Is someone trying to scare us off?'

Thea felt sudden rage course through her. Whatever their private thoughts, how dare those men talk about such things in front of the students? 'Not at all, Joy.' She did her best to keep her temper in check while reassuring the girls. 'That's idle talk, and we'd be best to ignore it, don't you agree?' She'd be damned if she let anyone scare these girls away. They had as much right to be there as the boys.

'Yes, Miss.'

There was a murmur of conversation and she held up her hand to silence them again. 'Please. There's nothing more to discuss at this stage. Finish your supper and then you're free until lights out.' She looked across the room and saw that the door that led to the kitchen was ajar. Standing behind it was Moira, the kitchenhand.

After the girls had gone to their rooms, Thea went to the kitchen, finding Moira wiping down the benches.

'Have you lived in the town for long, Moira?' she asked.

The woman stopped wiping. 'All my life.'

'So, you'd be aware of the house's history?'

'A little. It's been many different things over the years.'

'Is there anything that I should know?'

'Well . . .' She hesitated.

'Yes?'

'Some people reckon it's cursed. I don't, of course,' she said quickly. 'Else I wouldn't be working here, would I?'

'What kind of a curse?' Thea asked.

'Well, no one can settle here. They say the house wants something. Or wants to be rid of something.'

Great, first Pope and Battle, and now the house.

'What on earth do you mean by that?' she asked.

'There have been fires . . .'

'Yes, but any old house, especially one that dates back several hundred years, would likely have experienced a fire at some point in time,' she argued.

'And the ghost,' Moira added.

'Oh, I know about that, but honestly . . . aren't those kinds of stories made up to attract business, not keep it away?' Thea replied, her voice calmer than she felt.

Moira shrugged.

'Tell me, do you know anything about a maid who once worked here . . . I think she might have been accused of witchcraft. Not long after the house was first built.'

'Never heard of that,' Moira answered. 'But it wouldn't surprise me. There's any number of women who were accused of witchery around these parts. That's why no one goes to Grovely Wood after dark if they can help it.'

'Yes,' said Thea. 'The maid's name was in a book about the Handsel sisters.'

'P'raps you might be able to find out more?' Moira suggested.

'I'm going to try,' said Thea. She hesitated before adding, 'There was a symbol in the book too.'

'Oh yes?'

'Of an arrow.'

Moira flicked her left wrist self-consciously.

'Do you know any more about that, Moira?' Thea asked softly.

'The women of the old families . . .' she began. 'The ones that can trace their ancestors in the town and hereabouts more than several centuries back . . .'

'Go on.'

'I suppose we all support each other, kind of like a network. We recognise each other by it. My mother has hers on a necklace . . .'

'A network?'

'Yes.'

TWENTY-NINE

Now

Thea made another appointment at the records office, more curious than ever to try to get to the bottom of things. As she opened the second folder, her eyes lit on a newspaper cutting. It was folded and yellowed with age and as she spread it open, the headline blared: 'Up in smoke: woman killed in fire at historic Oxleigh house.' She pored over the faded print, which told of a fire that was believed to have started in the kitchen but that the cause was unknown. A man in his early thirties and two young girls had escaped the blaze, rescued by a couple of courageous neighbours, but firemen had tragically found the mother deceased when they entered the smouldering bedroom several hours later.

She checked the date: 15 October 1969. Fifty years ago next week. Thea remembered the earlier fire she had read about in the book in the school library. Two fires. Moira had mentioned that. It wasn't such an unusual thing in a centuries-old house, she reminded herself sternly. But two dead women as a result? Even over a span of several centuries, that was more of a concern.

The items in the folder then skipped forward to the 1980s, with a deed of purchase showing that the house had changed hands. Again, not unexpected, but it did appear to have had a number of owners, especially in recent times. No one had stayed there for long it seemed.

It was as though the layers of the house's history were pressed together like a book, with some of the print – past events – leaching through the pages. It occurred to her that the top one, on which the new history was being written, was now partly her story – hers and the girls'.

It was nearly closing by the time Thea reached the end of the folder, and she spent the final few minutes flipping through the remaining pages. What intrigued her most were the beginnings of the house. Call it a historian's instinct, but she couldn't shake a nagging feeling that something had happened then, something in its early years. She needed to find that book again, the one from the school library; perhaps the answers she sought would be there.

She turned to the final page. Another newspaper report, this time from 2001. 'Singular Spectres' blared the headline from the *Oxleigh Gazette*. It was a story on the number of ghosts reported to have been seen in the county. It led with a report from a guest staying at Silk House – from a time when it was a hotel – who claimed her room was haunted. By a young woman sitting on the end of her bed. Wearing a hooded cloak.

As Thea read this, she found herself barely able to breathe. She looked away, at the prosaic surroundings of the small room, and then back again to make sure she had seen what she thought she had. No mistake. A detailed description of the cloaked woman – she'd only seen in a dream, she reminded herself – sitting on the end of the bed. Thea went to the window and looked out. While she had been in the records office, the sky had turned a lowering grey, rain threatening in the thick clouds that blotted out the sun. It was as though there were a lid on the land, closing in and pressing down, stifling her.

When it was time to leave, she pulled on a pair of woollen gloves and wrapped a scarf about her neck, wondering about the implications of what she had discovered. Was the house really haunted? Was there a connection to a maid accused of witchcraft? Did she even believe such a thing was possible? And, more importantly, if she did, what was she supposed to do about it? She shivered in the cold air and hurried to Claire's car, blasting the heater as soon as she had turned the engine over, but it was a long while before she felt warm again.

~

'I wonder if I might have a word?' Thea asked, coming across Gareth Pope in the staffroom the next morning.

The PE teacher, who was in the process of making himself a coffee, turned towards her, kettle in hand, almost spilling hot water over his shoes. He made a last-minute correction and hit the mug as he had originally intended. He filled it and then raised his eyebrows at her.

'Want one?' he asked.

Thea shook her head. 'I'll get straight to the point. While I have no patience for idle gossip, I have been made aware of the fact that you and Mr Battle share a common belief that the girls are not cut out for Oxleigh College. That you have your doubts about the benefits of having girls at the school at all and have been voicing your opinions in their hearing.'

He looked astonished. 'Absolutely nothing of the sort. If anything I was defending them to old Battle. He's the one who's unhappy about the changes, not me.'

'There have been a number of incidents at Silk House, of which I am sure you are aware. If I were to find out that anyone from within the school had anything to do with them . . .'

He looked at her, bemused. 'Are you threatening me, Miss Rust?'

'I also understand there was a hockey practice yesterday,' she said, changing the subject. She had made her point.

He raised the mug to his lips, took a sip and contemplated her. 'I wondered why you had given it a miss.'

'It didn't appear on my schedule.' She did her best not to let her animosity show in her voice. 'And I am at a loss to understand how that could be.'

'You wouldn't be implying that I deliberately left you off the list, would you?' he asked.

'Well, did you?'

'I'm offended that you even have to ask. Of course I didn't. I'm not that petty.'

Before Thea could decide whether or not to believe him, Claire breezed into the staffroom, almost colliding with them both. 'Thea! I've got a free period later – fancy a catch-up?'

Thea nodded, turning away from Gareth. She needed to confide in someone about what was going on at the house, if only to convince herself she was reading more into events than was sensible.

~

'So, let me get this straight. Someone has poisoned the fish, you found mushrooms scattered on the ground, piles of dirt in your study, beetles in the tea, and you think you've seen a ghost?'

Claire was incredulous.

'Dreamed about a ghost,' Thea corrected her. 'There's a difference.'

'And several hundred years ago a maid living there was somehow involved in witchcraft? Look, I can understand that the fish thing is concerning, but the ghost?' She held up a hand. 'I know it was only a dream, but was she like the one I mentioned?'

Thea nodded. 'Kind of.'

'I thought you told me you don't believe in all that nonsense.'

'I don't, but you weren't the only one freaked out by whatever it was we saw as we were driving home from that party,' she reminded her.

'Okay, *that* was scary, but come on . . . We'd had a couple of drinks and it was pretty bloody misty. It could have been anything. It all seems a bit silly now.'

'I'd had a few glasses of mulled wine, but over about four hours,' Thea protested. 'And I know it wasn't just the mist. Besides that, I've heard footsteps on the stairs when I know there's no one but me in the house, the piano playing during the day when the girls are at school . . . I'm having trouble staying asleep at night – I keep waking up at midnight, two, three a.m. I'm not sure I can take much more of it, to be completely honest.'

They were walking side by side along the path that skirted the playing fields and led to Summerbourne. Claire stopped and turned to Thea. 'Do you think – and I mean this in the kindest possible way – that the pressure might be getting to you? After all, you've been thrown in at the deep end, expected to step into the new housemistress's shoes and look after fourteen teenage girls, all of whom are new to the school, as are you. A school, I might add, that has never seen girls in its classrooms until now. We're doing our best to drag the place into the twenty-first century, but it was never going to be easy.'

'Thirteen,' Thea reminded her. 'Thirteen girls. Anyway, I've been wondering if it might be sabotage. The fish thing, I mean. I know there are some people at the school who really don't want us here – Mr Battle, for one.'

'I suppose it's possible,' she said, pursing her lips. 'But, really? I've always thought Battle's bark was far worse than his bite, but then I guess you never really know what anyone's capable of until they're pushed. Are you going to bring it up with Dr Fox?'

Thea's shoulders drooped. 'He's already decided that I'm a liability after what happened with Sabrina. Adding my paranoia to that isn't going to improve his opinion of me. Besides, I don't have any proof of anything, and Mr Battle's been at the school forever, when I've only been here five minutes. I don't want to make things worse. But it's not only me I'm worried about – what if the girls aren't safe there, in the house? There's definitely something that doesn't want us there.' She stopped. 'Oh Christ, now I really do sound as though I've lost the plot.'

Claire regarded her seriously. 'We should call on a friend of mine. Fiona Spanswick. She's not far away, actually.' She got out her phone and tapped out a quick text.

Her phone beeped in reply a few moments later.

'Great, we can drop by now. She's only up the road. We can be there in fifteen minutes, tops.'

Mystified, Thea followed her friend along the path, eventually reaching Summerbourne and coming to a halt outside a small thatched cottage.

An elegant woman dressed in a soft, oversized black sweater, well-cut trousers and velvet slippers answered the door. Her fine salt-and-pepper hair was caught up in a loose chignon and pearls glowed at her earlobes. She greeted Claire like an old friend, enveloping her in a hug, and then smiled warmly at Thea as Claire introduced her.

'Sorry to call out of the blue, but we were passing and I thought . . . well, actually I thought you might be able to help us out,' Claire said as they came into the kitchen.

Was the woman some kind of counsellor? Thea flinched. She *really* didn't want to talk about herself, and certainly not to a stranger.

'Oh yes?' Fiona asked, filling a kettle at the sink and getting three mugs down from a cupboard.

'Sorry, Thea, I should have explained. Fiona is the curate at St Margaret's, the church in Oxleigh,' said Claire. 'She and my mother have been friends for years. Fiona's been like an auntie to me since I've been living here.'

'Don't you have to wear a uniform – a collar, or something?' Thea asked.

Fiona smiled indulgently. 'Not always.'

Thea was still none the wiser as to how Fiona might help.

'There's more to the job than hatching, matching and dispatching,' she said as if she'd read Thea's thoughts. She put the mugs on the table and indicated a jug near Thea's elbow. 'Not that many people would know. Help yourself to milk and sugar. I should have some bikkies here somewhere as well.' She turned her back and began rummaging in a cupboard.

Thea went to reach for a mug and started as she saw the design on each of them. Watercolour images of star-shaped purple flowers. Almost exactly the same as the ones on the strip of silk that she had found in the old book.

'My little joke to myself,' said Fiona who had turned back and caught Thea staring at them. 'Belladonna. Deadly nightshade.'

Thea flinched at the mention of the plant, but Fiona, who was busy ripping open a packet of biscuits and tipping them onto a plate, didn't seem to have noticed.

'Gingersnap?' she offered, pushing the plate towards Thea as she took a seat opposite them. 'Go on, they're really good.' She leaned forward, wrapping her hands around a mug, covering up the flowers. 'Now, what can I do for you?'

Haltingly, for she felt a little foolish talking about the events in the calmness of Fiona's cottage, Thea told her what had been going on. 'The likely explanation is that someone is trying to scare us off,' she said. 'Or maybe some of the boys are playing tricks. But part of me wonders if there might be a different cause.' Thea couldn't believe she was entertaining the idea of something paranormal. A few months ago she would have scoffed at the idea, but now, with everything that had gone on, she wasn't so certain. 'And there's the soil.'

'The soil?'

'It keeps coming up from the floorboards in my study. Battle – the porter – said it reminded him of the earth that's sometimes used at burials.'

'I see,' said Fiona when she had finished. She flicked a sidelong glance at Claire and then returned her attention to Thea, as if weighing her next words carefully. 'I'd say you've a restless soul.'

Thea sat back in surprise. *Restless?*

'An evil spirit,' said Claire dramatically, her eyes wide.

Fiona tutted. 'Not necessarily, Claire,' she chided. 'But there's definitely something that's disturbing the peace, by the sounds of it. Sometimes it can seem as if there is – for want of a better word – a *presence* in a place, particularly an old building, or one where something catastrophic might have happened.'

'I've been trying to investigate its history,' Thea interrupted.

'And?'

'Well, there was a fire, in the 1960s. A woman died. Then centuries before I think a maid might have been accused of witchcraft, but I can't find out much more. And there *were* reports of other people seeing a ghost, but that was ages ago. Actually, there were two fires – one several hundred years ago, and a woman died then too. You don't think they could be connected?' she asked.

'*Two* catastrophic events,' said Claire.

There isn't going to be a third, Thea vowed silently. *Not if I can help it.*

'It's possible, I suppose,' said Fiona. 'Anyway, as I was saying, certain people are more sensitive to such things, they pick up on vibrations that most of us don't.' She blew on her tea, rippling its surface. 'It's as if they act as a channel to the past, or sometimes the spirit can even attach itself to them.'

Claire whistled. 'That's a bit bonkers.'

Thea shuddered. She was surprised to hear such opinions coming from a woman of religious conviction, especially one as normal-seeming as Fiona, but then maybe it actually made some kind of sense. If Fiona believed in a higher power, then surely it stood to reason that she might believe in other unseen forces too.

'And you think that I might be such a person?' she asked.

'It's certainly a possibility.'

'So, what can I do? I'm worried about the effect this might start to have on the girls.'

'Not to mention yourself, my dear. Now, what Claire knows, but you most probably don't, is that I am part of a team within the diocese known as the Ministry of Deliverance.' She smiled benignly, the outer edges of her eyes crinkling. 'It sounds rather ominous, but I promise it isn't.'

'I've never heard of such a thing,' Thea said, mystified.

'We don't exactly advertise. Think of it as a healing ministry, if that helps. There is both major and minor deliverance. I undertake the minor sort: essentially, I help cleanse a building – or a person – of the spirits that might be said to haunt it,' Fiona said. 'It happens more often than most people realise. Sometimes there is an energy left behind in the fabric of a building, in the bricks and mortar, that needs clearing.'

'You mean like a poltergeist?' Thea asked.

Fiona nodded, putting down her mug and shifting in her seat. 'Kind of.'

'And what's a major deliverance?'

'Above my pay grade, my dear. Essentially, demonic possession.'

'Exorcism?'

A chill ran through Thea as Claire uttered the word.

'We prefer deliverance ministry,' said Fiona in a matter-of-fact tone.

Thea was astounded that such things even existed, but decided that at this point she would give anything a go. 'It will have to be when the girls are at school. Actually, when there's no one there. There's another woman, the housekeeper, but I don't think she'll be too amenable to such a thing.'

'Of course. Be assured of my discretion.'

They decided on a time the following week when the house was likely to be unoccupied, and on the Dame's day off. 'It'll take at least a couple of hours,' said Fiona. 'It's a large building and I will need access to every room. I will have a couple of helpers with me as well; they've all done this kind of thing before.'

'And what if it doesn't work?' Thea asked.

'Then I can refer you to a psychologist.'

'It's not in my head,' Thea insisted. 'I'm not making this up.'

'I believe you, my dear,' Fiona reassured her. 'I'm here to help.'

As they were making arrangements, Thea caught sight of a clock on the wall. 'Oh Christ – whoops, sorry. We have to get back. I'm supposed to be teaching the Upper Fifths in twenty minutes.'

They left in a flurry of thank-yous and goodbyes, but as the door was about to close on them a glint of something caught Thea's eye and she glanced down. The silver embroidery on Fiona's slippers. She hadn't been able to make out the design earlier, but now it was starkly clear. Arrows. The same as on the keys, the Dame's brooch, Moira's tattoo, and the stone at the lookout. The network of women. Thea didn't know whether to be reassured or concerned that Fiona seemed to be one of them.

THIRTY

May 1769, Oxleigh

'Have you seen her? Alice, I mean?' Rowan asked Prudence when she returned to the house.

She had come from the butcher's, waiting outside until Tommy emerged with his handcart, about to make his deliveries. 'I fear that you have been avoiding me,' she had said bluntly.

He stopped, pulled his cart over to the side of the road.

'I swear I have not,' he said. 'The other boy has been taken ill and I have been doing his work as well as my own. I've not finished until long after dark these past weeks.'

'Tommy.'

She could scarce bear to see the hurt enter his eyes at her distant tone.

'Rowan, what is it? I believed we were friends. Rowan?' he asked again when she did not reply. 'I cannot imagine that I have done anything to upset you but if I have, then do tell me and I can make my apologies.'

He was so sincere that she had almost believed him.

She kicked at a clump of tansy with the toe of her boot. 'You . . . and Alice,' she said, unable to contain herself any longer.

'Me and Alice?' he asked, a bewildered expression on his face. 'We have but a passing acquaintance. Has something happened to her?'

'Surely she has told you herself.' Rowan glared in his direction but her fierceness seemed to bounce off him and he continued to appear puzzled.

'No. I have not spoken with her. Not recently, that is.'

'She is with child,' she whispered, mindful of passers-by.

Now he seemed genuinely shocked. 'I still do not understand why that should be any business of mine.'

'Oh come now, are you certain of that?'

Realisation and then anger flashed across his face. 'I do not know who has been spreading such rumours but if I find out I will give them the drubbing they deserve.' He was indignant. 'I cannot credit that you believe such twattle. I thought better of you, Rowan Caswell. Who told you this?' he added, insistent. 'Who?'

His expression was as clear and cold as a pail of well water. She should never have doubted him. She shook her head. 'I appear to have been mistaken, my apologies. I must go.' She stepped past him and fled towards the house, not hearing him call after her.

'Alice? Is she about?' Rowan demanded of Prudence again. The lady's maid had recovered from the illness that had kept her abed, though she now conducted herself with an even sourer expression than the one she had when Rowan had first arrived at the merchant's house.

Prudence sat in front of a bowl of apples, peeling the skin from them in long strips and chewing the end of one. 'I believe she is attending to the mistress,' she replied calmly. 'What is it you require so urgently of her?'

'I lent her my mittens,' said Rowan. 'And it is fair freezing outside without them. 'Tis a bitter wind that is blowing.' She shivered to make the lie more believable.

Prudence raised an eyebrow but returned to the apple in her hand. 'Well, you are inside now. Come and warm yourself by the fire if you're cold. But mind you don't stay too long, for the table needs setting for the mistress's dinner. You can ask Alice about the mittens this afternoon.'

'Yes,' replied Rowan, placing a cloth on the range before resting her hands on it. 'I will not have need of them before then.'

Prudence clucked. 'I hope that is all it is about. Do not think that I haven't noticed that the two of you are barely civil with each other. When he returns, the master will not tolerate an uneasy household.'

That is if he was ever there to see it, thought Rowan in annoyance, for they had not heard from him for nearly a fortnight, though he had been expected to return from this latest journey within a week.

Rowan had to wait to confront Alice until much later that day, eventually coming upon her in the mistress's bedchamber as Alice was readying it for the night. 'I saw Tommy today,' Rowan said, watching her reaction carefully. 'He claims to have no knowledge of your situation. Tell me, how can that be?' Rowan only just managed to keep her temper in check.

'He is lying,' said Alice quickly, but Rowan heard the tiniest hesitation in her voice.

Rowan said nothing, waiting to hear more.

'He has forsaken me, will have nothing more to do with me. Curse him to the heavens.'

Alice sat down abruptly on the bed that she had been airing and Rowan noticed a tear glint on her eyelash and then track its way along the plane of her cheek. Rowan's earlier anger left her. 'I am expected to believe you? Come now, I am not that much of a simpleton. But I know you are no common doxy.' Rowan sat down next to Alice, who did not move away at her nearness. 'Who is it really? The master?' she hazarded.

'I pray you might show me a little kindness,' said Alice, her hands twisting rapidly in her lap. 'Though I likely do not deserve it. Can I trust you to tell no one?'

Rowan took her hand, squeezed it gently. 'You know you can.'

'You were correct in your first guess,' she said choking back a sob. ''Tis his. He insisted that Mistress Hollander was no use to him, that he wished we could be together, that he desired me above all others. But all that has changed now that she is with child. He has what he wants – a legitimate heir.'

'Oh Alice,' said Rowan, as the implication of her words sank in.

'He cannot find out the truth of my condition, for he will cast me out, of that I have no doubt. And I have nowhere to go.' She sobbed harder now. 'I can't go to St Peter and Paul.'

Rowan shuddered at the thought of the town's workhouse – named after two of the apostles, but as far from saintly as one could possibly imagine – on the edges of the town. She'd been in Oxleigh long enough to hear tales of the beatings and near-starvation conditions within its thick stone walls. Alice would not last the year there, she was sure of it, such was the rate of sickness and disease.

'You know what it is to want to make something of yourself. Would you deny me that chance?' Alice begged.

'I am not the one who got into this position,' Rowan said, although even as she said it, she felt some sympathy for the girl. If Patrick Hollander had wanted Alice, there would have been little the maid could have done to stop him, willing or not. She thought hard. 'I doubt that we could conceal the nature of your condition for long. And you certainly could not go away to have the baby.'

'You are able to make a draught to bring about a baby; are you yet able to brew one to help loosen one not yet fully formed?' Alice asked, taking great hitching gulps of air.

Rowan sucked in a breath. It was the one request she most feared, for it would trouble her conscience greatly to be responsible for snuffing out a life before it had scarce begun. She remembered her mother being called upon for just such a medicine, the narrowing of her eyes and the set of her shoulders as she prepared it. 'I thought you were suspicious of such sorcery?' Rowan replied, not giving her an answer one way or the other. 'You have been the first to accuse me in times past.'

'I know. I am so very sorry for that. You must believe me,' Alice pleaded with her.

'There's plenty of women found themselves in trouble,' her mother had said. 'But I cannot say such a thing pleases me, and there is a danger if it has gone too long.'

Rowan tried to remember how long exactly that was. 'When did you last have your courses?' she asked Alice.

'Early this new year.'

What would her mother have done, if presented with this? Not for the first time, Rowan wished she were there to dispense advice. It was one thing to be asked to help with the creating of life, but another entirely to assist in the ending of it.

'Can you do it?' Alice asked, her expression a mix of fear and hope. 'Is there still time?'

Not quite believing she was doing so, Rowan nodded slowly. It was for the best for both Alice and Caroline, for were Caroline to discover her husband's perfidy it might destroy her, would likely destroy the entire household. 'We must be quick, for every day that passes, the baby grows stronger within you. It is not without considerable risk. Are you certain that this is what you want?'

Alice slumped on the bed. 'What choice do I have?'

'As you wish. I will search for the ingredients, though I may need to obtain some from the apothecary. Have you the money to pay?'

Alice nodded, sniffing. 'I have a little saved. How much will you charge?'

Rowan looked at her in sympathy. 'I will make no charge. But the apothecary will.'

'Thank you.' Her voice was meek, small, no hint of the sneer it so often contained. She was about to say something else, but Rowan cut her off. 'Let us hope that it is not too late,' she said. 'For if it is there will be trouble for us both.'

~

The next morning there was still no sign nor word of her master's return. Rowan was relieved to have only light duties while he was away, for she was able to hurry through her morning tasks and then make her way to the apothecary's shop. First, however, she went to the churchyard, for the vital ingredient growing there. She would need to dry it and grind it to a powder, but would only require a tiny amount for the draught to do its work. Indeed, if she used too much it could cause death and not only in that which was unwanted.

Rowan saw the tree as soon as she entered the iron gate. Tall, dense and evergreen, with thick needle-like leaves and crimson berries. The leaves were poisonous, but the berries were her desire. She was on the point of reaching up to gather a handful when she saw a movement from behind a tombstone. She hesitated, for she did not wish to be caught in the act. Were someone to see her gathering yew berries it would be enough to start a wildfire of rumour that could perhaps even see her driven from the town.

The clergyman appeared. 'Do you require assistance?' he asked. Then, looking at her closely, 'I don't believe we have made each other's acquaintance.'

'Rowan Caswell, sir,' she said, giving him a deferential bob. 'I am the maid-of-all-work at Hollander's. The silk merchant.'

'I do indeed know Mr Hollander, though I wish perhaps he were more regular in his attendance at church,' he replied.

'Well, he travels often, sir.'

'So I understand. Now what might your business be here today?'

Rowan cast around for an explanation. She had no wish to reveal her purpose to a minister – he would surely bring the full wrath of the Lord down upon her if he had the slightest suspicion.

'A shortcut,' she said, thinking even as she did so that it sounded a poor excuse. 'To the watermill.'

He frowned at her and she held her breath. Would he believe her tale?

'I suppose there is no harm in that,' he said, still regarding her suspiciously.

'Good day to you, sir,' Rowan said, gathering her skirts and continuing onwards. She was forced to walk past the tree, didn't dare to glance back to see if he was watching her progress.

She made her way to the river path and ambled slowly along. After sufficient minutes had elapsed for it to be acceptable for her to return, as if indeed she had been to the watermill, she turned around and once again entered the church gate. This time she looked about carefully and, finding no sign of anyone, reached up and snatched some of the berries, hiding them in the pocket that hung from her waist.

She left them on the hearth in front of the kitchen fire overnight and judged that they would be sufficiently dried by the next morning. She explained their existence to Prudence as ingredients for a tincture for seven-year itch, and although the cook raised her eyebrows she did not say anything. After that, the draught would not take long to make. Rowan hoped she remembered her mother's instructions, the exact amount of each ingredient and how long to leave it before using. How and when it should be taken. What the effects would be.

She had some difficulty persuading the apothecary to supply her with the two remaining herbs she needed.

'Did you not come to me several months ago with a request? Pennyroyal and dittany, I believe it was?'

'Aye, sir.'

'And now you desire dried rue and more pennyroyal?' The sharpness of his glance told her that he had worked out what she was preparing. 'I fail to understand why you visit me again, clearly seeking an entirely different outcome from that of your first visit. Has your mistress bid you come again?'

Rowan shook her head. 'It . . . it is not for her.'

He sighed heavily. 'Very well,' he said, reaching for a ladder that rested at the back of the shop. 'But if it becomes known that I supplied ingredients in such a compound . . .' he threatened. 'If anything should go awry . . .'

'Not a soul will know,' she promised as she passed him a number of thin coins. 'I swear on my life.'

'And should that happen, I have never seen you before, nor will I again. This is not a kind of business I wish to involve myself in. But here,' he handed her a small volume bound in scarlet leather. '*Pow'rful Plants.* This will instruct you further.'

Rowan had not the courage to tell him that she could read very little. She would have only her memory of her mother's instructions on how to make this particular draught to rely on. She prayed it would be sufficient.

~

The next day, when she was satisfied that the herbs were ready, Rowan mixed the tincture with a small cupful of brandy that she had siphoned from the decanter that sat atop the master's escritoire. She gave it to Alice, with instructions to take a spoonful, morning and night, for a week. 'Let us hope it loosens your . . . problem. Do not be surprised if there is more blood than usual in your courses. You may have need of extra rags. And be sure to keep this hidden.'

The maid's face was pale. 'What if it does not work?' she asked.

'Then I am afraid that I cannot help you.'

THIRTY-ONE

May 1769, Oxleigh

Rowan was sweeping the passageway at the front of the house when the delivery arrived. She saw Jeremiah sever the string binding the parcel with a sharp pair of fabric shears and begin to unwrap the paper. As she swept through the shop floor, she drew closer to the bench, taking sidelong glances as often as she dared, curious to see what design this new fabric might portray, for proximity to the business of her employer had only served to increase her fascination with silks, taffetys and the like and the fine gowns that were made from such luxurious fabrics. Too often, she wondered what it might feel like to dress in such finery. At night she lulled herself to sleep with the imagining of it, how people might stop and stare at a fair-haired young woman in a glittering gown, that the young woman was her. She knew that it was a silly maid's fancy, but her dreams were filled with the lustre and rustle of silk.

Jeremiah pulled the fabric from the paper and rolled it onto the bench where it shimmered as if it were a living thing. Rowan stilled in her sweeping and blinked several times, at first not crediting her own eyes.

It was of the most sumptuous pale silk, woven through with silver, and Rowan found herself entranced by its dangerous beauty. But it was not the colour or the sheen of the fabric that caused Rowan to lose the breath from her lungs. It was the pattern itself, or rather the combination of herbs and flowers that twisted and curled across its snowy expanse, for they were the deep purple blooms of belladonna and monkshood, and the frothy white flowers of hemlock, intertwined with pink foxglove bells as luminous as if they had been plucked from the verge that morning. She was filled with a deep foreboding, yet she could not look away. 'Witches' weeds,' she whispered to herself. She was on the point of reaching out towards it when a voice interrupted her.

'What is this?'

She started, for Caroline had appeared in the doorway and Rowan had expected her mistress to be occupied with breakfast.

'I came to enquire if there was more milk for the porridge. What is this fabric, Jeremiah?' she asked, coming closer and pinching a fold of it between her fingers. 'I must know at once.' It seemed Caroline was as drawn to it as Rowan was.

'I am uncertain, mistress,' he replied. 'I have not yet consulted the order book.'

'I should very much like to have this for myself,' she said. 'I shall require a new gown for the upcoming Oxleigh cotillion and this is an ingenious design that pleases me greatly.' High colour flushed her cheeks and her eyes glittered at the prospect.

'Tell me, Rowan, you have knowledge of plants and the like. The foxglove I recognise, but what is the purple flower?'

Rowan hesitated, then spoke up. 'There are two, mistress. Belladonna and monkshood. They are powerful plants and a most fearful poison, especially when combined as they are here.'

Caroline laughed, and the sound chilled Rowan to the bone. 'What a novel idea! I'll warrant that no one has thought of such a thing before now.'

'Yes, mistress.' Rowan wanted to warn her of the danger she could see, for dark shadows had once again gathered in the room, though the sun shone brightly outside. She dared not reveal the full extent of her doubts for fear of suspicion falling on herself, and in any case, did not think her mistress would choose to believe her, for she gazed upon the fabric as if transfixed.

'I have no doubt that Mr Hollander will be amenable. Be sure to put it to one side for me.' She pulled her hand away with some reluctance.

'Very good, mistress,' Jeremiah said, retrieving the fabric and wrapping it again.

~

Later that afternoon, Rowan found herself back in the shop, which was closed for the dinner break. She wanted to see it once more, to reassure herself that it was merely a length of fabric, that she had been fanciful in imagining its sinister power. It lay on the counter, and as she unfurled the wrapping, she caught her breath. It was even more alluring than she remembered. She could see a tiny spider in a corner of the pattern, a beetle in another. Scarcely believing what she was doing, she grasped the pair of shears that lay on the counter and carefully snipped a strip about four inches wide from the end of the cloth, severing a spider's leg but capturing the belladonna and foxgloves. She replaced the shears, wrapped up the parcel and stuffed the purloined silk in her pocket. Hurrying from the room, she left the house and walked briskly in the direction of the millpond, for guilt at her action had settled in her stomach like a stone and she wished to take herself far from the house. If she were to be found out . . .

~

'Mistress Hollander wishes to see you.' Alice eyed Rowan from across the kitchen, and Rowan, who had returned from emptying the slops from the water closet, felt a fresh surge of the guilt that had kept her awake much of the night before.

Had her mistress discovered the theft? Was she to be thrown onto the street? Sent before the Salisbury assizes? She could not believe that she had been so foolish as to steal even the smallest snippet of fabric. She half-thought that she had taken the scissors to it in the hope that she might be able to work a spell to lessen its power, for she sensed a dark magic about it. However, the truth was that she wasn't entirely certain why she had taken it – the fabric seemed to wield a power over her that she could not begin to explain. It was as if the devil himself had cast his favour upon it.

When she had washed her hands in the scullery and tidied her hair away under her cap, she ascended the stairs to the morning room, approaching with trepidation. She stood near the door and gave a slight cough to alert her mistress to her presence.

'Ah, Rowan, come in, please. I have an errand for you.' Caroline smiled and Rowan's racing heart slowed. She found she was able to breathe again.

'Yes, mistress.'

'Take the fabric that arrived yesterday and deliver it to the mantua-maker. There is no time to waste, for it is a matter of weeks until the cotillion. Tell her that I shall call upon her forthwith to be fitted.'

Rowan hesitated, knowing that Jeremiah would not yet be at the shop.

'Get along then, girl. You have my permission to retrieve the parcel. I shall inform Jeremiah as to its whereabouts when I see him next.'

Rowan bobbed her understanding. 'Yes, mistress.'

When she slipped into the darkened shop, shadows once more seemed to chase her as she drew near to the shelves at the back. She scanned them for the fabric. At first, she could not see it, but then there was the crumpled, refolded paper on the top shelf. She reached up to retrieve it, staggering under the weight, for it was far heavier than she had expected and she had to hold it in her arms almost as one might carry an infant.

It was only a few yards to Mistress Pennyfeather's further along the high street. The mantua-maker's door was closed, and Rowan had to rap her knuckles hard upon it several times before it was answered.

'I'm come from the merchant's house, from Mistress Hollander,' she said to the young girl who opened the door. 'She bade me deliver this to Mistress Pennyfeather.'

''Tis awful early,' the girl replied. 'But you will find her already at work. You'd best come in.'

Rowan followed her into a room at the back of the house, where the mantua-maker sat, a dark vessel amid a sea of colourful silks.

Rowan explained the reason for her errand and placed the parcel on a table, her fingers trailing along it, reluctant to let it go, for its hold on her was tenacious. She remembered again the strip she had hidden under her mattress.

'She will need to come and see me to be fitted without delay,' said the mantua-maker without ceasing her stitching. 'For I already have several other gowns to complete and she has left me with little time in which to work.'

Rowan left, promising that her mistress would call in a few hours' time.

The mantua-maker worked day and night in the weeks leading up to the cotillion, for she was one of only two in the town and almost every woman attending the annual event had ordered a new gown. The town was a prosperous one, and each merchant desired to show off his good fortune, and what better way to do it than on the back of his wife?

Hollander's Fine Silks was also awash with customers, and both Jeremiah and Mr Hollander were kept busy supplying orders. 'I fear we shall have not a scrap of silk left to sell if this continues,' Jeremiah complained to Rowan as she swept the floors one morning.

'But if trade is brisk, then that surely is a good thing?' she replied.

He gave her a thin smile. 'One would hope so.'

~

Her mistress's gown was delivered early one afternoon. Caroline had gone out to call on a friend, and so was not the first to see it. Together – for the package weighed a great deal – Rowan and Alice carried it up to her chamber, laying it on the bed and unwrapping it.

When they had straightened it out flat against the coverlet, they both stood back, speechless. The fabric caught the light, the silver thread glistening like the gossamer of a spider's web and the bright purple and pink flowers stark against the cream background. The skirt was full, with a long train of fabric at the back that fell in folds from the shoulders. The waist was considerably larger than Caroline's other gowns, for she was now well into her confinement, but the bodice had been made with extra panels that could be removed once she returned to her normal size. 'I will not let that fact stop me from going,' Rowan had heard her declare to her husband as he questioned whether she might think again on her plans to attend the cotillion. 'I promise I shall begin my lying-in the very next day,' she had pleaded. 'But let me have a little fun first.' Patrick Hollander, for once, had not attempted to exert his will over her.

'It is as if it carries a light of its own,' Alice breathed, once they had regarded it for quite some time.

'Look, here,' Rowan said. 'The curve of the flowers is like that of the bodice; how clever.'

It was several moments before they could tear themselves away, but a bellow from Prudence had Alice scurrying down the back stairs towards the kitchen.

Rowan lingered a few moments longer, mesmerised. Then, before she knew what she was doing, she had untied the strings of her apron and loosened the fasteners on the front of her grey work dress, letting it drop to the floor.

As she stepped into the new gown, a shudder coursed through her. She knew she would certainly be beaten if she were caught, perhaps worse, and she was fearful of the power of the flowers, but she could do nothing to stop herself. Rowan was a similar height to her mistress, but slightly broader, and although the fabric stretched tightly across her shoulders and she did not have panniers at her hips, the gown fitted tolerably well, though she had to hold in the extra fabric at the waist. A small sigh escaped her lips, for the feel of the silk on her bare arms was deliciously cool in the warm room. The lace at the elbows and neck frothed like the cow parsley that grew in the hedgerows. Clad in such a fine gown, Rowan was a different person, a girl almost without blemish.

She took the few steps to the looking glass and pulled her cap from her head. As she removed the pins keeping it in place, her white-blonde hair fell about her shoulders, catching the light like the silver thread in the gown.

She turned to see the effect of the sack-back and its waterfall of fabric that cascaded from the shoulders and as she did so caught a shadow in a corner of the glass. A feeling of doom, as sudden and unexpected as a thunderclap, gripped her. The gown no longer seemed so alluring, for it was as if it were almost trying to possess her, as if a malevolent spirit were at work.

With trembling fingers, she unhooked the bodice and stepped out of the skirts, her fingernail catching on one of the tiny black spiders woven into the design. It was all she could do not to tear the material from her body in her haste to be free of it. She knew then that there was evil in the gown, whether in the design or the weaving of it, or both.

Should she warn her mistress? She knew she had little hope of convincing her to wear a different gown. And would it merely cause her to question exactly what kind of foresight her maid possessed, to claim that evil had been woven into such beautiful fabric?

Rowan carefully spread out the dress on the bed, smoothing out any wrinkles before hurriedly dressing in her own clothes. Never had her mousy wool skirts offered such reassurance.

~

By the week's end, Rowan had managed to convince herself that her fears were the result of an overwrought imagination, and that it was foolish to believe that evil could be captured in threads of silk, a design of flowers – no matter how deadly those flowers might be.

On the Saturday afternoon, Alice helped her mistress prepare for the cotillion, while earlier Rowan had laid out her master's favourite waistcoat – the one with the orange flowers that he had worn on the day he hired her – and a clean pair of breeches. Hearing a commotion in the passageway, she slipped from the kitchen to catch a glimpse of them as they left the house. Even in the dim light, the gown glowed and Rowan saw her mistress's face lit up with excitement. Patrick Hollander, too, gazed upon his wife admiringly. 'Only the best for my wife. You shall be the belle of the ball, my dear.'

Caroline laughed, 'Oh, hush now. With nary a waist to show for it, I think that unlikely.' But Rowan could see that she was pleased nonetheless.

A few minutes after her master and mistress had departed, Rowan took the opportunity to slip out the back door and along the passage that ran alongside the house next door. The evening was a fine one, and the sun had only just begun to set. The lively chatter of birds flying home to roost filled the air, which was scented with apple blossom from the trees at the bottom of the garden.

She hurried towards the river, where she had arranged to meet Tommy, for as well as wanting to see him, she had to share the burden of Alice's misfortune with someone.

He gathered her into his arms and she returned the embrace, savouring the feeling of comfort she found there. 'I spoke to Alice and she admitted that she had been lying when she said that you were responsible.'

'Why would she do such a thing in the first place? She is no better than a strumpet . . . begging your pardon.'

'I do not think it is that simple,' Rowan said.

'Who is it, then?'

Rowan hesitated, drew away from his arms. ''Tis Master Hollander.'

Tommy let out a breath. 'What is she to do?'

'She asked for my assistance . . .' Rowan bit her lip.

'Your assistance?' he asked. 'But what . . .' Then the realisation of her words began to dawn upon him. ''Tis not right. That's meddling with nature, that is.'

'What was I supposed to do? If I did not help her she would be thrown out, end up in the workhouse or worse, and she could make all manner of accusations against me; I know she is capable of such a thing. And then I would most likely be dismissed as well, for Master Hollander will not tolerate even a breath of such trouble. I am bound up in it.'

'But you would surely find work elsewhere,' he said, reaching for her hands.

'I am not so certain of that – some in the town have already come to suspect my knowledge, and it wouldn't take much for them to shun me entirely, to place the blame on me for disrupting the household. Anyway, it is too late – 'tis done.'

He regarded her for a while, making up his mind on the matter. Rowan held her breath.

'I'll stand by you no matter what happens,' he said eventually.

She breathed out and smiled gratefully at him. 'Tommy Dean, you are a true gentleman.'

'Unlike some who were born to that station,' he said darkly.

THIRTY-TWO

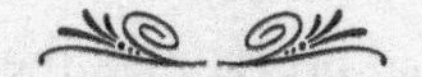

Now

Thea couldn't believe she'd agreed to it. The more she thought about it, the more it seemed utterly preposterous. Exorcism? People – and not just people, but ministers of the cloth – really did such things? This wasn't the Middle Ages, for heaven's sake, it was 2019. Superstition should have long been cast off. And yet, there was a small part of her that wondered – hoped, even – that it might just work, that the inexplicable, inconvenient and downright creepy happenings would stop and they could all get on with the business of school life. *Sometimes you don't need to see the evidence, to have all the facts, to believe in it*, she told herself. *You simply have to trust.*

Now, half an hour before Fiona was due to arrive, Thea sat in the empty house, listening to its creaks and groans, the gurgle of hot water pipes and the whistle of the wind as it rattled the windows in their frames. Her father would have scoffed at it all. She could hear his voice. 'Superstitious nonsense,' he would have said. Until recently, she would have agreed with him.

Earlier in the week, the fishpond had been drained, the water replaced and the dead plants removed. Thea had made reference to it in an email to Dr Fox but she did not mention her suspicions regarding Mr Battle. All she had was his ongoing animosity and Joy's report that he had proclaimed the girls wouldn't last the full school year. If she were to accuse the porter, she would need concrete evidence of any action on his part, not merely hearsay. The pest inspector's report had come back as inconclusive, but at her insistence they had returned and sprayed Thea's study anyway. She'd not been back in the room since.

Startled by the knock on the door, even though it was one she had been expecting, Thea leapt up to answer it.

When Fiona entered the house, wearing the traditional long, black cassock and white collar of her calling, she unzipped a small holdall and removed a rounded metal pot that had chains attached to its centre. 'A thurible,' she explained. 'We use it to burn incense and cleanse the space. Oh, knickers!'

'What?' Had Thea heard correctly? *Knickers?*

'Thought for a moment I'd forgotten the incense. But here it is.' She beamed back at Thea. 'Be assured that I will touch nothing, either with it or my hands.'

'Is it just you?' Thea asked. 'You mentioned there would be some others to help?'

'Oh, don't worry, they'll be here later,' said Fiona merrily before disappearing into the depths of the house, leaving a musky trail of incense in her wake.

She was gone for more than an hour, moving from room to room, and Thea caught a glance of her swinging the thurible as if in a dance, muttering what sounded like a chant. Soon, the house reeked of sandalwood and smoke. Thea glanced at her watch. There were still several hours before the Dame was due back from her afternoon off and the girls would return after prep and dinner. She hoped she would have time to air the place before then.

Thea stayed in the sitting room, pretending to read, but really waiting for Fiona to finish. The whole thing had an air of unreality about it. The incense and the chanting all seemed faintly ridiculous and amateur, and yet she wanted to believe that it would work, with an intensity that surprised her. As Fiona moved into the kitchen, Thea was unable to stand the tension any longer. She went to investigate, finding the back door open.

In the dusky light, she saw the curate standing at the far side of the parterre and, almost hidden behind the trees at the back of the garden, she was surprised to see the Dame, shrouded by a tattered yet voluminous cape, ever-present glasses shading her eyes. She was about to go to her, to try to explain, but then three women, whom Thea had never seen before, appeared through the back gate.

'What –' she began.

Fiona held up a hand for silence and waved the women towards her. 'Join us. Thea, over there, if you please.' She indicated a position further around the parterre, and Thea, still no clearer as to what was going on, did as she was bid. She reached her position and only then did it dawn on her where each of them was standing. Five women. Five points to the pentacle.

As she looked over Fiona's shoulder, Thea saw the Dame loitering in the shadows. *What must she be making of it all?* she wondered, but had no chance to speak to her as Fiona began to chant again, softly under her breath. Thea couldn't make out the words, didn't know if it was prayer or incantation. She stood there fighting the urge to leave, to run as far away as she could from the place, for she didn't understand any of it. It was so far from the cut-and-dried facts that she was used to, that she believed in.

One of the women reached for her hand, squeezed it reassuringly, and as she did so, Thea felt Fiona take the other. Here they were in a small back garden, stars beginning to prick the sky, the moon full and luminous. Five women holding hands in a circle in a garden after dark.

In another time, they would have been burned at the stake for less.

~

Afterwards, when everyone had left, there was another knock on the door. She went to answer it, thinking that Fiona must have forgotten something, but was surprised to see Mr Dickens standing in front of her.

'Ah, Miss Rust. I'm glad I've caught you. Forgive me for intruding, but –' He held out a brown paper-wrapped rectangle. 'I found it. The book: the one you wanted.'

'But I thought you said it wasn't allowed to leave the library?'

Thea didn't get a reply to her question, for he pressed the package into her hands, raised a finger to his lips and turned to leave. 'I must be off.'

She shut the door, grateful that he hadn't appeared earlier, for goodness knows what he would have made of the scene in the garden. Thea had been unable to find the Dame but knew she would certainly have to explain things to her at some point. She didn't want news of it to reach the headmaster's ears, for she doubted that he would be sympathetic.

When she eventually reached her bedroom that night, she found the door ajar and incense still hanging thickly in the air up there. She flicked on a lamp and immediately noticed something different about the room. Everything was as neat as she had left it, with one exception: the tin had fallen off the shelf and lay on its side, halfway across the room. It had probably been knocked over by Fiona, despite her promise not to touch anything. As Thea picked it up, checking that it had not come unscrewed, and set it straight, a thought flashed into her mind: might it have something to do with the disturbances in the house? She sighed, as another thought, one that had lingered in the back of her mind since she arrived here, pushed its way forward. *I have to do it. I should have dealt with it weeks ago.* But not tonight. Soon, though.

Thea reached for the book Mr Dickens had brought her and lay back on the bed, flicking through the pages until she found the part where she had left off. The type was dense and she strained to read it, but she persisted as the minutes ticked away, until it was past midnight. When she reached the final chapter she could hardly believe what it described.

~

That night she dreamed of the woman again. They were in Thea's study, though it looked older, the paintwork was a different colour, and there was no sign of Thea's desk or bookcase. Strands of fair hair, not dark as before, had escaped the hood of her cloak, though Thea could not make out her face. She seemed to be pointing to the wall.

Thea woke in a cold sweat and glanced at her watch. Two a.m. The same time she'd woken almost every night since she'd been there. Clearly Fiona's 'cleansing ritual' hadn't had the desired effect. Again, there was the distant sound of a piano, and she squinted across to the smart alarm to see if that was where the music was coming from, but it didn't appear to be. Surely no one would be playing downstairs at this time? She was about to get out of bed to investigate when she remembered. A piano. Of course. She had read earlier about the delivery of a pianoforte – the town's first. It had been a gift for the lady of the house.

Someone, or something, was trying to tell her something. She was beginning to have an idea who, but she still had no idea what.

THIRTY-THREE

July 1769, Oxleigh

Rowan woke to find a lantern shining directly into her eyes and Alice leaning over her, pulling her by the shoulders. 'Come quickly. Quickly, I said,' she urged in a whisper.

'What . . . What is it?' Rowan asked, blinking in the half-light.

'There's blood, so much blood.' She gave a half-sob.

Was it the tincture? Surely it would have taken effect before now? 'You should be lying down, Alice,' Rowan said. 'Too much activity will make it worse.'

Alice shook her head violently. ''Tis not me.'

'Someone from the town, then?' Rowan asked. 'Come to ask for help?'

Alice shook her head again, pulling her towards the door.

In that moment Rowan knew: there could only be one other so affected. As they descended the stairs, her mistress's wails became louder, the sound echoing chillingly through the darkened house. Once, in the summer before her father died, she had been out in the fields with him early one morning when they had come across a leveret, its hind leg caught in a trap. The noise coming from her mistress's chamber put her in mind of the high-pitched keening of the young hare as it thrashed against the rusty metal.

As they ran, Rowan remembered the gown her mistress had worn to the assembly rooms the fortnight before and then, with dread, the feeling that had come over her when she had tried it on. She mouthed a prayer under her breath, hoping she was mistaken.

'What's that?' Alice asked, holding the lantern up to Rowan's face.

'Nothing,' she replied, stilling the movement of her lips.

The sight that greeted them was one Rowan wished never to see again. It was as she imagined a slaughterhouse might be, for her mistress's sheets were painted with blood, dark as pitch in the dim light. She gagged at the smell that pervaded the chamber, her flesh crawling as she remembered the last time she had been in the presence of such an odour, a reek that was burned into her memory. Her mother had assisted at a birth, and had taken Rowan with her to help, but the baby's head had been stuck too long and her mother had been unable to stop the bleeding. Neither patient had survived.

It took all of Rowan's determination to force herself across the threshold and into the room. She reached the ewer on the dresser to one side of her mistress's bed and moistened the square of cloth placed there. While Alice stood back, Rowan approached the head of the bed, stepping aside a puddle of vomit on the Turkey rug and placing the cloth on her mistress's forehead, holding it firmly against her thrashing.

'Alice, is that you?' Caroline cried out as she felt the cloth.

'Rowan, mistress,' she replied, her voice low. 'Where is the pain?' she asked.

A deep guttural groan and then she answered. 'My belly, my shoulders . . . it hurts like I have the devil himself inside me trying to come out.'

Rowan bid Alice bring the lantern closer and did her best to assess the bleeding. The coverlet was thrown back and there were patches of brighter blood against the older, darker stains that had soaked the sheets.

'Tell me it is not the baby,' Caroline begged. 'Anything but that.'

'May I?' Rowan asked, pressing gently on her mistress's stomach, feeling below her ribs and then lower still.

Caroline gave another scream that would have woken the whole house, those in the street too, had the windows not been shut. Then, a noise at the chamber door: Prudence, a gown wrapped about her. 'What occurs?' she asked, her eyes widening as she took in the scene. 'I'll fetch some water, we need to get her clean.'

Before Prudence left, Rowan went across to the cook and spoke softly in her ear. Prudence nodded as she understood what Rowan was telling her.

Alice let out a low moan. 'It is all her doing –' She pointed at Rowan. 'She sees things that others do not. It is a bad magic. I caught her whispering the words of a spell earlier.'

'Is this true?' asked Prudence, looking sharply at Rowan.

Rowan's eyes darted between the two of them, furious with Alice and upset that Prudence did not dismiss the accusation outright. 'Don't be ridiculous,' she said, finding her voice. 'It was nought but a prayer. Now, hush. We must not cause the mistress upset. Let us do as Prudence suggests and clean her as best we can,' she added. 'And bring as many clouts as you have to hand. She is burning up.'

Despite her young age, Rowan took control of the situation; it was as if her mother's hands were guiding her as she assessed her mistress's condition.

Prudence returned, and they set to work removing the bloodied sheets and replacing them with clean ones, being as gentle with Caroline as they were able. Rowan could see that there did not appear to be any more fresh blood, nor sign of the infant and she murmured another, grateful, prayer. 'Should we call for the barber-surgeon?' Prudence asked.

'No!' cried Rowan, for she had heard of the terrible harm that such men could inflict, that they were no better than a butcher.

'The doctor, then?'

Rowan nodded reluctantly and Prudence commanded Alice, who still hovered by the door, to make at once for the medic's house. Rowan went to her attic room to dress, leaving Prudence with their mistress.

When she returned to the bedchamber, she took one of the cloths that Prudence had brought and soaked it in a fresh bowl of water, wringing it out and laying it across her mistress's brow, which was as hot as the coals from the fire. Caroline opened her eyes briefly at her touch, but they were blank, unseeing, and rolled back into her head. In that moment Rowan feared for her mistress's life, for her spirit seemed all but extinguished. As they waited for the doctor, Rowan sang to her, an old song she'd heard as a young girl. '*When the moon shines bright on his fair face, when the wind calls him home, when the frost is gone from the ground, then will my love return.*' As she sang, her thoughts turned to the master, and when he might come home, for he had left Oxleigh two days after the cotillion, claiming business in Bath once again.

When the doctor arrived, he banished everyone but Rowan from the room while she explained how they had found her mistress. 'Open the shutters at once, for we must rid the air of the putrid miasma that has taken hold,' he barked. 'Where is Mr Hollander?'

'Away, sir. We know not when he will return,' Rowan said as she hastened to do as he asked. The sun was up now and the noise of the street, the wheels of carts and stagecoaches grinding over the cobbles, horses neighing and flower-sellers calling out their wares, flew into the room with the cold air. It seemed cruelly unfair that the rest of the town carried on, going about its business as on any other day, while her mistress lay suspended between this world and the next.

'May God speed him home,' he said, drawing near to the bed and taking careful observation of his patient. Then, 'Give her barley water and beef tea if she will take it, and send someone to the apothecary for salt of wormwood. I will call again tomorrow.'

'And the baby?' Rowan asked.

'I cannot feel movement,' he said. 'But that in itself is not a conclusion.'

When the doctor had gone, Rowan returned to her mistress's side, frustrated that such a highly regarded medical man had been unable to do more for her. The fever still burned strong, causing her body to shudder and shake as if she had the palsy. The breeze that came in from the window cooled her not one bit.

Rowan tended to her all that day, and there was still no sign of Patrick Hollander. Prudence brought broth and a cold plate for Rowan, the furrow of her forehead deepening as she regarded them both.

Much later, as the light faded from the window, Rowan closed the shutters and lit the oil lamp. She bent over to place it on the table next to the bed and noticed that her mistress no longer shivered with fever. She was shrunken and pale, blanched to the colour of her sheets, and her fair hair was dark with sweat, but her breathing had calmed and her face had become serene again. Her eyes fluttered open and Rowan drew back, embarrassed at having been caught so close to her.

'Mistress,' she said.

'Drink,' Caroline whispered.

Rowan reached for the bowl of broth and spooned a little into her mouth. It was as if she were feeding a hatchling, so small were her mistress's sips.

The effort appeared to exhaust her and, after no more than half a cupful, Caroline lay back on her pillows and slept once more.

Alice, who had been absent the best part of the day sent to the apothecary and on other errands, peered into the room. 'How . . . how is she?'

'Better, I think,' Rowan said quietly. 'The bleeding has stopped. She must rest.'

'Has she . . .'

'What?' asked Rowan.

'Does she . . .'

'Out with it,' she said, annoyed at the interruption and still angry at Alice's earlier accusation.

'Has she lost the child?'

'There was so much blood that it is indeed a possibility that it no longer lives within her.'

Rowan could not read the expression on her face, but something about Alice's demeanour disturbed her. She seemed almost pleased.

~

The next morning the doctor returned and, after a perfunctory examination, pronounced Mistress Hollander over the worst of her fever. He instructed Rowan to continue the doses of wormwood, diluted in water. 'It is not certain yet whether the child still grows,' he said as he took his leave. 'But I believe Mistress Hollander is saved. For now.'

Moments after the doctor had gone, there was a commotion in the street outside the house, followed by the slam of the front door and the sound of boots thudding fast and heavy on the staircase. Caroline raised herself slightly from her reclining position. 'My husband?'

Patrick Hollander burst into the bedchamber as if a man possessed. 'I saw him in the street!' he cried. 'The doctor. What occurs? Are you quite all right, my dear?'

Rowan stilled the gasp of surprise that rose from her throat, for he little resembled the man she had come to know as her master. His hair was awry, his normally white breeches filthy with mud, his jacket half off his body and his waistcoat torn. He looked as though he had been set upon by highwaymen and come off much the worse for it.

Caroline did not appear to notice his dishevelled appearance, instead summoned a faint smile for him. 'A weakness, that is all. I am much recovered.'

Patrick looked from his wife to Rowan and Alice. 'Is this true? Nothing more serious? The baby?'

Rowan did not reply. It was not her place to contradict her mistress, no matter the untruths she spoke.

'Do not worry after me. A little blood, that was all,' Caroline insisted.

'But the baby?'

'Should be just fine,' she interrupted him. 'I merely have to be patient, rest and wait.'

'Wait? What for?' he demanded.

'For him – or her – to grow strong, of course,' she said. 'But what has happened to you? Your clothes . . .'

Patrick sat down heavily on the bed. 'Our coach met with misfortune, that is all. Overturned on the road not far from Melksham. We had to drag it out of a ditch. But there is no need to dwell on such matters. Bath was most agreeable and I am happy to report that I have secured a lease on a fine building in the midst of the town. I am returned to arrange the delivery of stock henceforth.'

'And who shall tend to the shop there?' Caroline asked.

'Why, myself, of course.'

'So, you will be gone from us again?' Disappointment marred her face.

'Aye, on the morrow, for I must return at once.'

'And here?'

'Jeremiah does an admirable job of serving our customers. Do not worry yourself about such things. For certainly you have never had need to do so before.' He reached for her hand and squeezed it gently.

Rowan turned to leave, but as she did so she caught Alice's stricken expression and followed her gaze to where it rested on their master. Seconds later, a horrifying thought occurred to her. Could Alice have used the draught she had made up for her on their mistress? She dared not contemplate such a vile thing, for if it were true then she was to blame as well.

THIRTY-FOUR

Now

Aside from the stormy day of the ill-fated hike, it had been an unseasonably dry autumn. Thea had been watching the weather forecast with a careful eye, wondering when this supposedly damp country would get the rain for which it was so well known. So far there had been nothing heavier than mist, but only a steady downpour and darkness would do, for they would not only obscure her presence but also allow her actions to go unnoticed. The rain would wash away any evidence.

Before she had left Melbourne, her mother had pressed the anonymous tin into Thea's hands, asked her to take it with her. A final filial duty.

That week, the forecast was for a low-pressure system approaching from the west, coming over the rolling downs flanking the town, and indeed the Sunday afternoon brought steel-grey clouds and the air hung heavy with the promise of rain.

Throughout the day, Thea became increasingly jittery, pacing her small room, unable to concentrate. It was with relief that she watched the sky grow dark and listened to the sound of raindrops pelting the windowpanes. Distracted, she went through her night-time duties and then, when she judged the girls to be asleep and with little chance of waking, she zipped up her jacket, sliding a torch into one of its capacious pockets and the tin into another. The tin was heavier than it looked and it pulled the jacket awkwardly down on one side, but she ignored this and crept down the stairs.

Quietly, so as not to wake the sleeping house, she laced up her boots and eased open the front door. Almost immediately, the rain began to blow in, forming small puddles on the flagstone floor.

Time to get the thing done, and then perhaps she might finally sleep easier.

It was nearly closing time at the pubs and a faint light could be seen from some, but the high street was almost deserted. Oxleigh was practically a ghost town, lamps casting dancing shadows onto the puddled pavements. Thea pulled the drawstring on her hood tight to her scalp, put her head down and walked determinedly towards the school. The rain needled her face, stinging the exposed skin and she had to wipe her glasses several times to clear them.

Damn.

She had reached the entrance but the tall wrought-iron gates were locked. As she rattled them in frustration, she berated herself for not checking the time they were secured for the night. She flicked on her torch, using the beam to scan the gates for any other means of entry.

Nothing.

Then, as the beam shone on the left-hand side she noticed a small side gate cut into the main gates. It was obscured during the day, when the gates were drawn back against the wall. She drew closer. It too was fastened with a heavy padlock, but as she shone the torch on it, she noticed a symbol. The quiver of arrows. Might it be? She reached in her pocket for her keys and selected the one with the arrows on it, the one she now realised she had been unable to find a lock for. She nearly cheered when it slipped smoothly into the chamber and she was able to pass through the gate, into the school grounds without further mishap. She hurried onwards, leaving the padlock unsecured for her return.

Thea marched along the path, zig-zagging to avoid the worst of the puddles. The rain still came down in gusty sheets, blowing sideways onto her glasses and making it hard to see where she was going, but she carried on regardless. Her jeans had long become soaked but her jacket at least was proving to be resistant to the downpour. The tin knocked painfully against her thigh as she walked, a reminder, not that she needed one, of the task ahead.

Soon she was on the playing fields – the hockey pitches where Gareth had tried and failed to best her and the girls only weeks before. These same pitches were used as tennis courts and a cricket oval in summer, the place her father had spoken of so fondly.

A single floodlight had been left on, illuminating part of the fields, but Thea stayed in the shadows, not risking the possibility of CCTV cameras scanning the grounds.

She stood for a moment, feeling the rain trickle into the gap of her collar and down her front. Then she reached into her pocket and pulled out the tin. It was a plain grey cylinder about the size of a small telescope, and nothing about its exterior gave a hint as to the contents. She wrapped her hands around the smooth surface, raised it upwards and unscrewed the lid.

Whenever she thought of her father, love, frustration, regret, hurt and anger were bound up together, a tangled skein that, she knew now, would probably never be unravelled.

Steadying her shaking hands, she angled the tin and shook it towards the earth. A greyish-brown powdery rubble streamed out and immediately disappeared into the grass, exactly as she had hoped. Merely dust, returned to the earth. A tear slid down her cheek and mingled with the rain on her face. Her father had wanted to toughen Thea and her sister against the world, make them warriors. He hadn't quite succeeded.

The rain continued to pour down, unrelenting, as the last of the ashes sifted from the tin. She tipped it over and shook it to be sure, then held it up, collecting rainwater before rinsing it clean until not a speck of dust remained.

It was done. She was soaked through to her skin, her jacket having finally succumbed to the rain, but she barely noticed it. The weight that had pressed down on her for so many months had dissolved along with his ashes: as though she had released herself from the past.

She didn't notice a dark figure across the pitch until she heard the shout.

'Thea!'

Gareth, dressed in waterproofs, his face obscured by an umbrella, was coming towards her.

'Christ on a bike,' she muttered to herself. The last person she wanted to see. 'What are you doing here?' she hissed when he reached her. Rain dripped off the collar of his jacket and his eyelashes had clumped together like starbursts.

'I was just about to ask you that. I saw you leave the house. I was having a beer in the pub down the street.'

'And you followed me?' She was incredulous.

'Guilty as charged, I'm afraid.' He held up a hand. 'I admit I was curious as to what might bring you out on such a foul night, but it wasn't my intention to scare you.'

'Well, you did,' she said, bristling.

'I'm sorry.' He held out the umbrella towards her, a peace offering. 'I didn't mean to disturb you. I waited until you'd finished. Don't worry. Your secret's safe with me.'

She eyed him warily.

'Come on, let's get out of here before we both catch our death of cold.'

'I don't need your help,' she said stubbornly.

He grinned and was about to answer when another shout echoed across the fields. Thea looked up. 'Battle!'

The porter was moving at a not inconsiderable speed, scuttling towards them like a demented crab. Thea blinked. She'd no idea he was capable of moving so fast.

'Oi!' he shouted again. 'What do you two think you're doing?'

Gareth grabbed Thea's hand. 'Quick! Before he catches us.'

'How did you get in here?' Mr Battle shouted as they began to flee. She could almost feel the waves of disapproval and annoyance radiating off him.

Thea didn't have time to think. She followed Gareth as if by blind instinct, a bubble of laughter welling up at the ridiculousness of it all. She was a responsible teacher, not a wayward schoolgirl.

She turned her head and through the smear of her glasses saw the porter coming closer. 'You were the one who gave me the key!' she called, before nearly doubling over with mirth.

They raced towards the gate, leaving him gasping in their wake. Thea nearly ignored the next shout, but she halted at its note of pain and turned to see the porter clutching at his chest. 'Wait!' she called to Gareth. 'I think something's wrong.'

Gareth stopped a few paces from her. 'We'd better see if he's all right.'

Thea watched Mr Battle sink to his knees. Without a moment's hesitation, Gareth sprinted back towards him, Thea following close behind. 'We'll lay him on his side,' he said, shielding the porter with his umbrella as Thea caught up. 'I don't like the look of him.'

Mr Battle seemed so much smaller, lying helpless on the ground. Even in the semi-darkness, Thea could see that his face was an unhealthy grey. She pulled her phone from her pocket and dialled.

'It's nine-nine-nine,' Gareth reminded her.

'Yes, yes,' she said, feeling a rush of guilt that she was the cause of all this.

Less than quarter of an hour later, lights and sirens lit up the darkness and Thea saw the figure of the headmaster striding across the fields. Even in a dressing gown and wellington boots he cast an imposing presence.

Before Dr Fox could ask, Gareth stepped in and briefly explained the situation, omitting to mention why they had been on school grounds at that late hour.

'Right. I'll get dressed and then go to the hospital. No need for you both to come; you should go back to your houses.'

He didn't ask any more questions, but Thea knew that eventually they would have to explain their presence on the school grounds at nearly midnight.

The paramedics eased Mr Battle onto a stretcher and fitted an oxygen mask before loading him carefully into the ambulance. 'We'll have you up to St Anne's in a jiffy,' she heard one of them say.

Thea stood watching as they drove away, unsure what to do next. If Mr Battle didn't recover . . . If he did recover and tell the headmaster what she'd been up to . . .

'Come on,' Gareth said, interrupting her catastrophising. 'I know exactly what we need.'

THIRTY-FIVE

July 1769, London

'I must go,' Mary announced as she stormed into the house. Two months had passed since she had sent the bolt of silk to Hollander's and there had been no response. 'I cannot believe I was so foolish as to trust him,' she fumed. 'I will not allow him to get away with this.'

'What?' Frances asked from where she sat at the table, a half-darned stocking forgotten in her fingers. 'Where must you go?'

'To Oxleigh, of course. For I cannot stay here a moment longer. I need to be certain for myself that Mr Hollander received the silk and to find out exactly why I have heard nothing in return.'

'Will any good come of it, sister?' Frances said gently. 'I have had my doubts about him since our first meeting, for he struck me as altogether too slippery a character.'

'And you did not think to warn me more sternly of this at the time?'

Frances shrugged. 'You were – we were – desperate.'

Mary shook her head violently, drops of rain flying from her cloak and wetting the floor. 'I cannot afford to let this lie, for the sake of my pride as much as the hope of being able to recover our mother's necklace. I shall not be taken for a fool. Unlike Mr Le Maître, I cannot wait months in the hopes of payment. I am booked on tomorrow morning's stage and will be there by Wednesday. I must make haste and prepare my trunk, for there is no time to waste.'

Mary packed the cloth featuring the columbine and traveller's joy alongside her drawings, wrapping them carefully in several layers of plain linen. She added several ordinary gowns suitable for travelling, a couple of chemises, stockings and so on. On the top she placed a set of sheets, for the inn where the coach would stop overnight could not be guaranteed to be free of bugs among the bedding and Frances had advised taking her own.

That night, Mary found herself restlessly pacing the floor, her cheeks burning and her thoughts churning, for now she had resolved to act she could not settle to anything. She rehearsed the words she would say to Mr Hollander. Would she be angry, self-righteous even, as a man would, or should she be calmer, reason with him more gently? She knew the latter would likely be a more successful course of action, though she longed to rage at him for flaunting their agreement. She would not be cast aside, disregarded, ignored any longer. The fact of her being a woman did not give him the right to renege on his agreement and evade his debts.

The rain ceased its drumming against the windowpanes and as darkness fell it sputtered to a slow drizzle, lifting Mary's hopes that it would continue to ease and that the coach would not be held up, for the journey would be long enough without the prospect of further delay.

She had little knowledge of the country to the south-west of London, but Frances assured her it was pleasant and generally flat going. 'I wish I could travel with you, but I am committed to the hospital,' she fretted.

'We can scarce afford the fare for one of us,' Mary replied. 'Besides, I am perfectly capable of confronting him on my own.' She stoked the anger burning within her until it was a flame that would not easily be doused.

As Mary prepared to leave the following morning, Frances pressed a small package into her hands. 'Some food, for the journey. God speed and may He protect and guide you.'

Mary fought the flare of doubt that rose in her chest. There was a chance, however slight, that something untoward had happened to Mr Hollander, he could have been taken ill . . . there could be an easy explanation for the lack of communication. Perhaps even at this very moment he was on his way to London once more. Oh, how terrible it would be if she missed him in this way.

No, she reminded herself, that was the least likely thing, and she could not sit around and wait for her fate to be decided. Her patience was exhausted. She could not bear to remain ignorant another moment.

~

Mary had taken but one other long journey in her life, the one from her childhood home in York to her sister's in Spitalfields the year before, and she remembered a similar sense of dislocation after so many hours of travel when she finally arrived in Oxleigh. The coaching inn in front of her was a grand building of honeyed stone, and she was struck by how far away she was from all that was familiar. Before she had time to dwell on it, however, she had been deposited near the doorway together with her trunk and her valise, and her travelling companions were but a cloud of dust in the distance, headed for the Bath Road.

The light was fading, for it was now late in the afternoon. She knew her hair to be awry, her travelling clothes rumpled and she had no desire to be at a disadvantage when confronting the man who had caused her such anguish. She resolved to seek him out the following morning, early, before he had time to be abroad.

When she reached her room, she paid little heed to its pleasant aspect over rolling hills and instead she lay upon the bed, relieved to no longer be in perpetual motion, for her bones felt as though they had been rattled loose from their joints.

Later, after a meal of cold meat and bread had been brought up, she opened her trunk and took out the bolt of cloth, handling it carefully so as not to sully it. She spread it out on the bed and marvelled again at its luminous beauty. The mere sight of it gave her courage.

The church bell sounded and she judged that there was less than a half-hour left of twilight. Convincing herself that the town was sufficiently safe for her to make a quick investigation of its high street, in search of the merchant's house, she hastily wrapped up the cloth and set it aside before venturing from the inn.

Mary gathered her cloak about her and hurried along, past several more inns, a shoemaker, a chandler and a saddlery, a milliner, a grocer, two butchers and a liquor merchant, the trade they conducted picked out in bold letters on the doors or on signs above the windows. It was a prosperous town, but that did not surprise her, for she knew it to be a popular stopping place on the way to Bath, where society gentlemen and women took the waters and mingled in the new assembly rooms. She had nearly reached the end and was beginning to be concerned that she had missed the shop she sought, when there it was, right in front of her, a bright illustration of bolts of silk and a pair of shears. Her heart began to beat faster at the thought that she might soon encounter Patrick Hollander, to beard the lion in his den.

Pretending to peruse the merchandise, she peered into the window, rearing back when she caught a glimpse of a man in the gloomy room. He was not the one she sought, however. This man was thinner, with a stooped back and shoulders folded inwards over a sunken chest like the wings of a bat. He looked up, as if conscious of her scrutiny, and she walked on, pretending urgent business further along the street.

When her racing heart had slowed somewhat, she crossed the road, gathering her skirts to avoid the mud, and walked back along the other side, sneaking another glance at the shop from a distance.

Now she had seen the place, the fury that burned in her grew even greater. Patrick Hollander had ignored her; he had made promises that he did not keep and she would not stand for it. The morning could not come soon enough.

THIRTY-SIX

Now

They entered the pub by a side door. Thea was surprised to see the place more than half-full despite it being officially after closing time. A few people stopped talking at their arrival but soon went back to their beer and conversation when they recognised Gareth. A couple raised their drinks to him.

It was a relief to be out of the rain, and Thea hung her coat on a hook by the door, watching as rivulets of water streamed onto the carpet. Gareth returned from the bar with two quarter-full tumblers and a small beer towel. He handed her the towel and she took off her steamed-up glasses and gratefully wiped the dampness from her face and hair.

They found a booth tucked away in a corner, next to a fire that kicked out a welcome heat, and sat opposite each other on old wooden settles.

'Do you think he'll be all right?' she asked. 'I feel terrible. If he hadn't been chasing me . . . Christ, I could have killed him.' She'd really gone and done it now; felt sure the headmaster would dismiss her before the week was out.

'Thea,' Gareth said sternly. 'This isn't the first time it's happened.'

'The first time what's happened?'

'The first time Battle's had a bit of a turn.'

'That wasn't a "bit of a turn",' she said, astonished. 'It looked more like a heart attack.'

'He's an old man,' Gareth said, so softly that she had to lean closer to hear him over the noise of the other drinkers. 'Truth is, the job's been too much for him for years now, but Foxy's kept him on out of loyalty. Battle's been at the school ever since anyone can remember. Should have been claiming his pension decades ago.'

'Does he have a family? A wife?'

Gareth shook his head. 'The school is his family, I reckon.' He clinked his glass to hers. 'Care to tell me about what was going on back there?' he asked, taking a sip of his drink. 'Though of course, if you'd rather not . . .'

Thea shook her head. 'My dad.' Her voice was thick, clotted with unshed tears.

'Of course. The late Henry Rust.'

'You know about him?'

'Everyone does. Head boy. Legendary school sportsman. Went on to play cricket for Australia, didn't he?'

'New South Wales, actually.'

'I know it was only recent. That's got to be tough on you.' He sat back, considering her for a moment, and she saw kindness soften his eyes. 'You're not the only one who had a sports-mad father.'

'Oh yes?'

'My dad was a rugby tragic – I'm named after Gareth Edwards, Wales's greatest scrum-half, greatest player ever; well, according to Dad, anyway. It was a source of eternal disappointment to him that I chose hockey over rugby.' He grimaced. 'Didn't much like getting hurt.'

Thea smiled. She knew all about fathers and their impossibly high standards.

'So, you're a chip off the old block, then?' he asked.

'Oh, I'm not sure about that.'

'You're too modest. I underestimated your skills and experience. I looked you up – very impressive. I feel bad about giving you a hard time. I'm sorry, Thea.' He gently placed a hand over hers and Thea found its dry warmth unaccountably comforting.

'I need to apologise too,' she said with a rueful expression. 'I jumped to conclusions, said some things I probably shouldn't have.'

'Truce?' Gareth's expression was earnest.

'Truce.' She held up her glass, chinking it against his before taking a swig. The whisky blazed a fiery trail down her throat, warming her from the inside. Her shivering stopped.

'What drives you?' he asked, leaning towards her, a look of genuine interest on his face.

'I'm sorry?'

'What drives you to excel?'

'Fear of failure?' She smiled slightly. 'No, actually, that's not entirely true. I guess I wanted to make the old man proud of me,' she said.

'And did you?'

She put her glass down. 'I really don't know. He wasn't an easy man to get close to. I don't think even my mother knew him very well. I suppose part of my reason for coming here was to search for clues, anything that might give me a bit of insight . . . I'm not sure there's much more need for me to stay here though, and I reckon Dr Fox will probably agree after what's just occurred.'

But as she said the words, she realised that wasn't the case at all. She did want to stay. Not as a nonsensical way of somehow earning her father's respect or understanding him, but because she had become fond of the girls, the school, even, and the good things it stood for.

Thea took another sip of her drink and lapsed into silence. Her fingers and feet began to thaw, the feeling prickling back into them. She stared at her hands as she flexed them, seeing a smaller version of her father's square-tipped fingers.

'I didn't always like him.' There it was. The truth. Finally uttered out loud. What was the trite saying – *The truth will set you free*? Well, the jury was still out on that one. 'And it's been hard to stop feeling guilty about that.' She finished her drink and put it on the table with a *thunk*. 'Another?'

'We are not our parents, Thea. We don't have to be them. And anyway, they were never perfect. Far from it in some cases.'

'I know.' She finally understood that.

'It might not look as though much changes,' he said, glancing up at the low ceiling and ancient beams. 'But it does.'

She got up to order another round of drinks.

'And what about your mother? Brothers? Sisters?' he asked when she returned. 'No boyfriend to lean on?'

Thea gave an awkward laugh. 'Let's just say that I'm better at hockey than relationships.'

~

The next afternoon, although visiting hours had finished half an hour earlier, Thea slipped past the nurses' station and along the corridor to the ward where Mr Battle lay. Once inside, she tiptoed to the only occupied bed. There was an arrangement of purple lilies, the same as the one in Mr Dickens's buttonhole, on the nightstand nearest him, but little else punctuated the antiseptic grey and cool blue.

His eyes were closed, so she waited a while as he slept. As she made to leave, he snapped to attention, his gaze fixed on hers.

'Sorry if I'm disturbing you. I just . . .' she faltered. 'I came to see how you were doing.'

He grunted and gave a terse laugh. 'You haven't killed me yet.'

Thea smiled. 'I'm so sorry.'

'Nothing gets past me,' he said, a faint note of pride in his voice.

'So I'm beginning to learn,' she said ruefully. 'How are you feeling?'

'Never better.'

'So I can see.'

He paused, swallowing. 'It's my life. The school.'

Thea nodded. Tears of sympathy pricked her eyelids. She knew it had cost him to admit that.

'And I can't say I'm happy about the changes. *Tradition*,' he said, biting down on the word. 'That used to stand for something, not that you'd probably know much about that. Being from the colonies and all.'

Thea ignored the barb, knew he was baiting her, just as he had done the first time they'd met, though this time she realised it was meant to tease not taunt. 'It still does,' she replied. 'The school isn't losing anything. It's only gaining. Do you think you might perhaps be confusing tradition with history? One can evolve, you know.'

Battle spluttered, and she thought for one awful moment that she might have pushed him too far, but his breathing quietened and he motioned to the cup of water by his bedside. She reached for it, holding it to his lips as he swallowed.

THIRTY-SEVEN

July 1769, Oxleigh

Unable to lie abed a moment longer, Mary rose as the sun began to clear the horizon, swiftly washing her face before dressing with care. She cinched her stays over her chemise, laced the bodice of her gown over her stomacher and shook out the creases in her skirt from where it had been packed in her trunk. After buttoning her sleeves, she combed out her hair before pinning it under her bonnet, grimacing at the frayed brim and outmoded style of her headwear.

Her stomach was wound in far too tight a knot to accept any breakfast, though she did sip a little of the tea that was offered to her when she descended the stairs and entered the dining room. As it was still early, the room was quiet, with only a few other guests already about. She forced herself to drink as she waited for the clock to sound the hour. When it struck eight times, she knew she could wait no longer and returned to her room to collect the second length of fabric that Bridget O'Neill had woven.

Mary walked along the high street with a determined expression that belied the roiling in her stomach. It was market day and the centre of the street was taken up with all manner of stalls, so she kept to the edges, skirting the flower-sellers and the cheesemongers, the bakers and those with baskets of eggs and river fish. When she reached the front door of the merchant's house, she didn't allow herself to hesitate, rapping soundly with her fist.

At first there was no movement within, but after she knocked once more, she heard footsteps approaching.

A maid with a curious scar across one eye came to the door. 'We do not open for another hour or more, if it's the shop you are after,' she said, her vowels soft and rounded.

'No, no. I am after Patrick Hollander. He is the mercer, is he not?'

The girl nodded, and said yes he was. 'But I am afraid that he is not hereabouts.'

Mary could not believe her ears. She hadn't allowed herself to think of him not being there, had gambled everything on confronting him that morning. She thought despairingly of her mother's beautiful necklace in the greedy hands of the pawnbroker.

'He has been gone these two days past,' the maid added.

'But I have come from London,' she said, unable to keep the desperation from cracking her voice. She did her best to marshal her scattered wits, to assemble her thoughts into some kind of order. 'My name is Mary-Louise Stephenson.'

The maid regarded her blankly. 'Was he expecting you?'

'We are in business together. At least –' She indicated the bundle under her arm. 'That is what I was led to believe.' Mary spoke more loudly than she had intended and the maid looked over her shoulder into the street, where a number of passers-by were starting to stare at her curiously. 'He should have been in receipt of the first of my fabrics, a purple flower pattern.'

The maid startled. 'You had better come in,' she said. 'I can ask my mistress what might be done.'

Mary found herself ushered up a staircase and into a large morning room where a fire burned brightly in the grate. 'She may be a short while, for she is not yet risen. She has been indisposed . . .' The maid's voice trailed off in embarrassment and Mary felt all at once quite out of place. The inappropriateness of her errand, at such an hour, struck her. Women of her station in life, however impoverished, did not call unannounced.

'Perhaps I might . . .' she ventured. But it was too late, for the girl had left the room. Mary carefully placed the bolt of fabric on the chaise next to her, undoing its wrapping and spreading it out. She glanced around, noting the luxurious window hangings and the thickness of the rug under her feet. Patrick Hollander was a man of some considerable means. That he lived in such comfort, all the while apparently callously disregarding her, sparked the flame of her anger back into life, steadied her resolve.

When Mistress Hollander entered the room, Mary could see that she was obviously with child, her embroidered stomacher doing little to hide the swell of her belly.

'I beg your pardon for calling at such an early hour –' she began, getting to her feet.

'Not at all. I have been most curious to meet the designer of such entrancing silk,' Caroline said as she sat down, inviting Mary to do the same. 'I understand from my maid that you are responsible for the belladonna fabric design?'

Mary nodded. 'I am pleased to learn that it did arrive, for I have had no communication from Mr Hollander in regard to payment for my – and my weaver's – work. I have also brought the second design that he commissioned.'

'Yes, I can see.' Caroline reached over to inspect the fabric that Mary had displayed, running delicate fingers across its surface. 'I am most desirous of having this design as well. I shall have Jeremiah, our shopkeeper, arrange for you to be paid.'

Mary allowed herself a small smile and her shoulders, which had been taut with the strain of her errand, eased. Perhaps in dealing with Mistress Hollander she would be fairly treated at last? 'That is most pleasing to hear. However, there is the fact of the other length of fabric, for which I have not been recompensed.' Mary didn't like raising the subject of money with a gentlewoman such as Mrs Hollander, particularly one in her condition, but she pressed on regardless of both of their sensibilities, for the idea of returning to Spitalfields with the matter unresolved was unthinkable.

'I am afraid that I cannot assist with that,' she replied. 'For I am ignorant of your arrangement with my husband in that regard. You will have to wait until he returns. He is away to Devizes, I believe, for a supply of cassimere and drugget. Perhaps call again tomorrow?' She stifled a yawn and it became clear to Mary that her welcome at the merchant's house was wearing thin. She was left with no choice but to accept payment for the silk she had brought, and to wait on Mr Hollander for the other.

Mary left the merchant's house with a note and a clutch of guineas in her pocket from the sale of her fabric. Though she had negotiated only gently with Mrs Hollander, she had been pleased to be fairly paid. The money would go some way towards paying back the pawnbroker and she would be able to afford a few more nights at the inn, for she was determined to stay and confront Patrick Hollander. Having made the journey to Oxleigh, she was not about to leave having been only partly successful in her mission. She wanted to see him for herself, to find out why he had broken their agreement.

~

As Rowan returned to the morning room her attention was immediately caught by the fabric that was displayed on the chaise next to her mistress. Pale and lustrous, it seemed to concentrate all the light in the room, drawing her eye to its irresistible beauty. She did not feel the same sense of disquiet upon contemplating this design as she had with the other one; indeed, this delicate pattern of wildflowers was positively joyous.

'Exceptional, isn't it?' said Caroline. 'She is a woman of unusual talent.'

Rowan nodded in agreement.

~

When Mary left the merchant's house, she had no desire to return to her lodgings immediately, for it was still early, and so she decided to explore the surrounds. She wandered the length of the high street and then continued past where the cobbles ended along a dirt path that led out of the town. A swift-flowing river ran alongside the path, just far enough away to prevent unwitting travellers from falling in. It wasn't long before she reached a mill, its wide paddlewheel turned by the fast-flowing millrace. The noise from the machinery and the grinding stones and the water was almost overwhelming, but she was mesmerised by the rushing water.

After a while she turned to leave, but stopped as she saw a young woman standing almost directly behind her on the track. 'Oh!' she cried, for she had imagined herself alone. 'You are the maid from the merchant's house. Did you follow me?'

There was no answer.

'It cannot be coincidence that I come upon you here.'

Rowan bobbed a curtsey. 'Begging your pardon, mistress, but it is the fabric – the first design. I saw it when it arrived . . .' She hesitated. 'I wanted to warn you. It is only that those plants contain a dark magic. 'Tis bad luck to meddle with them unless you have the knowledge.'

Mary scoffed. 'It is mere weaving. What possible harm could come to the wearer of such fabric? Mistress Hollander seemed pleased enough with it. And who are you, a serving maid, to question that?'

Rowan cast a furtive glance around and hurried past. 'Good day to you, my lady.'

'One moment,' said Mary, for a thought had recently occurred to her.

'Yes, mistress?' Rowan turned back to face her.

'I was saddened to hear of the passing of Mr Hollander's mother. I do hope she did not suffer.'

Rowan looked at her blankly. 'I'm afraid I am unaware of such an occurrence, mistress, though I have been at the merchant's house not even a year. Perhaps it was before my arrival? I confess I have never heard my master speak of his mother.'

'I see. Then I must have been mistaken.' Mary's suspicions were confirmed. She was indeed dealing with a liar and a cheat. As to the maid's superstitious warning about the fabric – well, that was nonsense. Nevertheless, she felt a momentary misgiving as she recalled her sister's words about the design, of her desire to be rid of it from the house.

THIRTY-EIGHT

July 1769, Oxleigh

The following day, Rowan was blacking the steps in front of the merchant's house, and did not notice the pattern-drawer, Mary Stephenson, approach until she stood directly in front of her.

'I heard tell that Mr Hollander is returned,' Mary said as Rowan paused in her efforts, tucking an errant strand of hair underneath her cap.

Rowan gave a slight nod. 'He is much preoccupied,' she said, knowing that her master was in one of his more capricious moods, having upturned one of the dinner dishes the previous day on discovering that the meat was not cooked to his liking.

'Well, I have even more to preoccupy him,' said Mary, marching up to the door to the shop and pushing it open.

Though she had nearly finished her task, Rowan tarried a while, curious as to what might happen. She did not have to wait long, for the door remained propped open and she could readily see into the shopfront, where Jeremiah was helping her master select the bolts of fabric that he was to take to Bath later in the week. She nearly jumped backwards into the path of a cart at her master's shout of surprise when Miss Stephenson entered, but then, despite risking a reprimand or worse, she slipped in and tucked herself behind the open doorway, where she was in a position to overhear everything.

'Madam.' After his initial outburst, Patrick Hollander's voice was controlled. 'I confess I hardly expected to see you in these parts, come so far from London.'

Rowan heard the steel in Mary's voice as she answered him. 'I should not have cause to come were it not for your complete abandonment of our agreement. An agreement made in good faith, I might add, for I took you to be a gentleman of your word. Did you set out to cheat me?'

'In truth I did not,' he said, sounding astonished. 'You have my assurance of that.'

'I fear that is worth little,' Mary scoffed.

He looked blankly at her. 'Miss Stephenson, I confess I became convinced that *you* had reconsidered our agreement, for I had heard nothing at all further. Indeed, were I not so taken up with other matters of business, I surely should have returned to demand the coin I advanced you, on my next visit to the capital.'

'But I sent the fabric. *Months* ago.'

'And your proof is?' he opened his hands, threw his arms wide. 'For it is nowhere hereabouts.'

Patrick appeared bemused.

'Surely you cannot deny that you received it. Your own wife has informed me that she admired it so much that it was fashioned into a gown for her.'

'I do know the fabric you speak of,' he admitted, realisation showing on his face. 'But as I was not here when it arrived, I had no inkling that it was your work.'

Mary could not help but make a disbelieving sound in her throat at such a flimsy denial. 'Would your man not have recorded its arrival in your absence?'

Patrick shrugged. 'There is nothing in the order book.'

Rowan could not believe what she was hearing. Despite her feelings towards her master he was still her employer and because of that she owed him loyalty, but the realisation that she found herself in a house of liars and cheats vexed her honest soul.

'But I have your wife's assurance that it was delivered. Does that not count?'

'Miss Stephenson,' Patrick said. 'My wife has been under a great deal of strain, her condition . . . And as you can see, I am taken up with other matters at the present. Perhaps you might call again tomorrow afternoon when I have had the opportunity to review the ledger and we can rectify this little misunderstanding.'

'It might be a trivial misunderstanding to you, sir, but to me it is my livelihood.'

'Of course, I have no doubt that this will be satisfactorily resolved, but I really cannot help you until I have conducted a further investigation.'

Rowan forced herself to hold her tongue as she overheard Mary agreeing to return the following day. She knew that her master was leaving for Bath the following morning and that he would not be there when Mary was to call again. Like a cunning spider, Patrick Hollander was weaving a web of lies, but would he be the one caught in his own trap?

~

Later, Rowan made her way to the butcher and placed Prudence's order for more mutton, still mulling over the knowledge of her master's perfidy. The butcher regarded her unhappily. 'The account is some three months outstanding. Please inform your master that this is the last time I can supply his order until I receive payment.'

As Rowan left, it began to dawn on her that this was more than an oversight. She remembered seeing Prudence arguing with the greengrocer only the week before. When Prudence noticed that she was within earshot, she had explained it away as potatoes riddled with mealworms, but now Rowan was not so sure. Was money – the lack of it – the cause of her master's erratic behaviour? Had he gambled away their fortune? Or had he overreached himself in Bath? Or did he simply have so little grip on the reality of things?

Rowan did not return directly to the merchant's house, calling instead at the coaching inns at the far end of the high street. She had no luck at the first one, but at the second was told to wait in the dining room while the innkeeper went in search of Miss Stephenson.

'Oh, it's you.' Mary stood in front of Rowan. 'Do you carry a message from Mr Hollander perhaps? Has he reconciled his accounts?' she asked, a hopeful expression lighting her face.

Rowan shook her head, glanced about and noticed that the innkeeper loitered across the room, doubtless hoping to glean some gossip. 'Might we go somewhere more private?' she asked in a low voice. 'Please, it is in your interest to hear what I have to say.'

'Very well. It is rather pleasant out, but let me fetch my cloak in any case.'

'I shall wait for you near the church – the one at the far end of town.'

Mary nodded in agreement and Rowan hastened from the inn.

She did not have long to wait, as she soon saw the figure of Mary Stephenson several yards away. From a distance her cloak could have been the same as Rowan's, but as she drew closer Rowan saw that it was made from far finer fabric, albeit moth-eaten in places.

'Well,' Mary said, standing in front of her, 'what is it that you have to tell me?'

Rowan had become a gambler, her words were her dice, though even before she spoke she was not certain there was a winning side to be had. 'When I overheard Mr Hollander say that he did not believe he had received the fabric, I could no longer remain silent. How could he not have recognised it? It is a design apart from anything I have ever seen.'

Mary flinched.

'He is not to be trusted,' Rowan continued in a whisper, her eyes darting about to make sure she was not overheard.

Mary seemed confused. 'But you are his servant. Why risk your position to tell me this? And why would he lie to me, when he has promised to see me on the morrow?'

'He intends to leave for Bath at first light,' Rowan confessed.

'He *what*?' Mary's eyes hardened. 'I still do not understand. Why does he toy with me so? If he does not like my work, why commission me in the first place? He does nothing but waste all of our time.'

'If you please, mistress, I do believe him to be deranged.'

'Deranged? How so?'

'Inconstant. He has but a loose grip on the present, let alone the past. Forgets what he has promised. It is as if he wishes to make one happy in the moment, but then denies it henceforth.' Rowan stopped there, convinced that she had said too much. She had not forgotten her mother's stories of the scold's bridle, and though Rowan knew they were no longer used, there would still be dreadful consequences of speaking about her master in such a way were he to discover her disloyalty.

'How can he conduct a business in this manner? It is preposterous.'

'Everything is not as it seems in that house, and I thought it only proper to warn you.'

'The way you warned me about the danger of my design?' Mary asked, pacing up and down in front of Rowan. 'I cannot return to London and tell my sister I have failed in my endeavours.' Mary turned, her hands clenched, her jaw set. 'I will not be made a fool of, damn him! He will regret his actions, I will make sure of it.'

'Please,' said Rowan. 'He cannot know that it was I who told you.'

Mary's expression softened. 'You have risked plenty, and for that I am most grateful. He shall not know what brings my swift return. Here,' – she held out a copper – 'for your trouble. I am sorry; it is all I can spare.'

Rowan shook her head. 'I did not come to you in hopes of recompense,' she said. 'Only out of a sense for what is right.'

'Very well.'

'I must away, for I will be missed if I am gone too long.' She hurried from the churchyard, conjuring an excuse on her lips should Prudence enquire after her absence.

~

Mary paced, not caring that her skirts had become muddied from the path. How utterly foolish she was to have been duped by such a man. She cursed herself for being so trusting of his word, for being dazzled – she now admitted – by his apparent wealth, by his good looks and charming manner. It seemed they were naught but a sham.

She would not be the fool he took her for. She would place more of her work eventually – the whispers of the draw boys and apprentices and the reaction of Mrs Hollander to her designs were proof of her talent. She wasn't about to stop believing in herself after a single misstep, but she would be far less trusting in her future dealings.

THIRTY-NINE

July 1769, Oxleigh

An unnatural quiet had descended upon the town and Rowan went about her duties with an uncharacteristic slowness, lingering over simple tasks and taking long pauses between them. The growing tension in the air felt like the hours before a thunderstorm broke. The master was absent once again. Rowan, who had seen him head in the direction of the tavern at the end of the high street, privately suspected he had made his way to the card tables.

Before he left, Patrick had instructed her to repack his trunk with fresh clothes for his departure, but once that was done, she found she could not summon the energy for her normal tasks. She was tired of the lies, the undercurrent of deception that had seeped into the house, poisoning the air like a canker. No one seemed spared it. Even Prudence had been avoiding her lately.

Could this be because of Alice's accusations? She had done her best to help Alice, but the maid appeared to wish her nothing but ill.

Rowan could hardly wait for the afternoon to arrive and as the bell began to strike two, she was already throwing her cloak over her dress, for indeed the sky was the purple of a bruise and seemed ready to rain at a moment's notice. She slipped out of the back door and followed the side passage that led to the high street. A few yards along, she saw two familiar figures: her master and Miss Stephenson, standing underneath the sign of The Seven Stars. She could not hear what they were saying, but she pulled the hood of her cloak further over her head to avoid being seen by them. She needn't have worried, for neither would have noticed her, so intent were they on each other. As she drew closer, idling at a shopfront, she risked another glance. They appeared to be arguing, and at that moment, she saw her master grasp Miss Stephenson by the wrist and pull her along the street. She knew at once that they were headed in the direction of the river. A sudden vision of the swirling millrace filled her mind, a red shape caught in the whitewater at the centre of the pool. Something terrible would befall the woman from London; Rowan felt it as if it were a knife to her belly.

Tommy called after her from the doorway of the butcher's shop, but she ignored him, forging on.

The pair were out of sight now, but Rowan walked rapidly along the street and veered into a narrow lane that would bring her to the mill from the other direction. Her cloak snagged on a gorse bush causing her to stumble and tear a stocking, but she pressed on, running now in an effort to reach the mill first.

She gasped with the effort of running, her breath coming in great gulps, but did not let up, even as her chest began to burn. But when she reached the riverbank, someone else entirely stood before her.

Her mistress. Caroline. Wrapped in a scarlet velvet cloak, her fair hair loose about her shoulders. She had a wild look in her eyes, as if she had lost all reason, and Rowan noticed that her hands shook as if with a palsy when she raised them before her.

'Should you be abroad, mistress?' Rowan gasped.

'You knew?' Caroline demanded, ignoring her concerns.

'Knew what?' Rowan, fearing her betrayal had come to light, steeled herself to take her punishment, whatever it might entail. She swallowed a lump that had risen in her throat, ready for the worst. But the name her mistress said next was not the one she had expected to hear.

'Alice and my husband.'

Rowan regarded her dumbly, unable to confirm or deny her mistress's suspicions, feeling a wave of relief that her own sins had not yet come to light.

'I must know the truth.' Caroline spoke through gritted teeth. 'I have searched the town, every tavern and alley. Is he this way?'

'I followed them – him,' said Rowan. 'Come, let us keep looking.'

They reached the river, and both could see the couple some way ahead on the path in front of them, near where the water widened at the millpond.

Mary-Louise, the silk designer and her master.

Rowan and Caroline pressed on. As they drew closer, Rowan could see that they were both making jerky movements, their heads drawn forward, eyes wide; arms gesticulating wildly. Patrick Hollander seemed unsteady on his feet, staggering as if drunk. His stock was awry and his pockets pulled out as if to show they concealed nothing. The noise of the millrace meant that she could not hear a word that was said, though the animosity between the pair was clear enough.

Her master raised his arms as if in submission, but in doing so caught Miss Stephenson on the shoulder. She rocked backwards, so close to the water that Rowan gasped. She saw her master's mouth move, but she could not hear his words.

'Patrick!' Caroline screamed, loud enough to be heard over the rush of the water.

Patrick and Mary both stopped, as if astonished to discover that they were not alone.

Rowan watched as Caroline gathered her skirts and, despite her increased girth, hastened towards them. As she reached her husband, she placed a hand on his arm, but he threw it off and Caroline reeled at the force of it. Unbalanced, she stumbled backwards, then tripped over her cloak, which had become tangled about her feet.

Rowan watched in frozen silence as one moment her mistress was standing there, and the next she was gone, down like a felled oak, plunging into the churning water, swallowed up in an instant.

Patrick bellowed after her.

Rowan stood, rooted to the spot, watching as he threw off his jacket and waded into the pond, shouting his wife's name.

Rowan felt thick-witted, as if in a fog, her ears filled with the roaring sound of the water. Time seemed to slow, honey dripping from a comb, as she stood at the edge and fretted, watching her master wade deeper into the pond. Finally, she found her voice, though the words she screamed as he disappeared into the water were foreign to her, sounded even to her ears like a curse. All she could see of Caroline was her cloak floating on the surface, her earlier vision made a dreadful truth.

Then, Tommy was by her side. She didn't stop to ask how he came to be there, simply pointed to the cloak. Without hesitation he, too, cast off his jacket and waded in as Mary moved further away, scanning the water downstream.

Patrick was deeper, in the centre of the pond now, ducking down where the cloak had swirled, but each time he came up empty-handed. 'Caroline!' he shouted, his eyes wild as he searched the water beneath him. 'Caroline! Show yourself!' Three, four, five times Rowan watched him dive. He looked towards the bank. 'I cannot . . . I cannot see,' he called out to them. 'I cannot find her! It is as though she has been sucked into a whirlpool.' Then, he disappeared again and again but did not come up a twelfth time.

Tommy was in the water too, had reached the spot where Patrick had been and began to duck down into the churning water.

After a long moment he surfaced, turned towards Rowan, wiped the water from his eyes and shook his head. Not giving up, he continued to dive.

'She's here!' Mary shouted. She had run further along the bank where the pool joined the river and the water was calmer. 'Over here!' she pointed.

Rowan abandoned her position by the edge of the pond and ran towards the river. She could see the red cloak, dark like spilled blood, under the water.

Caring no longer for the fact that she feared the water, Rowan ran along the path, cast off her own cloak and waded in. She stumbled and almost fell, drawn dangerously deeper as the water caught her skirts. She struggled on, not thinking of her own safety, taking great wracking breaths until she reached her mistress. Holding underneath her arms, Rowan pulled her towards the calmer water. Mary waded in and helped drag Caroline, wrapped about with chickweed so fine it looked like lace, closer to the bank.

Together they wiped the weed from her face, leaned in to see if there was the slightest chance that the spark of life might not have left her.

'He pushed her,' Mary gasped. 'I saw it. He might not have meant to, but he pushed her in. He nearly did for me as well.' She shook with shock and the cold, her arms and skirts running with rivers of water. 'He is the devil himself.' She reached an arm around Rowan. 'Are you quite well? You yourself could have drowned.'

Teeth chattering, Rowan felt the woman's warmth beneath her soaked clothing, a small comfort.

They held Caroline free of the water, unsure of what to do. For a few moments there was nothing, then, after what seemed like an age, Rowan saw a slight breath escape her mistress's lips.

Relief surged through her as the breaths came more regularly. Together, she and Mary pulled her onto the riverbank. Once she was convinced that her mistress had clung to life, Rowan sat back on her heels, unable to comprehend everything that had happened in the space of a few terrible minutes.

'We must get her home,' she said when she had regained her composure.

'But how?' Mary asked.

'Fetch help. The butcher has a cart.' Rowan was unafraid to take charge now.

Mary stood up, wrung out her skirt as best she could, then left at a halting pace – for her petticoats and underclothes clung wetly to her legs – towards the town.

Rowan cast around for Tommy, fearing the worst. She didn't dare take a breath herself until she had seen him. Finally, his sleek head popped up as an otter's might and he splashed to the surface. In her relief she was distracted by movement on the far bank. Her master's body had rolled on its side, and for a moment Rowan imagined it must have been the current pushing him thus, that it was a corpse coughed up by the river. She let out a shriek when she saw him sit upright, shake the water out of his hair, lean forward and choke a stream of water onto the bank. 'Tommy!' she screamed. 'Help him.' Despite everything he had done and not done, she could not see a person go unaided when they were in need of assistance. Besides, she knew that when he eventually came to understand what had happened, Patrick Hollander would have to live with his actions.

That, she knew, was a far greater punishment than any other one could conceive.

FORTY

July 1769, Oxleigh

Caroline lay in her bedchamber, her breathing shallow and laboured. She had been helped from the river by the butcher and another apprentice summoned by Mary Stephenson. Though more used to animal carcasses, they loaded her onto the cart with surprising gentleness as Rowan, Tommy and Mary looked on. Patrick staggered towards them, letting out a great howl of rage and anguish as he saw his wife's unmoving form. 'She is not . . .' he slurred. 'She cannot be . . .' Tommy grasped his arm, holding him back from the cart as they got underway. 'They have her now,' he said. 'You'll do best to summon the doctor.'

Patrick shrugged himself free of Tommy's grasp and took off unsteadily after the cart.

When they reached the house, the butcher and apprentice carried Caroline upstairs to her chamber. Alice removed her waterlogged gown and Rowan placed her hands on her mistress's barrel of a belly, praying that life still grew therein. She crossed herself as they tucked the sheet around the unresponsive form and waited for the doctor.

He arrived within the hour, insisted they leave the room and then emerged a short time later wearing a sombre expression. Rowan saw him go to the parlour to speak with her master, didn't need to hear his words to know that her mistress might never wake up.

~

Mary had returned to her lodgings only after Rowan had reassured her that there was nothing more for her to do. Her gown was wet through and covered in mud, but she barely noticed the chill of it for her body and mind were as if stupefied. It was as though the horror she had recently witnessed was at arm's length, had been but a bad dream, for it was too awful to contemplate. She feared that Mistress Hollander might not survive; she had never seen a face so drained of colour. Her skin had been pale grey, and the sight of it remained in Mary's mind as she staggered along the high street, oblivious to the concerned and curious glances thrown her way. Teeth chattering, she stumbled into her room and peeled her gown from her body before fumbling with the laces of her stays, disrobing entirely and crawling under the blankets. It was a long while before the shivering stopped.

Much later a knock woke her and Mary hastily threw on a clean chemise. 'Who's there?' she asked.

'Heard what happened,' said the innkeeper's wife as Mary opened the door a crack. ''Twere a terrible tragedy. Who would credit it?' She shook her head ruefully, sucked her teeth and stood there, clearly hoping for more gossip on the matter.

Mary was silent. She seemed to have forgotten the art of speech entirely.

Realising she would get no answer, the woman offered up the tray she was carrying. 'This should warm you up. There's been a letter delivered here too. Addressed to you. It went to The Seven Stars first, but then they thought to try here.'

Mary regarded the tray without much curiosity but stood back and let the woman enter.

After she had spooned some of the soup, nearly choking as it burned down her throat, Mary's eyes slid to the letter and registered the familiar writing.

~

Three days Caroline lay in her bed, growing ever paler, a faint rattle coming from her lungs with every breath, while her husband sat vigil by her bedside, refusing to leave it, nor able to touch the food that Rowan carried up for him.

Rowan visited the apothecary, asked if he knew of anything that might speed her mistress's recovery, but he had nothing to offer. 'Time,' he said gravely. 'Only time will tell.'

On the second day a letter arrived at the merchant's house, addressed to Rowan. It put her in something of a confusion, for she had never received such a thing. She thought fleetingly of her brothers and prayed that nothing untoward had happened to them, for tragedy, it seemed to her at that moment, was everywhere. 'I do not recognise the hand,' she said, taking it to Prudence, for the cook was a better reader than she.

''Tis from Miss Stephenson,' Prudence said after she had broken the seal. She held the paper in her meaty fingers and peered at it short-sightedly. 'She says she must return to London, for she has had word from her sister that there are mercers asking to see her designs.' She turned to the next page. 'She says she will pray for Mrs Hollander and asks you to send news when you are able. There is an address here.' Prudence refolded the paper, handed it back to Rowan and took a slug of gin from her beaker.

~

Early on the fourth morning, Patrick was finally persuaded to leave his wife's chamber while Rowan and Alice saw to their patient. As Rowan lifted the sheets she saw a movement under her mistress's nightgown. A pulsing of her belly. She placed her hand there, felt the movement again. 'I believe the baby is coming.'

'What?' asked Alice. 'It still lives?'

'It is too soon,' Rowan whispered. 'Too soon.'

'Should I fetch the doctor?' Alice asked.

'No, this is woman's work. Send for the midwife.'

~

The birthing was quick. Less than an hour, Rowan reckoned, going by the sound of the church bell, which only chimed once. She had been present at several births with her mother, but none like this, none where the woman did not cry out or curse. Caroline was silent, her eyes rolled so far back in her head that all Rowan could see were the whites. The midwife said little, asking for more cloths and then, at the end, for Rowan to hold her mistress's legs apart so that she could pull the new life from her.

Rowan had never seen so tiny a newborn; scarce bigger than a rabbit, as skinny as one too, and the thick hair covering her skin made her look more like a monkey than a human child. Rowan's heart twisted for one born so early, before her time.

The midwife presented the poor mite, swaddled in muslin, to the master after the process was over. Caroline Hollander had not once come to her senses during the delivery, remaining as unreachable as she had been since the day they had pulled her from the river.

The master sat on a chair next to the bed, holding the child but numb, barely taking in the fact that he had a daughter.

'Do you have a name for her, sir?' the midwife asked as she tidied the room.

He looked between Rowan and the midwife as if seeing them for the first time.

'Diana,' he whispered. 'Diana Grace.'

Rowan turned her attention to the baby. The pinkness of her features was darkening, and before her eyes she turned a deeper shade, almost blue. Snuffled for breath.

'The poor wee thing,' the midwife said gently.

Prudence stood at the doorway. 'She must be christened.'

But Patrick Hollander would have none of it. 'Let me be, woman!' he cried. 'For I cannot think straight.' He looked around the darkened room, his gaze resting on the motionless form of his wife on the bed beside him. 'I so desperately wanted a child, but never, never like this,' he whispered. 'I am wholly to blame.' He handed the infant to Rowan and stumbled from the room, careening down the stairs, slamming the front door behind him.

'Let us hope he has gone to the parsonage,' said Rowan.

'I rather fear he might have gone to the tavern instead,' said Prudence, watching his progress from the window.

They both turned at the sound of the midwife's gasp of horror. Saw the sheet that covered their mistress was now soaked red with blood. 'I can feel no beat,' said the midwife, her finger to Caroline's neck. 'She is gone from us.'

Less than an hour after her mother left the world, Diana, cradled in Rowan's arms, took a final breath, her skin now as pale as marble.

~

Though he agreed to the funeral of his wife, Patrick would not let go of the babe. When a tiny coffin – smaller even than a hatbox – was delivered along with the one for Caroline, he took possession of it and ordered them all from the house.

On their return, there was no sign of it, and none of them, not Prudence nor Jeremiah nor Alice nor Rowan dared approach Patrick to enquire as to its whereabouts.

FORTY-ONE

July 1769, Oxleigh

Though Patrick Hollander's body recovered from his near-drowning and the loss of his wife and child, his spirit did not. His former boundless confidence had been shattered, and he moved with the gait of a broken man, one who no longer understood or even wanted to be a part of the world about him. Rowan watched on as he stood in the churchyard, shaking like a poplar in the breeze, on the morning of his wife's funeral. There was, of course, no question that he would be held to account for his part in the tragedy. Though she, Mary and Tommy had seen exactly what had happened, neither she nor Tommy would have dared speak out, and Mary was long gone, returned to London.

Caroline was buried in the gown made from the fabric she had so delighted in; the tangle of deathly flowers her funeral shroud. Rowan found herself unable to shake the guilt at her part in the tragic events; indeed, it felt as if it were a heavy robe she was condemned to wear forever. She had failed to warn her mistress strongly enough about the dangers she sensed, the evil woven into the gown, had not been able to prevent her from wearing it. That she had also made up a tincture to still the life that grew in Alice's belly, but may in fact have contributed to the death of her mistress's infant, left her consumed by guilt and remorse.

One evening, when the master was out, Rowan could bear it no more. Standing at the top of the servants' staircase, beyond the door that closed it off, she waited in the shadows for Alice as she crept up to bed. As she was about to pass, Rowan reached for the maid's wrist, using all her strength to hold her pinned against the wall. 'Tell me,' she hissed, bringing her face close. 'The draught. Did you use it on our mistress?'

Alice writhed against her grip, but Rowan was not about to let her go until she heard the truth. 'Witch,' the older girl spat.

'How dare you call me that?' Rowan replied. 'You were all too eager for my help not so long ago, weren't you? Now,' she said, tightening her grip until Alice moaned in pain, 'tell me the truth.'

Alice shook her head violently but Rowan held her fast, waiting for an answer.

'You were the one who made the draught. Perhaps you should have been more careful with it,' Alice eventually replied.

Rowan seethed as her suspicions were confirmed. 'How *could* you use such a thing for your own evil ends, and worse, try to place the blame on me when our mistress took ill?' she asked. 'Were you ever actually in need of it yourself?' As she uttered the words, the final piece of the puzzle dawned on her.

Alice laughed. 'You fell for my pathetic act, didn't you? You credulous clot. I had you completely convinced.' She mimed holding her stomach and laughed again, a bitter, hollow sound. 'If she had lost the child, then Patrick would have been free to come back to me. I had no choice but to do it.'

Alice's eyes glittered in the moonlight, and in that moment Rowan fancied she saw a trace of madness in their depths. She loosened her grip, all out of fight. She had been completely outfoxed by Alice. 'I feel sorry for you,' she said. 'You fool yourself more than you did me. Don't you see that he would never acknowledge you, a mere maid? Did he ever make such an assurance?'

Alice's expression darkened at Rowan's words. 'I know he would have, had he the chance. I would have given him reason to.'

'But you didn't, did you? For despite your lies to me, you did not grow his child within you.'

Alice twisted again, taking advantage of Rowan's distraction and wrenched herself free. She stumbled and fell heavily against the door. It was not properly closed, and so swung back against her weight, banging against the wall. In the split-second that followed, she overbalanced and then she began to fall, calling out as she did so. The movement seemed almost a dance, a tumble of skirts, petticoats and bloomers. Her cap came off and her hair escaped, flying about her face. Try as Rowan did – and she surely did – to reach out and save her, she was too late, and was left grasping thin air as Alice toppled down the steep stairs, before coming to rest with a heavy bump against the banister.

Rowan peered into the gloom, seeing a heaped tangle of arms and legs on the landing far below. Alice lay quite still, and even from where Rowan stood she could see that the maid's neck was twisted at a most unnatural angle.

A chilling silence filled the house.

Then, the bang of another door and the uneven sound of someone ascending the staircase from far below.

'I heard everything,' Prudence puffed once she reached the scene.

'It was an accident, honest it was,' Rowan said. 'You must believe me. I meant her no harm.' She shook with terror at the thought that she had now been the cause of another death.

'Aye, girl, I know that.' Prudence caught her breath and stooped over Alice, a hand at her neck.

'What should we do?'

'I'll fetch someone who won't ask any questions,' she said, surprising Rowan with her quick thinking.

Prudence straightened up, giving a final despairing look at Alice and hastened down the stairs.

She returned a while later, bringing Tommy with her.

At Prudence's instruction, the three of them carried Alice's body down the remaining stairs and out of the back door, where his cart was waiting.

'You'd do this for me?' Rowan whispered as they covered Alice's body with an old sheet.

'Of course. For Prudence, and for you,' he reassured her. 'Don't worry, Prudence told me everything. You are not to blame, not in the slightest.'

'But where will you take her?'

'Best you don't ask,' Tommy replied.

'Make sure no one sees you,' Prudence warned as he wheeled the cart down to the end of the garden.

He gave them an acknowledging nod and disappeared into the blackness.

After he had gone, Prudence and Rowan went to the kitchen, where Prudence retrieved the bottle kept on the sideboard and poured them both a cup of gin. Rowan choked on the bitter liquid, but forced it down. It would help numb her, for a while anyway, though she knew there was no way she would sleep that night. Neither of them would.

'I'll tell the master that she's skipped out on us all,' Prudence said, taking a hefty swig. There was still no sign of him, and Rowan surmised that if previous nights were anything to go by, he would not return until the early hours of the morning. 'Say she's gone to a family in Summerbourne. He'll not be surprised, I'll wager.'

'But what about her things?' asked Rowan.

'Nothing that a good bonfire won't do away with.'

'But her family? Won't they miss her?'

'She didn't have none,' said Prudence. 'Came to us from the workhouse.'

Rowan knew then why Alice had been so terrified of going back there.

'I hope –' Rowan's voice wobbled. 'I hope you don't think I'm to blame for . . . everything.'

'Hush, child. How could I think that? Alice got what was coming to her, one way or the other.' Prudence drained her glass. 'There's been too much death in this house, that I know,' she said grimly. 'We will not speak of it again.'

~

Prudence's words offered Rowan some comfort, but she could not shake the worry that Alice's body might be found, and that her part in the tragedy would be revealed. The following day, a loud knock on the door brought two men to the merchant's house, demanding to see the master. Rowan did not recognise them from the town and, with a growing sense of foreboding, she eavesdropped at the parlour door, keeping to the shadows so she would not be discovered.

'We're here to investigate allegations that you are harbouring a criminal,' one of them said.

'That is utterly preposterous,' Patrick replied. 'For there is only me and my servants, all of whom I can vouch for. Do you really come to torment a man who has so recently suffered the loss of his wife?'

Rowan saw shame on the men's faces, but they continued nonetheless. 'We seek a young woman. Rowan Caswell,' one of them said.

Rowan froze, feeling herself go hot and cold all over. They had come for her.

'There is a maid in my employ of that name, but I assure you she is no criminal. I am quite prepared to attest to that.'

Despite his words, Rowan held her breath, torn between wanting to discover more, and the desire to flee for her life.

'We have information to the contrary. That she purports to supply supposed "healing nostrums", with fearful consequences. That she is in fact a poison-maker.'

'I know of no such activity,' Patrick said. 'And I very much doubt that it would occur under this roof, for it is well known that I do not tolerate such things.'

'Then you agree that we want no such practices in this town. Has the maid been in your employ for long?'

'Long enough for me to know that she is a good and able servant,' Patrick said.

'Nevertheless, might you summon her?'

Patrick sighed heavily, and then agreed to their request. 'You must question her here, in my presence. I will not have her taken away.'

As the men muttered among themselves, Rowan slipped from the shadows and hurried to the kitchen, finding Prudence returning from the scullery.

'There are men with the master,' she gasped. 'They wish to question me.'

'About Alice?' Prudence's eyes bored into her.

'No, they accuse me of being a poisoner.' She collapsed onto a chair.

Prudence reached for Rowan's arm and steadied her. 'Who are these men?'

Rowan shook her head. 'I have never seen them before. The master insisted that they are mistaken, but they are not convinced.'

As they wondered what to do, a shout came from upstairs, summoning Rowan.

'Help me?' Rowan pleaded.

'Take courage and face them, for it is too late to run.'

'No, sir,' Rowan replied, her eyes cast down demurely as the first of the two men questioned her. 'I have no knowledge of such matters.' She clamped her boots together to stop her legs from trembling under her skirts and giving her away.

'Tell me, where is your proof?' Patrick looked as if it had only then occurred to him to ask.

Rowan noticed that for the first time the men looked less confident of their position.

'At the moment, we are acting on an allegation, sir.'

'Pfft,' he said. 'And who is making such an allegation?'

'A rumour reached our ears and we were compelled to investigate.'

'Well, I – and the maid here – have sworn that there is no basis for this.' He stood up and went to the door. 'Prudence?' he called. 'Prudence, come in, please.'

Prudence had followed Rowan up the stairs but remained loitering in the hallway, and she bustled through the door only a moment after being summoned. 'Yes, master?'

'These gentlemen,' he said, 'have come with accusations that a member of this household is a poisoner.'

'Such a thing is an impossibility, master,' said Prudence, pretending to be shocked. 'For we are a God-fearing, respectful household that wishes no harm to man nor beast.'

'Indeed,' said Patrick. And then to the men, 'I told you there was no cause for suspicion. Now be away, and leave a poor man to grieve the loss of his wife in peace.'

The men did not look entirely persuaded of Rowan's innocence but were left with little choice but to back down. 'Very well. If you are prepared to swear to her good conduct, we shall let the matter rest, for now.'

'If you are found to have misled us in any way, the consequences will be most serious,' added the second man.

'I find that I no longer care, for far worse things have been done to me in recent weeks than you are likely able to imagine. Prudence, please see the gentlemen out.'

'Th-thank you, sir,' stammered Rowan when the front door had slammed, 'for favouring me.'

Patrick swept out of the room without replying.

~

The altercation seemed to briefly revive the master, but as the days passed and the shop bell rarely rang, he sank once more into despondency. He barely registered Prudence telling him of Alice's departure, saying only that it was for the best, for he could no longer afford her wages. The friends he had once entertained abandoned him, for the breath of scandal hung heavily over the house, and he rarely left the parlour, asking for meals to be served to him there, staying up late into the night over a bottle or two or more.

Few now called for Rowan, for it seemed that news of the accusations made against her were known by all in the town. She was thankful to be left alone, for she lived with the fear that the men would come back, with proof this time, or worse, that her part in Alice's death would come to light. She worried that the master might not be able to pay her too, come the quarter year, but a new loyalty towards him prevented her from looking for work elsewhere. Besides, half the town seemed set against anyone connected to the merchant's house.

She had plenty of time to wonder what her master might have done with the tiny coffin, for it was a puzzle she could not solve. One afternoon, as he sat in the parlour staring fixedly into the fireplace, she plucked up the courage to ask him about it.

'The baby, sir?' she asked. 'Diana Grace? Shouldn't she be buried in the churchyard?'

'What?' he roared, his ill temper ignited once more. 'How dare you speak to me about my daughter? It is *no* business of yours. She is with God, as is my wife. Be gone from my sight.'

'Aye, sir,' she said, backing away from him. 'Forgive me; I shouldn't have mentioned it.'

Rowan knew that he was lying, but she had no choice but to do as she was bid.

~

In late September, as the leaves had begun to turn and the chill of winter threaded the air, Patrick dismissed Jeremiah. 'In truth, we no longer have the custom,' he said, stating what was obvious to them both. Dust gathered on empty shelves where fabric was once displayed and the house grew silent, although sometimes – if she listened hard enough – Rowan fancied she could hear the melancholy notes of a pianoforte. The lullaby her mother had once sung. She swiftly dismissed such imaginings, for there was no one to play the instrument now.

Tommy had stopped calling to deliver meat, for the master ate so little that it was hardly needed, but one afternoon, as Rowan returned from the fields to the south of the town – she avoided the river now – she came upon him in the street. She nodded to him as he passed, not expecting him to stop, especially after their last encounter. Indeed, the entire town now did its best to avoid the remaining inhabitants of the merchant's house.

'Rowan,' he called, when she was several paces past him.

She stopped and turned around, watching as he walked towards her.

'How are you keeping?' he gave her a tentative smile.

'Well enough.' She made as to move on.

'Can we not be friends again?' he asked.

Rowan felt a momentary flicker of hope, as if the world were not all ashes. 'I'm not certain that is a wise idea,' she said. 'I am not a person many wish to have as a friend.'

He pulled his cap from his head and twisted it nervously in his hands. 'I care not what others think.'

She returned his smile. 'That is good to hear.'

'Actually, perhaps we might be more than friends?' He hesitated, as if steeling himself for disappointment, then continued on. 'May I court you, Rowan Caswell?'

'Are you sure?' she blurted, taken by surprise at the bluntness of his words. 'After everything that has happened?'

'I would not ask if I weren't.'

'Well then, I should like that, Tommy Dean,' she replied. 'Very much.'

FORTY-TWO

Now

'Mr Battle.' Thea stood in front of the porter, having raced over to the school a week later at a summons from the headmaster.

'Miss Rust.'

Thea smiled to see his customary expression of faint disdain. He must be feeling better. 'Glad to see you back,' she said. 'I have an appointment with the headmaster.'

He raised an eyebrow, but said nothing.

'He asked to see me rather urgently,' she added.

'One moment.' He picked up a phone receiver and murmured something unintelligible into it before eventually replacing it and nodding at her.

Thea took it as a sign to proceed and continued past him.

'We will be moving you and the girls as soon as we can arrange it,' said Dr Fox when she entered his office.

'I'm sorry?' Thea's thoughts were scattered. It was not what she had been expecting to hear.

'There is an issue . . . with the groundwater at Silk House. A ruptured pipe is apparently what caused the fish and the plants to die. There is only a slight risk to you and the girls, but nonetheless I feel it prudent to keep you all away from the area until the problem is resolved, which may take quite some time. We will be clearing George House, distributing those boys among the other houses. It should be ready late next week, but in the meantime, the garden is to be strictly out of bounds to all students and staff.'

'I see. Of course, headmaster.' She was relieved that he had apparently moved on from her encounter with Mr Battle, something he had upbraided her for the day after the event.

'Mr Battle will ensure that you are informed at every step.'

As she left the headmaster's office, she was pleased to see Claire, her bright clothes a splash of colour against the grey stone buildings. 'We're moving,' she said as she caught up with her.

'What?'

'The girls and I are leaving Silk House. There's a problem with the plumbing apparently, that's what caused the fish to die.' Thea explained the rest of the headmaster's solution.

Claire wrapped an arm around Thea's shoulders and squeezed her. 'I think that will be for the best. It was never ideal having the girls so far from the main school.'

'But I'm not actually sure I want to leave Silk House quite yet. I'm convinced there is something there that needs resolving.'

'What exactly?' Claire was puzzled.

'I wish I knew.' Despite Fiona's cleansing, Thea still felt uneasy there, especially when she was on the top floor, in her room or her study. Now she only had a few days left to get to the bottom of it.

'Don't overthink things, I say,' Claire tried to reassure her. 'Very soon it won't be your problem.'

But Thea knew she wouldn't be able to let it go that easily. On her way to classes, she called in at the library and was amused to find Mr Dickens almost completely obscured, only the tuft of his hair showing above a stack of books.

'Ah, Miss Rust!' He seemed delighted to see her, and Thea smiled to see that he sported yet another purple flower pinned to his lapel, this one a calla lily. He must have a hothouse, she mused, for even she knew that such things didn't normally bloom in winter.

'I have something to show you,' he said, shuffling the stacks of books and extricating himself from his desk. He led her towards the back of the library, turning left at the last moment and opening a small door that might have led to a cupboard but in fact turned out to be a tiny room, its shelves lined with hundreds of boxes. The air was dry and cold and she wrapped her arms about herself as he ushered her in. 'This is where we keep some of the oldest documents relating to the college – details of its history, and deeds of establishment and so on.'

Thea nodded, now mystified.

'When you asked about information on Silk House, I didn't think we had much more than that one book, but even so I thought I'd see if there was anything from around the time it was built.' He pulled out an archive box inscribed with the dates *1750–1850*. 'There's not a lot – obviously, as it was two hundred and fifty years ago and a hundred-odd years before the college was founded. The present headmaster's house was once a coaching inn.'

Of course. She knew that the town had prospered in the eighteenth century, due to its situation on the Bath Road.

'Somewhat miraculously, we have a few items of interest from this time.' With a flourish that would have impressed a magician, Mr Dickens opened the box, and Thea peered inside, seeing a couple of old books sitting on top of what looked to be a stack of ledgers. 'Remarkable that these have survived,' he added, handing the first book to Thea.

'*Tom Jones*,' Thea said, checking the spine. 'If this is a first edition Fielding, it's probably worth a fortune.' Her mouth hung open in shock.

'I know – don't tell anyone.' His eyes gleamed. 'But that's not all.' He pulled out the ledgers and placed them precariously on a pile of folders as Thea waited. 'This,' he said, reaching into the bottom of the box and pulling out a painted portrait miniature. 'Caroline Hollander. Wife of Patrick Hollander, the first residents of Silk House. I took the liberty of doing a little research myself. It appears that she died in tragic circumstances.'

'I know, it's mentioned in the book. It says she fell into the millpond. The water soaked her gown – it would have been as heavy as lead – and, of course, in those days she would never have learned to swim,' she said. 'There was a rumour that her husband pushed her, but he was never openly accused. The tragedy broke him, ruined his life and eventually his business.'

'She was only twenty-four,' he said.

'And pregnant,' she added.

When Thea returned to the house, it was late afternoon and the place was deserted. She climbed the stairs to her study.

There they were once more. The house had been vacuumed that morning – the cleaners came twice a week – but again, the wretched piles of dirt. She knew now that no amount of fumigation would stop them appearing. After her discussion with Mr Dickens she had begun to form an idea as to their significance. If she and the girls were to move out next week, she couldn't wait any longer to solve the mystery. She would do it the best way she knew – by taking matters into her own hands and going in search of concrete evidence. It was time to stop being afraid of what she might find.

She walked over to the far end of the room, where the wall met the floorboards, and where it bowed slightly when she leaned on it. She pulled her phone out of her pocket and thumbed through the photos, finding the close-up of the plans from the records office, and zoomed in on the attic rooms. The ink was faint but she could make out the tracing of a small cupboard, a hidey hole of some sort perhaps. There was something in there, she felt sure of it.

She pressed the wall again, saw a crack form at both edges. She grabbed a metal ruler from her desk and slid the sharp edge along the crack, deepening it. Unlike the rest of the room, which was brick finished with lime plaster, it looked as if, here, a large rectangle of board had been placed over the brickwork. As she pushed, it separated from the wall with a loud crack, and she used the ruler to help slide it out of the way. She blinked and coughed as a shower of dust rained down.

A few centimetres behind the board was a brick wall.

FORTY-THREE

July 1790, Oxleigh

Twenty years after she last walked out of the merchant's house, Rowan Dean – Rowan Caswell as she once was – stood on the doorstep. The sign of the shears no longer hung above the lintel, and dust clouded the once sparkling windows.

'I can only let you in for a few minutes,' said the shopkeeper next door who'd come to open up for her. 'As a favour to Mr Dean. Why'd you want to see the place anyway?'

'I worked here once. I wanted to make a final farewell, I suppose. Before it changes.' She had heard a rumour that an ostler wished to buy it, for the demand for inns in the town showed no sign of abating as the fashionable class stopped off on their way to take the waters at Bath.

The last time she had seen Patrick Hollander, late the year before, he had been emerging from The Seven Stars and she had hardly recognised him. She had been shocked by his staggering gait and filthy clothes. Rumour had it that he had never recovered from the loss of his wife. He was far from the young dandy she had encountered on the village green more than two decades before but, she supposed, she too had changed. She was a rounder woman now, not the skinny maid she had once been. Three children and the benefits of being a butcher's wife had added padding to her frame, although she wore it well. This particular day she had on a gown woven with a pattern of tiny daisies – feverfew, one of her favourite healing flowers, and a pattern from the hand of Mary-Louise Stephenson, now London's most noted silk designer. She thought of the beautiful silks that had once been sold in the merchant's house, how she had coveted the feel of them, dreaming of wearing something so beautiful, never imagining such a desire would come true. It seemed such a long time ago now.

She had wed Tommy the summer after the tragedy, and it was with few misgivings that she gave up her position tending to Mr Hollander to move into a small cottage on the edge of the town and begin her married life. The merchant's house had become a dark place, with shadows gathering in every corner, and she had not been able to leave it fast enough. Often a cold shiver had passed right through her, though the windows were tightly fastened and there was no breeze to be had. She sometimes imagined she felt Alice in bed next to her at night, though she knew it was a foolish notion. She hadn't slept easy until the night of her marriage, under a different roof, and though she fully expected it, no word ever came of the discovery of the body of a young maid.

'There you go,' he said, unlocking the front door and pushing it open. Rowan covered her mouth as she stepped inside, for the air was stuffy and smelled sourly of unwashed clothes and long-abandoned chamber-pots. The walls were yellowed by smoke and the rugs that once lay upon the floors were nowhere to be seen. The fine furniture, the lavishly upholstered chaises, the rich silk curtains and oak sideboards were also gone.

Rowan took her time, moving from room to room, as memories of her days at the house came rushing back. She had been happy to begin with, pleased to be well treated, and to earn her own money for the first time, had taken pride in her work and had loved being surrounded by such beautiful silk, such vibrant colours. But as she entered her former mistress's chamber, other memories flooded back and she recalled the blood and the screams and then the deathly quiet that descended upon the house. Rowan sat upon the bed and closed her eyes. Though her marriage was a happy one, and her children brought her much joy, she had remained uneasy about the events at the merchant's house. She had often lain awake troubled by guilt that she had unwittingly set in motion the events that led to her mistress's death. Of course, there were others who bore more of the blame, she knew that, but she had not been able to make peace with herself entirely.

As she sat, the melancholy notes of a lullaby floated into the room. Her eyes still closed, she fancied she felt a presence sitting beside her. Her mistress. She was trying to tell her something. Holding her breath, Rowan strained to make sense of the feeling. Then, the flash of a picture in her mind's eye. It was the same vision of a pale, waxy infant she'd had many years before, but this time there was a tiny coffin, a silver breastplate. She knew then what her mistress required of her.

Rowan opened her eyes at the sound of footsteps on the oak staircase.

'You really must leave now.'

It was the shopkeeper.

'Of course,' she said, rising from the bed and glancing about her one last time. She would have to return, though she knew not when, for she must see that the coffin was properly buried. She had to find a way to put things to rest.

FORTY-FOUR

Now

Solid brick. Great. Thea sat for a moment, then ran her fingers along the surface. Some of the bricks were a different colour from the others, and it appeared that they had never been mortared. As she pressed against them, she felt a slight movement, a few millimetres, but enough to set her thinking.

She went back to her bedroom and grabbed one of the hockey sticks, an old one, not her favourite – *obviously*, as the girls would say.

Her heart had begun to thump in her chest and her hands were tense on the strapping, but a few well-placed thwacks was all it took for Thea to push several of the bricks through into the cavity behind. A few more and she had cleared a space big enough for her to squeeze her head through. She didn't dare clear a larger hole, didn't know what it might do to the rest of the wall. She used the torch on her phone to shine a light into the space. The air was thick with dust from her efforts and she had to wait a few moments for it to settle. Then she looked again, leaning through the hole she had made, the hand holding her phone stretched out in front of her.

Cobwebs laced the air and she checked for spiders, but saw none. At first the space seemed to be empty, but then she saw something that made her jolt against the bricks and drop her phone into the cavity. The torch continued to shine, however, illuminating a small box, the shape of which meant only one thing.

She withdrew from the space, sat back on her heels and contemplated the hole. Then she picked up her hockey stick again and – more carefully this time – dislodged a couple more of the bricks, widening the opening until it was large enough for her to reach in and retrieve the box.

It was heavier than it looked and she grimaced as the rough edge of one of the bricks scraped along her arm when she pulled it through the hole. The wood splintered, crumbled and began to disintegrate beneath her fingers; underneath she could feel cold metal.

Lead. Of course. Coffins were often lined with lead in earlier times.

A small plaque sat on the top. A breastplate covered in dust, dark and tarnished, but as she rubbed at it, a faint script emerged.

Diana Grace Hollander. July 1769.

It had to be Caroline's daughter – the date pretty much confirmed it.

She placed the coffin on the floor in front of her and contemplated the fact that it had quite possibly lain there undisturbed for two hundred and fifty years. As a historian, she was thrilled by the discovery: this was the type of artefact any archaeologist would salivate over. But, though she knew infant mortality was all too common in the eighteenth century, it nonetheless pierced her to see the evidence of such a pitifully short life. What could have happened for the coffin – an expensive one, no less – to be bricked away in the house and not buried in consecrated ground? She was well aware she might never find out.

The correct course of action would be to inform the headmaster, but something held her back. She knew how much the school valued its privacy, and a discovery such as this would have the media swarming. Eventually, reluctantly, she lifted the coffin back through the opening, reaching forward to grab her phone as she did so. She stacked the removed bricks to one side, replaced the plasterboard so that it covered the hole she had made and left the room.

A decision of this weight needed some consideration.

~

When Thea woke up the next morning, after a fitful night plagued by dreams of row upon row of babies all wrapped up like Egyptian mummies, only their faces showing, black holes for eyes, she knew what should be done. And there was only one person she could confide in, who might possibly be able to help.

Fiona answered the door wearing an incongruous Christmas apron, over which her clerical collar could just be seen. 'Hello,' she said, welcoming Thea inside. 'I didn't think I'd be seeing you again so soon. What can I help with? Presuming, that is, this isn't merely a social call?' The smile on her face was warm and open and Thea knew then that she had come to exactly the right place.

Fiona led her to a bright sunroom and they each took an armchair facing a sweeping view of rolling hills, Grovely Wood a dark smudge on the horizon.

Thea told the curate what she had found, and everything she now believed.

'How absolutely fascinating,' she said when Thea had finished speaking. 'I can hardly believe it.'

'I think I know what I should do, but I'd welcome your opinion.'

Fiona paused, considering. 'There are three possible solutions,' she said finally. 'First off, I don't see that there's any point in contacting the police. From what you say, it's been there far too long for any good to come of that course of action. And of course, that would mean it wouldn't stay quiet.'

Thea nodded in agreement.

'Secondly, you could speak to the headmaster, and leave it in his hands. Or . . .'

'Or could I bring it to you?' Thea asked hopefully. 'Perhaps it might be possible to bury it in consecrated ground? I think that's what the piles of dirt are saying.' She couldn't logically explain it, but she felt sure that properly burying the tiny coffin would put an end to the disturbances in the house.

Fiona sucked in her cheeks. 'Well, it could be a bit of an administrative nightmare, to be honest.'

Thea's spirits sank.

'But not entirely impossible.' She gave Thea an enigmatic half-smile. 'I think if we handle things quietly, it might be the best way. I'll have a word with the boss.'

'You mean God?' Thea asked.

'No,' she laughed. 'Reverend James. Though I might seek His guidance too.'

'I am convinced that we should not involve anyone else,' Thea said. 'It wouldn't serve history, nor Diana's remains.'

Fiona gave her a short nod. 'Agreed.'

~

Thea got the call later that evening. 'I've found a solution to our dilemma. Bring the package to the churchyard at dawn,' Fiona said. 'There's a funeral here tomorrow. A local family who have a crypt in the churchyard. It'll be open first thing, and I can slip in then. No one will be any the wiser.'

'Are you sure?' Thea asked. 'It won't get you into trouble?'

'Let me worry about that.'

~

The sun had not yet risen as Thea made her way to the church. She carried the box covered in a tea towel, and then innocuously in a shopping bag. It weighed a ton, and she had to concentrate to hold it level so as not to disturb the contents. She just hoped she wouldn't be spotted by anyone she knew.

Fiona waited by the moss-covered crypt, its heavy door ajar. As Thea approached, her shiver was not entirely due to the seeping cold, for she didn't much care for hanging out in dark churchyards.

Before the curate took delivery of the package she leaned over it and made the sign of the cross, then unwrapped it and read the inscription.

'Only two hundred and fifty years late,' said Thea, trying to lighten the atmosphere.

Fiona gave her a reassuring smile as she held the coffin in her arms and spoke softly. 'Almighty God, our Heavenly Father, I now commit the body of Diana to her place of rest. "Go back you child of earth, for a thousand years in Your sight are as yesterday . . ."'

After a few more brief sentences, Fiona gestured to Thea to follow her. Thea didn't fancy being in a dank crypt, no matter what the reason and so she hung back, watching Fiona disappear into the darkness. The curate reappeared a moment later. 'You need to come in, Thea; it's the only way.'

Fiona took her hand and, scarcely believing that she was doing it, Thea walked inside. There was a musty smell and the air was even more frigid than it was in the churchyard.

When her eyes had adjusted, Thea cast about but could not see the tiny coffin. 'Has it . . . Where has it gone?' she whispered.

Fiona shook her head and pointed to a spot in the far corner. Ah, there it was, dwarfed by the caskets surrounding it. It looked so pitifully small. Thea swallowed the lump that rose in her throat.

Fiona began to chant in a high soprano as she pulled Thea deeper into the crypt with her. Reaching the tiny casket, she sprinkled holy water and chanted a final prayer, then bowed her head.

Singing over the bones, thought Thea, unaccountably moved by the ceremony. An ancient way of mourning the dead in so many cultures.

Finally, Fiona indicated that they could leave. 'She's at rest,' she said, gathering Thea in a hug as they emerged into the fresh air. When Fiona released her, Thea heard the dawn chorus begin to tune up, the first chirrups carrying sweetly on the still air like the notes of a piano. The sky began to lighten and the mist to clear. It was going to be a beautiful day.

FORTY-FIVE

Now

'Remember, remember . . .' chanted the girls as they walked in lines towards the school. It was a little over a fortnight since Thea had scattered her father's ashes, just over a week since her discovery of the tiny coffin belonging to Diana Hollander.

The fifth of November: that infamous day in 1605 when Guy Fawkes was discovered as the ringleader of a plot to blow up the Houses of Parliament. On Bonfire Night, according to Claire who had filled Thea in, the school celebrated by building a pyre on a disused field at the far reaches of the grounds. Earlier in the week, as the girls played hockey, Thea had seen Mr Battle supervising the outdoor staff in its construction in a roped-off area. He'd been given strict instructions to keep all exertion to a minimum, according to Gareth, but was clearly having trouble with the doctor's orders. 'Keep those girls away from here,' he barked at her as they ran past, 'or there'll be no end of trouble, mark my words'. She gave him a smile and was pleased to see the corners of his mouth twitch in response.

The floodlights were on, casting shadows over the grounds and as they reached the field, she saw that a straw man – the guy – was now perched atop the enormous pile of branches and sticks and old bits of wood. For a moment it looked to Thea as if Battle himself were atop the mound, for the stuffed man wore a similar old-fashioned frock coat.

'Parkin?' Claire materialised in front of her, wearing a black velvet cape fastened at the neck with thick ribbons and brandishing a tin of a dark, sticky-looking cake.

Thea helped herself to a slice and took a bite, tasting spices and treacle and feeling the crumbs stick like cement to her teeth. Claire had disappeared, swallowed up by the throng of children and teachers. Loud chatter filled the air and Thea struggled to keep her eyes on all of the girls. Worried that she had lost a couple, she looked across to see Fenella, Sabrina and Joy standing in line with a group of boys near a long trestle table laden with silver foil-wrapped baked potatoes, piles of grated cheese and tubs of sour cream. Next to that was a large urn, bowls of marshmallows and hundreds of mugs in racks, ready for hot chocolate. She watched as Fenella threw her head back, laughing at something that one of the boys had said. The excitement was infectious and Thea's mood, subdued since the night on the playing fields and at the crypt, lifted.

After everyone had filled their bellies with potato and many were chewing on treacle toffee – 'Mind your fillings,' warned Claire – the call went out that the fire was about to be lit. The students were ushered to a safe distance away, behind the ropes, with teachers watching over them. Mr Battle lifted the cordon and approached the towering structure. He was dwarfed by it. Thea saw the spark of a lighter, the flare as he lit tapers and thrust them into the heart of the pile, again and again.

A moment of complete silence, then a gasp as the fire took, its crackle and snap increasing in volume until it roared in Thea's ears, as though it might consume her if she let it.

'Quite something,' said Gareth, coming to stand beside her.

'Yes,' she replied, shouting to be heard over the roar of the bonfire. And suddenly she remembered a day, forgotten until that moment, a family holiday, she must have been about ten years old, Pip eight. A car journey, everyone hot, tired and sticky from the January heat and an ineffective air conditioner. They had been not far from Beechworth, north of Melbourne, returning from visiting their grandparents, she and her sister lolling in the back seat, sticky with sunscreen and the residue of pine-lime Splices, as the radio warned of record temperatures, the danger of fire. The air was an odd dusky orange and the smell of smoke seeped in even through the closed windows, making the asthmatic Pip cough and wheeze. She remembered her mother's worried expression as she looked past them and out the back window. Flakes of ash falling like snow on the car. Her father told a story – a sketch from *Monty Python* – turned to reassure them with a smile, made even her mother laugh. But Thea had seen the whiteness of his knuckles as his hands gripped the steering wheel, felt his relief when they reached home safely. A bright pebble of a memory.

'You okay?' he asked, seeing her distant expression.

'Fine, really,' she replied, throwing him a reassuring smile.

Eventually, when the bonfire was nothing more than a skeletal heap of glowing embers, the teachers began to collect their charges. The housemasters led the students back to their respective boarding houses and gradually the field emptied, until only the girls and a few of the teachers who were on clean-up duty remained.

'We must be off now,' Thea said, calling the girls to her. 'Fenella, can you fetch Sabrina and Morgan? I think they were near the food tables with some of the boys.' The girl nodded and went to collect them. When they had all gathered, they walked back towards the school gates.

'Straight upstairs now.' She ushered them through the door of Silk House and towards the cloakroom. As they noisily removed their coats and shoes and hurried up the stairs, Thea saw the kitchen door creak open. 'Hello?' she called. 'Dame Hicks, is that you?' She hadn't seen the housekeeper all day and was starting to wonder where she might be.

There was an answering sound, but it wasn't a human one.

FORTY-SIX

Now

The cat slunk towards her, meowing furiously.

'Isis!' said Thea, bending down to stroke her. 'Where's your mistress, hey?' As she stroked the cat's neck, she felt something attached to its collar. It was hard to make out in the dim light but Thea's fingers found the end of a thin ribbon and she pulled it, loosening the knot that had been tied in it. Isis gave a small hiss of protest, and then scampered away, leaving a heavy, coin-shaped object in Thea's hands.

She ran her fingers across its surface, then brought it closer to her face, to see it better.

The Dame's brooch. Thea had never known her to be without it.

She kicked off her muddy boots and took swift steps towards the Dame's room at the back of the house. She hesitated when she reached the door. If the Dame had gone to bed early, Thea didn't want to disturb her. A faint light was coming from the gap at the bottom of the door, convincing Thea that the Dame must be there.

She would return the brooch in the morning.

~

The Dame failed to appear after breakfast and so once Thea had seen the girls off to school, she went to the room at the back of the house once more. She knocked, waited, knocked again, but there was no reply.

Frustrated, she reached for the door handle, expecting it to be locked. To her surprise it turned in her hand and she gently pushed open the door. 'Hello?'

Her voice sounded hollow in the empty room. As she peered inside, she gasped at the blast of cold air that came towards her and the sight of the room.

Save for the furniture and a quilt rolled up at the end of the bed, there was little evidence that anyone had occupied the place. A faint smell of herbs hung in the air and as Thea looked towards the window, she saw the pot of salve sitting on top of a worn red leather book. And there, was also a scrap of something beside it.

The fabric! She held it up to the window. It was almost transparent in the light, the woven plants seeming as though they were suspended in mid-air.

Thea picked up the book, which threatened to split at the binding. *Pow'rful Plants: a guide*. She opened it, startled to see the name *Rowan Caswell* written in faded copperplate in the top corner of the flyleaf. She put it down again and looked helplessly around the room. Where could the Dame have gone? They weren't due to move to the new boarding house until later in the week, so why had the Dame's room already been emptied? And why did she have a book belonging to a former maid at the house? A book that was hundreds of years old?

None of it made any sense.

Hearing a knock on the front door, she left the room, and went to answer it. She blinked as she saw a lanky dark-haired man standing on the step. He looked familiar but it was a moment before she could place him.

'Jeff,' he said, and as he smiled she saw his rickety teeth.

'Of course, the photographer! Hello, how are you? I'm afraid the girls aren't here at the moment.'

'Oh no, I've only come to drop these off.' He held out a large brown envelope. 'Sorry it's taken so long, but I've been slammed. Beginning of a school year and all that.' He pushed his hair out of his eyes. 'There's a copy for each of the girls. I had to do a tiny bit of Photoshopping,' he said apologetically.

'Oh?'

'Yes, there was a strange shadow on all of the frames. I left one of them untouched so you could see it – it's on the top.'

Thea said goodbye, and slid her thumb along the edge of the envelope. Sure enough, there was one print on top of the pile that was different from the others. Exactly where the Dame had been standing when they were in the garden was a white, blurred shape. The only sign that she had ever been there.

As if at the turn of a key, a realisation clicked into place.

Had she ever seen the Dame in the company of anyone else? Apart from that morning in the garden, she had never been in a room at the same time as the girls – not for meals, not first thing in the morning as they left for school, not last thing at night when they went to bed. Had anyone else at the school ever actually mentioned her? Moira, or any of the other kitchen staff? Claire? Dr Fox? Thea searched her memory, but couldn't find a single instance.

How could she have been so blind?

She told herself that there was no way she could have simply imagined the woman: the Dame had given her the salve, talked to her, reassured her . . . but had Thea ever touched her, felt the warmth of her skin, the substance behind her clothes?

She shook her head, trying to reconcile what was real and what was not, convincing herself that she hadn't gone mad. Not totally.

Without bothering to take the house keys with her, Thea raced along the path to Summerbourne, seized by a sudden need to escape the claustrophobic house. To get some fresh air and perspective. As she crossed the top of the high street, she found her way blocked by a Mini that had come off the worse from an encounter with a large four-wheel drive. A police car was already there, its lights slowly revolving, and although there was a group of shocked passengers, no one seemed to be badly hurt. To avoid it she cut through the churchyard, thought perhaps she might even find Fiona there and that it might help to talk to her about everything, might calm her down.

As she walked along the path, music floated through an open window, a choir rehearsing a requiem: she'd seen the posters advertising the concert a few weeks earlier. The voices soared and dipped, swirling around the gravestones, giving the place a peaceful ambience that was miles away from the traffic snarled on the high street.

A spray of lilies resting on one of the graves caught Thea's attention. Drawn to it, she slowed her steps for a moment. The stone was modest, small and rounded, age-spotted with yellowy-green lichen.

Her breath left her as she deciphered the worn inscription.

Sacred to the memory of Rowan Dean née Caswell. Beloved wife of Thomas Dean. Mother of Lucy, William and Grace. Born 31 October 1754. Died 5 November 1804. Aged 51 Years.

She ran her fingers over the chiselled stone, as if to prove to herself that she wasn't imagining things, that it was real. Rowan Caswell had lived – for those times, anyway – a long life. And had been buried in consecrated ground – so the accusations of witchcraft hadn't stuck. Somehow that was comforting.

The date of the woman's death was the same as yesterday's. Two hundred and fifteen years earlier. At the top of the stone was a pentacle, and at the bottom an arrow in a design that exactly matched the brooch the Dame had worn.

A network of women who look out for each other.

It made a strange kind of sense.

~

'What's that you've got there?' Claire asked, pointing to the book in Thea's hand.

They were in the staffroom after classes that afternoon and Thea was preparing to walk back to Silk House.

'It's a history of the silk merchant's house – Silk House. It mentions that maid I told you about, the one who was accused of witchcraft, so it fits right in with my studies. And I think I found her grave in the church earlier.'

'A reason to stay perhaps?' Gareth asked hopefully as he joined them.

'Yep,' said Thea with a broad grin. 'I'd say there are plenty of reasons.'

The sun was setting, colouring the sky a glorious orange and tinting the clouds rose-gold, and so Thea decided to walk back to the house via the river. As she came to the edge of the playing fields, she took the path that ran parallel to the river, eventually coming upon the back of Silk House. When she reached the gate to the garden, she decided instead to continue along, all the way to Summerbourne, still mulling over the strangeness of her discovery that morning.

She heard the rushing water of the millrace, noticing a fork in the path as it curved down to the water. The river there was overhung by a thick tangle of brambles, dense with thorns and bare of fruit. She avoided that path and turned towards the village, so she didn't see the shadowy form of a dark-haired maid crouching among the bindweed and the nettles.

Acknowledgments

One of the first movies I ever saw was a ghost story where children from the past haunt an old country house. *The Amazing Mr Blunden* had a lasting effect, both chilling and thrilling me, and lodging firmly in my memory. Perhaps partly because of this, I have long wanted to write a book where past events leak through time to the present day.

The germ of an idea for this story came from a display in the Victoria & Albert Museum. I've made many visits to the museum over the years, particularly when I lived in London, and the costume section is my absolute favourite. On a visit about three years ago, I spotted an extraordinary eighteenth-century silk gown on display and could not drag my eyes away from it. The cream background of the fabric was woven with sprays of flowers and it had a glow that appeared undimmed despite its several hundred years of existence. I took a photo and made a note of the designer, Anna Maria Garthwaite, later discovering that she was a renowned silk designer at a time when men more usually fulfilled that role. I began to imagine how hard it must have been for her to forge her way as a woman in a male-dominated trade.

I grew up in an English market town, where there is a restored silk merchant's house, and so revisiting there gave me another thread (ahem) for my story, and I would like to thank Lynda Nunn for her liaison assistance and Ilse Nikolsky of The Merchant's House, Marlborough for her help with my queries as to life there in the eighteenth century. Marlborough is also home to a highly regarded public school, and I should stress that the school I imagined here bears no relation whatsoever to that one.

I know that Wiltshire is not alone in being a place where witches were said to practise dark magic in centuries past, but as I researched further, I came upon many instances of women in the county – often poor and elderly, often working as healers and herbalists – accused of witchcraft, blamed when crops failed or illness afflicted the towns and villages. This persecution continued throughout the fifteenth, sixteenth, seventeenth and early eighteenth centuries, and some of the stories of what happened to those women are still well known there today; the story of the Handsel sisters is one of them.

My interest in the powers of medicinal and poisonous plants led me to imagine what a fabric woven with such plants might look like. It seemed fitting to combine a story about an unusual and powerful length of fabric with notions of herbalism and suspicions of witchcraft.

Before she died, my mother was a minister in the Church of England for a number of years. She had a special interest in exorcism, and underwent additional training in this area. A natural storyteller, she often had me transfixed by her stories of the power of spirits and the manifested thoughts of the human mind.

I'm also fascinated by the notion that traumatic events can leave a mark on a place, that the energy can be felt even centuries later, and so I began to imagine an old house haunted by the ghosts of its past, and where characters in the present are able to help put to rest unquiet souls.

Thanks, as ever, to my patient and encouraging husband, Andy, to my always enthusiastic agent Margaret Connolly, and to everyone at Hachette Australia for their continued support of my work. Special thanks to Alex Craig, for her ability to see the wood from the trees in the first draft she read, and her invaluable suggestions as to how to improve the manuscript, and also to Celine Kelly and Claire de Medici for their keen insight and direction. Thanks also to Becky, for story brainstorming help exactly when I needed it. And finally, there is one person whose opinion of my work matters to me more than anyone else's: I am so delighted by Rebecca Saunders' overwhelming enthusiasm for this manuscript, and consider myself incredibly fortunate to have her as my publisher and editor.

If you loved *The Silk House*, discover Kayte Nunn's other spellbinding novels . . .

Discovery. Desire. Deception.

When Anna discovers a box hidden in her late grandmother's house, containing water colours of exotic plants, an old diary and a handful of seeds, she finds herself thrust into a centuries-old mystery that will send her halfway across the world.

In 1886, Elizabeth Trebithick is determined to fulfil her father's dying wish and continue his life's work as a plant-hunter. But when she embarks on a perilous journey to discover a rare and miraculous flower, she discovers that betrayal can follow you anywhere . . .

A forbidden love. A dangerous secret.

1951. Esther Durrant, a young mother, is committed to a remote Cornish asylum by her husband – but can captivity lead to freedom?

2018. When marine scientist Rachel Parker is forced to take shelter on an isolated island off the Cornish Coast during a research posting, she discovers a collection of hidden love letters. Determined to find their recipient, Rachel sets in motion a chain of events that threatens to reveal secrets kept buried for more than sixty years . . .